TWIN CONNECTIONS

By the same author

Lovenotes

Twin Connections

Justine Valenti

Heywood Books

© Justine Valenti 1983

First published in Great Britain
by Sphere Books Ltd in 1983

ISBN 1 85481 019 7

This edition published in 1989 by
Heywood Books Limited
55 Clissold Crescent
London N16 9AR

Printed in Great Britain by
Cox & Wyman Ltd, Reading

1

'What terrible timing,' Fern Brunner repeated, between forkfuls of her salmon-and-dill omelette.

'Stop worrying.' Lud Haley smiled reassuringly at his assistant director.

As the waiter cleared the table, Fern lit a cigarette and tensely exhaled a cloud of smoke.

'Of course I'm worrying. One of us has to. You still haven't told me how we're going to start rehearsals in two weeks without Gina. And you can't come up with a single other name.'

'Someone else will want the part.'

'Oh, dozens will want it, but we have to find just the right someone.' Fern continued to express her anxieties about being on schedule and on budget for the television series Lud and she were in New York to direct. They had just learned that their female lead was having to honour a previous contract for a feature film and had returned to Los Angeles.

'Dessert?' Lud questioned Fern as the waiter rolled up the cart.

'Not at lunch. I don't dare.' She patted her stomach.

Lud ordered chocolate pecan pie for himself and strawberries for her. 'Not fattening. Relax, Fern, and just enjoy being in one of the most attractive spaces in New York.'

'I'm trying.' The food was delicious, and she would be having a terrific time if she weren't so concerned about who was going to play Suzanne.

Joanna's was a large and comfortable restaurant. Situated in an old cast-iron building, it had been done up to resemble a Paris bistro, with huge mirrors on pale green walls, flower-shaped sconces, and an Art Nouveau frieze under the high ceiling.

Fern sighed and popped a strawberry into her mouth. 'Ed Storman must be having a fit.'

'Of course he is. Producers specialise in fits. Fortunately, the pilot was screened overseas, and we've already got commitments and secured advance distribution. Who the star is doesn't matter so much over there. The audience responded to the story line, not to Gina. She's a big deal mostly in her own mind.'

'But don't we have to redo the pilot for the American networks?'

'Of course.'

'And what about the backers?'

'Just round up the extras, love, and coordinate as only you know how. Ed and I will worry about backers.'

While he spoke, Lud noticed the bejewelled, fur-coated young matrons down from Westchester who swept past him leaving expensive scent lingering in his nostrils. His discerning eye picked out the fashion designers in their hand-knitted sweaters and extravagant pants; the transparent-skinned anorexic models, drinking Perrier, toying with cold lobster, and delicately spearing truffles from the potato salad; the naughty-eyed girls brought here by their middle-aged married lovers because the place was off the beaten track; and the expensively dressed professional women, briefcases leaning against their ankles, talking seriously to each other but acutely aware of every male around them.

Fern sipped the last of her wine and lit another cigarette, feeling she was silly to be so concerned: Lud would land on his feet. After all, his unerring instinct for talent had made him one of the most promising television directors in Hollywood at only thirty-two, and she felt terrifically privileged to be his assistant director for this new series.

A couple nearing Lud's table, on their way out of the restaurant, caught his eye. The man was stocky, bespectacled, thick-nosed, and, in Lud's view, didn't rate the striking young woman with him. The director cast a

practised eye over high cheekbones in an oval face, framed
with layers of soft, caramel-coloured hair. Her figure was
the sort that would retain a Modigliani-like slimness on
film. And her age, about thirty, was just right, too.

'To show you, my little Fern, that Haley never sleeps,
have a look at that lady over there who carries herself so
well. That's how I see Suzanne.'

Fern turned and squinted, her vision blurred without
her contacts, which she had removed because her eyes
burned from smoking endless cigarettes.

'Well, she's certainly attractive. The clothes do great
things for her.'

The blonde was wearing an Adolfo white knit suit with
braided navy piping over a navy silk blouse adorned with
pearls. A mink-lined navy cape was slung over her
shoulder.

As the couple drew closer, the blonde began to look
familiar to Fern. 'I'll be damned!' Jumping up, she edged
forward with arms outstretched.

'Good lord,' the blonde murmured to her companion,
'there's someone from my home town. This may take
time.'

'Okay, babe. No rush. I'll go on. Meeting at two-
thirty.'

'Nadine! It must be ten, no, twelve years.' Fern wrapped
her arms around her old friend and then stepped back.
'Don't tell me I've changed that much, Naddie. You don't
recognise me?'

'Of course, Fern, but – '

'Oh, you must join us. Nadine Lennox, meet Lud
Haley, director of *Wanted, To Share*.'

Wincing at Fern's gaucheness, Lud smiled and stood up,
wondering about the other woman's slight frown. Was it
because of that silly introduction?

'Lud, this is so exciting. Our farm was only ten miles
from the Lennox place, which in Texas means right next
door. We had so much fun right from the day the twins
and I were big enough to make mud pies together. And we
went straight through school and on to college, didn't we,

3

Naddie. I was simply devastated when we lost touch. I headed for Hollywood, as you know. My daddy died and then we sold the farm.'

While Fern rattled on, Lud observed Lennox, noting the intelligent hazel eyes, now taking on a sardonic edge, a nearly perfect nose, and a slightly too wide mouth. She missed being beautiful but only just.

'I'm not married yet, Naddie. That's a story in itself, to go with being Lud's assistant director,' Fern said proudly. 'But you must be married. Oh, tell me everything.'

There was a pause.

'Well, to start with, I'm Joanna.' The quiet voice was tinged with irony.

Seeing Lud's curious glance, she added, 'As in Nadine-and-Joanna, not the owner of this restaurant.'

Fern clapped her hand over her mouth, muffling her 'Oh, shit.' Her milky, freckled skin reddened as she sought to rectify her stupid mistake. 'Hell, nobody could ever tell the twins apart unless they were side by side. And me without my contacts.'

'Nadine is here in New York as well,' Joanna continued in her low, silky voice. 'She's kept her married name, Barrett, and she has two children.'

Fern was furious with herself for not having known immediately. Nadine would never have given her such a cool greeting.

'Does Joanna often lunch at Joanna's?' Lud asked her.

She smiled, and rose on his beauty scale from an eight to a nine and a half. 'Today is my first time. In fact, I was taken here because of the name.'

'Joanna what? Still Lennox?' He wanted to hear more of her voice.

'Again Lennox.'

'I'm going to the little girls' room,' Fern mumbled, snatching her handbag and disappearing into the alcove next to the bar.

It was obvious to Lud that Fern much preferred the missing Nadine to her twin, who was also aware of it.

4

In fact, Joanna was feeling acutely uncomfortable. She started to stand up. 'I really must be getting back.'

'Hey, don't rush away. Fern only went to put her eyes back in. At least finish your brandy.'

Joanna realised it would be awkward to leave without a token sip of what he had ordered for her.

'I see that being a twin can have its problems, but I always thought it would be great fun, especially as I'm an only child.'

No, not always fun. Whenever she was mistaken for Nadine, Joanna had the sinking feeling that it was because the person wanted her to be Nadine, as Fern did. In spite of the coincidental name of the restaurant, Fern hadn't made the association.

Joanna couldn't admit all of this to the smiling stranger sitting opposite her.

Shyly she smiled back. 'I suppose I should be used to it by this time, but it's still a shock when somebody calls me Nadine. There's always a split second when I'm not sure myself.'

Lud looked at her with growing interest. 'Did you and your sister used to tease people, pretending to be each other?'

'No. People were confused enough, and there weren't a lot of people on the farm to tease.'

He could hardly visualise Joanna as a farmgirl. Fern, in spite of having been brain-washed in college and sun-dried in California, still had wisps of hay around the edges, but not this elegant lady.

'I'm trying to picture you picking cotton.'

'Well, I did milk the cows, groom the horses, help harvest the wheat – '

'And struck gold.'

'Something like that.' Her smile was mysterious.

Intrigued, Lud looked at her steadily for a long moment through his deep-set, dark-blue eyes ringed with exceptionally thick lashes.

Joanna felt a strange fluttering in her stomach that was more than the cognac sliding down. At the same time that

5

he made her feel special, she was a little uneasy at the intense way he was looking at her, as if fine-combing her features for some imperfection.

Automatically her hand moved to smooth her hair. Did she need some more lipstick? Or was he mentally doing a little plastic surgery?

He observed her gesture. 'I'm sorry for staring at you like that, Joanna. In fact, the talent scout in me is thinking that you'd be the perfect type to play the lead in a television series I'm directing. It's about a very talented lady lawyer, Suzanne, who's been forced on the conservative old firm of Otis, Otis, and Goldsmith.'

Joanna looked pained. 'I'm not an actress,' she said quickly, 'so that lets me out.'

'Can't be sure you're not if you've never tried – '

'I could never even consider it,' she interrupted.

He looked at her curiously. 'I only said you looked right for the part, not that you have to go after it. You don't seem to think much of actresses, and maybe not much of directors, either.'

Joanna flushed. 'I'm so sorry. That came out all wrong. I quite admire actors, actresses, *and* directors. But I see myself only as a spectator.'

'In that case, come and spectate with me tonight. I have tickets for a Broadway preview. And then you can tell me over supper why acting scares you so much.'

Of course acting didn't scare her. But it was a nice invitation, and she wished she could accept.

'Thanks, but I'm flying to Amsterdam tonight. Oh,' she exclaimed, consulting her watch. 'I must be getting back to work.'

'Just a moment, Joanna. Please.'

She marvelled at the way she sank back in her seat, held spellbound by his glance and the seductive nuance in his tone. He must be one hell of a director.

She returned his look in spite of herself.

'I get the feeling you're your own boss, Joanna.'

'No, I'm afraid not.'

'Well, how about telling whoever that your lunchmate was particularly fascinating and the service was slow.'

Joanna was amused. 'My boss will agree about my lunchmate but he knows that the service was impeccable, since he's the one who bought me lunch.'

'Aha. Let me guess. He's in the rag trade, and you've just shown him a portfolio of designs that will sweep away the names of Saint-Laurent, De La Renta – no? How about this. He manufactures dinnerware, and you've invented something new and fabulous that will make the name of Lennox synonymous with fine china everywhere and smash Delft's reputation to smithereens.'

She laughed at his preposterous imagination.

'Okay, seriously, Joanna, you're a headhunter sent abroad to recruit talented females for highpowered jobs–'

'The truth is far more mundane,' she broke in hastily. 'I'm only an art editor in the book division of Omega Publishing, and I'm going to Amsterdam in connection with our travel series.'

'That doesn't sound mundane to me. When people are paid to travel it's to make important decisions. I seem to remember, though, that Omega doesn't like to give women responsible jobs.'

Lud was baiting her. He had obviously read about the action several women had brought against the huge publishing empire a couple of years back, which they had won out of court. In fact, Joanna was the first female art director ever to be appointed at Omega.

Lud wormed her title out of her and then leaned forward, his vitality so palpable that he made her jump.

'The moment I saw you I recognised the quintessential new woman, tough-minded and determined, but totally feminine. That's the way I see my lawyer. Lovely-looking, with an attractive voice. You know, you carry yourself like a veteran of the camera. I suppose it must be natural.'

The glow Joanna had been feeling at his compliments faded at the mention of a camera.

'I really must go.' She started to get up.

'Okay, okay, we'll talk about my brilliant career. I'm sure you're consumed with curiosity.'

Joanna sat back again, feeling absurd. She was popping up and down like a jack-in-the-box. This man affected her very strangely.

'So far, in addition to some minor pieces, I've directed several episodes of *Starsky and Hutch*, two two-hour specials on musicals of the thirties and forties, and finally, that incomparable sitcom, *Wanted, To Share*.'

She smiled tentatively. 'So Fern said. That ran quite a while, didn't it?'

'Three years. Well, it was a good idea. Famous star's daughter left with no money but big beach house suffers through a procession of roommates, gets into all sorts of hilarious situations – goddamn it, you really don't know what I'm talking about, do you? And I've been flattering myself that my name is a household word.'

'I'm sure it is,' Joanna said quickly, 'and the fault is mine. I just hardly seem to have time to watch television.'

'And certainly not sitcoms. I was only teasing. I don't blame you. What I can say is that *Sister In Law* is several cuts above sitcom.'

'I'm sure it will be a great success, and I'll make it a point to watch every episode,' Joanna assured him.

Irony seemed to be her speciality. 'But what-did-I-say-my-name-is, huh?'

'Well, Haley, as a matter of fact I didn't quite catch the first part. Is that L-u-d?'

'*Jawohl*, as in Ludvig.' He pronounced it Loodvig, clicking his heels together smartly under the table. 'Mother is not only what you might call a gifted amateur pianist, she's also a Beethoven freak. She plonks away at *The Moonlight Sonata* and thinks she's really groovin'. Oh, well, it could have been worse. She could have swooned over Ditters von Dittersdorf. You have a beautiful smile, Joanna. When will you be back from Amsterdam?'

'In about two weeks,' she murmured, flustered by his abrupt change of tone.

8

Suddenly she noticed Fern hovering near the alcove, smoking and apparently waiting for her to leave.

Joanna got up from her chair firmly. 'Now I really must go. It's way after two, and they'll be missing me.'

'I'll be missing you,' Lud murmured into her ear as he draped her cape over her shoulders.

She felt a faint shiver of desire. Impossible. She hardly knew this man.

He gave her another of his luminous looks that promised initiation into undreamed of mysteries. 'I'll call you, Joanna. Or you call me.' He handed her his card.

'Yes. Thanks,' she heard herself saying. Was she mad, or what, to let him see how intrigued she was. In fact, it had been ages since she had been truly interested in any man. Maybe that was why she found him so electrifying.

No, that wasn't it. As he escorted her past the other tables she realised that every woman in the place, accompanied or otherwise, glanced at Lud with admiring interest. Why? He wasn't particularly tall or handsome. His eyes became extraordinary only when he used them in a special way. His hair was plain old brown, though fashionably curly, and his features were ordinary. His skin, in fact, was not noticeably smooth, but what might have made another man almost ugly only intensified his masculinity.

Maybe it was his energy and the self-assured way he wore his expensive casual clothes – the butter-soft tan suede suit, the white cashmere turtleneck, the designer boots.

Lud brushed her cheek with his lips. 'Later, Joanna.'

Unable to risk a last look at him, she fled into the street, glanced at his card, and slipped it into her handbag.

You have a beautiful smile, Joanna.

When the twins were eight years old, they were picked by representatives of the Dallas television station to do commercials. Aunt Sally, who had come to live with them after their mother's death, was terribly excited by the

9

prospect as she drove them to the studio in their beat-up station wagon.

The twins were dressed in fine new clothes of the kind they had never touched before. Their hair was curled and tied with ribbons, and special makeup was applied to their faces.

Joanna didn't mind that part. A glance in the mirror made her feel just fine. It was when she was standing in front of the hot cameras, with a man telling her to smile, that she felt awkward. The director was pushing and pulling the girls here and there, talking about profiles and angles. While Nadine basked in the attention and never stopped smiling, Joanna withdrew further and further.

'Okay, honey, Joanna, come forward here, that's right. Take a long swallow from the glass. That's it. And smile. It tastes good, doesn't it? See, look at your twin.'

Joanna tried to smile, but she didn't like Doc Pepper at all. To her it tasted like a mixture of prune juice and cherry cough syrup. She would much rather be drinking a coke.

The twins were shown cue cards with large printing on them, telling them what to say. Nadine spoke first, and then Joanna.

'C'mon, honey, put a little oomph into. And smile.'

Joanna did her best, but her voice sounded funny. Anyway, she didn't see how she could smile and speak at the same time.

'Okay, that's all for now.'

Joanna and Nadine were sent back to their dressing room so that the makeup girl could fuss with their faces and hair again.

Joanna, finishing first, wandered out and approached the camera, curious about how it worked.

The producer and director were in a huddle, their backs to her. 'Make sure the lines go to the one who talks naturally. What's her name, Nadine. The other one sounds like she's reading, and her smile's too forced.'

Joanna stepped back, devastated. She rushed over to her aunt. 'I want to go home.'

Her aunt shook her. 'Jo, don't you dare start. No sassing me or anybody else. This is our chance to get our hands on some real money. If you mess this up, gal, I'm gonna whup you and your daddy's gonna whup you, hear?'

'Nadine and Joanna,' the director called.

Sullenly Joanna walked where they told her to go, stood where they put her, and smiled the best she could, but she hated being ordered around like a dog or a donkey. She didn't want to be the hind end of Nadine-and-Joanna. She wanted to be herself, wear her own clothes, think her own thoughts, and speak her own words. And someday she would, she vowed.

Joanna hailed a taxi. She was being an idiot. In two weeks Lud would have cast his lawyer, and that would be that.

'Shame on you, Lud Haley.'

He grinned. 'Just doing my job, Fern, just doing my job.'

'If that had been Nadine, I could understand it.'

'Tell me all – as if I could stop you now.'

Fern, inured to his teasing, was about to launch into her tale when the waiter approached, and Lud busied himself with the bill.

Stealing a look at herself in one of the mirrors, Fern liked what she saw, even if she would never be as pretty as the Lennox twins. She was pleased that her short-cropped red hair made her look younger than thirty-four, and that her tailored clothes indicated she belonged on the directorial side of the camera.

Fern was particularly sensitive about that point because when she had first arrived in Hollywood she had been a mass of fluffs, frills, and musical comedy ambitions. But after a decade of chorus lines and commercials, she had jumped at the offer of a job as production assistant to the rising director, Lud Haley. Overnight she had changed her clothes and her image, dusted off her degree from the University of Texas, and made herself indispensable by her relentless efficiency.

11

In the taxi returning to the Astoria Studio in Long Island City, Fern told Lud all about the Lennox twins: how television scouts had come to Tyler, where they went to school, and picked the twins out for commercials.

'They started to make pots of money at a time my daddy was hardly working.'

'Pots? Really?'

'Well, it became pots after it was invested in oil. Aunt Sally took charge of it all, and I think she was shrewd when it came to money. Anyway, oil was eventually found right on their land. Hell, they were millionaires by the time we got to college.'

'Interesting. What kind of commercials did they do?'

'Oh, all sorts. Breakfast cereal, soda pop, kids' clothing. As they got older it was shampoo and drive-in movies. All through those years Nadine was my best friend, always sharing with me and not a bit spoiled by her good luck. Unfortunately, the Brunners remained dirt poor. My daddy used to say that our land was so rocky he could walk from one end to the other and never touch the ground. No oil, either, and no spending money for me. I wouldn't have had a stitch on my back if Naddie hadn't given me some of the clothes she got to keep from the commercials. In fact, I wouldn't even have made it to college if Nadine hadn't lent me some money.'

'Only Nadine?'

'You'd better believe it,' Fern said heatedly. 'Nadine is a honey pie. The other one has always been a bitch.'

2

Nadine sat at her desk at home working on pen-and-ink spot illustrations. Try as she might she couldn't seem to concentrate, and the drawing was going very slowly.

When the phone rang she jumped up to answer it, glad of the excuse.

'Hi, I'm going to stop by tonight on my way to the airport.'

'Tonight? Oh, Joanna, I didn't realise you were leaving already.'

'I did say Wednesday – '

'Oh. I thought today was Tuesday.'

Nadine tried to get back to work but she simply couldn't. Well, it was only ten in the morning. There was plenty of time.

'Lilly,' she called, going into the living room. Her day helper wasn't there. Nadine tried the dining room, master bedroom, and the rooms of her two children.

Then Nadine remembered that Lilly had gone out shopping.

'I must be losing my grip,' Nadine said aloud into the silence. Funny. When the children were at home the large apartment seemed crowded and noisy. And yet when she was there alone she felt so isolated.

When Carl and she had bought this place he had insisted on having a decorator do it up with modern furnishings. There were two large brown leather sofas and several low-slung chairs easier to sink into than rise from. The dressers and tables were low, too, impossible to get at without kneeling and stooping.

Nadine had never cared for modern but she hadn't had the energy to argue with her husband. After she and Carl

13

had split up she had thought she would make changes, but somehow she never seemed to get around to it. Suddenly she visualised the wonderful antiques in Joanna's apartment and immediately became depressed.

Again the phone rang. This time it was Nadine's hairdresser reminding her of an eleven o'clock appointment. Of course she had forgotten. It was no good writing things on her calendar if she didn't remember to look at it.

'I need a trim,' Nadine told her hairdresser, a girl in her twenties. 'Maybe cut some fluffy bangs, just for a change.' She peered critically at herself in the mirror. 'My sister wears hers that way and I really like the look.'

It gave Nadine a lift to chat with her hairdresser about the latest styles in makeup, clothes, and about new films in town. Not for the first time, Nadine wished someone would offer her some sort of job where she could be with people. Maybe when the kids got a little older she would try to find something.

She decided to stop at the children's department in Bergdorf's and pick up a few things for Jeff and Kate. On her way out she popped into sportswear just to see if anything appealed, and wound up with an armful of clothes to try on.

'Those black pants look wonderful on you,' the chunky salesgirl told her wistfully. 'Imagine being thin enough to wear velvet.'

Nadine smiled at her. 'Lucky inheritance is what it is.' Instead of the black pants she chose the crimson ones, and to go with them a white silk shirt with a mandarin neck.

'That's terrific,' the salesgirl confirmed.

Nadine thought so too. She had admired the same combination when her sister had worn it just before Christmas.

Climbing into a taxi, Nadine gave her address as Park Avenue and Seventieth.

'It's awfully cold out there,' she called through the grill. 'Though I guess it's about right for January.'

The young driver turned and grinned. 'No English,' he apologised.

Nadine talked to her doorman for ten minutes, and then dropped in to see a neighbour. After a cup of coffee, her neighbour, a speech therapist, apologetically told Nadine she was expecting a patient.

At home Nadine unpacked her purchases and put on her new outfit.

Suddenly she heard the key in the lock and the voices of Lilly and her children.

God, was it after three already?

Joanna worked on the eleventh floor of the Omega Building, at Second Avenue and Fifty-second Street. Her office was spacious, allowing her to have, in addition to her desk, a large working table next to her drawing board and several chairs for visitors. Bulletin boards hung on two walls where she pinned layouts, proofs, stats of photographs, and production schedules. A third wall had a built-in bookcase holding all the volumes she had worked on during her thirteen years with the company.

Omega Publishing was a huge concern, with branches in all the major cities of Europe. In addition to their crafts and hobbies books, where she had started, Omega published an encyclopaedia, an almanac, and expensive glossy books on nature, gardening, and travel. There was also a children's division, a record division, and a videotape division.

As art director for travel books, Joanna was responsible for book and jacket designs, layouts, and selection of type, photographs and illustrations. Unlike the usual portable travel book full of practical information, the volumes she was working on were intended for reading and aesthetic enjoyment before, after, or instead of the actual trip: they included sections on history, geology, archaeology, geography, art, literature, science, and customs of the country. Text and illustrations were about equally divided.

Written in the language of each country by Omega staff

15

based in the capitals, each book was then translated and produced in a slightly different form for United States distribution. So far France, Britain, and Italy had been completed and Holland was in the works. Joanna always travelled abroad to supervise the layouts and colour proofs and in general liaise with her foreign counterpart.

When she returned to her desk from the restaurant, Joanna felt a little woozy because she rarely drank at lunch. This had been a special goodbye from her boss because he had so liked her jacket design for the Holland book. And afterwards she had drunk that brandy with Lud Haley.

While Joanna put galleys and layouts into her attaché case she thought about Lud and what an attractive man he was.

Lisa, her young secretary, bounced into her office carrying a thin white florist's box and a bud vase already filled with water, showing her usual efficiency.

'Someone has an admirer.' Lisa smiled knowingly and departed.

Joanna looked up in surprise. Who could be sending her flowers?

Feeling absurdly excited, she opened the box. There, nestling in its white tissue paper, was one beautiful scarlet rose.

Delighted, she took it out and put it into the vase.

She answered her ringing phone with, 'Hello, Joanna Lennox.'

'Hello, Joanna Lennox,' a seductive male voice repeated. 'The card, if there were one, would say, "To match your perfection. With love, Lud Haley."'

'Oh!' she exclaimed, flustered. 'Thank you. It – it only just arrived this minute.'

'Of course. That's the way I timed it. I wanted you to know that I'm thinking of you, Joanna, and that I'd like to promise you a rose garden.'

She felt a delicious shiver. 'What a lovely thought. Roses are my favourites. Tyler, in Texas, is rose country, and we used to grow acres of them.'

'Aha. Mysterious vibrations are helping me to get to know you. And I hope to know you better.'

'I'd like that,' she murmured, warmth flowing through her.

'For you, life should always be a bed of roses, and I'm volunteering to pick out the thorns. Remember that, Joanna. *Bon voyage*.'

The moment Nadine opened her door, Joanna forgot about Lud and her encounter with Fern because she was staring at herself.

'You've cut your hair,' Joanna cried, trying not to sound reproachful. 'Doesn't Michael prefer it long?'

'I guess so, but I like it this way. Anyway, I'm sort of phasing him out.'

'Are you? I thought you were interested. He seemed very pleasant – '

' – but boring.' Nadine sighed. 'And if I'm not sure of someone I can't go on seeing him because the children may get too attached.'

'The trouble with you – ' Joanna began.

' – is that I don't know what I want,' Nadine finished, smiling a little defensively.

Nadine was certainly blasé about men. Well, she could afford to be. She knew how to have them lining up around the block for her.

Joanna, regarding her sister's outfit, almost identical to the one she owned, felt touched at the flattery of emulation, but at the same time she was faintly dismayed.

'How are the drawings coming? I'd like to take them with me.'

'I'm not finished yet but I've made a start,' Nadine said quickly. 'I can give you a few. I just don't know where the day disappears.'

Joanna smiled. 'How can you, when you don't even know what day it is?'

Nadine acknowledged her sister's teasing by a helpless shrug. 'Okay, don't rub it in, Miss Highly Organised. I'll

17

bet running an art department is easier than being a single parent. I miss having someone grown up to talk to.'

'I know, but you chose it.' Joanna's voice was noncommittal, but if *she* had been married to Carl . . .

'Well, no, he chose it,' Nadine countered, 'by choosing to travel all the time. He didn't have to refuse CBS's offer to work in New York.'

'He likes being a foreign correspondent. You knew that from the beginning.'

'I thought he'd compromise after the children were born. I couldn't disrupt their lives. A year here, a year there, in dangerous places.' So Nadine had preferred to divorce Carl four years ago. It had always seemed to Joanna an extraordinary solution.

'God, I'm worn out, Jan. The kids have been pestering me all afternoon.'

'Where are the little monsters? They can pester me as much as they like.'

'Easy for you to say. You see Jeff and Kate only for fun and games, but if they were yours, with you day in and day out –'

Joanna flinched.

Nadine saw the pain in her sister's eyes. 'That was stupid and thoughtless. I'm sorry. I guess I'm sort of feeling guilty for not finishing my drawings.'

'I know.' Joanna smiled sadly, brushing away the reminder of her three miscarriages. 'I hate to put pressure on you, but we really do need those spots. We're way past our deadline.'

'I'll have them done by Monday and deliver them to the office myself, I swear to God, Jan,' Nadine said, invoking a childhood promise and smiling conspiratorially.

'You do that, Dini.' Joanna returned the smile.

Jeff and Kate came whooping down the long foyer, galloped into the living room, and began to jump all over their aunt, vying for her attention.

Jeff was a sturdy seven, big for his age, with straight brown hair and brown eyes, and a warm, wonderful smile.

18

Kate, a year younger, had her mother's leggy appearance, as well as her silky blonde hair and green-flecked hazel eyes. A very pretty child, she promised to be a beauty, but at that age she disliked feminine things and tended to copy her brother.

'Come and see my new electronic game, Aunt Joanna,' Jeff said, pulling her by the hand.

'I can't now, Jeff. I'm on my way to the airport.'

'Oh, wow, take me, take me,' he clamoured, while Kate chimed in.

'Not this time.' Joanna smiled indulgently at them. 'I'll be busy working. And you two behave like a couple of puppies.'

'We *are* a couple of puppies. Woof, woof,' Kate screeched.

'You're not, you're a parakeet,' Jeff insisted, making a low, dog-like growl.

Joanna laughed and kissed her niece and nephew, holding each close. They were very precious to her and she spent several minutes listening, talking and playing. 'Let me say a word to Mom now, please, because I have to go soon.'

They started to object but Joanna was firm.

'How long will you be away?' Nadine dropped into an easy chair.

'Couple of weeks, I guess.'

That long? Nadine felt suddenly forlorn.

The children turned on the television.

'Lower, please,' Joanna requested.

Jeff made a face but turned the knob.

'Oh,' Joanna began, turning to her sister, 'did you call her about –'

'Yes. Called her yesterday. She's okay but she's worried about him. His health is so-so. High blood pressure and the heart not too good. He's walking around in his old threadbare suit, saying –'

'"It'll see me to the pearly gates, 'cause it won't be long now."' Joanna mimicked their father in the Texas country accent both women had lost years ago.

Nadine smiled. 'She's been trying to get him to move into town.'

'I suppose he won't hear of it, though how he can bear to live in that broken-down shack with the oil derricks all around I can't imagine. I guess he's too old to change.'

'"This here's the land of my daddy,"' Nadine began.

'" – and I'm gonna hold on to it like a coyote thievin' a chicken,"' Joanna finished.

The children had been listening to the exchange. Kate, puzzled, finally asked, 'Who's him? Who's her?'

'Grandpa Lennox and Aunt Sally, of course,' Nadine replied.

'How do you know, Mommy?' Kate challenged.

'Oh, we just do, darling.'

'Because they're twins,' Jeff enlightened his sister.

'I wish I were twins,' Kate said wistfully.

'Well I don't,' her brother shouted, ''cause then there'd be two yous to bother me.'

Kate ignored her brother, got up from the floor, and climbed into Joanna's lap. 'Why are you going away?'

'Because she has to work, dummy. You don't know anything.'

'That's enough, Jeff.' Joanna knew that the children really cared for one another in spite of the bickering.

'Are you going to Africa like Daddy?' Kate wanted to know.

'No. Amsterdam.'

'I wish Daddy would come home,' Kate said sulkily.

'He can't, silly, he's working. He was on the nine o'clock news last night,' Jeff said importantly. 'And as soon as I'm old enough he's going to take me with him.'

Joanna got up. 'I must get to the airport. Take care, precious pet.' She kissed Kate, and hugged Jeff tightly. 'Bye, big Jeff. I'll see you soon.'

Nadine walked Joanna to the door. 'Jeff's getting more like Carl every day. Sometimes he gets an expression on his face or makes a gesture that reminds me so much of him it's uncanny, because Carl doesn't see the children for months at a time.'

'Really? That seldom? I thought he came to New York every couple of months.'

Nadine shrugged. 'If he does, I don't hear about it. However I may feel about Carl, he's their father and I know they miss him. Jan, I'm going to miss you.'

Joanna smiled. 'Me too.'

'Not you. You won't think twice about me. You'll be too busy,' Nadine said dejectedly, wishing she were going along.

Joanna, reflecting, suddenly laughed. 'Do you know, I can't remember a single day of my life that I haven't thought about you, whether we were together or not.' She hugged Nadine. 'Hey, bones, you've – '

'Only a couple of pounds. I don't remember to eat when I'm by myself.'

'Well, eat with someone, then. Michael, or somebody from the top of the list, dying to take you to dinner. You could charm any man into feeding you nectar and ambrosia, but please ask for steak, okay?' Joanna was a little worried, knowing her sister was feeling very lonely.

'Okay.' Nadine smiled bravely.

'That's better. You know, you can do whatever you really make up your mind to do.'

'I guess so, but come back soon anyway,' Nadine said in a small voice, kissing her.

I've got to make an effort to pull my life together.

Yet, when Nadine saw her sister wave from the hall, she experienced a painful emptiness, as if half of her had departed in the elevator.

When Nadine and Joanna had registered for the University of Texas Joanna was going to major in art, Nadine in drama. Joanna, as always, was scathing about acting. 'I have enough trouble being myself without pretending to be someone else.'

Nadine felt quite different. From the first time she had appeared in front of the television cameras she had wanted

21

to be a star, with her name in lights, acclaimed by millions.

The trouble was that when she thought of being separated from her sister for several hours a day she would feel an emptiness in the pit of her stomach and a cloud of depression would settle over her. The twins had never before been parted for more than minutes at a time.

The first few weeks at college were fraught with conflict for Nadine in spite of the supporting presence of Fern Brunner. Fern sat next to her in all her classes and did her best to take Joanna's place but it wasn't possible.

Nadine resented the way her sister was thriving at art school away from her. Joanna would return to their room in the boarding house and pore over her assignments, while Nadine sat with a play open on her knees trying to concentrate.

Then Nadine was given the part of Blanche Du Bois in a production of *A Streetcar Named Desire* which her class was going to present for the drama department at the end of the first semester.

Fern was more excited than she was. 'Naddie, you've got so much talent you're going to make it to Broadway for sure.'

Although she had never had any trouble memorising lines before, that time Nadine suffered agonies.

One day they were rehearsing the scene where Blanche first comes to visit Stella and realises her sister is sexually fulfilled by her husband, even though Stanley Kowalski is a brute by Blanche's standards. Nadine accurately projected the superiority Blanche felt towards her sister, tinged with envy and an underlying anxiety.

But when it came to the part where Blanche says she's not going to put up at a hotel because she wants to be near her sister, Nadine halted, her mind a blank.

Although the teacher cued her, she simply kept forgetting. When she had to repeat, after the teacher, that she couldn't be alone because she wasn't very well, Nadine found the words too close to her real-life truth. Suddenly she was so acutely in need of Joanna that she trembled and broke into a sweat. Grabbing her books, Nadine fled from the classroom.

Fern chased after her. 'Naddie, for goodness sake, what are you doing?'

Catching up with her, Fern talked her out of leaving the drama department on the spot. But Nadine, try as she might, never could learn the part and she had to give it up. She felt humiliated by her failure and more uncertain of herself than ever.

Before the end of the term she switched her major to art and put aside her dreams of stardom in exchange for feeling secure and complete again by attending the same classes as her sister.

Nadine had never completely got over her fear of being separated from Joanna. Listlessly she dragged herself back to the living room.

The children had pulled in some of their toys.

'Kate, if you're watching television you don't need your Lego set. And Jeff, that electronic game makes such a racket you can't possibly hear the programme.'

The children ignored her. Someday soon she would have to show them she meant what she said, but it upset her terribly to have scenes. She couldn't take the noise, the crying, and especially the final declaration both children would make that they hated her.

Nadine sighed deeply. Lucky Joanna, to have a job to absorb her and no other responsibilities. She didn't know how well off she was without children.

Nadine kicked off her shoes. She needed to relax a little before she could get back to the illustrations.

Seeing Kate and Jeff absorbed in their toys, she switched the channel to a romantic comedy just beginning with George Segal and Glenda Jackson. Monitoring Jackson's performance critically, Nadine imagined herself in the role. Although she had planned to watch the movie for only fifteen minutes, she stayed with it for the entire two hours.

3

The flight attendant poured champagne for Joanna and Abby.

'To Omega,' Abby toasted, 'for sending us VIPs first class.'

Although it was not strictly necessary for Abby Cassell to go to Amsterdam, Joanna had decided to include her assistant and friend in the trip as a reward for her hard work.

Abby was small and dark and one hundred percent vivacious. Although she never missed an opportunity to flirt, when she settled down to work she was willing, capable, and loyal. Abby was fun to have around; tales of her exploits with men were as diverting as soap opera. At least she could see her own absurdities in the pursuit of love and never minded Joanna's gentle teasing.

When Joanna was married, Abby had been her next-door neighbour and the two women had become friends. Joanna had brought Abby to Omega as her assistant two years previously.

While Joanna rummaged in her attaché case for the galleys she was planning to finish reading, Abby struck up a conversation with a man across the aisle.

Joanna was secretly a little envious of her friend's ability to steadfastly believe that somewhere, just around the corner, or maybe in the next airplane seat, was Mr Right. Though she was twenty-nine and unmarried, Abby still approached each affair with unflagging optimism. When she was let down she simply picked herself up, brushed herself off, and went on to the next adventure.

Not so Joanna. The breakup with her husband, Ben Magid, three years before, had left gaping wounds that had never healed. Joanna still turned down most dates. And when she did occasionally accept an invitation, or even more rarely a night in bed, she felt flat afterwards. For a long while she would let her emotions and her body lie fallow. Her job, her sister and the children were the important, constant things in her life.

Hearing Abby laughing with the man across the aisle disturbed Joanna, preventing her from concentrating on her work. After she had read the same paragraph twice she realised she wasn't absorbing a word about how the Dutch had wrested a country from a watery marshland. Instead, she was reliving her encounter with Lud Haley. She felt again the scrutiny of those hypnotic eyes, heard his sexy voice on the phone, and smelled the perfume of that perfect rose. *I'd like to promise you a rose garden, Joanna.*

'Joanna.' Abby tugging at her arm made her jump. 'I've met the most unusual man. Don't look now, he's gone to the john. Did you happen to notice?'

'Not really.' Joanna smiled. 'True love at last?'

'You never can tell,' Abby said happily. 'His name is Willem and he's Dutch. Lives in The Hague. Anyway, he's going to be in Amsterdam for a couple of days and he's offered to show us around. I think he's awfully nice.'

When she met him Joanna didn't agree. She could barely be polite to the nervous Willem, forty-fiveish, who wore his remaining strands of hair plastered horizontally across his head. He grew tulip bulbs, an occupation he managed to make duller than necessary.

'Well, what do you think?' Abby asked Joanna later over dinner.

'That he's looking for a one-night Amsterdam connection before returning to his Katinka of the tulip fields. Sorry, but that's my honest impression.'

'Oh. You think he's married?'

'Uh huh. If you want a diversion go ahead. But please leave me out, and remember, don't write yourself a lasting romantic part in this saga, which is likely to be Gone with the Windmill.'

Abby put down her fork and roared. 'You're probably

25

right. I do have a way of picking impossible men. But it's such fun while it lasts.'

Joanna swallowed that remark with her lemon mousse and wished she could be as casual as Abby.

'I guess,' Abby mused, 'you could call Willem my any-port-in-a-storm. A safe port, anyway. I mean, he's not the type to strangle you in your bed or anything. But he's not a hunk or a heart-thump either.'

Part of the fun for Abby was categorising and pigeon-holing. Joanna found it hard to keep track.

'Tell me again the difference between a hunk and a heart-thump.'

'A hunk is somebody sort of muscle-bound, with a mind to match, but you don't care. I mean, you try not to talk and even less to listen. You just feel, and wow is it good. A heart-thump is more than just a physical delight. It's someone you like every which way, someone you can't resist even if he's married or neurotic or whatever. Someone who literally makes your heart go thump thump.'

Joanna thought of Lud Haley and she felt a warmth start in her toes and work its way tantalisingly up through the rest of her. By Abby's definition, he was Joanna's 'heart-thump'. In fact, she suspected he might be a womaniser, which would be okay for Abby, who changed her men as regularly as pantyhose, but not for Joanna.

'I'm going up to the lounge,' Abby said. 'Want to come?'

Joanna noted that Willem was not in his seat. 'No, thanks. I'll just finish these galleys.'

Abby hesitated. 'Do you need help?'

'Not really. I'm marking natural breaks in the text where we can put spots. I'll show you later.'

Joanna had once been to Amsterdam with Ben, and they had stayed at the Hilton. This time she had selected the Krasnapolsky, on the Central Dam, not far from the Omega offices.

It was Abby's first trip to The Netherlands. As she

26

looked out at the landscape on the way from Schiphol Airport she exclaimed to Joanna, 'Everything's so incredibly flat.'

'True. Hardly a molehill to make a mountain of, even if you wanted to.'

'What I do want is to dive into a hot bath and then a drink, to warm me up. Oh, look at the canals. Aren't they wonderful?'

'They certainly are. The Venice of the North, as the brochures say.'

'In that case bring on the singing gondoliers.'

The double room Joanna and Abby were sharing at the Krasnapolsky was cheerful and comfortably furnished in beige-and-gold tones, with bentwood-and-cane chairs and wicker furniture. Since neither of the women had been able to sleep much on the plane, they had a nap. Afterwards they explored the area near the hotel, which included a view of the Royal Palace.

'It was built on more than thirteen thousand piles,' Joanna told Abby, 'just to give you an idea of how marshy the land is underneath.'

Noise and bustle attracted the women to the Kalverstraat, the principal shopping street.

Abby dragged Joanna into a store selling wooden shoes. 'I always wanted to try a pair.'

They did and fell in love with them. The friends left the store wearing their purchases and giggling as they clopped along the street.

Although Abby wanted to sample the nightlife, Joanna convinced her to return to the hotel because they were due at Omega early the following day.

As they prepared for bed, Abby said, 'Funny, Willem hasn't called. He seemed so keen.'

'Maybe it's my fault for not striking the right note of enthusiasm.'

'Never mind. Someone else will turn up. Someone always does.'

The Amsterdam branch of Omega, with its staff of eight,

was tiny by New York standards. Joanna and Abby were to be working with Hans Terboch, editorial director, and Pieter Hynckes, his art director.

Joanna could see that Terboch, a portly fellow in his mid-fifties, very much resented having to defer to an American female young enough to be his daughter.

From the moment he saw the American layout, starting with the frontispiece and title page, Terboch voiced vigorous objections. Joanna pointed out two main reasons for the changes. The difference between Dutch and English meant altered spacing in text and captions. Also, the American audience, far less knowledgeable than native readers, would get more out of the type of photo that was boringly familiar to the Dutch.

'Certainly,' Terboch granted coldly, 'but this one of girls in traditional costume in the tulip fields makes me shudder... And you can't have that illustration on page six breaking up text that way...'

Pieter Hynckes, younger and more flexible and with a better eye than his boss, put in a quiet comment of support for Joanna, which drew an icy glare from Terboch. He continued to demand modification of every suggested change.

Abby, who was taking notes and keeping the pages organised, grew incensed. 'God, what an m.c.p.,' she whispered heatedly to Joanna during a moment alone. 'I don't know how you keep from kicking him where it would do the most good.'

'By thinking finished product. The book has to look good and sell a lot of copies. So we have to disregard the bad vibes from Mr Terboch and try to get around his objections. I guess he's the victim of his age and lowland upbringing, which we must try to rise above.'

'I admire you for making jokes, but I'd really like to dip his head in the canal until he yells uncle. I guess I'd better shut up.'

'Yes, Abby, please do. Especially during lunch.'

'Oh, hell, do we have to?'

Terboch escorted Pieter, Joanna, and Abby to an

elaborately formal restaurant where the waiters were dressed in white tie and tails.

'I don't believe this,' Abby moaned into Joanna's ear.

'Pretty fancy,' Joanna agreed. 'I just wanted something light, like a salad.'

'Forget it. It's going to be a banquet and cost the earth. I hope they don't make us go Dutch.'

'Shh,' Joanna hissed, stifling her laughter.

'If I may take the liberty of ordering for the young ladies,' Terboch stated, rather than asked.

'Please do,' Joanna responded, smiling agreeably. What she ate was inconsequential compared with the book she would take back. She could afford to allow him small victories.

The women stoically chewed their way through herring fillets on toast followed by pickled minced beef with apple and red cabbage, washing it down with cold Dutch beer.

Any attempt of Abby's to lighten the serious conversation was met by Terboch's uncomprehending frown and Joanna's elbow in her ribs.

In the ladies' room Abby exploded. 'That creep really takes the cake or the *koek* or whatever they call it. All I can say is "Thank God it's Friday". It *is* Friday, isn't it? I mean, we haven't lost it over the Atlantic or anything?'

'It's Friday, all right. Terboch goes off early for the weekend, so you may be able to spend the afternoon charming the red-cheeked Pieter.'

'You have something there,' Abby said complacently, applying lipstick. 'Little Pieter has definite possibilities and a real cute accent.'

'Just be discreet, please.'

'Aren't I always?'

They were right about Pieter. Without his boss the young man was pleasant and cooperative, and the work went without a hitch. That afternoon they got through four chapters.

'Isn't it nice of Pieter to offer to show us around town tomorrow, Joanna? Or are you going to say he's married too?'

'Nope. Much too shy and sweet. Anyway, he's certainly nicer than any-old-port-in-a-storm Willem.'

'Miles nicer,' Abby agreed. 'I could even see him as a heart-thump.'

Pieter took them sightseeing in a very handsome little power boat owned by Omega. It negotiated the labyrinthine canals under, it seemed to Joanna, most of the thousand and one bridges Amsterdam was reputed to have. Abby was in her element, able to combine nonstop questions and comments with suggestive glances and even more suggestive remarks.

Joanna left her to it, absorbed by the beautiful architecture of the houses fronting on the canals. Extended from some of the houses' top gables were heavy beams with big hooks attached; reminders of the days when Amsterdam had been a trading centre and ropes had pulled up baskets of spices and silks directly from the boats.

Joanna had very fond memories of Amsterdam, even though when she had been here with Ben their relationship had begun to turn sour. Now she was able to see the city through her own eyes, though she secretly thought it might be great fun to be with somebody who could share her experience – somebody like Lud Haley.

'I'm hungry,' Abby told Pieter, 'and now the sun's vanished and it's getting cold. How about a drink and some of that famous pea soup?'

Pieter found a cafe and ordered three jenevers, served chilled in shot glasses. 'Dutch gin, very strong,' he explained.

Abby grinned impudently at him. 'Just watch us.'

The women quaffed their drinks in two gulps.

'It's neat, neat,' Joanna joked, 'and here comes the pea soup. Reminds me of London fogs I have known and loved.'

Abby's easy laughter made Pieter smile although he really didn't catch on.

Later, while they were studying Rembrandt's 'Night Watch' at the Riijksmuseum, Abby's roving eye picked out a familiar figure. She moved forward and touched the arm of a tall, lean man.

'Dominic? Of all people, of all places. Are you really real?'

'If you want to be sure, give us a kiss, love,' he mimicked in Cockney, planting one on her cheek.

'Joanna, look what I found,' Abby announced, pulling Dominic by the hand. 'You remember cousin Dominic, don't you?'

'Of course. Hello,' Joanna murmured. Dominic Graham was not a man one easily forgot. Aside from his regal bearing, he had an unusual face, with prominent cheekbones, thin, aristocratic features, and a healthy, ruddy complexion. A shock of dark hair gave him a rakish English look.

'How nice to see you again, Joanna.'

She shook his hand and smiled shyly.

Abby introduced the two men, who exchanged a few words.

'You are British?' Pieter questioned.

'English, actually,' he replied, at the same time that Abby said, 'As British as tea and crumpets.'

They looked at each other and laughed.

'The English are British, of course,' Dominic explained, 'but we usually don't use the terms interchangeably. If I were Scots or Welsh or Irish I might resent being called English – '

'But since you're English you're not keen to be taken for anything but,' Joanna joined the banter.

Dominic smiled, his grey eyes cool and penetrating. 'You have me there. I confess to a measure of pride in being English, which is probably a little defensive because I've lived in the States so long.'

'How long have you been in Amsterdam?' Abby broke in, 'and how long are you staying?'

'Came over for a medical conference a week ago, and I'm leaving the day after tomorrow.'

'Oh, hell, just when we got here.' Abby linked arms with Dominic and Pieter. 'Dom used to be married to my dancer cousin, Alexis. They met in Britain when she was on tour. That was about ten years ago. He's a doctor, the kind that finds babies under cabbage leaves.' Giggling merrily at the perplexed look on Pieter's face, she explained that Dr Dominic Graham was the head of obstetrics at St Anne's Hospital in New York.

'If you've all seen enough for one afternoon, I'd like to buy everyone a drink,' Dominic said.

'Great,' Abby responded enthusiastically. 'I'm glad somebody around here isn't completely carried away by art, with a capital A. Besides, my feet are crying out for a rest.'

Dominic offered his arm so that Joanna could walk on his other side.

'I haven't seen you in ages, Joanna, not since a party at Abby's a couple of years ago, I believe.'

'I guess that's right.' Joanna remembered the evening only vaguely. It seemed to her that Dominic had still been married then.

'Abby was so happy when you offered her a job as your assistant. She fills me in from time to time on the doings at Omega, the petty annoyances, the office politics we're all so familiar with.'

'Can there be "office politics" in a hospital?'

'There certainly can. The props may be different but the power plays are the same. Too many doctors think they're only slightly below the status of the supreme medicine man in the sky, and egos get bruised all over the place. Especially because the hierarchy at a hospital is so rigid. You know, intern, resident, consultant, head of department...'

Dominic talked on, in his attractive Oxbridge accent, making Joanna smile with his amusing descriptions of doctors' animosities.

'And how is Nadine?'

'Just fine.' Joanna sighed involuntarily. Even on the other side of the ocean she couldn't escape being the Joanna of Nadine-and-Joanna.

32

'I run into your sister occasionally in Central Park with the children. Kate and Jeff are growing up beautifully.'

'Yes, they are.' Joanna's face muscles relaxed.

'I delivered both of Joanna's sister's children,' Dominic explained to Pieter. 'It's nice to keep track.'

To postpone the inevitable mention of the twin business, Joanna hastened to talk about her niece and nephew. 'Jeff is a whiz with anything mechanical, and Kate draws so beautifully she'll be ready to work in our department in a few years.'

'Oh, thanks a lot,' Abby snorted. 'Then I lose out to nepotism – or rather nieceotism.'

Joanna laughed and her eyes locked with Dominic's. Embarrassed, she quickly switched her glance to Abby. 'By then you'll be married and living in Westchester, creating your own candidates for nepotism.'

Over drinks, Dominic drew Pieter out, asking about aspects of Dutch politics and way of life.

Abby, becoming restless, steered the conversation to lighter and more desultory quipping and flirting.

'Tell me, Pieter, in absolute confidence,' Abby giggled, after two jenevers, 'Is Mr Terboch always so deadly serious?'

Pieter considered. 'You believe so? To me he is fair to work with and lively enough. But I suppose you think we Dutch don't go in much for joking, not in your way.'

'For good reasons, I imagine,' Dominic mused. 'Keeping a country from being reclaimed by the sea is serious business, and anyone not on his toes would soon have floundered in very deep water.'

Joanna, smiling and again meeting Dominic's piercing eyes, lowered hers first.

'Of course there is our Calvinistic religion,' Pieter went on.

'Well, I don't get it,' Abby said. 'During the sixties this was hippy paradise. The drug scene, porn, all kinds of weird behaviour, the worse the better.'

'One of life's little paradoxes,' Dominic explained. 'The careful, punctual Dutch are amazingly tolerant of differ-

33

ences, though the dropouts went much too far in making a mess of this city. The last couple of years have been much better.'

'Damn. I've got here too late, as usual,' Abby grumbled. 'Wherever I go, people always say, "Oh, it's different now, spoiled, touristy, dirty, cleaned up, whatever. You should have seen it last year, ten years ago, two centuries ago".'

'Poor baby.' Dominic smiled at her. 'I think we can still manage to give you a glimpse of Amsterdam's underside, can't we Pieter?'

'Yes, but it is time to leave for the restaurant now,' he insisted rather stolidly.

'Pieter is taking us to an Indonesian place,' Abby said to Dominic. 'You're coming with us, I hope.'

'Yes, please join us,' Pieter echoed.

'I'd like that, thank you, if Joanna doesn't mind.'

'No, of course not.' In fact, she preferred to have him along, the presence of a fourth person making her feel less awkward while Abby did her seductive number on Pieter.

Abby was the only one among them who had never experienced a genuine Indonesian *rijstaffel*, and she was bewildered at the array of more than twenty small dishes accompanying the rice, all set out to be shared.

'Pork satay,' Pieter pointed out, 'shrimps in hot pepper.' He ordered cold beer for everyone.

After dinner, Abby took Pieter's arm. 'Okay, enough of this tame stuff, lead me to the ladies of the night.'

'Very well, if you wish,' Pieter agreed, blushing.

The four of them joined the droves of tourists who came to witness the phenomenon of prostitutes sitting behind red-lighted windows. Dressed in provocative silky lingerie, the women read magazines, polished their nails, or simply looked out, smiling invitingly at the passing parade.

'It's crazy,' Joanna remarked to Abby. 'All this is acceptable, but if you come two minutes late for a dinner reservation the captain acts as if you've murdered your mother.'

'If you come late for dinner, you probably have,' Pieter said.

Abby, delighted, gave him a kiss. 'Who says the Dutch have no sense of humour.'

Again Joanna found herself laughing with Dominic, sharing the moment, and she had stopped being flustered.

'Amsterdam,' Pieter was explaining, 'used to be a shipping centre, and ships meant sailors looking for diversion. Now the tourists look for diversion. Of course this district is regulated by the government.'

'That's all right then,' Joanna said sardonically.

'Does this scene bother you?' Dominic's eyes probed hers curiously.

Joanna shrugged. 'If women want to earn their living this way, that's their business. I just find it sad.'

'Well, I don't,' Abby said. 'At least these women can make a choice. They sit in their own living rooms and they can say yea or nay. I think it's fabulous. And I'm amazed at how young most of them are, and how pretty. That one over there is just plain stunning. Don't you think so, Dominic?'

'Not really.'

'Which one turns you on?'

'None of that lot.'

'You're just too cheap to pay,' Abby teased.

Dominic gave her a playful swipe. 'And you're an *enfant terrible*.'

'That's your fault for not taming me,' she threw back, fixing him with wickedly flirtatious eyes.

He raised his eyebrows mockingly. 'Shocking, madam.'

'I've seen enough here, Pieter,' Abby declared. 'How about a club, something really sinful.'

Pieter agreed, apparently bewitched by Abby and flattered at her attentions. The sort of nightclub Abby craved didn't interest Joanna at all.

Dominic glanced at her. 'At this point I'd rather have a quiet brandy. Joanna, would you care to join me?'

Before she could reply, Abby said, 'Okay, you old fogies, go ahead and have your brandy. Pieter and I are going to paint this town red – I mean redder.'

Abby obviously wanted to be alone with Pieter, and Joanna was grateful to have an option. 'A drink would be nice, thank you, Dominic.'

'I'm at the Krasnapolsky,' Joanna told him in the taxi.

'Yes, so Abby said. They have an American bar, I believe. Not terribly exciting. Actually, I know an offbeat place, a local watering hole that scarcely ever sees a tourist. It means a short drive outside of the city.'

'As long as it's not halfway to Luxembourg. By midnight I'll be dozing.'

'I promise to have you back at your hotel before the second yawn. Okay?'

'Okay.' She smiled and relaxed. Until today Joanna had known Abby's cousin-by-marriage only slightly. He was much better acquainted with Nadine. Having had the impression that Dominic was rather dull, Joanna was finding his company surprisingly pleasant. Especially as he didn't think it necessary to keep up a constant conversation. She was grateful for the interval of silence during the ride because she felt a little stiff from her efforts to be sociable all evening. Now she was able to look out of the window at the glittering lights of the city, and then at the flat, quiet countryside dotted with houses. Her heartbeat increased as she thought suddenly of Lud Haley, and what it might be like to see Amsterdam with him.

Dominic helped Joanna out of the taxi and led her into a windmill. 'The name of this place translates as The Old Mill, not surprisingly. Although it's converted it still retains windmill features.'

'How charming,' Joanna exclaimed as they took seats at the round wooden bar. 'You were right about the natives. We're the only ones gawking.'

'I hope it remains that way because this place has the makings of a spectacle. The works in the tower have been removed to make room for seats, and the bartenders hoist drinks by means of that pulley.'

While they waited for their jenevers, Joanna watched in fascination as trays of drinks were raised to the upper storey so quickly that not one drop of liquid in the glasses was spilled, although it hardly seemed possible.

Their drinks arrived in stemmed glasses with no feet. Instead, the stems were rounded so as to fit into holes imbedded in the bar itself.

'That's ingenious,' Joanna observed.

'And practical. The Dutch can really knock back the booze. I guess this system keeps the drinks upright even if the drinkers are atilt.'

She laughed and lifted her glass. '*Skol.*'

'That's Danish. You mean *Proost.*'

'Do I? As in Marcel? Sounds French to me.'

He grinned. 'We'll be American, then. Here's looking at you, kid.' His imitation of Bogart delivering his famous line was credible, accompanied by a suitably romantic facial expression.

Joanna touched her glass to his and smiled a little uncomfortably. 'How did you happen to find this place?'

'We were taken here by a couple of Dutch doctors at our conference.'

'I see. What was the conference about?'

'New theories about birth traumas.'

Seeing the fleeting look of dismay on Joanna's face, Dominic did not elaborate. 'How's your drink?'

'Just perfect, thanks.'

'Although I invited you for a brandy, I've wound up drinking the national drink. I guess I usually do. Ouzo in Greece, Pernod in France, Campari in Italy, malt whisky in Britain, martinis in America.'

'I do too. A martini would be awfully out of place here. Are you going to stop over in England?'

'I've already been. Spent a few days in Sussex with my sister and her husband as well as some time in London looking up old friends.'

37

During a pause, Joanna looked around her curiously. 'I wonder what it would be like to grow up in a round house like this windmill. Must give a person quite a different view of the world.'

'It must. Well-rounded, rather than square, wouldn't you say? I began life in an Elizabethan half-timbered house, so to the young me a roof over one's head meant thatch.'

'How marvellous. I was in Rye, for a day, and fell in love with those houses. I found them so exotic.'

'It may strike you as improbable but for me the height of exoticism when I first got to New York was a penthouse on the forty-first floor, surrounded on three sides by terrace and with a view of the East River.'

'Not improbable at all, to a farmgirl coming from a wooden shack in Texas on land almost as flat as this is. I'd probably be very different if I'd been born at the foot of the Rockies and had grown up looking at towering peaks.'

'Or even the towering peaks of Manhattan,' Dominic added.

'True. Which reminds me that very few people I meet in New York were actually born there. Home has its virtues, of course, but I always knew I'd be a New Yorker even before I ever got to the place.'

'Me too. From my first day I felt at home in Manhattan, in spite of the language they call, unaccountably, English, and the noise, and the people keeping to a pace that boggled my mind until I caught up. Much as I love visiting England, I don't think I could live there again.'

'I feel the same about Texas.'

Dominic lifted his glass. 'Let's drink to the Big Apple, then, and to getting together there over a martini so we can talk about Amsterdam.'

Joanna laughed without replying. Dominic was fun, but when she thought of drinking martinis in New York, Lud Haley was the person who came to mind.

4

'Ooh, what a luxury to have breakfast in bed,' Abby declared, sipping her coffee. 'Though I could use a little more sleep. Didn't get home until the wee hours, but Pieter's coming by at eleven to pick me up. We had such a smashing time last night. Went to a place where they do everything you can imagine in the way of sex, and in public, too. After that warm-up Pieter invited me back to his place, but of course I wouldn't go on the first date.'

Joanna smiled. 'Since today will be the second date, does it mean you won't be sleeping here tonight?'

'I hope so,' Abby said, so fervently that Joanna laughed.

'Hope you will or won't?'

Abby flung a pillow at her. 'Won't. I'd better get showered and dressed. You're welcome to come with us, of course. We're driving to The Hague and we'll probably have dinner there.'

'No, thanks. You really don't need a crowd, Abby, and I'll be fine by myself, honest.'

While Abby was in the shower the phone rang.

'Good morning, Joanna. Dominic. It's my last day in Amsterdam and I decided to do something I've never got round to, namely seeing the city on a bicycle like a native. Does the idea appeal to you?'

'Yes, it does sound like fun, as long as I don't have to ride tandem.'

'I guarantee you your own wheels. Abby is invited too, of course, though I seem to recall that cycling is not her favourite form of exercise.'

Joanna smiled to herself because she had a fair idea of what was. 'Abby's going driving with Pieter.'

Joanna arranged to meet Dominic in the hotel lobby.

'Did I hear the phone?' Abby asked, emerging from the bathroom wrapped in a towel.

'Yes. Dominic, suggesting a bike ride through the city.'

'Wow. You said yes, of course.' Abby threw her a knowing smirk.

'I said yes to the ride, but you can forget the rest of what you're thinking.'

'Nothing bad. Just that it's great Dom's so interested in you. You know, since he's been on the market women have been breaking down his door for a chance to grab the most eligible man in New York.'

'Yes, I can imagine he'd have his choice, but I'm not in the running and that's voluntary.'

'Why not? Jesus, he's terrific.'

'Did his wife leave him?'

'No. He left her. Alexis was a sensation seeker. She needed to be admired twenty-four hours a day, preferably by twenty-four different men.'

While Abby rattled on, Joanna was trying to remember whether or not Dominic had ever dated Nadine. She seemed to recall that her sister had turned him down.

'Dominic's very nice but I'll keep it light, if you don't mind.'

Abby looked at her closely. 'Anybody else heavy on the horizon?'

'Maybe,' was all Joanna would reveal, but she couldn't help smiling mysteriously.

'Well, I can't imagine what another man could have that Dominic doesn't. In fact, Dom has been my alltime heart-thump for years. He just doesn't take me seriously.'

Neither did Joanna. In fact, she didn't want to take Abby at all right now. She wanted to have another cup of coffee and think about the extraordinary eyes of Lud Haley.

*

'I haven't been on a bike in so long that I'm wobbling,' Joanna said anxiously.

'You'll get used to it. Just follow me on to a quiet street. Take as long as you like until you feel quite comfortable,' Dominic advised.

It was a cool, crisp day, and the sun peeped from behind fleecy clouds every few minutes, sending gleaming shafts of light on the water of the canals.

Joanna had initially felt cold in her suede jacket and trousers, but her exertions were making her extremely warm.

'There you go, Joanna. You've got the hang of it already.'

'Yes, this is much better,' she agreed, relieved. She didn't want to be a drag.

'Okay, we're off.' Dominic effortlessly pedalled on to a major street slowly enough so that Joanna could keep up. Every few moments he looked around and noted that she was a perfectly competent cyclist.

Joanna was one of the few American women he had come across who was modest about her accomplishments. Personal reticence was something the English took for granted, and Dominic still couldn't get used to what he often thought of as boasting. He found it especially unappealing in women. Joanna, of course, wasn't unappealing in any way.

'How do you keep from getting your wheels caught in the trolley tracks?' Joanna panted, when they stopped for a light. 'I'm petrified that I'm going to get stuck and go flying into the air.'

'Don't worry, I'll catch you. Or a flying Dutchman will, anyway. You're doing just fine. I suspect you're more experienced at this than you let on.'

'No, not really. We had a relic of boy's bike back home. My sister and I learned on it, but that took some doing,' Joanna continued, as she and Dominic rode side by side on a tree-lined street alongside a canal. 'The tricky thing was the bike had no brakes. We would yell, "Y'all git," as we

41

jumped down, trying to stop it with our feet, and usually managing to smash into a tree or something.'

'At least you know what to do should your brakes fail.'

'Anyway, I had a bike at college and rode it around Austin. Nothing more ambitious than that. I can't see myself on one of those ten-speed jobs the bicycle freaks ride, pedalling like mad.'

'Like this?' Although his bike was only three-speed, Dominic suddenly hunched over the handlebars and took off like a streak.

'Oh, wow, look at him go,' Joanna said aloud, laughing.

He waited for her to catch up, grinning with embarrassment at the way he had been unable to resist showing off. And after he had just been thinking unkind thoughts about that sort of thing, too.

'That was certainly impressive,' Joanna granted, smiling at him.

'Thanks. Actually, I'm not the bicycle freak you may think. I was being facetious. I couldn't keep that up for ten minutes. It's been many years, about eighteen, I blush to admit, since I tooled around Oxford. And I used to take cycling holidays on the Continent with my friends.'

'I see. Switzerland?'

'Not quite.' He smiled at her and pedalled away, Joanna following. She was enjoying herself enormously and feeling very healthy. She was glad she could ride as well as ever, even if she wasn't in Dominic's class.

Watching him from behind, she could picture him manoeuvring around Oxford, wearing his Shetland sweater under a tweed jacket, his hair windblown over those ruddy English cheeks.

After a while they stopped at a herring stall. Dominic ordered two herrings and held each by the tail, as Joanna looked on in dismay.

He laughed at her expression. 'No, madam, no knife and fork. Just take yours, like this, and down the hatch.'

'Oh, God, I can't.'

'Of course you can. Come on now, be big and brave.'

Joanna finally took hold of the herring gingerly and dangled it in front of her face.

'That's it, but hold it up a little and tilt your head back so that it misses your nose. It tastes better than it smells.'

'It better!' Taking a deep breath, she bit into the herring. Dominic laughed. 'Okay?'

'Hey, it's pretty good.'

'I thought you'd change your mind. How about a second helping?'

'No, thanks. It's not that good. I'd like something to wash it down with, and off my face.'

Dominic found them a little cafe.

They resumed their ride, stopping at a stall where a man was baking small round waffles. When they were ready, he sandwiched two with a sticky caramel filling.

Joanna ate hers greedily. 'Now that's a Dutch custom I could get used to. What's this called?'

'The vendor says it's a *schtropevaffel*.'

'Mm. Very onomatopoeic, especially when your teeth stick together.'

'I see you have a sweet tooth. Nadine, I seem to recall, can take sweets or leave them. I'd expect identical twins to be more alike in this respect.'

Joanna had the distinct feeling that he was with her mainly because she was Nadine's twin. Well, he wouldn't be the first man to feel that way.

Although they broke up their bike tour with a visit to the Van Gogh Museum, by late afternoon Joanna felt she had pedalled through every 'straat' and 'gracht' in Amsterdam.

'I'll take the bikes back, Joanna. You look as if you could use a hot soak, to loosen up those muscles.'

'I think I will. Thanks, Dominic, for a lovely day.'

'It can extend into evening as well, if you'd care to join me for dinner.'

Joanna hesitated. It really wouldn't be fair to let him think that her interest in him was in any way personal.

'Thanks, but I think I'll have a quiet evening in my room.'

'Well, I'll be at my hotel, the Sonesta, if you should change your mind.'

Dominic walked away wheeling both bicycles and knowing Joanna wouldn't call him. He felt somewhat let down. Had he imagined that at times she had been particularly responsive to him? Most probably she treated everyone with the same kindness and bright appreciation of humour. She was witty herself.

In any event, it was obvious that she didn't find him appealing, and he would do well to stop being so juvenile as to wish for something he couldn't have.

5

The phone was ringing as Joanna entered her apartment. It was Nadine.

'Yes, everything went well,' said Joanna, 'but I'm really exhausted. Couldn't sleep on the plane, and I'm barely conscious. Can we talk tomorrow? Lunch will be great.'

Joanna opened the living room window briefly, inhaling the fresh cold air. Then, kicking off her shoes, she lay down on the couch and relaxed her body inch by inch.

Her apartment, on the top floor of an elegant old brownstone on Seventy-third and Madison, was small but cosy, her place of refuge. After her divorce from Ben, Joanna had found it unbearable to remain in their large place, which was only a few doors away from Nadine. She had sold it with all the furnishings in spite of her sister's objections.

This apartment, originally a sublet, had been listed on the office bulletin board. A few months after she had rented it, the owner had decided to sell, and Joanna had jumped at the chance.

She had enjoyed collecting the furniture herself after Ben's insistence on ordinary department-store stuff. In the living room there was a comfortable modular sofa covered in beige suede. Accents of colour were provided by a muted Persian rug and paintings of Schiele and Klimt. There was a Tiffany lamp, low mahogany bookcases and side tables and a marble cocktail table, as well as a Mission rocking chair. Her small collection of pre-Columbian figures adorned shelves in front of the windows, amid a jungle of plants.

In the dining area adjoining the kitchen, one wall papered with a William Morris Art Nouveau pattern

45

served as a backdrop for the early nineteenth-century French bleached oak dining table and four English side chairs. Her small den contained a rolltop desk, drawing board, and a floor-to-ceiling oak bookcase. In the bedroom an early American quilt covered the platform bed, flanked by 1920s night tables of glass and chrome. On the floor was a one-of-a-kind beige rug in a modern pattern. The white walls were hung with paintings by Hartsley and Hopper, and drawings by Picasso.

After a hot bath, Joanna got into bed and watched the news on television. A filming crew was shown on location and Joanna thought of Lud Haley. She hoped he would call her because, rose or no rose, she was very shy about making the first move after a two-week absence.

In the morning Joanna dressed warmly in fleecy boots over grey flannel trousers, a yellow cashmere sweater, and a tweed jacket under her mauve down coat. She left the house early enough to walk to work.

The sun cast a pale light without much warmth, but Joanna felt energetic, working up to an easy stride, her breath steaming into the icy January air.

Picking up four containers of coffee, she took the lift up to the eleventh floor. It was only a few minutes past nine.

Joanna put one coffee on her secretary's desk, one in Abby's cubicle, and took her own and the remaining container to the office of her boss, Irwin Kranick, Editor-in-Chief and Project Manager of the Travel Books Division. He was already at his desk, surrounded by a sea of pasteups.

For ten of her thirteen years at Omega, Joanna had worked with Winnie and they were old buddies.

'*Dag, Mijnheer,*' she greeted him in Dutch.

'Hey, babe, how're you doing? Welcome back. On the dot, and with coffee, too. More than I can say for your shadow. Abby just called to report she'll be late. Overslept.'

'Well, she deserves a little more sleep.' Joanna fell into

a seat. 'She's been working like a serf to get the layouts into shape for today's meeting. What a time we had with Terboch. He turned out to be as immovable as the boy at the dyke, questioning the most trivial changes. He hates not having total control...'

'Yeah, he sounds like a pain. We've had our own troubles with the Switzerland manuscript...'

Winnie's round, plain-featured face and homey speech made him seem like a Bronx shopkeeper, an image that was deceptive. He was a strong ideas man who had devised the travel series and he had a lot of clout at the company.

'Okay, enough business for now. What's happening with you, kiddo? You're looking secretly happy, as if you'd met that special someone over there.'

'No,' Joanna said lightly, 'but I did have a wonderful time. Amsterdam is quite fascinating...'

Abby wandered in, yawning, and took a swig of her coffee. 'It was just fabulous, Winnie. You've really got to get yourself over there.'

He shrugged. 'I'll stay over here if it's all the same to you. My folks barely escaped the holocaust, so the old country doesn't hold any special charms for Kranick survivors.'

'But you're the one who thought up the whole series,' Abby persisted. 'I don't understand.'

'Nothing to understand. I can find out what's there without making the trip in person. It's called professionalism, and knowing how to delegate work.'

The truth was that he had a pathological fear of flying, and travelling by ship wasn't much better because he got seasick.

'You two were happy enough to do the Europe bit.'

'And how. You can send me back any time,' Abby granted, 'only I could use another twelve hours sleep.'

Winnie smiled at her shrewdly. 'I'll bet you had a Dutch treat or two.'

Abby giggled. 'I'll say. There was this really sweet art director – oh, there's my phone.'

'Go and take a snooze at your desk,' Winnie called after her.

'Are you kidding? I can see the pile of work from here.'

'She didn't go overboard, I hope,' Winnie said to Joanna when Abby had left. 'What did you two get up to anyway?'

Joanna smiled. Winnie was hopelessly nosy, but she felt more comfortable with him than with most other people. When he had taken over the travel book section her initial impression of him as a clown had been reversed during their first week together. Ten years older than she, Winnie was steeped in New York smarts. Also, he thought Joanna was terrific, and from the beginning had assumed the role of father-cum-big-brother. He had been instrumental in getting Joanna her promotion.

Winnie was a bachelor and never dated as far as Joanna knew. He had women friends, like her, but that seemed to be all. She didn't think he was gay. Possibly he was neuter, too much involved with his old parents and paralysed by periodic bouts of hypochondria. In any case, his personal life, if he had one, was not open for discussion. He preferred to advise Joanna about hers. Sometimes he pushed his way into her affairs more than she would have liked. Still, his support had been invaluable when she went though the agony of her breakup with Ben.

'Come on, give. Uncle Winnie's waiting.'

'Okay, okay,' Joanna gave in, smiling. She filled him in briefly about Abby's flirtation with Pieter and in the course of the story Dominic's name had to be mentioned.

'Aha.' Winnie gave her a knowing look.

'No aha about it. Just a pleasant interlude.'

'If it was so pleasant, why not continue it in New York? I've met the guy a couple of times, and in my opinion, you could do worse.'

Joanna smiled. 'I know you'd like nothing better than to arrange a marriage for me old-world style but I'm going to have to decline that particular honour. Anyway, there's the possibility of someone else, but of course it's only speculation at this point.'

She summarised her meeting with Lud and mentioned the rose he had sent her. 'It may not mean anything much.'

'Of course it means something. Listen, you've got a lot on the ball, and any man with eyes could see that.'

She kissed Winnie's cheek in a sisterly way. 'Thanks for the pep talk. Now, can I go and do some work, please, boss?'

'Yeah. Scram.'

Lisa had put a pile of pink telephone messages on Joanna's desk, and she read them from the top slowly and ritualistically, feeling a stab of disappointment that Lud's name wasn't among the callers.

Joanna, arriving before her sister at the Italian restaurant, was seated at a table near the wrap-around window. As soon as Nadine joined her, the twins, as always, became the object of admiring stares.

Nadine looked radiant in a teal blue cashmere sweater dress adorned with an antique gold rope chain. She seemed so unlike the unenergetic woman she had been recently that Joanna could only gape at her with delight. 'You look terrific.'

'I feel terrific. Oh, Jan, so much has happened. I almost called you in Amsterdam but then I decided I'd wait until the screen test.'

'Screen test?'

'Yes. I've never really given up on my dream of being an actress, but I felt I was too old to start with drama school again and without it I couldn't ever find my way to a role. Well, by a wonderful stroke of luck a role has found its way to me.'

A warning bell went off in Joanna's head and an odd feeling began to arch up her backbone.

'Remember Fern Brunner? She's in New York, of all places. You know, old Bossy Missy, you used to call her.

49

Out of the blue she phoned me and wanted me to meet a television director she's working for...'

Out of the blue.

Joanna felt her insides crumble.

'... All so quick. "Put on your best duds, Naddie,"' Nadine mimicked with deadly accuracy, '"and get your tail over here. You're going to be a star."'

Three trendily dressed young men stopped outside the restaurant to read the menu but wound up gawking at the twins. They grinned and made admiring gestures. Joanna looked away but Nadine, revelling in the limelight, kept smiling as she continued her animated narrative.

For a moment Joanna saw her sister as others saw her: a vivid, exciting, self-confident woman, basking in the knowledge that she was beautiful. Joanna felt like a blurred, paler print of the original. She had never been able to let herself go the way Nadine did. A little hard knob within Joanna always cautioned reserve, directing her to hold back something of herself. Because if she gave everything and it was rejected she would have nothing left.

'... So attractive, so dynamic. He's already made quite a splash but he's going to go to the absolute top, I can tell. Wait until you meet him. His name is –'

'Lud Haley,' Joanna supplied.

'But that's remarkable!'

'Not really.' Trying to keep the anguish out of her voice, Joanna told her sister about meeting Fern and Lud.

'And you never said a word! Come to think of it, neither did they. Well, they're so frantically busy. You, I suppose, forgot because the last thing you'd be interested in is a part in a television series.'

'It was mentioned to me in any case,' Joanna murmured, her ears burning. She knew it was mean of her to minimise Nadine's accomplishment.

But her sister only laughed with delight. 'I'll bet you told Lud what he could do with the role.'

Joanna, remembering her defensiveness, had reason to regret it.

'What's the matter? You didn't want the part, did you?'

Joanna shook her head. *I wanted the man.* Now she knew for certain that her first instinct about Lud had been correct. He had been merely casting the part. A rose was only a rose. Lud had no interest in her, hadn't even mentioned to Nadine that he had met her.

'Jan, what is it?'

Joanna squeezed her sister's hand across the table. 'Don't mind me. Just tired from the trip. I'm really glad for you, Dini. I know you'll do splendidly.'

'I hope so. I'm going to have to study and work like I never did in my life.' Too excited to eat, she left most of her food untouched. Joanna did the same because she was feeling so unreasonably depressed. Conflicting emotions were turning somersaults within her. Yes, she was genuinely pleased that Nadine would at last be doing something exciting for herself. Joanna hadn't quite realised the extent of her sister's acting ambitions and she thought guiltily that her own disdain for the profession might have had a negative influence. Her sister was a different person when she was happy and enthusiastic.

If only all this had come about some other way, without involving Lud Haley. If he were not a director . . . but of course it was fated to be so. Nadine had always been lucky in love.

Joanna could imagine Lud's first reaction to her sister. He must have seen Joanna plus, Joanna to the nth power.

She excused herself right after coffee, claiming a huge backlog of work.

At the staff meeting Joanna went over the layouts, but by the end she had a raging headache and just wanted to go home.

Winnie stopped by her office. 'What's happening? This morning's bride looks like this afternoon's widow. He hasn't called, is that it?'

'I don't want to talk about it, please.'

'You always say that when you're aggravated, but you

51

know that talking helps. So give.' He eased his bulk into a chair.

'Come on, kiddo. Catholics confess to their priest and Jews confess to anyone who'll listen. But you WASPS swallow it down until it burns a hole in your gut.'

'Winnie, please.'

He took off his thick glasses and looked at Joanna with compassionate eyes. 'It just hurts me to see you unhappy, that's all.' He spoke tenderly as a father might to his little girl, as Joanna's father didn't speak to her. She was touched.

'There's not much to tell. Fern called Nadine, introduced her to Lud Haley, and to make it short, she was offered the star role in his series.'

Joanna had never confided to anybody the extent of her troubled feelings about herself in relation to her sister, but Winnie perceived some of it. 'And?'

'And nothing. Isn't that enough?'

'Not the way I see it. So your sister is working for the director. So what? If that guy liked you before, he'll like you now. Just because you and Nadine look alike and sound alike doesn't mean you are alike.'

'Well, first impressions count and Nadine is so comfortable with new people, so self-confident. It always takes me longer,' she finished wistfully.

Winnie didn't immediately reply. Watching Joanna put on her coat, he was thinking that men could be such fools. Yes, Nadine had a pleasant surface charm, but Joanna had everything.

'Never mind, princess, you'll meet your prince someday. If not this Lud, someone else will come along, I promise you.'

She smiled wryly and picked up her attaché case. 'Then I won't worry.'

What Joanna didn't voice was her fear that her prince might very well choose her sister.

52

6

Joanna had arrived in New York in the autumn of 1968, intrigued and a little scared. Ever since her teenage years New York had been the city of her dreams, the place where 'bachelor girls' had exciting careers, lived in glamorous apartments with views over the city and dated handsome, sophisticated men, eventually choosing a husband among them.

Of course, before all these wonderful things happened to Joanna, she had had to find a place to live and a job. She took a room at the Martha Washington Hotel for women on East Thirtieth Street and began to look for work as a magazine art assistant.

In fact, she had left Texas rather suddenly, needing to flee from the hurt of Nadine's engagement. Since separation was inevitable, Joanna had decided to make the first move. Besides, she wanted to establish her own identity and get started on the career she had promised herself as a child.

During her first week in New York she had realised how really backward she was, how ill-equipped to cope with her new surroundings. Her college city, Austin, with a population of less than two hundred thousand, was a small town in comparison, a place where total strangers often said, 'Howdy, y'all' on the street without meaning to be personal. Although she had been to Dallas for her television work, she had never spent much time there. Dallas hadn't captured her imagination the way New York had.

The thing that had struck Joanna immediately was that New York had more to offer the rich than the poor. If she could have got her hands on her money she would have been able to live at the Plaza, shop on Fifth Avenue, and learn the city at her leisure instead of having to find a job within weeks or return home.

Although the twins' television earnings had always been turned over to their aunt, who saw that the money was properly invested, their father, A.W. Lennox, had been designated the trustee. Joanna and Nadine had assumed they would get control of their funds at twenty-one, but they learned that they would have to wait four more years because their father believed that young people – especially females – had no sense at all. What A.W. wanted for his daughters was marriage to men of good families with money of their own. Nadine was already on her way to fulfilling her father's aspirations but Joanna, the maverick, received scant sympathy from him. He had opposed her trip to New York and had grudgingly parted with only a few dollars.

The pressure to start earning was a problem for Joanna, adding to her anxiety of being alone in a strange city, a place where nobody knew or cared. She longed to fit in and felt sure she would, given a little time. But at the beginning she was so achingly lonely, alternating between feeling relief at being a singleton for once and missing Nadine terribly.

On a Friday evening, after three weeks of frustrated job hunting, Joanna roamed the Shubert Alley area, trying to work up the courage to go to the theatre by herself. She was bewildered by the people jostling her, the leering men who tried to pick her up, the brassy neon lights, and the smells of junk food.

Outside Town Hall she got caught up in a crush of people and she paused to look at the concert advertisement. Julian Bream was playing sixteenth-century music on the lute that evening.

On her way to the box office, Joanna noticed a man holding up two tickets.

'For you, half price,' he said.

'I'm afraid I need only one,' she apologised in her gentle drawl.

54

'That's okay. One ticket for a buck fifty.'

She bought the ticket. Her seat was in the tenth row in the centre. Looking at her stub, she saw that she had paid much less than half price and she grew warm with embarrassment and gratitude, especially when she saw that the ticket seller was just sitting down next to her.

'How's the seat?'

'Just fine, but you didn't charge me enough.'

He grinned. 'Let's call it a welcome to New York from one out-of-towner to another.'

'Well, thank you,' she murmured shyly. 'I expected you'd sell the other ticket.'

'Me too, but my only customer was an old man reeking of garlic. I couldn't do that to such a lovely young lady so I decided to join you after all. I hope you don't mind.'

'No, of course not.' In fact she was pleased, drawn to his open manner, friendly brown eyes, and sincere way of speaking. He seemed very different from other men she had been meeting.

'Michigan's my home. I'd guess you to be from the southwest. Texas, maybe?'

'Oh, Lordy, it really shows.'

'Only because I've been there, ma'am.'

A wave of homesickness brought tears to Joanna's eyes as she listened to her companion tell of his travels through Texas, among other places. He was a freelance journalist with an interest in politics. And he, too, was supporting Hubert Humphrey for president.

During the intermission she and her neighbour talked about the wonderful music and of Bream's technique. Little by little her new friend drew her out, undoubtedly sensing her loneliness. Before Joanna realised it, she had told him of her situation.

'I was in a similar spot three years back when I first got here. You've been looking for a job the hard way.'

His name was Carl Barrett and he invited her to lunch the next day, suggesting she give up on magazines and leave her resumé and a covering letter with book publishers that had large art departments.

Within two weeks Joanna had a job at Omega and a furnished studio in a walkup on West Seventy-fourth Street, not far from where Carl lived.

Joanna began to date Carl regularly and they advanced from the good-night kiss to passionate embraces on her sofa. Joanna, who was still a virgin, was grateful that he wasn't rushing her.

At the University of Texas, even in the mid-sixties, the new sexual freedom had not totally permeated. Texas was Baptist country, and the Lennox twins couldn't escape its restrictions because their aunt found them a room in a boarding house for women students run by a Baptist lady. That meant no liquor on the premises, a strict eleven pm curfew, monthly reports to the boarders' families, and no male of any age allowed beyond the front porch.

Of course an enterprising co-ed could go off for daytime or early-evening adventures in the back of a car or at a motel. Nadine, who dated all the time, never discussed any sexual episodes she might have had with her Joe Bobs or TCs whom she whipped through as quickly and impersonally as a tornado.

Although the sisters were extremely close and exchanged or perceived one another's feelings on many subjects, each had a reluctance to share thoughts about sex. Joanna believed that Nadine was so popular she could put boys off and never have to go all the way.

Wearing the school colours of orange and white, Joanna and Nadine attended football games and sang *The Eyes of Texas Are Upon You*, rooting for the Longhorns, which Nadine did with abandon, Joanna with great restraint. It was only a game, after all, but to avoid isolation she tagged along with Nadine in her social pursuits, as Nadine had followed Joanna's lead academically.

Joanna consumed hamburgers, cokes, and gooey sundaes in university hangouts on Guadalupe, known as the Drag. She went to drive-in movies, to picnics at Barton Springs, and drank bourbon-and-beer boilermakers at sorority parties – usually with some boy Nadine's date had dragged along for her. What Joanna did avoid – and it lost her many a second date – were the goodnight kisses and half-hearted fumblings in cars, the suggestions to 'go somewhere private'.

Was there something wrong with her? Or were Joanna's dates unexciting because they were so unlike her secret fantasy boyfriends she had modelled on characters in the *New Yorker* magazine short stories?

Shortly before graduation Nadine became engaged to the son of a wealthy West Texas rancher. And Joanna felt lost. For the first time in their lives her sister was spending more time with her boyfriend than with her. Joanna wanted to be independent, but Nadine's new friend was a blow to her anyway. And her fleeting speculations about the extent of her sister's sexual involvement only upset her more. Joanna felt confused and unable to clarify her own passions, or lack of them.

Going to New York was the best thing she could have done. There everything was different and *New Yorker* stories came alive. Joanna was soon acquitting herself well on the job and she was also falling in love. In New York there were no troublesome comparisons with Nadine to undermine her confidence.

By the time Joanna and Carl had progressed to full-fledged sex she had learned that she was normally responsive after all. It felt wonderful to be kissed and caressed intimately. Carl was right for her, whereas all the others had been wrong.

Carl was her first love, as well as lover, and she greatly respected his opinions. He advised her on clothes, took her to restaurants, plays, concerts and jazz clubs, and showed her how to survive in the city. Within three months the shy, naive Texas girl had become a New Yorker and began to embrace the exciting city with enthusiasm.

Joanna wrote glowing letters to her family, mentioning her romance and hinting at a forthcoming engagement, though of course concealing the sexual side of the affair.

Nadine was strangely subdued on the telephone, and in her infrequent letters she kept saying how much she missed her sister. Of course Joanna missed Nadine too. But she was busy, and on her tight budget, Joanna didn't dare take time off from the new job to go home for a visit. If only Carl would propose soon. She dreamed of a double wedding, something the sisters had planned from childhood.

One morning Joanna awoke to her doorbell ringing. It was barely seven. Sleepily she got out of bed and opened the door. There stood Nadine clutching a suitcase.

The sisters hugged and kissed, laughed and cried, their words tumbling over each other, their close communication resumed instantaneously.

'I broke my engagement,' Nadine explained, over coffee. 'I just couldn't live way out there on a ranch and never do anything exciting or see you.'

That last was the important part, though Nadine didn't emphasise it. Shortly after Joanna left, Nadine had discovered she was no longer in love. She dragged herself around feeling as if she had lost a limb. Desperately she had fought her panic. Her fiancé was a magnificent specimen, rich, handsome, a football hero, the catch of the decade. How her father and aunt had begged her not to give him up. They pointed out that he had everything. And he did, but Nadine simply couldn't commit herself to a life that didn't include Joanna.

Though thrilled to have her sister actually sitting in her little apartment, Joanna also felt a flicker of fear. Nadine had always been more dependent on her than the other way around. But to give up her fiancé! Joanna couldn't imagine doing the same thing to rush to Nadine.

Then she wondered if Nadine's presence would make a difference in her life. Would Joanna, as in the past, retreat in the face of her sister's overshadowing personality? How would Carl and Nadine get along?

Ashamed of such doubts, Joanna hugged Nadine again. She had missed her sister more than she had been able to admit to herself all this time. 'We'll find you a job and an apartment. Oh, and wait until you meet *him*.'

Joanna was nervous and proud at the same time. Her sister and lover were friendly to each other but slightly guarded. Carl, a quiet-spoken man interested in politics and travel, was as different from Nadine's football hero as he could possibly be, not Nadine's type at all.

But as soon as the sisters were alone Nadine approved in glowing terms. 'He's a real fine fella, Joanna, just right for you. I only hope I do as well.'

'You? Of course you will. Even better,' Joanna finished generously, although she could imagine nobody better than Carl.

Nadine moved into a studio a block away from Joanna and found a job as a photo researcher at an ad agency. As always she made a tremendous splash wherever she went. Within a month of her arrival Nadine was happily juggling several men.

It was like old times, except that Joanna had both her lover and sister. And she was promoted to art assistant. She had never been so happy.

Joanna and Nadine saw each other constantly, in either a threesome or foursome. Carl treated her sister with kindness and gallantry, but he was always openly affectionate with Joanna in front of Nadine, which was wonderfully reassuring.

When he went off on a three-week European assignment Joanna missed him terribly but consoled herself that as soon as he returned they would finally announce their engagement. He had implied as much.

Nadine suggested that Joanna come on a double date with her. 'It'll be such fun, better than mooning at home. My date knows someone who's dying to meet you.'

'Oh, Nadine, I couldn't. I'm nearly engaged.'

'So what? It's just a casual date. You don't have to do anything you don't want to just because a guy buys you dinner. Anyway, until you have that ring on your finger you should play the field. A little jealousy never hurt. You don't want him to take you for granted.'

'Carl doesn't take me for granted,' Joanna objected, shocked. Immediately afterwards she wondered if it could be true.

She let herself be persuaded to go on the date because she

trusted her sister's superior understanding of men. Not that she enjoyed herself. As of old, it was two guys comparing and contrasting 'the twins', and as usual, she felt she couldn't measure up to Nadine.

The next night Joanna received a frantic transatlantic call. 'I tried you until one am last night, New York time – '

'I'm so sorry, darling. I was expecting your call to-night – '

'Where the hell were you?'

'Only out with Nadine and some friends...'

Nadine had been absolutely right. That was Carl's first indication that he could be jealous. However, Joanna was afraid to repeat the experiment. She was in love, and game-playing wasn't her sort of thing.

When Carl returned, he was suspicious and cool. Joanna, terrified of losing him, went overboard to reassure him of her total devotion. She boldly initiated oral sex, hoping to bind him more closely to her, but it was a mistake. He accused her of infidelity and didn't believe her denials. The result was a growing coolness on his part and no further talk of an engagement.

'You know,' Nadine said after a while, 'I'm not sure he's really serious about you, Joanna. Maybe he's stringing you along.'

Immediately defensive, Joanna shrugged. 'That's ridiculous. Anyway, we're okay as we are. There's no rush.' In spite of her words, Joanna's happiness collapsed. Nadine had said what she had been thinking herself. And her sister should know. Nobody kept Nadine dangling. She had had several proposals, but she flitted from man to man, examining, judging, and discarding at whim.

Joanna's old fear of being unlovable began to surface, and she tried to convince herself that she didn't care, didn't want to marry someone who didn't want to marry her.

Their easy lovemaking began to change. Carl spent less time arousing her and climaxed much sooner, sometimes leaving her hanging. She was too hurt to say anything. As he grew cooler, she grew cooler, although it was killing her. Joanna could flourish only in a loving atmosphere. Where rejection and dissatisfaction were even hinted at, she withdrew into hurt silence.

Only once, after a disappointing episode in bed, did she lower her pride enough to ask him if anything was wrong between them. He said nothing was, and changed the subject.

Unable to confide in Nadine because she knew her sister would tell her to drop Carl, Joanna kept hoping things would improve. Finally they did, one glorious weekend. Carl was unusually solicitous, gentle, and as attentive to her sensual needs as in the very beginning. Joanna felt loved again, and her hopes soared.

She regretted very much that he was leaving to spend three days in Washington but scrupulously avoided saying or doing anything to spoil their rediscovered passion.

The evening she expected him to return, Joanna put on the dress he liked best, prepared his favourite Texas barbecued ribs and rice and chilled the beer and the glasses.

Suddenly her sister burst into her apartment, such a look of agitation on her face that Joanna became alarmed.

'What's wrong?' Joanna rushed to Nadine, who pulled away sharply.

'Oh, Jan, I simply don't know how to tell you. I don't even know how it could have happened.'

'What? What's happened?'

'Carl – he isn't still in Washington. He came home yesterday and has been staying at my place. Oh, Joanna, we've fallen in love.'

Joanna froze into stone.

'I told him from the beginning it was impossible, that I couldn't do this to you ... but these things just happen sometimes... You weren't going anywhere with each other ... I tried to warn you... I discouraged him but he was so persistent ... called me day and night ... waited on my doorstep... He never let me alone.'

Through the shock, Joanna managed to do as she had always done – she pretended not to care. Her ego had been so badly bruised in regard to men as she was growing up that she had learned to protect it by shrugging off the things that wounded her.

'I guess we were cooling off and I didn't realise it until now,' she said in a tight voice.

'Oh, Joanna, I feel awful.' Nadine didn't look awful, however, she looked flushed with excitement, and vastly relieved that her sister was taking the blow so well.

'Don't be upset,' Joanna murmured, automatically comforting her sister as usual. 'It's all for the best, I suppose. Better to find this out now than later.'

Nadine believed her because she wanted to and it relieved any guilt she might be feeling.

The full impact hit Joanna in the next couple of days, and the anguish was unbearable. She hated Carl. And she hated her sister, but at the same time she couldn't stop caring altogether because Nadine was like a part of herself.

Joanna thrashed about in the prison of her twinness. Although she couldn't imagine breaking away for good, she had to go somewhere else for a while.

Using the holiday time she had been saving up for her honeymoon, she went to a tennis resort in New England. Pounding the ball relentlessly over the net hour after hour helped her to deal with her pain and anger.

One of the tennis-playing guests, Ben Magid, took an immediate interest in Joanna. He was very handsome and assertive. She didn't know where to turn, so Ben guided her expertly towards him. One evening, when she had had a few more drinks than usual, she went to bed with Ben. Her action was a desperate attempt to expunge the old love and to make her feel that she was desirable to somebody.

Ben assured her she was to him. She told herself that he had many admirable qualities, and she felt secure with him. He was a senior chemist for American Cyanamid, and although he worked and lived in New Jersey he immediately made plans to move to New York to be closer to Joanna.

She could picture the surprise on Nadine's face when she brought home such a handsome, respectable man.

Five months later Joanna and Ben Magid were married in a double ceremony with Nadine and Carl Barrett.

7

Nadine became so wrapped up in her work that she had very little time for anything else. It was a relief to Joanna not to see very much of her sister. Kate and Jeff, bewildered by the sudden loss of their mother's attention, turned to their aunt. Although Nadine hired a full-time housekeeper, Mrs Wilson, to take care of the children, Joanna stopped by every evening after work and spent a couple of hours playing with her niece and nephew. If she had no other plans she often remained to have supper with them and read them bedtime stories.

Winnie, who thought Joanna was withdrawing too much because of the hurt over Lud, invited her to the theatre and the opera. Winnie loved to eat well and sometimes he picked Joanna up at Nadine's to take her to a late dinner after the children were asleep.

Because Mrs Wilson wasn't feeling well one evening, Joanna stayed until Nadine returned, late and full of apologies, but overflowing with talk of the series. 'It's such a meaty role. Suzanne is exactly the kind of woman I'd like to be. She was a whiz at law school, encouraged by her father who had no sons. Anyway, she joins this law firm, with its chauvinist partners who hate having to hire a woman. She's brilliant but feminine . . .'

As Joanna listened a strong feeling of merged identity took over. Nadine's part was also hers. She was Suzanne, sitting in the courtroom and defending an impossible client, one the other lawyers shunned. Suzanne had pored over endless law texts, looking for loopholes. To her colleagues' astonishment, she won the case.

The connection Joanna was feeling with Nadine snapped the moment Lud Haley's name was mentioned.

'He's fabulous, Joanna, so tactful and really kind. I've heard about tyrannical directors who either have their actresses in a temper or in tears . . .'

Joanna was unable to conceal her painful reaction.

'Last night we had dinner in a really great place – what's the matter?' Nadine looked with concern at her sister's drawn face.

'Nothing.'

'You're working too hard and not playing enough, I think. And now taking over the kids, which I love you for, is making things worse. They can be with Mrs Wilson perfectly all right. You never get out, see anyone – '

'Of course I do. I had dinner out myself last night with – '

'Winnie. He doesn't count. It's like being with – '

' – a girlfriend, I know. But he's so sweet to me.'

'Never mind Winnie. One of the cast, Megan, is having a party in a couple of days. Come with me, Joanna. You'd enjoy it and meet everyone I keep talking about.'

Joanna shook her head.

'But why not?' Nadine cried impatiently. 'What's wrong with you, anyway? You're moping around like someone just died or something. You're as bad as I was a few weeks back. Listen, if I'm up it doesn't mean you have to be down. Now, give me one good reason not to come to the party.'

'A cast party – I won't know anyone.'

'You will. I'll be there, Fern will be there – '

'Terrific. How can I pass up that exquisite pleasure?'

'Oh, come on. Even if you don't like her she's not exactly poison.'

Exactly poison was how Joanna thought of Fern Brunner.

'She'll only be one of a cast of dozens. Everyone is dying to meet my twin.'

'Nadine, I don't want to go to the party, really and truly, so please drop it. I'd rather sit with Kate and Jeff.' Joanna stood up and slipped into her coat.

Nadine gave up. 'Okay, I'm not going to fight with you,

but it's silly to go on nursing the hurts Ben gave you. It was years ago. Anyone else would be over it by now.'

At home, Joanna felt herself on the verge of tears. Aspects of her life with her husband – painful times she thought she had forgotten – came back with startling clarity. She could visualise how Ben had looked, sitting in his chair across their vast living room, reading a technical journal, his perfect features as cold and abstracted as his mind. Trying to get emotionally close to Ben had been like looking for warmth in an iceberg.

Since her divorce, it had often occurred to Joanna that she should have recognised from the start that Ben was someone *not* to marry. Nadine had never liked him and Nadine knew a bad guy when she met one.

Joanna turned on the television, knowing she would never get to sleep counting up all the traumas of her marriage. She tuned into a Spanish station. The staccato words she didn't understand acted as a dulling white sound and she dozed off with the set on.

Joanna had arranged to be at her sister's by nine. Nadine wanted to give the kids supper and spend time alone with them for a change before putting them to bed.

Joanna ate a quick sandwich, then changed from her office clothes to a pair of black velvet jeans and a hand-crocheted écru sweater. Slipping on her sheepskin jacket and grabbing a book of Eudora Welty's short stories, Joanna walked to Nadine's.

When the door to the apartment was opened Joanna thought she had got off at the wrong floor. An attractive blond man stared at her for a moment, grinned, kissed her cheek, and drew her into the foyer. From the din, it was apparent to Joanna that a party was in progress.

'You're Nadine's twin, of course. Jim Sweeney. Pleased to meet you. The resemblance is just remarkable.'

Joanna's face was burning. Feeling slightly foolish she took off her jacket and put her book on the hall table.

In the living room a crowd of bright, laughing, attractive

people were milling around, drinks in their hands. As they noticed Joanna they did a double take.

Nadine, rushing to make introductions, saw her sister's reproachful look. 'At the last minute Megan's roommate got the flu, honest, and it seemed simpler to move everything over here. Megan, come and meet Joanna.'

Nadine was wearing black satin pants and a cream-coloured ruffled satin blouse. The textures differed but the colours were the same as Joanna's. The coincidence was common enough; the twins often chose similar outfits or colour combinations without knowing what the other was going to wear.

Joanna's stomach tensed up and her smile felt stuck across her face with Superglue. She drank her glass of wine much too quickly. But Nadine had been right about the friendliness of the cast and crew, who were very warm to her. Everyone kissed everyone else endlessly. The two people she couldn't pick out were Lud Haley and Fern Brunner. Joanna hoped they had the flu and didn't care that she was being cruel. If they didn't turn up – and she drank enough wine – she might even enjoy this party.

The smell of pot was so thick it was possible to get high just by breathing, but when she was passed a joint Joanna took a couple of pokes to be sociable.

As soon as the disco music began, everyone started to dance in place, miraculously pairing off, just like in a musical. Joanna, talking to Ace, found herself dancing with him. It was very amusing. She was glad the floor was rather crowded because she didn't really consider herself a dancer. Not like Nadine, who threw herself totally into the rhythm, her motions beautifully coordinated and sexy. Of course, she adored every minute of being on exhibit.

Joanna felt somewhat self-conscious because she was bound to be compared with her sister. Then she noticed that the dancers were gradually moving to the sides of the room until the only people dancing were Joanna and Nadine with their partners. It was a musical after all. Olivia Newton-John and John Travolta.

Joanna, glancing at her sister, had a moment of pure

identification. She began to dance as she never had before, tailoring her movements to Nadine's.

When the number ended and everyone cheered the twins' performance, Nadine, basking in the attention, put her arm around her sister's waist.

Joanna was feeling rather reckless after letting go the way she had. Just then, through the smoke and the crowd, she picked out the features of Lud Haley and a dull pounding began in her chest.

'Lud,' Nadine cried, kissing him. 'It's about time. I thought you were going to stand me up. You've met my sister, Joanna, of course.'

'Of course.' His eyes were as deep-set, as dark blue, as intense as Joanna had recalled.

Somehow Nadine vanished during the next few moments and Lud was saying, 'All alone by the telephone, and when it rings it's never you, Joanna.'

The way he said her name sent a ripple of excitement through her. She struck a flippant pose. 'I must have lost your card.'

'Lost it? Or tore it up?'

She smiled ruefully. 'Whatever.'

'The subject was roses, remember? We were going to explore all the possibilities over that dinner I owe you.'

'I don't think so, under the circumstances.'

His eyes burned with intensity. 'Well, I do. We have unfinished business, or rather, pleasure. My business is with your sister.'

Joanna raised one eyebrow.

'I mean it. I admit that when we first met I was thinking about you for Suzanne, among other things. But now that's irrelevant. It leaves you and me free for the – other things.' He said the last words in a low, seductive voice.

Joanna felt a weakness in her knees, and when she saw the promise in his eyes she became a pin drawn to a magnet. He was unbearably attractive in his dark brown leather jacket over a maroon sweater, his hair curling just over the collar.

'Oh, Lud, I have to speak to you.' Fern elbowed her way

towards them. The two women acknowledged each other with a hostile nod.

'Not now, Fern.'

Fern knew Lud was never to be opposed when he used that tone of voice with her and she moved away, fuming. He was starting with Joanna again, even after she had warned him.

Nadine came out of the kitchen with some mixers and was gratified that the party was really swinging. Observing Joanna and Lud in conversation she moved over to join them. Why, when there were so many unattached men here, did her sister not circulate?

'Ah, let me have a good look at the two of you together. Mm hm, mm hm. I don't think I'd ever mistake either of you for the other. Although the features are nearly identical, there's a different expression around the mouth and eyes – '

'Nadine, phone,' someone shouted.

She excused herself and went to answer it.

Joanna, almost reeling from what Lud was doing, looked apprehensively at him.

'Her mouth is more pouty. Yours, when it's not tense, has two little lines of humour right in the corners.' He touched them with his fingertip, sending a shudder up Joanna's spine.

'And Nadine's eyes go inward. She likes to be looked at. You prefer to do the looking and you see a lot.'

Joanna could have hugged him for perceiving that.

He came closer and took her arm lightly. 'This place is too public to talk. Dinner tomorrow. Say yes.'

'Yes.'

'Wonderful. I'll call you in the morning. I'd better, since you're so unreliable.'

He kissed her cheek and melted into the crowd.

Joanna spent a restless night alternating between elation and fear. Not only did she sense that Nadine was infatuated with Lud, but she didn't entirely believe his claim not to have a personal interest in her sister.

69

Joanna had never quite got over the Carl business. Even so many years later when she thought of him she felt pain. She should have been Carl's wife and the mother of Jeff and Kate. Whenever Joanna remembered how Nadine had let that marriage fall apart she felt like weeping.

At the time Carl switched from Joanna to Nadine, Joanna hadn't been able to determine if, as her sister had insisted, Carl really had gone after her without encouragement, or if Nadine had flirted with him as she did with most men, almost without thinking about it.

Joanna had always avoided knowingly competing with Nadine for the same man because she felt certain she would lose.

But suppose Lud really did prefer her? Had he any reason to lie? Lud had come on strongly to her before he met Nadine, and Joanna wanted him. If his interest was real she wasn't going to be such a fool as to hand him over to her sister.

8

Joanna met Lud for a drink in the Grill Room of the Four Seasons. He was already seated at a corner table. Behind him the shimmering chains that covered the window were undulating gently. How well Lud fitted into this contemporary setting, with its mixture of sensual warmth and cool chic.

He stood up and held the leather-and-chrome chair for Joanna, surveying her quickly and smiling with pleasure.

Lud was wearing an expensively tailored charcoal suit and a shirt and tie with subtle shadings of blue that made his eyes glint like lapis lazuli.

Joanna had chosen her own outfit for elegance rather than sexiness. The wheat colour of her Galanos nubby-silk tunic overblouse on its flatteringly clinging skirt was speckled subtly with olive, the green picked up in her Chinese jade necklace and matching earrings.

'Dear lady, relax. You're holding yourself as stiffly as if you were being tested for a role.'

'I believe I am – even if it's not lady lawyer.'

He smiled appreciatively. 'Sharp, but wrong. I made up my mind about you the first time we met. At the very least, can we agree to be friends?'

'At the very least,' she responded flippantly, to quell her heartbeat, 'I can agree to drink a martini, bone dry, on ice, with a twist.'

'Not of the knife, I hope.' Lud ordered two martinis.

'Please don't be upset at me for not phoning you, Joanna. Working on a new series is hell on earth, with so many problems that there is no time for personal life.'

'I'm not upset, but I play it as I see it. And what I see is Nadine and you.'

'There is no Nadine and me. There's only you and me, if you'll let us.'

'There's actress and director, spending endless hours together every day, creating a character – '

'Creating your character. That's the point exactly.'

Their drinks were served. Lud lifted his glass and touched hers. 'To the uniqueness of Joanna.'

Intimations of fear and desire changed places between her shoulder blades. She took a nervous sip of her drink and asked, 'What do you mean?'

Lud leaned closer. 'You were the one who seemed perfect for the role, not only because of the way you look but because of your style. I told you that at the time and won't bore you by repeating myself. In Nadine I saw the same general appearance and the potentiality for her to *act* the role you play naturally. That's why I hired her, and we're working like dogs to make it happen. Your sister will do just fine for the series, but only you, uniquely Joanna, will do for me.'

Beads of sensuality crept along Joanna's skin like droplets of warm rain.

'You can't know that, so soon – '

His hot fingers on her wrist sent a shock through her. If there were a heartquake scale equivalent to Richter's the tremor would have registered eight point six.

'I know women, Joanna. I can spot the mysterious charmer with nothing beneath the Mona Lisa smile, or the bubbling two-week good-time girl, or the type whose possibilities can be exhausted in one night.'

'Which little square do you check for me?' Joanna whispered.

'None Of The Above. A long time ago there was someone. Beautiful, intelligent, sensual, sweet, playful, *muy simpatico*. I was so overwhelmed by her and so stupidly young and fearful that I hesitated.'

Lud pushed his hands through his curly hair, his expression mournful. 'I lost her. No, not to another man. To eternity. She died, Joanna, and I never even had a chance – '

72

He swallowed and lifted his drink to hide the pain in his eyes.

Joanna was terribly touched.

'I've never been married,' he continued in a low voice, 'or lived with anyone for longer than six months. I've been searching for someone to satisfy my mind, my spirit, my body, to make me whole.' Lud raised his eyes and fixed them with intensity on Joanna.

Did he think that she could possibly be the one? Against her will Joanna felt herself drawn more and more to this man who was appealing to her out of the depths of his very soul.

'You don't remind me of her physically,' he murmured. 'She was small, a redhead. But from the moment we met I felt an affinity between us, Joanna. Your voice, your grace, your smile, your wry way of looking at things – oh, damn.'

He reached for her hands. 'Forget my sad story. This isn't a wake but a celebration of two kindred spirits beginning to explore infinity. I want you, Joanna.'

Drawn by his intensity, his flattery, his palpable sensuality, Joanna responded to him more than she had intended. She felt so happy with Lud that she was barely aware of drinking the second martini, of moving from the bar to the taxi to the Café Des Artistes.

They sat at a banquette under one of Howard Chandler Christy's distinctive murals, renditions of nude women that combined a quaint vanished innocence with lush sensuousness.

Fleetingly, when Joanna could tear her eyes from Lud's, she noted that many of the diners seemed to be couples in love.

'Taste this pâté. Out of this world,' Lud murmured, putting a morsel on toast and bringing it to her mouth.

She suddenly smiled.

'Share the joke?'

'I was thinking of the eating scene in Tom Jones, The Movie.'

Lud laughed and squeezed her hand. 'You're adorable.'

Later, when Joanna offered him a taste of her cake, a few crumbs clung to her fingers. Lud flicked at them with his tongue, sending rockets of desire upwards on the insides of her thighs.

Their conversation was laced with sensuality. A revelation here, a phrase there, the fragment of a poem, a vignette, a tableau, a boy, a girl, a pain, a pleasure.

After paying the bill, Lud leaned across the table and gently kissed Joanna's lips. With his arm around her, she floated out of the restaurant and into a taxi. Her heart began to doubleflip, and she simply leaned her head back and let the enchantment of the evening bathe her in pleasure.

He put his arm around her shoulders and lightly kissed her temple, moving his soft lips down to her cheeks. His touch was almost painful for being so insubstantial.

She couldn't speak, couldn't think, could only feel exquisite ripples of delight pulsating through her.

She knew they were going to his place in the East Fifties. Not only didn't she object, she could hardly wait to be in his bedroom.

With trembling fingers they undressed each other in the wondrous illumination of a single flickering white candle.

'Oh, Joanna!' Lud gazed at her with intense desire.

'Lud,' she whispered, greedily drinking in the shadowy contours of his muscular body, proud and hard and unabashedly wanting her.

He pulled her close, turning her around, and she felt his warm breath very lightly against the back of her neck, making her tremble. Softly he kissed her shoulders and back, stroking her arms very lightly with burning fingertips.

Joanna felt as if she had no bones in her body, only flesh that quivered at his touch.

74

He moved his hands over her firm breasts, stroking her nipples until they were erect. 'You're fantastic.'

Moving his hands to her hips, he kissed his way down her back and buttocks, then knelt and gently insinuated his flickering tongue between her legs.

Joanna swayed, her flesh on fire, and felt her knees giving way.

He lifted her and carried her to the bed.

Joanna responded to his rhythm like a madwoman. She crested quickly and then again, low moans escaping from her lips. He finally let himself go, his body exploding, while he murmured her name.

They devoured each other again and again until, towards morning, they slept, wrapped around one another and sculpted by passion into a pulsating work of art.

9

Joanna awoke to the touch of Lud's hands.

'I can't, I must get up ... work ... oh, Lud...'

His face was incredibly handsome in the intensity of passion. 'I love you, Joanna,' he said tightly, trying to hold back. 'I love you. God, how I love you.'

He grimaced and thrust deeply into her, calling her name and bringing her to climax with him.

Somehow she got to work, opened her mail, drank her coffee. Her phone rang.

'Have lunch with me.'

'But Lud, I'm supposed to go to the dentist.'

'Cancel. Why choose pain when you can have pleasure. I can't wait until tonight to see you.'

They met at a little bistro on First Avenue.

'How could you manage the time? All this way from Long Island City just for lunch.'

'No, for love and lunch. Three hours, I'd estimate.'

'I can only take an hour, so I'm afraid I'm limited to lunch,' she told him, smiling.

'Later, then,' he promised, giving her a bone-melting look.

'Lud have you – have you said anything to Nadine? About us, I mean.'

He grinned, surprised, and shook his head. 'I'm not in the habit of discussing my love life with the cast.'

Joanna would have to tell Nadine, and soon. 'I hope she won't be upset. She might have thought – well, many directors have affairs with their discoveries –'

'Not this director.' Lud placed his fingers gently on Joanna's lips and mouthed 'I love you' at her.

Joanna melted. Of course this wasn't real but she was going to hang on to every exquisite second.

When Joanna was back at her desk Abby came into her office and sank into a chair. 'I can't seem to do any real work today. Must be because it's Friday.'

'That must be it,' Joanna agreed, smiling mysteriously.

Abby stared at her with sudden recognition. 'You look like you're in love.'

'Don't be silly,' Joanna murmured, flushing. But pressed by Abby, she admitted she had just started an affair.

Abby's face lit up with vicarious interest and although she asked a dozen questions, Joanna gave her only the barest bones.

'Oh, wow. He sounds terrific.'

'So far.'

'And you mean Nadine is working with him and she doesn't know yet?'

Joanna's smile stiffened. 'No, but it only just happened – '

'Gab, gab, gab.' Winnie appeared in the doorway with page proofs. His antenna immediately told him something was going on. Scrutinising Joanna, he began to beam. 'Your prince came through, huh, kiddo? I want to hear all about it, later. But now I have to interrupt with a dirty word, like deadline.'

After work Joanna met Lud in the Monkey Bar, where the lighting was subdued, the piano music soft, and the ambiance wonderfully romantic.

They sat side by side at a banquette holding hands and grinning like adolescents.

'Did you get any work done this afternoon, Joanna?'

'Nothing inspired. Just slogged through the routine stuff. You?'

'I was practically comatose. Every time I looked at Nadine of course I thought of you. Don't frown. I don't

77

mean it that way, sweetheart, as you should know after last night. Unique Joanna, uniquely beloved by me.'

They sipped their drinks, hands clasped, eyes fastened on one another.

'Where would you like to have dinner, love?'

'I don't think I can, after all these nibbles. Are you very hungry?'

'Only for you.'

It was an unseasonably warm night. Arm in arm, Joanna and Lud strolled up to Central Park, where hansom cabs were lined up awaiting passengers.

Lud squeezed Joanna's arm. 'Let's do it.'

'Let's. But the driver must be wearing a top hat and boots.'

'And a black coat with a velvet collar.'

'The carriage must be elegant.'

'And pulled by a noble steed.'

'No plastic flowers.'

'No rock music.'

'That one,' they decided together.

As the carriage clopped through the park Lud kissed Joanna, exploring her mouth, caressing every crevice, and with his tongue outlining the contours of her lips. The sensuousness of his kisses awakened in her a pulsating desire for him.

'Your place or mine?'

'Yours,' she replied, thinking with a surge of apprehension that Nadine might call her at home.

By the time they reached his apartment they were both so aroused that they left a trail of their clothes in the carpeted foyer leading to the bedroom.

Lud lay Joanna gently back on the bed and began to kiss her feet, nibbling on her toes, moving his tongue and hands upward and stroking her body until it was burning.

Controlling her urgency, she rolled over and caressed him with a passion and freedom she hadn't felt or shown with anyone in ages.

They savoured the preliminaries as long as they could before joining their bodies and peaking explosively.

78

Hours later, Lud leaned on one elbow and looked at Joanna. 'How are you feeling?'

'Marvellous. A little hungry, even.'

'Good. Me too.'

They ate scrambled eggs and mushrooms in the living room. Lud opened a bottle of white wine.

'To think you have a living room after all,' she teased, 'and I'm finally allowed to sit in it.'

'Not for long.'

'We'll burn out quickly if we keep this up.'

'Never. Love leads to more love. Don't you know that?'

'You mean lust,' Joanna said carefully.

'I mean love, love.'

Joanna didn't argue, but neither did she trust. Time would tell.

Saturday morning Joanna phoned Nadine and said she would be right over.

'Did you have to do that so early?' Lud groaned. 'I was hoping for just a little more love –'

'I have to tell her,' Joanna insisted, pulling on her clothes over her still-wet body, having had a quick shower. She turned to face Lud, a growing feeling for him vying with her anxiety about Nadine. 'Twins have a special connection. If you and I are going to see much of each other –'

'If! What do you mean if?' Lud pulled her into his arms with mock anger. 'No ifs. Don't crush me just when I'm feeling on top of the world.'

Joanna responded to the hunger of his kisses but forced herself to pull away. 'I have to go to Nadine now. Please, Lud. Our closeness began in the womb, and that's the way it is. Please understand.'

'I do, my angel, I do.'

'Oh, and tomorrow I spend a few hours in the afternoon with Kate and Jeff. My niece and nephew. Every Sunday that's what I do.'

'And I'm not invited?'

'Well, not so soon. I don't want to confuse them.'

He looked sulky for a moment, almost like a small boy.

Joanna put her arms on his shoulders. 'It's only the afternoon, silly man. We can be together in the evening, if you really want to.'

'No ifs, I said. I want you today, and tomorrow, and forever after.'

Instead of going directly to Nadine's apartment Joanna phoned her from a nearby coffee shop, asking her sister to meet her. It was impossible for them to talk when the children were around.

Nadine settled herself in the booth across from Joanna and looked at her curiously. 'You've been avoiding me for days. What's going on?'

Nadine sounded irritable, increasing Joanna's qualms.

'I hope you won't be angry. But at the party last week – ' She stopped.

'Aha. You met someone.' Nadine relaxed. 'You're having a little thing, aren't you. Well, that's great. It's about time. Why should I be angry? Let's see if I can guess. The handsome Rick? I hope it's not Ace because he's more gay than straight – '

'It's Lud,' Joanna whispered.

Nadine's face went blank, then registered amazement. 'Lud? Lud Haley? You've been seeing Lud Haley?'

'Yes.'

'But you hardly had time to get to know him at the party.'

'True. But we talked for a long time when we first met at the restaurant, you know, with Fern. I told you about it. What I didn't tell you was that he had asked me out. Sent a rose to my office, and called. I thought it was because he wanted me to play Suzanne. Apparently I was wrong.' Joanna continued to explain, studying Nadine's expression and feeling vaguely guilty.

Nadine laughed. 'Why didn't you tell me you had a crush on Lud, for heaven's sake?'

A crush. It sounded so adolescent. Maybe it was. 'I hope

you don't mind. You speak of him in such glowing terms as a director. I wondered if you also had a romantic interest in him.'

'Did Lud say so?'

'No. He assured me your relationship was only business. Of course he speaks highly of you, of your acting . . .'

Nadine listened, a smile on her face. 'Acting is what's important to me right now. I'm so late getting started that I've really got to work at it. Well, you and Lud. It's certainly a surprise but I'm happy for both of you.'

Joanna breathed more freely. 'I'm relieved, because if it bothered you – ' She hesitated.

Nadine looked sharply at her sister. 'If it bothered me, what? You'd stop seeing him? Don't be silly. It probably would be harder for me to work with someone I was involved with. So don't give it a second thought.'

As soon as Joanna had left, Nadine's smile vanished. Lud and Joanna – it was preposterous. They hadn't the smallest thing in common. *She* was the actress, turning herself inside out to please him. *She* was vital to the success of the series. In fact, without her – hell! For what possible reason could he be having an affair with her sister?

Now that she thought about it, it was odd Lud hadn't mentioned having met Joanna first. Her sister had been the one to say so, but Nadine had brushed it off, apparently too lightly. Of course, she had been unable to believe that once Lud met her he could actually prefer Joanna. Such a thing had never happened before. How the devil had her sister made such a hit with the likes of Lud Haley?

Impulsively Nadine phoned Fern and arranged to have lunch with her.

An hour later the two women met at the Café Carlyle.

'Naddie, I'm so glad. On the set there's so damn much work, so little time. I'd like us to be the friends we used to be.'

'I know.' Nadine smiled brightly at Fern. 'It is hard work but I love it. Tell me a little about Lud. Sometimes I think he expects me to go much further than he says, to

sort of understand what he means without being told.
What's your opinion?'

Fern was thrilled at being asked. 'You just sort of have
to follow your instincts. If you miss he's bound to let you
know. But you're doing so well I don't think you need to
worry. You're able to concentrate, and that's the secret.
Certainly it's Lud's. Lordy, if he were directing a scene,
say, and a naked lady with three breasts happened to walk
by he'd never even notice.'

Nadine smiled to show appreciation of Fern's little joke.
'Does Lud really like women? I mean personally.'

'Are you kidding? He goes through women personally,
as you say, like they're going to disappear from the face
of the earth.'

Nadine expelled a sigh. 'You?'

Fern shook her head briskly. 'Never. I've always been
very businesslike. To be Lud's assistant director is the
plum job of the century and I'd rather die than spoil it. Like
having an affair and maybe getting the shove afterwards
because he wouldn't want me around every day. Anyway,
I've got someone in Los Angeles. Married and a Catholic,
but a dynamite guy, a producer. I see him a couple of times
during the week and on weekends when his wife goes off
to the fat farm.'

Nadine ordered a second gin and tonic and listened to
Fern's longwinded tale of her affair without showing her
impatience.

'You never told me,' Nadine said, when Fern finally
paused, 'that you had run into my sister before you got in
touch with me.'

'I didn't? I must have forgotten. I mean, I didn't even
know your married name until I heard it from Joanna.
Anyway, does it matter? You got the role.'

Nadine didn't reply.

Fern took a nibble of her chicken salad and, wiping her
mouth fastidiously on her napkin, eyed Nadine, wondering what she wanted. Maybe she still felt unsure of her
acting skills.

'In fact, Naddie, the day I met your sister I thought she

82

was you and that's why I introduced her to Lud in the first place. I knew you'd be a perfect Suzanne. I always had faith in you as an actress, but I guess I was the only one who encouraged you. Remember how hard I tried to get you to stay in the drama department?'

'Yes. And you were right. I should have.'

'Let's face it, Naddie, you and I were always special friends, weren't we?'

'Of course.' Nadine forced a laugh. 'When Lud talked to Joanna about acting she must have bitten his head off.'

Fern hesitated. Long experience had taught her not to talk against one twin to the other, not even to Nadine. But this was somehow different. Nadine seemed to be asking for Fern's special loyalty. And she would get it.

'In fact, to my surprise Joanna sounded interested in the series. Of course, when Lud uses those Svengali eyes on a girl he can make her forget that she doesn't want what he wants. And he likes his ego massaged. Joanna sat there eating up every word as if he were a guru or something. In fact, I had to leave the table. I couldn't stand to watch those two. Frankly, I was thinking of the series and I knew once he'd met you he'd give you the part.'

'Well, I'm glad you were right because I'm having a ball.'

Fern suddenly discerned a slight tremor in her friend's voice and knew something besides acting was bothering her. What?

The past few days Lud had seemed unusually energetic, but at the same time jumpy. That was the way he got when he was romancing someone. And he'd taken more than a two-hour lunch – of course! Lud was screwing Joanna. That had to be it. And Nadine knew. Probably Joanna had told her, the bitch. Now Fern could understand why Nadine had looked so relieved when Fern had clued her in on Lud's fickleness with the ladies.

Fern had always disliked and resented the sarcastic, unresponsive Joanna, wanting Nadine all to herself. And now Joanna had captured Lud, who ought to be Nadine's friend, damn it.

Nadine had a date with Jim Sweeney that evening and went through the motions of flirtation and conversation although her mind was elsewhere. Not that Jim really noticed. He saw and heard what he wanted to see and hear.

She did not invite Jim to come up for a nightcap, pleading she was tired. Jim was sweet and obviously enchanted by her. He would keep.

Before bed Nadine drank a stiff scotch and thought about her sister and Lud. Well, Joanna might have attracted the man but she wouldn't know how to hold him, as she hadn't known how to hold Carl or even that cold-blooded bore, Ben Magid.

Fern's parting words had been very reassuring. 'You know, Naddie, Lud's work is his life. It really has to be that way in this business, working crazy hours, travelling together, hanging around on the set until you get it right. That's why he's happiest when his romantic interest, so to speak, is right on the set with him. Sooner or later that's bound to happen. Of course, you can't force anything, but I'd sure keep it in mind, Naddie.'

10

Monday began as a nightmare for Lud. They were shooting a crucial episode on the Wall Street law office set. For the first time Suzanne realises she has made implacable enemies of two of the partners because she won a case both of them, with twenty-five years of experience, expected her to lose.

Nadine was playing the scene all wrong.

'No, no, cut,' Lud ordered, exasperated. 'Dear lady, you're hurt at the way these men are tearing into you. At the same time you're tough enough not to let them provoke you into quitting – '

'I know that. I was showing that,' Nadine interrupted shrilly.

'No, you weren't.' Lud took a deep breath and softened his tone. 'What you showed was coyness, and it's just not Suzanne. She didn't flirt her way into the job. She got it because of solid credentials. She has to be sympathetic. Millions of women will be watching her, identifying with her. Yes, she's beautiful and desirable. But she needs to be taken seriously as an attorney. The men out there in the audience have to believe she's being unfairly treated.'

I'm being unfairly treated! Nadine felt such rage rising that she had to dig her nails into her palms to keep from screaming at Lud. It was the first time he had spoken so harshly to her. She was so furious that she missed key words in what Lud was saying, sure that if there had been no Joanna he wouldn't be chewing her out now.

Fern, standing by, was agitated by a similar thought. She cursed Joanna under her breath but didn't dare to interfere.

'Can we take a break?' Nadine asked, her throat tight. 'I'd like you to explain – '

'What the hell do you think I've been doing for the past ten minutes?'

Nadine threw herself into a chair and covered her face with her hands.

Lud, sighing, went to Nadine and put his hand on her shaking shoulder. Telling the cast and crew to take twenty, he tried to control his impatience with Nadine.

She looked miserably up at him, her full lips trembling, her eyes wet. She may not have been playing Suzanne to his satisfaction but she was an expert at playing Nadine.

'I don't mean to be rough on you, sweetheart, but you really have to pay attention – '

'I do,' she said, a catch in her voice. 'But when you start shouting in front of everyone, and even the extras leave their card game to gawk I – I feel like a kid being bawled out, and I just want to run away and hide.' She rubbed at her eyes.

Lud put his arms around her shoulders. 'Come on, kid, I'll buy you coffee.'

Joanna had assured Lud that Nadine didn't mind their relationship, and he hadn't contradicted her even though he knew better. He knew women up and down, inside and out. There was no way Nadine was going to accept his affair with Joanna. It was plain old sibling rivalry garnished with female jealousy. Lud had never known a sister who didn't turn bitter and difficult when the other got what she wanted. And it was natural for an actress to want her director's undivided attention.

While Lud explained for the tenth time about Suzanne's character and reactions and how to convey them in front of the camera, he was conscious of the irony that it was Joanna who had Suzanne's sensibilities. Joanna should be playing the part and not this look-alike who, for all her talent and eagerness to succeed, didn't really understand the nuances. By an uncanny concidence, Joanna embodied all the exciting traits of the fictional Suzanne. In fact, Lud, who had dreamed up the series, had worked with the writer to fashion a heroine who conformed to his feminine ideal.

However, Nadine was his star, and her well-being was of primary importance. 'You're doing a great job, love, and I'm basically very pleased. But even the most talented actress sometimes misses. Otherwise nobody would need a director at all.'

'I know that. And I'm trying so hard – ' her voice broke.

Lud saw that something needed saying. 'It's important for you to understand that my friendship with Joanna has absolutely no bearing on our working together – '

'Of course not,' Nadine broke in tearfully. 'But she was your first choice for the part.'

'It's true that Joanna had the right look. But after I met you, I could see that you're the actress in the family.'

He hadn't exactly refuted Nadine's point but she didn't notice. She simply couldn't understand why Lud was sleeping with her sister instead of being madly in love with her.

Nadine now widened her lips into a smile and beamed at him, her eyes still glistening with stage tears. 'Don't think for a moment, Lud, that I'm envious of my sister. On the contrary, I've always felt a little guilty about her. She was so terribly shy that she suffered agonies when we did commercials and it was even worse when it came to boys. I usually had to get a date for her. On the whole Joanna had a rougher time than I did in every respect. You know, she needs to experience someone like you and have a decent relationship for once.'

'Oh? How about her husband?'

'Well, Ben was a scientist who wanted to be free to create. And my sister, wonderful as she is, can't really cater to a man because – oh.' Nadine put her hand over her mouth. 'That must sound like criticism of Joanna but I don't mean it that way. After all, she's my mirror image.'

Nadine, sensing that she may have said too much,

switched the conversation to the role again, recapitulating Lud's points and looking for reassurance.

He gave it to her.

When they reshot the scene Nadine improved her performance with each take. Lud decided he would have to treat Nadine like silk chiffon. It was going to take some effort to keep her happy as the leading lady in the series while Joanna was the leading lady in his life.

When Joanna and Lud went to '21', Sardi's, and Elaine's – places frequented by famous people, many of them in show business – Lud knew nearly everyone. It was a novel experience for Joanna, used to basically unsociable men like Carl and Ben, to see how popular Lud was. She felt a delicious elation when Lud and she periodically exchanged the heated looks of lovers who ultimately were going to feast upon each other. Their lovemaking was spectacular for its inventiveness. Lud was insatiable and made Joanna the same. She had never met anyone remotely like him. As the weeks went by, she grew to believe in his love and in hers for him.

From the first time Lud had picked her up at the office he had made a hit with Winnie and Abby. Lud conveyed an appreciation of Abby's charms without showing any inclination to sample them. And he immediately perceived the shrewdness, sophisticated tastes, and high intelligence behind Winnie's clowning. On his part, Winnie responded to Lud's obvious fondness for Joanna.

Abby was simply knocked out. 'He's super, tremendous, dynamite. I think a new adjective needs to be invented for your Lud.'

Hearing Abby speak so enthusiastically of her man pleased Joanna. Maybe her poor track record wasn't her fault. Maybe she had merely been unlucky.

The only thing bothering Joanna was that she and Lud never went out with Nadine and Jim.

'It's not a good idea,' Nadine explained. 'We're together too much as it is on the set. Everyone's tense at times, Lud too, and we snap at each other. Besides, you don't want the three of us to talk shop, do you?'

'I wouldn't mind at all,' Joanna assured her.

The truth was that Nadine couldn't bear to see Lud with her sister.

He, too, discouraged foursomes. 'If we've had a rough day it may spoil the evening. Or else being great pals off-camera might make it damn hard for me to be the necessary tyrant on the set.'

What Lud neglected to say was that he knew Nadine was flaunting her interest in Jim in an attempt to make him jealous. If Lud hadn't been so crazy about Joanna he would have been flattered that her twin was so taken with him. But as things stood, Nadine's infatuation was merely a nuisance, something to be handled delicately. *Sister In Law* was Lud's big chance to be taken seriously as a director of meaningful drama, and nothing and nobody was going to get in the way of his success.

The next two scenes went smoothly because they had reached the part where Suzanne falls in love with one of the partners, and Nadine needed little coaching to be flirtatious and seductive.

'Can you guess what today is?' Lud asked Joanna on the phone.

Her face grew warm. 'Yes. Two months exactly.'

'I thought you might have forgotten.'

'Impossible. I haven't been the same since.'

'I haven't either. I think this calls for a return of Joanna to "Joanna", scene of the crime sublime.'

They toasted each other with martinis at the marble-topped bar. Joanna couldn't resist kissing his cheek. She felt euphoric. After dinner Lud had promised to take her to the Vanguard to hear jazz.

In honour of the occasion, Lud had bought Joanna a gold bracelet at Tiffany's. She had bought him a Pierre Cardin gold ballpoint pen, which he took up and used to write on the cocktail napkin, 'I love you'.

The mood was broken when Lud noticed a bearded man

in a denim suit seated at a table with several others. 'There's
Frank Metcalf, a producer friend of mine. Hey, Frank?
Mind if we join you?'

Although Joanna wished they could have dined alone,
she found the others friendly and welcoming. Besides, she
had the secret pleasure of seeing Lud work his extraordinary charm on three people he had never met before –
Frank's wife and his lawyer and wife. The two women
especially were fascinated by Lud, laughing with delight at
everything he said and treating Joanna with respect tinged
with envy.

During coffee, Lud put his hand on Joanna's knee while
continuing his animated conversation. She sipped her
cognac and boldly ran her finger lightly over his thigh. He
increased his pressure and moved his fingers upward in a
subtle stroking motion. For several minutes they tantalised
each other, until Joanna was sure that if he moved his hand
any higher she would lose all control and drag him under
the table.

'Time to go,' he whispered hotly in her ear. 'But wait
a couple of moments.' He moved her hand so that she
could feel how aroused he was.

Lud gave Joanna's address to the taxi driver and then
pulled her close to him. They embraced passionately, their
hands all over each other.

'He can see us in the mirror.' Joanna indicated the
driver.

'Don't worry. Even we can't teach a New York cabbie
anything new.'

They went up the steps to her apartment in stages,
embracing at each landing and beginning to undo one
another's clothing.

Lud drew Joanna into the bathroom and began to run
a bath. 'Come here. Closer.' Putting his hand into the tub,
fragrant with bath oil, he wet her face and hair, moving his
fingers enticingly down to her neck, shoulder, breast,
belly.

When she began to sway he drew her into the tub with
him.

'Isn't it nice the tub's so old-fashioned and big,' she said.

'Not so big we can't be cosy.' He positioned himself facing her and pulled her on top of him.

Joanna, gluing her mouth to his, lost herself in passion, as he did too.

They washed each other, playing games with the soap and splashing until the floor was covered with puddles.

They took turns drying each other with the bath towel, then went to bed and began to make love again.

'Joanna, my sweet, sweet lover.'

'You're so wonderful.'

'And?' He stopped moving.

'Oh, don't stop, please.'

'Then tell me.'

'I – I love you.' She whispered the words for the first time.

'And I love *you*, love *you*, love *you*.'

Later, when they were lying peacefully in each other's arms, Lud asked, 'Do you love me really? When I'm not blackmailing you to say so.'

'Yes.' She sighed.

'But you have a problem with it?'

'I don't want to be disappointed.'

'As you were in the past?'

'Yes.'

'Do you want to talk about it?'

'Well, my first experience was with a man who – who – anyway, it just didn't work out. And Ben, my husband, had a lot of good qualities but we were wrong for each other.'

'Mm hm.' He waited for more.

Joanna stirred restlessly but didn't amplify.

Lud saw her discomfort. 'Joanna.' He sat up and took her face in his hands. 'After the series I'll be going back to Los Angeles. If I asked you to come with me, would you?'

She was caught offguard. 'I don't know. I haven't thought.'

91

'Think then, because the time will come, and I hope by then – ' He stopped and scrutinised her. 'The beautiful Lennox twins must find it hard to settle down with one man. I'll bet both of you have left a string of broken hearts from here to Texas.'

'Not me,' Joanna blurted out. 'Nadine is the heart-breaker.'

Lud was quiet for a moment. 'She's an actress. I suppose some men are easily taken in.'

He leaned over Joanna and kissed her nose. 'What takes me in is uncalculating honesty.'

'In that case I'd better admit that – that my first love was Carl Barrett, and he chose Nadine over me.'

All the pieces fell neatly into place. 'I see. Well, Carl's loss was my gain, exquisite Joanna.'

She glowed and kissed him tenderly. 'Right now, sleepy Joanna.'

'Sleep, then, and dream that when you open your eyes you will be even more loved than when you closed them.'

11

On Sunday Lud joined Joanna and the children at a puppet show in the Village. Kate and Jeff were shy with him and very demanding of their aunt.

'I want ice cream now,' Kate said after the show, tugging on Joanna's arm. 'Chocolate.'

'Butterscotch is better,' Jeff proclaimed. 'What flavour do you like?' he asked Lud.

'Uh, coffee.'

'Yuk.' The children began to make faces to go with their noises of disgust.

'Stop that, please.' Joanna, glancing at Lud, saw that he was irritated.

'You don't have any children, do you?' Jeff divined shrewdly.

Lud smiled. 'No. I'm not married.'

'Are you going to marry *her*?'

Joanna, embarrassed, saved Lud from having to answer by pointing out the ice cream shop.

Later, when the children were playing in the park, Lud said, 'You're wonderful with those two, and they love you almost as much as I do.'

She smiled. 'Genetically they're my half-children, much closer than an ordinary niece and nephew.'

'That's right. I never thought of that.'

'You're bored, aren't you? I guess they're not as disciplined as they should be. And they miss having a steady man in their life so they're kind of shy this first time.'

'Who says I'm bored? I've just had no experience so I don't know what to say to them. I'll probably learn when I have my own. Do you want kids, Joanna?'

'Yes.'

'Mine?' he whispered.

The answer to that was yes also, but she didn't dare to say so yet. Besides, what if it turned out that she couldn't?

Lud nuzzled her ear with his lips. 'I'd love you to have my child.'

Hastily Joanna got up to gather Kate and Jeff so that they could go home.

Later that week Lud told Joanna that he had arranged a squash game on Sunday afternoons. Although she was a little disappointed she also felt relieved. It really had been a strain. And there was no point in Lud's playing uncle to the children until he had made a commitment to their aunt.

Lud began to encounter problems with permits and personnel which put them way behind schedule. They were forced to work on Saturdays. Joanna helped Nadine by taking the children then because Mrs Wilson wanted the weekends off. 'No problem,' Joanna assured her sister. 'It's a pleasure to be with the little monsters.'

One Saturday when a heavy downpour cut short their walk in the park Joanna took the children into the nearest lunch place, a health food restaurant on Madison Avenue.

'I want a hamburger with lots of ketchup,' Kate demanded.

'Not in here. You can have a salad or a tuna sandwich, or maybe a vegetable plate – '

'I hate salads and stuff,' Jeff broke in to complain.

'Me too. It's yukkie. Let's go somewhere else, Aunt Joanna.'

'We can't,' she said firmly. 'It's pouring out there. You'll just have to suffer today. You eat too much junk food as it is.'

'I love junk food,' Kate affirmed loudly.

Joanna put her arm around her niece. 'Katie, my decision is final. Here we are, here we stay, bottom line.'

She tempered her firmness with a kiss on the head. 'Now, how about a tuna salad with tomato – '

Joanna felt a tap on her shoulder from behind. Turning, she saw Dominic Graham smiling at her. 'How are you, Nadine?' He leaned across and kissed her cheek, while the children tittered.

Joanna stiffened automatically.

Immediately he realised his mistake. 'Joanna, I'm so sorry. Seeing you with the children I made the assumption – ' He stopped, at a loss for a moment.

She had noted how much more open he had been when he thought she was her sister.

'Hey, Doc, I wish you'd come and sit next to me and even up the sides. You know – girls,' Jeff finished, making a face.

Joanna and Dominic laughed.

'Do you mind, Joanna?'

'No, please do.'

Dominic slid next to Jeff, who continued to call him Doc.

'Jeff, that's disrespectful,' Joanna began.

'Not at all,' Dominic said. 'I kind of like it. After all, we're very old friends.'

'I know why you eat here,' Kate said, nodding wisely. 'Because you're a doctor, and it's all vegetables and things.'

He laughed with delight, an attractive laugh, Joanna remembered.

'I actually like vegetables and things, Kate. Don't you?'

'Yukkie,' both children said at once.

'How about if we call them veggies, as the Brits do?'

'They're still yukkie. Yukkie veggies.' Jeff made a disgusted face.

Dominic and Joanna laughed, locking eyes. She looked down quickly and said, 'Enough of this. I'm going to have a salad.'

'Me too,' Dominic decided.

'With cucumber?' Kate wanted to know.

'Mm.'

Kate began to chant, 'Cucumber, cucumber – '

'Shut up,' Jeff commanded. 'You're a cucumber.'

'You're a carrot,' Kate giggled.

'You're a potato,' Jeff said to Joanna.

'And you're a stalk of broccoli,' she countered.

The children laughed. 'You're a stalk of broccoli, Doc.'

'Not me. I'm an artichoke.'

That evoked a wave of giggles, followed by questions. Dominic, trying to describe an artichoke, finally summoned the waitress and ordered one. 'Show and tell, kids, and then eat.'

The children howled at every word he uttered.

Joanna was finding Dominic disturbingly attractive. Doctors are taught to be charming, she told herself. Dominic was gaining her sympathy because of the way he treated Jeff and Kate, getting them to do anything by making it so much fun. He convinced them to eat some salad as well as the artichoke.

'This is the tricky part, the "choke", the section you cut away like this because it tastes like a mouthful of fur. And here's the best part.'

He gave Joanna the first portion. 'Have a piece of my heart, madam.'

'Delicious,' she pronounced, smiling quickly at the double meaning.

'Me next,' Kate implored. 'I'm a madam too.'

Dominic ruffled her hair.

When they left the restaurant the rain had stopped.

'Can we have ice cream? We were good, weren't we?'

'Yes, for a change.'

Dominic had insisted on paying the bill and was at the cashier. He gave Joanna a long look through the window and then smiled at her the way he had the last time they had met in Amsterdam. She suddenly felt a compulsion to get away.

'Thanks for the lunch,' she said quickly as he emerged

from the restaurant. 'We're going to make a quick trip for ice cream before the rain starts again.'

Dominic saw from the way Joanna took each child by the hand that he wasn't invited to join them, so he said goodbye and deliberately turned in the opposite direction. Now he was glad he hadn't phoned Joanna in New York, though he had been on the point of doing so several times. He felt that she gave him conflicting signals and he hesitated to put himself in a position to be turned down. This afternoon had confirmed that she was more reluctant than interested.

'Aunt Joanna, why couldn't Doc come with us?' Jeff asked.

'Because,' Joanna snapped, feeling she had been unnecessarily brusque with Dominic.

'Because why?' Kate wanted to know.

'Because I said so, that's why.' Joanna was irritated and annoyed with herself for it.

The children forgot Dominic and bit happily into their ice cream cones, which kept them occupied until Joanna got them home.

Nadine looked very happy. 'What a heavenly day. Everything went right, and Lud was so pleased. We've finally finished with a segment we've been filming all week. Hey, that looks good, kids. Save me a lick. Mm. Did you have fun?'

Both children talked at once, describing their lunch and their meeting with Dominic.

Joanna went up to the bar and mixed herself a scotch and water.

'. . . and she wouldn't let Doc come with us for ice cream,' Kate declared.

'Oh, watch out, you're dripping.' Nadine got a cloth and then sent the children to wash their hands.

She turned to look curiously at Joanna. 'Are they so much trouble that you need to hit the bottle?'

'No. They're fine. I'm just a little chilled from the rain.' That wasn't entirely true. She had suffered a twinge of fear at the way Nadine had looked when she mentioned Lud.

'Why did you drag the kids away from Dominic? Did he do something wrong?'

Joanna shrugged. 'Enough was enough. I think he was just being super polite in that English way, insisting on paying the bill. I didn't want to involve him in the ice cream mess as well.'

'Don't you like him? He's always been so nice to all of us – '

'I like him fine. For God's sake, stop picking, will you?'

'I'm not picking. What's with you this afternoon?'

'Nothing,' Joanna said glumly, the whisky having lowered her inhibitions. 'I just don't like the way you're always shoving me into male arms when I don't want to be there. Especially when you don't either. I have Lud, thank you. If you're so keen on Dominic, go out with him yourself.'

Later, when Joanna was having a drink with Lud and felt reassured of his love, she regretted having been so unreasonably sharp with Nadine.

Excusing herself, Joanna phoned her sister and apologised.

12

While Lud was directing a love scene between Suzanne and her lawyer friend, the actor, Rick, suddenly doubled over in pain. An ambulance was sent for, and they learned at the hospital that Rick had a ruptured appendix.

Lud decided to suspend production. 'We can't go on unless we know that Rick will be all right. A ruptured appendix can mean complications, though I hope to God not. I like the guy and he's doing well. But we might have to reshoot all his scenes with someone else if he doesn't recuperate in time.'

'But Lud, the schedule will be destroyed,' Fern objected.

'Can't be helped. We're going to be late whatever happens. We might as well take a two-week break. In fact, I insist on it.'

'What are you going to do?' she asked suspiciously.

'Don't worry your pretty head,' he responded lightly, blowing her a kiss. 'I'll be in touch.'

Nadine, watching Lud retreat, rushed up to Fern. 'But he can't just walk away.'

'Yes he can. He always does.'

'What do we do in the meantime?'

'Get our act together letter perfect. Knit sweaters. Play Russian roulette. Listen, the Great White Chief has spoken. There's no way we're going to change his mind.'

Nadine felt sure that Lud was going to spend the free time with Joanna, and the thought chilled her. She tried to reach her sister at the office but Joanna was out to lunch. By the time Nadine got home, though, a message was waiting for her.

Lud appeared at Joanna's office and explained what had happened. 'Tell your boss you're going on holiday. Right now.'

Joanna began to laugh. 'You're joking. I can't do that. We're just finishing the Holland book.'

'Abby can take over,' he declared, just as Abby walked into the office.

While Joanna continued to object, Lud held up her coat.

'But Winnie isn't even back from lunch. I can't.'

'You can. Abby would, wouldn't you?'

'Me? Are you kidding? I'm ready to come with you whether you want me or not.'

Lud waved to her on their way out.

Abby waved back, muttering, 'It should only happen to me.'

'Lud, this is impossible,' Joanna protested in the taxi bound for Kennedy Airport. 'I'll get fired.'

'Of course you won't. Don't you have a month's holiday coming?'

'Yes, but –'

'You're only taking half of what you're entitled to.'

'But –'

Lud engaged her in one of his compelling kisses.

'Oh, Lud, this is crazy. We have no bags. Where are we going?'

'Up into the wild blue yonder.'

It was insane, and yet she had never been so excited. For once in her life she was going to do something rash.

While Lud was buying the tickets, she rang Nadine's house and left a message. Then she called Winnie and tried to explain in a reasonable manner something that was entirely unreasonable.

There was a long silence.

'I've left instructions with Abby. She's perfectly capable of keeping the material flowing. It's just that Lud swept me out of my chair before I had time to think.'

'Okay. We'll manage. Have fun.' The phone clicked. Winnie was probably furious. If she had any sense she would go right back to the office. But her sense had been overpowered by her senses, all five totally attuned to Lud Haley.

'To us. Long may we love,' Lud toasted, touching his glass to Joanna's.

'And where are we going to do all this loving? Los Angeles?'

'You'll see.'

It wasn't until the plane was in the air and the captain announced their flight to Los Angeles *and* Honolulu that Joanna had a glimmer. 'Hawaii?'

'That depends on how nice you are to me between here and Los Angeles.'

She was ecstatic. Clever Lud, to transport them six thousand miles without a passport.

When the film came on, Lud used the darkened cabin as an excuse to fondle Joanna.

'Please stop.'

'Okay. I'll be upstairs in the flight deck lounge, if you want me.'

If she wanted him. Joanna tried to watch the movie but it was no use. Her whole body was tingling.

Lud was sharing the lounge with two well-dressed middle-aged couples. Glancing through *Business Week*, Lud nodded his head to Joanna, and she took a seat beside him. He smiled pleasantly.

'Are you enjoying the flight, Ms – ?'

'Lennox.' She smiled back at him. 'Yes, thank you, Mr – ?'

'Haley.' He shook her burning hand solemnly.

While the other occupants were deep in smoke and conversation, Joanna and Lud continued their pretence of having just met. One of the wives glanced at them from time to time and Joanna was sure she had an inkling of what was going on.

But Lud was turning his hot eyes on her, and she felt steam beginning to rise from her skin. Moving closer, Lud

101

avoided actually touching, but his body language was arousing her to an extraordinary pitch.

'I'm going to the john at the back of the lounge, Ms Lennox,' he whispered. 'Wait a moment and go into the other one but leave the door open.'

It was madness.

She did as he had requested, her heart pounding, afraid that someone would surprise her before Lud's hand reached out, took hers, and pulled her into his cubicle. He bolted the door.

'And now, Ms Lennox, we'll see if your beauty is only skin deep.'

Spurred by the playacting, the tiny space, the fear of discovery, they tore at each other's clothes and bodies. Lud leaned against the wall, bracing his legs, and lifted Joanna on to him. The excitement was intense, the climaxing quick and heady.

Within a few minutes Lud was back in the lounge, looking unruffled and impersonal, a newspaper on his knees.

Joanna, sure that the lady who had been observing them knew what they had been up to, sat down next to Lud and gave him a wicked smile. 'I'd like to get to know you better, Mr Haley.'

'Of course. First things first.'

Joanna realised that she actually knew very little of Lud's history. He told her that he was born in Los Angeles, that he had inherited money through his paternal grandfather and that he had started in television as a bit part actor. Lud's father, she now learned, was a tennis pro, had had a drinking problem and died young of sclerosis. His mother was married for the fourth time to a rich property developer and was presently in the Bahamas.

'No, I wasn't very close to my father. He was mostly wiped out with alcohol.'

'I take it you're close to your mother. She must be pleased with your success.'

'Sure, but she expected it.' He smiled disarmingly.

'Mother's a great lady. That's probably why I like women so much. Beware of the man who hates his mom.'

Joanna felt the stirrings of an old ache. 'Mine died in childbirth when we were young, and Daddy's sister came to live with us. She tried very hard, but I always felt my real mother would have understood me better – '

'We're going to be landing in L.A. soon, Ms Lennox.' Lud grinned and held out his hand, saying in a low voice, 'It was a pleasure to pleasure you. I may take you to Hawaii after all.'

Lud had called ahead from L.A. and managed to get them a room in the Royal Hawaiian Hotel at Waikiki. 'I've been to Hawaii many times. Stepfathers number three and four have business interests here. Come, my little *malihini*. Before we ensconce ourselves in the pink palace we're going to get some gear.'

At the Ala Moana shopping centre, Joanna and Lud draped each other with *leis*, and went from store to store buying madly with their credit cards like a couple of kids let loose in a toy department. Underwear, sandals, swim suits, jeans, straw hats; makeup, muumuus, and beautiful flowered print sarong dresses for her; shaving stuff, slacks, a white suit, and aloha sports shirts for him.

They changed their clothes in one of the shops and acquired two suitcases into which they stuffed their purchases.

'I feel as if we're on the lam after having robbed a bank,' Joanna said.

Lud picked a white hibiscus and put it behind her ear. 'Wait until you see our hideout.'

Joanna was entranced that they were staying at the famous pink stucco Royal Hawaiian, built in the twenties. The main entrance was on the lush garden side, under an archway.

As they followed the bellman with their luggage along the carpeted hall, Joanna could picture such celebrities as Mary Pickford and Douglas Fairbanks in their elaborate

103

suites in the days when the hotel catered to polo players, and afternoon tea dances were held on the veranda.

Joanna's and Lud's room was elegant, done in accents of white and pale blue, with a blue-and-white flowered spread on the white bed and a blue carpet on the floor.

'This is fabulous.' Joanna stood on the balcony looking at the endless expanse of Pacific. 'To think there's nothing between us and the Orient.'

The Mai Tais Lud had ordered came in large iced glasses, each garnished with a perfect small purple orchid and a tiny paper parasol spearing a chunk of fresh pineapple. The rum-based drinks were delicious.

As they sat on their lanai watching a magnificent sunset, Lud pointed out the land mass rising to the left. 'Diamond Head, an extinct volcano, once the home of Pele, the fire goddess.'

'It's stunning.'

'You're stunning, my own fire goddess,' he murmured, nibbling at her ear. 'Want another of these concoctions?'

'I couldn't. This is a drink, salad, and spectacle all in one. My orchid's going down for the third time.'

Lud laughed and pulled her insistently into his arms. 'Going down is wonderful. Let's do it.'

They did.

In a rented car Lud and Joanna toured the island of Oahu. They visited a complex of Polynesian villages, staffed with natives of each island, who demonstrated how to crack a coconut, dance the hula, and weave a grass skirt. They saw a Buddhist temple, a magnificent waterfall, and a blowhole in a lava ledge at the ocean, with seawater spurting out of it like a geyser. They ate pineapples, papayas, and wonderful native fish called *mahimahi* and *opakapaka*. Afterwards they gorged on such wicked desserts as macadamia nut cream pie, and rationalised their gluttony by assuring each other they would work off the calories during their long swims.

A blissfully happy Joanna surrendered to the luxury of the soft climate, the brilliant exotic flowers, the sweet

Hawaiian music rendered on guitar and ukelele, and the wonderfully relaxed life. For once she gave herself to an experience completely.

After a few days they flew to Maui, a gloriously green island of spectacular beauty.

Instead of a hotel Lud negotiated for a private mansion outside of Lahaina, an old fishing town that had been the playground for Hawaiian royalty in the eighteen fifties. The house, belonging to wealthy Hawaiian friends of Lud's stepfather's, was surrounded by a garden containing coconut palm, banana, guava, breadfruit, and papaya trees and a profusion of flowers.

Joanna wandered the paths, transfixed, until Lud led her into the house, with its lovely Hawaiian furnishings made of bamboo, koa, and monkey pod wood.

'And now we come to the most important room. How's that for a bed?'

Joanna stared with amusement at the huge, ornately carved four-poster. 'It's positively decadent.'

'I should hope so. Queen Emma and King Kamehamea IV slept here. Honest. And so will we, about an hour from now,' he finished, pulling her on to it.

The first morning, Joanna awoke from a dream that she had been swimming in a bed of flowers. In fact, Lud, wearing three *leis* hanging down his bare chest, was covering her with hibiscus and plumeria blossoms. He pinned an orchid in her hair and greeted her in Hawaiian.

'Good morning, Queen Joanna. I am here to serve you.'

Serve her he did, with food he cooked himself, and very well. They kept up the game of queen and her servant for the day, their eating and drinking interspersed with sunbathing, swimming, and lovemaking.

Anyone observing them on their private stretch of beach could have believed that Joanna, with her golden tan, her blonde hair streaked by the sun, and dressed in the briefest flowered bikini, was of royal birth. And Lud, his muscular body deeply bronzed, rode a surfboard as expertly as a native.

Arm in arm they strolled through Lahaina looking for antique scrimshaw in this once-prominent whaling port. Later they enjoyed drinks under a ceiling fan at the old Pioneer Inn and watched people cooling off in the shade of a huge, century-old banyan tree.

They rented a sloop and sailed to the small island of Molukai and back. Anchoring the boat above a coral reef, they swam nude and snorkelled. Lud strummed a uke and sang *Sweet Leilani* in Hawaiian, substituting Joanna for Leilani. Then they made love on deck under the stars. Joanna could have played native with Lud in Hawaii forever.

One night he awakened her at two. She asked no questions because she loved every surprise he sprung on her. Pulling sweaters over jeans, they filled a thermos with hot coffee and made some sandwiches.

Although she was only half awake, Joanna felt an anticipatory excitement as the car began to climb a road that twisted and turned. When the moon occasionally floated in front of the clouds she saw cinder cones and hardened lava deposits all around her, creating the illusion that they were driving to the end of the world.

Lud had timed their ascent perfectly. They got out of the car at an observation point ten thousand feet up on Mount Haleakala just as the first light of dawn appeared to the east.

Lud put his arm around a shivering Joanna. 'Hang in there, it won't be long.'

As the yellow globe began to rise, he gestured at it in encouragement. 'Come on, baby, that's it, you can do it.'

Joanna laughed and hugged him.

They subsided into awed silence as the morning light illuminated the enormous volcanic crater just ahead of them.

'It's a lunar landscape like something out of Yves Tanguy,' Joanna marvelled.

106

'I know. Incredible. The floor of the crater is about twenty-five square miles. Manhattan could fit into it. You know, Haleakawa is considered dormant, not extinct. The last volcanic action was only a couple of hundred years ago and it could erupt again at any time.'

'Just like us,' she murmured, squeezing his hand.

'Watch that stuff. We're here to see the sights, not provide them.'

They drank their coffee while sitting on a rock and admiring the rare silversword plant found only on volcanoes.

Joanna was sorry it was their last day on Maui. She had lost track of time. One doesn't watch the calendar in paradise.

They flew back to Honolulu, and Lud made some phone calls.

'We're back in business. Rick's okay and ready to work next week. Tomorrow, L.A.'

Lud had a spacious rented apartment in Beverly Hills in addition to a house he owned on the beach at Malibu. Joanna, driving in his cream-coloured Mercedes, was for the first time aware of how rich he was. Lud's persona altered there, to her amusement. In his open-neck sport shirt, slacks, loafers and crew neck sweater, his eyes concealed behind large dark glasses, he looked the very picture of a successful Hollywood director.

For the next couple of days Joanna was transported to the unfamiliar, fascinating world of the television industry, tagging along with Lud and his producer, Ed Storman, head of the most successful independent television production company in L.A. This was her first opportunity to see Lud in action. When she had once suggested visiting him on the set in New York he had gently dissuaded her, joking that he wouldn't be able to concentrate. His real reason was that Nadine's performance would fall apart if Joanna were allowed to be there.

At lunch, agents, actors, and writers joined them at their

table at La Serre and talked nonstop about rising production costs, strikes, the changing audience, the new technologies.

Dinner at Chasen's could last into the wee hours, over more talk. When they finally left the restaurant, Joanna was surprised to see stars carrying bundles of groceries emerging from Hughes, a twenty-four-hour supermarket across the street.

As a result of all the talk, Joanna learned that *Sister In Law* was being handled differently from most series. Normally, the first episode would be screened as a television film, or pilot, and if the public reaction was favourable, the network would agree to finance the series. However, the screening of the pilot of *Sister In Law* had been delayed because of a strike. Then the star had left. In the meantime, on the strength of the pilot, the series had been sold overseas. Ed Storman had decided to proceed with private backing and was planning to present the completed series to the networks for, he hoped, a great deal of money.

On Friday night one of Lud's director friends threw a huge bash in his honour and Joanna found herself in a milieu she had only read about or seen in films. Everyone was tanned, spectacularly dressed and supremely self-confident. As Lud's woman, she was kissed and fussed over and treated almost like a celebrity herself. However, she was bothered by the number of people who assumed they had met her before.

'Did you have another friend who looked like me?' she asked Lud. 'You haven't been sneaking off to L.A. with Nadine, have you?'

'No, ma'am. It's just that to all those jaded eyes all beautiful women look alike. Just as well, in this case. If they realised how uniquely Joanna you are they'd never let you out of here.'

13

Joanna made it into her office at eight-thirty and attacked the pile of papers on her desk. She was relieved to see that the Holland book had gone to press without her. And no reason that it shouldn't have. Nobody was indispensable.

Winnie and Abby arrived at the same time, Abby squealing at how tanned and well Joanna looked, and going into raptures over the sarong she had bought for her in Honolulu.

Winnie examined his gift, an antique woodcarving. 'Thanks. It's beautiful. Next time you go AWOL try to stop off in Israel. My mother's been wanting a genuine mezzuzah from Jerusalem.'

Winnie's humour was tinged with a sharp edge. Joanna saw that he was angry.

Later she apologised for the way she had run out on him. 'I know it was bizarre but I just couldn't help myself – '

'That's the part that bothers me, babe. It's not that I don't want you to be happy. But you're too happy, if you see what I'm getting at. It's unreal. I'm afraid for you when you come off the high and find out that this Lud of yours, with all his charms, is still only a man with a man's weaknesses.'

'Whew. Heavy.' Nevertheless, Joanna smiled brilliantly at her boss. 'All I can say is eighty percent less pleasure will still be twenty percent more than I've ever had with anyone else. Anyway, I'll work day and night to make up for going off like that. The book looks fine but I can see the Kranick touch. You had to do my share, didn't you?'

'Forget it. You'll do mine next time.'

Joanna ploughed through her work, disappointed that

109

Lud didn't phone. Of course he must be frantically busy the first day back on the set, but she felt let down anyway. Nadine didn't call either, not even at lunchtime. Joanna, working like mad on the Switzerland book, ate a yoghurt at her desk. She stayed until six-thirty and then took a taxi directly to Nadine's bearing the gifts she had brought back: an antique coral necklace and earrings and several toys for Jeff and Kate.

Mrs Wilson opened the door and told Joanna that Nadine was resting after work, not feeling well. The children were having supper at a friend's.

Joanna rushed into the bedroom. 'Nadine, what's wrong?'

'Only a lousy cold,' her sister said huskily. 'I've had it all week. And today I couldn't do a thing in front of the camera.'

'I'm sorry you're not feeling well, but you sound so sexy – '

'Sure, but Suzanne's presenting a case in court. She can't croak like a frog.' Nadine looked at her beautifully tanned sister resentfully. 'How could you just go off that way without a word?'

'I phoned. Don't tell me you didn't get my message?'

'Yeah, but it didn't say where you went or who with.'

'I didn't know where myself until we were halfway to Hawaii. Surely you knew I was with Lud.'

Nadine blinked rapidly and began to cough. Her chest was heavily congested.

'I don't like the sound of that. Have you seen the doctor?'

'It's a little late to be concerned, after running out on me. Since you started dating him you're like another person. I've never known you to be so selfish, especially towards Jeff and Kate. They were so disappointed to miss two Sundays.'

Joanna's heart contracted. She sat down on the bed. 'I'm sorry, Nadine, I'll make it up to them. But I just had to go. I can't even explain it. Didn't you get my postcards?'

Nadine blew her nose without replying, glaring at her

110

sister over her tissue. It was galling. Joanna, bursting with health and happiness after a romantic idyll in Hawaii with Lud. While she had been left here alone with no work to occupy her and nobody to help with the children.

And now Joanna was handing her a present.

In a fury, Nadine hurled the box across the room. 'I can't be bought off with a crummy gift.'

Joanna was stunned.

'No sooner did I tell you I had a part in a television series and had met a fantastic man than you did your number.'

'*I* did a number?'

'Damn right you did. New York is full of men. Omega alone employs hundreds, but you had to choose Lud Haley.'

Joanna felt a horrible sinking sensation. 'He chose me. I told you all this – '

'You told me a lot of crap. When you got back from Europe he didn't call you, did he? Because in the meantime he'd met me. We went to dinner together. We were getting to know each other, slowly. But you couldn't leave him alone. You had to go after him at the party – '

'I didn't even want to go to the goddamn party!' Joanna raised her voice angrily.

Nadine sneezed and buried her nose in a handkerchief. For someone who hadn't wanted to go to a party, Joanna had managed to walk off with the most desirable man in the place.

Joanna took several deep breaths in an attempt to control her anger. So this was the way Nadine really felt. She had only pretended to be happy that Joanna was seeing Lud. Her sister was more of an actress than she had ever dreamed and a hypocrite too.

Nadine, coughing and sniffling, vented her rage on the box of tissues. She could have kicked herself. Because she had been so intent on being given the role of Suzanne and playing it to perfection she had behaved like a star-struck idiot, not aware that Lud was only waiting for a positive response to his interest in her. In the meantime, her twin had come along and zeroed in, flattering him, no doubt, making herself so available that he would have had to be made of stone to refuse. And by some miracle, she was managing to hold on to him – so far.

Joanna had succeeded in calming down. 'There's nothing to be gained from talking about it now, Nadine. I'm sorry you feel I trespassed on your territory, but if you were interested in Lud you should have told me from the start. Since you didn't, I refuse to feel guilty for what's happened.'

'I can see that,' Nadine croaked, unable to capture the proper sarcastic tone. 'But you're not as innocent as you pretend. Maybe the Lud thing is to get back at me because I've always been more successful with men.'

'Nadine, for heaven's sake! I fell in love with him, pure and simple. It's a *feeling*. It has nothing to do with you.'

Bullshit. Nadine knew very well that Joanna had never forgiven her for Carl. Ironically, if her sister knew what a favour Nadine had done her she would be thanking her now.

'I think you'd better go,' Nadine sniffled.

Joanna stood up slowly. 'I have some presents for Kate and Jeff.'

'They're with their friends. Won't be back for at least an hour.'

Joanna began to burn with humiliation. Was Nadine going to punish her by keeping her from her niece and nephew? Why pick this particular time to let her have it? Of course the answer was obvious. Nadine was feeling sick and sorry for herself.

The old feeling of protectiveness towards Nadine washed over Joanna and she hovered in the doorway. 'Do you need anything? Shouldn't I at least call the doctor? Or the chemist to get something for that cough?'

'Stop it, stop putting on the good sister act. If you cared about me you wouldn't have run off to Hawaii. God, you didn't even phone me once. Two seconds to scribble a postcard was all the time you could spare me. You didn't care that I might be worried or lonely. And it all goes back to Carl, doesn't it?'

This was the first time since revealing their affair so long ago that Nadine had openly mentioned Carl in connection with Joanna.

Joanna felt a sudden stab of pain at the memory. 'My feeling for Lud has nothing to do with Carl,' she said in a low voice. 'Anyway, it's hardly the same thing. You and Carl began when he and I were nearly engaged.'

'Come off it! It was just about over between you when I got here, but you'd rather think it was my fault than yours.'

'What do you mean?'

'I mean that you never knew how to make a man feel important. That's why he picked me.'

'Oh no it's not.'

'Oh yes it is.'

'I can't listen to this for another moment.'

'Then don't. I'm not keeping you here.'

Joanna walked angrily out of the bedroom to get her coat. While she was putting it on, she heard Nadine talking on the phone. 'Daddy? Yes, it's me, with a cold. No, nothing to worry about, I'll be fine. I just wanted to call and say hi, see how you're doing . . .'

Joanna left the apartment overwhelmed by an old feeling of jealousy so strong it took her breath away. She *knew* why Carl had picked Nadine over her. It was for the same reason that their father preferred her sister, as did ninety-nine out of one hundred other men.

Joanna's earliest memories of her father were warm ones. Although he wasn't around much, when he was at home he played with both his daughters. What Joanna especially remembered was taking turns at having a piggyback ride.

Joanna was a happy child, totally close and loving to Nadine, who was always there to talk to, to play with, and even to sleep with in the same bed. She had never felt any jealousy towards Nadine for the first six years of their lives. Then their mother's death changed everything.

The two little girls clung to each other, frightened by the hushed whispers in their ramshackle farmhouse and the

113

scurrying of neighbour ladies, bringing in plates of fried chicken and hominy grits to feed them and their father, who had retreated into sullen, angry silence.

After a couple of weeks, Aunt Sally, Daddy's much younger unmarried sister came to live with them. She was a take-charge person, and at first Joanna was vastly relieved to have meals prepared on time, and clothes washed and ironed. She was glad to be told when to get up and when to go to bed.

But Aunt Sally had none of her sister-in-law's delicacy. Joanna, imagining her mother in heaven, visualised a pretty, pale woman who spoke with the soft voice and accent of her once-rich, refined, upper-East-Texas family. Dressed all in white, she would forever float lightly and a little sadly among the clouds, sometimes playing the dulcimer and singing the plaintive songs of her youth.

Aunt Sally, like Daddy, was cut from denim rather than dimity. She was small and stocky, with a coarse-grained complexion and plain features. After her sweetheart had been killed during World War II she had remained at home until her parents died. Characterising her sister-in-law as 'high-falutin',' Sally had preferred to live on a cousin's farm. But when her brother was left with two motherless girls she agreed to come and keep house for him and 'the twins', as she kept calling them.

Aunt Sally didn't play the dulcimer, or read books, or notice that Nadine was better at singing and dancing, Joanna at drawing.

Aunt Sally did pick up a difference their mother had never mentioned. Pointing out that Nadine was slightly smaller and thinner, Aunt Sally said about ten times every day, 'Jo, y'all got to look out for your little twin. She's delicate, like your poor Mama, and you got to take care she won't get carried to heaven before her time.'

Joanna was puzzled. She didn't see that Nadine was any more delicate than she was. Didn't they do the same chores and play the same games? Aunt Sally couldn't even tell them apart unless she identified their different clothing or saw them together.

114

Questioning her aunt, Joanna was told, 'Of course you're stronger, born first, and weighed more too. Poor Naddie was only a little mite of a thing. Nearly got taken before she ever opened her eyes.'

Joanna was only dimly beginning to understand what being born meant. Their intended baby brother had died along with their mother. Joanna wanted to talk about birth and death with her sister, but whenever she tried Nadine would pick that moment to get something in her eye or complain of a stomach ache, or just run away.

Although Nadine had never been a complainer, she now whined and demanded special treatment.

'C'mon, Dini,' Joanna would say, 'y'all can heft the milk pail just as good as me – '

'I can't,' Nadine would object. 'It's too durn heavy, Jan. Aunt Sally says y'all have to help me.'

As Nadine did less and less, Joanna had to do more, and it rankled. On top of that, although she tried her best to please her aunt, Sally liked Nadine better, and hugged and kissed her more. Joanna wanted affection too but she held back, afraid of asking and not getting. There wasn't enough of anything to go around. Daddy was spending eighteen hours a day trying to make a living from his land, but it yielded very little.

Once, watching Daddy putting on his jacket to go back to work, Joanna rushed up and threw her arms around him.

'Hey, gal, git off of me,' he said morosely, disentangling her from his overalls. 'No time for playing.'

Joanna drew away, the pain of the rejection translated into sullenness.

'Why not?' she asked.

'Because I got me some land so poor it won't even sprout black-eyed peas.'

As he left she heard him mumbling about being cursed with daughters instead of being blessed with sons. She began to wish she were a boy so that she could be of more help on the farm. Maybe then her father would want her.

And yet whenever he sat still long enough, Nadine was the one who got to bounce in his lap, the one who was petted. She would smile fetchingly and act cute until it made Joanna want to throw up.

Just before the twins were to start the first grade, Aunt Sally took them into Tyler and bought them identical outfits. Their mother hadn't dressed them alike, and Joanna felt peculiar when she looked at her sister. Where did she end and Nadine begin?

'Jo,' Aunt Sally told her, handing her the two lunch-boxes on the first day of school, 'y'all take care of your little sister, hear?'

Joanna was afraid to sass her aunt but she smouldered with resentment.

Aunt Sally dropped the girls in front of the schoolhouse in Tyler and drove away in the old station wagon. She had too many chores at home to wait around. After all, the teachers were there to see to the children.

Nadine looked at Joanna and tears filled her eyes.

Joanna grabbed her sister's hand and pulled her into the yard, so close to tears herself that her throat felt as if she had swallowed a plum without chewing it.

Dozens of children clustered around them. 'Hey, lookee here. Twins.'

The girls were unused to towns and large groups of children. Joanna became tense at being in the centre of a crowd. Feeling her stomach twist into a knot, she held tightly to Nadine's hand and was silent. Nadine, however, loved the attention and boldly answered all the questions flung at them.

Then Joanna saw Fern Brunner pushing towards them. Bossy Missy, with eyes like a ferret, was always trying to get between Joanna and her sister. Fern was loud and shameless, and she made it clear in a short time that Nadine was her 'best friend'.

To Joanna's relief the teachers finally broke up the circle and conducted the children to their classrooms.

That part was fine. Joanna was fascinated with the reader she was given and her new notebook and pencil. She was interested in what the teacher said and riveted by the way she wrote on the blackboard and then magically erased the chalk.

But during recess Joanna was back in the schoolyard, surrounded by children made more aggressive because of enforced stillness at their desks. Some of them actually poked Joanna to see if she was different from them.

While Nadine continued to get right into the spirit, willing to stand back to back with her sister so that the kids could see the difference in height, Joanna felt sick to her stomach. She had been unable to eat a bite of her lunch.

Finally she escaped from the gang and stood leaning disconsolately against the wall of the schoolhouse. Then she spotted Fern coming towards her with two of the older kids, a brother and sister.

Joanna quickly scooted around the corner so that they couldn't see her.

'How do y'all like them twin sisters, Betty Sue?' Fern asked.

'I like Nadine real good.'

'Me too,' Fern agreed. 'The other one's a sourpuss. Which one do y'all think is prettier, BJ?'

'Golly, no use asking him. He hates girls, don't you, BJ?'

'Only if they sass me like you. Between them two twins, Nadine is the pretty one all right.'

The argument with Nadine had punctured Joanna's euphoria. She was back in the real world, with Lud so busy she didn't see him until Wednesday, and then she couldn't keep from blurting out the reason for her quarrel with her sister.

'Lud, did you take her out to dinner while I was in Europe? She said you were interested in her but she didn't encourage you.'

Lud frowned and took Joanna's hand. 'I took her to dinner, yes. Interested in her as a woman, no. She wasn't interested in me either, not really, not until she heard about us. I'm not sure if that's the reason or if it's only the usual

117

silly, temporary fix an actress sometimes gets on her director. It's meaningless. You're my love, Joanna, please believe that. And if you want to do something for me, make up with Nadine. She's all hurt feelings and temperament. It's hell on the role and the rest of the cast. You're the one whose head is together. Please make the first move.'

Of course Joanna agreed to call her sister.

However, Lud remained tense and preoccupied. There was no lovemaking that night. Joanna was disappointed even though she understood. She had grown so used to Lud's constant good humour and intense passion.

Spoiled, that's what I am, she thought.

From the next day Joanna called Nadine several times, but on each occasion her sister put down the phone.

To make Joanna feel worse, on Friday afternoon Lud, claiming exhaustion, cancelled their evening together. Having so looked forward to seeing him, Joanna really wilted.

Abby insisted that the two should go out to dinner together, since she was 'between men', as she put it. Abby didn't know of the quarrel between Joanna and her sister and assumed the trouble was with Lud only.

'After such a heavenly couple of weeks, coming back to earth is bound to be a downer.'

'I suppose so, but to call off tonight at the last minute –'

'That's typical. Men. At first they can't see you enough or make love enough. That's my story over and over. To start with I'm a little standoffish. After all, I hardly know the guy. Then, just when I'm really getting turned on to him, boom, he cuts me back from four times a day to twice a week, like it or lump it.'

'But why?'

'Because men and women are different, that's why.' Abby, working on her second Bloody Mary, leaned forward confidentially. 'Women are nest-builders. We're into procreation so we need a stable life.'

'But Abby, you're usually the one who cuts out.'

'Sure, but my reason is as soon as I get turned on they get turned off. And then I split because I know it can only get worse. I've made a study of the subject, Joanna, and believe me, men just aren't into *intimacy*. Not nowadays. It scares the shit out of them.'

Joanna excused herself right after dinner and went home. She undressed, got into bed, and turned on the television. There was a rerun of Lud's old series, *Wanted, To Share*. The episode she watched was frothy and marginally amusing. Mostly it made her long for the director so acutely she nearly phoned him.

By Saturday morning Joanna had hit her lowest point. She and Lud were supposed to have dinner with his producer. Ed Storman had just flown in from L.A., and she was dreading having to spend the whole evening talking business. Of course she had agreed, rather than risk not seeing Lud at all.

Just when she decided to try Nadine one more time, the phone rang.

'I'm sorry for everything and for hanging up on you.' Nadine sounded contrite. 'Don't move. I'm coming over.'

Her cold was gone, and she looked alive and happy again.

'It was such a silly argument, Jan. I was tense, premenstrual. I started my period this morning and feel so much better. Forget what I said about Lud and everything. I didn't mean it. It's just that I felt so left out – the two of you going off and me all alone, stuck with the kids. Even Jim went to Chicago to see his folks. He's back, of course, and I'm feeling much better.'

Joanna caught her breath. She had missed her period. For the first time since she had gone to Hawaii she realised that not only hadn't she taken her pills with her, it had never even crossed her mind until this moment.

After Nadine had left, Joanna found half of her last month's supply of pills still in the pack, and she was a week late. She really could be pregnant.

Was forgetting her pills simply carelessness? Or at least

119

not making other arrangements in Hawaii? Or did she have an unconscious wish to be pregnant by Lud? She began to feel a warm glow, remembering that Lud had once told her he would love her to have his child.

Of course it was too soon to tell for sure. Excitement, change of climate, the quarrel with Nadine – almost anything could have thrown her off. She would just have to wait and see.

The dinner with Ed Storman and his wife turned out to be enjoyable after all, mostly because Lud was his usual amusing self, and he beamed passionate looks at Joanna that made her burn with desire.

When they finally got to bed they were as intensely sensual towards each other as ever.

Sunday was wonderful from start to finish. Joanna took Jeff and Kate rowing in Central Park and shared their excitement and pleasure. How glorious it would be to have a child of her own to make happy. Lud's child. She would adore it with every breath of love within her.

Sunday night Joanna cooked dinner for Lud which they ate by candlelight. The thought that she might be pregnant was oddly arousing to her.

Before dessert they were tearing off their clothes. Much later they ate their strawberries and cream in bed.

Abby was wrong about men in general and Lud in particular. Joanna felt closer to him than ever and more certain with every moment that their love was going to produce the child they both wanted.

Lud lay on his back, his arm around Joanna, feeling a sense of peace for the first time since returning to New York. Things were going reasonably well at last. Nadine was acting again instead of acting up, though it had taken a hell of a lot of doing. And Joanna was so beautiful, so passionate.

'Good night, sweetheart,' he murmured. 'Dream of me loving you.'

Nadine sat in front of her mirror rehearsing her part. She was elated by her grasp of the role at last. Only yesterday

120

her director had told her she had made a brilliant improvement.

She looked good, too. Her hair felt silky again, her skin creamy, and her eyes were bright with happiness.

The crew would soon be filming in New Hampshire. Surely Joanna wouldn't be coming with them, having so recently returned to her job. Besides, if Nadine asked her in just the right way she would stay around to watch out for the children.

Nadine was the one who was important to Lud's career, not Joanna. That had already been tested and proven.

Nadine lost herself in her recurring daydream: As the biggest star in television, she is able to choose any role she wants but insists on working only with one man, the famous director Lud Haley. Who also happens to be her husband.

14

Joanna awoke every morning convinced that she was pregnant, and the knowledge exhilarated her. She had plenty of time to indulge in her fantasy because Lud's schedule had accelerated to the point where they were seeing each other only on Saturday and Sunday and, once, on Wednesday. But it didn't matter. When they were together Lud was magnificent.

Wherever she went, Joanna smiled at mothers-to-be and at mothers-that-were, peering into carriages and behaving like a perfect fool over strange babies.

She began to drink milk, eat more cheese and take vitamins, and she tried to rest a great deal. In fact, she was feeling good until Lud told her, on Sunday night, that he would be leaving in a couple of weeks to film on location in New Hampshire. It was something that had been set up at the very beginning, when Gina was still the star of the series.

'May I come with you, Lud?'

'Sorry, angel. Much as I'd love to have you, the schedule will be hectic. I've already told the cast that spouses, roommates, offspring are out. No room at the inn and no time for diversions.'

Joanna felt uneasy, a moment later scolding herself for her foolishness. 'How long will you be away?'

'Three, four days, if all goes well. Monday through Thursday, something like that.'

Joanna said no more. She was hardly seeing Lud during the week anyway. Besides, Nadine was dating Jim Sweeney, and he would be in New Hampshire, so what was Joanna worrying about?

She was worrying nevertheless. Although she had been

postponing seeing a doctor, she would have to attend to it very soon.

This was the part that dismayed her. To have to find a doctor, relate her depressing history of miscarriages, be told, perhaps, that she would have to spend time resting in bed... And what if she really wasn't pregnant at all? What if it were a growth of some kind, or simply a deep wish translated into a hysterical false symptom?

To combat her restlessness and anxiety, Joanna decided to play some tennis at her club on Monday evening.

Her first game was a doubles match, all women. Joanna was a strong player, and after a short warm-up she and her partner easily beat their opponents two games out of three.

Joanna drank a glass of tomato juice at the bar with her partner and agreed to play a game of singles with her.

As she was leaving she backed into Dominic Graham. 'Oh. Hi. I'm so sorry,' she said, flustered.

'It was my fault, Joanna. I hope I didn't damage any vital parts.'

'No. If you'll excuse me, please. Game,' she muttered, moving quickly away. Something was disturbing her, something from the past that was on the tip of her memory.

'Gee,' her partner commented, 'he looks nice but I guess he must be an ogre or something, the way you split.'

'Of course he's nice. Very.' Then why was her pulse racing? She felt as frightened as a highly superstitious person who had just walked under a ladder and into the path of a black cat.

Her anxiety wasn't helped by noticing Dominic playing a game of men's doubles on the adjoining court.

Whap. Joanna hit her first serve into the net and her next off the court and into Dominic's. In fact, he retrieved the ball and sent it neatly back to her.

She nodded her thanks and immediately looked away, trying to concentrate on her game, but it fell to pieces. She was hitting hard but wild. Her opponent had more control. Her shots went where she placed them and Joanna

123

was having to dash all over the court. She lost the first two sets. She was perspiring and wondered if she ought to stop playing. Suddenly the court began to spin, and she lost her balance.

Down she went and blacked out.

In a moment Dominic was at her side, explaining to her worried opponent that he was a doctor. He took Joanna's pulse, frowned, and listened to her heartbeat.

In a few moments Joanna was conscious. 'I'm fine, really. I was just dizzy for a moment.' She felt mortified and insisted on getting up, although allowing Dominic to lead her to a chair and bring her a glass of water.

He was looking at her with a mixture of concern and dismay. 'When was the last time you had a checkup?'

'I don't really remember.'

'See your doctor, Joanna, as soon as possible.'

'You think it's serious?' She wondered if he suspected a pregnancy but was too delicate to say so.

'No, probably not, but do it anyway.' Dominic gave her a faint smile. 'Can't have you wilting on the courts that way.'

'I spoiled your game. I'm so sorry.'

'Don't be silly. Look, let me take you home. Get a good night's sleep and have yourself looked at tomorrow. That's my professional advice.'

A chill went through Joanna as she remembered what it was about him that had been bothering her.

'I'll be all right,' she said in a tight, frightened voice, starting to move away.

'Joanna! At least let me get you a taxi. No, really, I insist.'

'I have to change.'

'Right. I'll meet you outside.'

Joanna found herself trembling in the dressing room. Biting her lip, she made an effort to control herself. She thought of Lud, of how happy he would be when she told him. Now she was absolutely sure. The only other time in her life she had fainted had been when she was pregnant.

Dominic, still in his tennis gear, was standing at the

kerb. 'Don't know where all the bloody taxis have got to.'

He caught Joanna staring at him, and he smiled. 'I look ridiculous, I know, like a fugitive from Wimbledon.'

Joanna touched his arm guiltily. 'I appreciate your efforts but I wish you'd go back to your game. I'm fine now, honest, and I'm sure a taxi will come along.'

'No, my dear, out of the question. Let it never be said that I left a damsel in distress.'

A taxi pulled up and Dominic opened the door with a flourish.

'Thanks,' she murmured, getting in.

Dominic touched her cheek for a moment before closing the door.

Joanna leaned her head back, her thoughts whirling. She remembered another time when Dominic had not come to the rescue of a damsel in distress.

When Joanna became pregnant for the third time she wanted to change doctors.

Nadine suggested Dr Dominic Graham. 'He's wonderful, really.'

'I feel funny about him as a doctor. I've met him at Abby's parties with his wife.'

'Does that matter? Abby recommended him to you for me.'

'That's different. You didn't know him socially first.'

'So what? I know him socially now. The point is that Dominic's a terrific doctor. Not only competent but so sympathetic, always there when you need him.' While Nadine spoke two-year-old Kate climbed into her lap to be cuddled.

'Okay,' Joanna said. 'I guess I am being sillly. Oh, Dini, if only I can have this baby!'

Nadine handed Kate to her sister. 'Of course you will, Jan, Dominic will see to it.'

Joanna made an appointment with his nurse.

In the waiting room of his office she noted a few poorly dressed patients among the obviously affluent.

When Joanna was ushered into Dr Graham's office, he looked up, startled.

'I'm Nadine Barrett's sister?' Joanna made it a question, Texas style, feeling very ill at ease.

'Yes, of course. I remember you very well, Joanna. I just didn't make the connection between you and Mrs Ben Magid.' He indicated a seat. 'What can I do for you?'

'Well,' she began, 'I'm sure I'm pregnant. And I've had two miscarriages within the last four years. For no particular reason.' Joanna gave him a few details.

Had Nadine said Dr Graham was sympathetic? Caring? He seemed hardly to be listening.

'I'm going to interrupt you, Joanna, to say that I'm not taking on any new pregnancies at present. If it were a matter of a checkup or a prescription I'd be happy to oblige, but I'm afraid I have as many pregnant patients as I honestly feel I can attend to properly.'

He smiled apologetically. 'I'm terribly sorry. But I can recommend you to a fine obstetrician.'

Joanna sat motionless, feeling a hot flush suffuse her skin. As he wrote the particulars on a piece of paper she looked resentfully at him. He had accepted Nadine but rejected her. He even took on Medicaid patients. Surely one more pregnant woman couldn't make that much of a difference.

As soon as Joanna was outside his office she crumpled his piece of paper into a ball. She would find her own doctor.

She did, an older man, very experienced. But it did no good. She miscarried anyway.

At the time, Joanna had felt on a gut level that if Dr Graham had been her doctor she, like Nadine, would have had her baby.

The day following her fainting spell, Joanna sat in her new doctor's waiting room marvelling at how she had blocked out the memory of Dominic's rejection of her as a patient. No doubt the reason he had given her at the time had been a truthful one but anxiety had caused her to be oversensitive, to feel that he had favoured her sister over her.

Joanna immediately responded to Dr Theodore Halloran. He had a shock of red hair and a full red beard, and he appeared younger than he probably was, but so knowledgeable, so unpatriarchal. He explained everything she wanted to know, treating her like an intelligent being who was in touch with her own body.

Within two days he had confirmed her pregnancy. Joanna felt confident she wouldn't miscarry this time. Her attitude was different, and so was the father.

She was a little uneasy to learn that her new doctor coincidentally was associated with St Anne's because she feared she might keep running into Dominic there. Well, with luck she would only be at the hospital during her confinement.

Joanna decided not to say anything to anyone for a little while longer. She wanted to be sure nothing would go wrong.

Nadine, with a twin's sixth sense, was aware of a beatific expression on her sister's face. Could Joanna be pregnant? That would be the worst possible thing that could happen. Lud might stay with Joanna if she was going to have his child. That was one area in which her sister had an advantage over her. She already had Carl's two children, whereas Joanna . . .

Whereas Joanna, even if she was pregnant, probably would lose the baby.

Nadine immediately felt contrite. She wanted Joanna to have children – just as long as Lud was not the father.

The more Nadine thought about it, the more sure she was that it couldn't be true. The very first person Joanna would tell would be her sister.

15

Winnie invited Joanna and Lud to an art opening featuring American sculptors at the Whitney Museum, which was packed with patrons of the arts as well as a number of prominent artists and collectors.

Joanna, wearing a Mary McFadden cream-coloured pleated dress, was glad it had no waistline to reveal that her own was already beginning to thicken slightly. Moving through the throng with Lud and Winnie, she made a note to come back by herself at another time so that she could look more carefully at the works.

Dominic Graham, a museum member himself, had brought Abby with him to the opening. He saw Joanna before she saw him, and glumly observed the loving looks she was exchanging with the curly-haired man at her side.

'Oh, look, Dom, there's Joanna and Winnie.'

'Yes, I see them. A little decorum, if you please. That means not shouting across the room,' he said dryly.

Abby made him a mock salute. 'Yes, sir. But don't you intend to say hello?'

'In good time.'

Abby, forgetting Dominic's interest in Joanna in Amsterdam, barrelled ahead in her usual fashion. 'That smashing guy with Joanna is Lud Haley, her new big love. Is he ever. He's got it all: brains, talent, wit, charm. I wish he had a brother; even a father.'

Dominic forced a smile, while thinking that he wouldn't describe Lud Haley as smashing, but the reason was probably jealousy. He looked trendy, fashionable. Dominic noted the appealing smile, the easy confidence.

128

Perhaps a touch of flamboyance. A television director. So that was what Joanna liked.

Dominic wished he could have avoided her entirely, but Abby took his hand and resolutely pulled him towards the trio.

For Joanna he had a cool nod and the merest suggestion of a smile. Dominic shook hands with Winnie and then with Lud, who greeted him with a few light words before beginning to joke with Abby. Dominic was happy to talk to Winnie, while Joanna, somewhat uncomfortable because of Dominic's presence, edged away from all of them and tried to concentrate on the exhibit. She refused another glass of champagne. It was spooky the way Dominic kept turning up wherever she went. She hoped by the time she rejoined the little group he would have wandered away, but he was still talking to Winnie.

A striking young woman rushed up to Lud and flung her arms around him dramatically. She was an actress, of course, and they knew endless people in common.

Lud, the moment she paused for breath, introduced her to Joanna and the others, but the newcomer barely nodded, saving all her attentions for him. She was wearing a gold lamé halter top, which showed a wide expanse of flawless back and midriff, and matching culottes.

Joanna had a frightening preview of what being with Lud in Hollywood might be like. Of course he couldn't be downright rude to the lady, but did he have to smile and look as if he not only didn't mind her extravagant behaviour but actually found it amusing? It was particularly mortifying to Joanna that Dominic was there to observe it all – not that she ought to care what he thought.

Without much subtlety, the actress was manoeuvring Lud away from his friends, and Joanna found herself pushed closer to Dominic and separated from the others by a new crush of people who were converging on a waiter holding a tray of champagne glasses.

Dominic, forced to say something, began to discuss a sculpture that was nearby. 'I find this piece quite interest-

129

ing. At least the sculptor has done his own welding, rather than transport an auto wreck and arrange it as "art".'

Joanna listened politely and agreed with him, relieved that he hadn't asked her if she had seen a doctor.

She kept looking over at Lud, hoping the awful actress would move on and display herself to some other man. In the next moment Joanna told herself she was being awfully silly to expect Lud to pay constant attention to her, especially in public. She smiled to herself when she recalled one or two of his private attentions.

Dominic, observing her with pained interest, thought that like most happily pregnant women, Joanna looked beautiful. He had been worried about her the day she had fainted, but it hadn't occurred to him she might be pregnant. When, coincidentally, he had later that week seen her name on Ted Halloran's list of patients Dominic had felt unreasonably depressed.

Now, watching Joanna's anxious eyes on Lud, the man who undoubtedly was responsible for her condition, Dominic could scarcely imagine any man lucky enough to be Joanna's lover publicly forsaking her for such an unworthy diversion. Dominic had the idle thought that Lud would have quite liked Alexis.

A large man, pushing his way through the throng, crushed Joanna against a stone sculpture without even noticing.

'Do watch where you're going,' Dominic said sharply to the man, who muttered an apology.

Dominic rescued Joanna, taking her arm. 'This is impossible, and there's no proper ventilation, either.'

'I'm all right.' But she wasn't. She had a sudden moment of vertigo and stumbled against Dominic.

He drew her to the stairwell, where it was ten degrees cooler, peeled off his jacket, and placed it on the top step. Firmly he sat her there and put her head down between her knees.

In moments the dizziness passed. Joanna looked up. 'I'm all right now, thanks.' She suddenly knew that he knew she was pregnant. Quickly she looked down at her middle.

Dominic smiled. 'No, my dear, it doesn't show. It happens I saw Dr Halloran's list of patients, since my assistant makes the hospital schedule up months in advance.'

Joanna felt shy and vulnerable. 'Please don't tell Abby or anyone. I wanted to wait until I was sure nothing would go wrong this time.' She stopped herself from going on. There was no reason for Dominic to remember her history of miscarriages.

Apparently he did remember. He pressed her shoulder with sympathy. 'Of course. I understand. But the father has to have a blood test. I wouldn't wait too long, Joanna.'

'I won't.' She stood up, looking with dismay at his crushed jacket. 'Oh. I'm so sorry.'

'It doesn't matter. I'll tell Lud you're waiting for him here.'

Before she could object, Dominic snatched his jacket and vanished into the gallery.

He made his way towards the group, relieved to see that Lud was now alone with Winnie and Abby, all of them looking around for the missing members of the party.

'Joanna is near the stairs,' Dominic told Lud coolly.

Lud frowned, thanked him, and left.

Dominic willed himself to be pleased for them both and forego the taste of sour grapes.

When Lud found Joanna he held her close. 'I'm sorry we got separated, love. Cindy's like a steamroller. It's impossible to get away without demolishing her fragile ego. Yes, I know she comes on strong but it's only an act. I can't tell you how many times she's supposed to have taken an overdose.'

Winnie appeared and the three left the museum together.

Joanna's evening was spoiled, however. For the first time she was fearful of the future. She had been concentrating so much on the confirmation of the pregnancy that she hadn't thought of some practical consequences. If she could hardly hold Lud's attention now, how would she compete with the stunning, exotic women of Hollywood when she became gross and ponderous during the course of the pregnancy?

'I hope you won't mind keeping an eye on the children while I'm in New Hampshire,' Nadine told her sister on the phone.

Joanna heard the excitement in Nadine's voice, and dark thoughts tugged at her well-being. Nadine, alone with Lud in New Hampshire – but of course that wouldn't be true. Jim would be there, and the rest of the cast and crew.

Although Joanna kept telling herself she was being ridiculous, she couldn't stop worrying.

16

Joanna had a call from Dr Halloran's nurse reminding her that the baby's father should have a blood test. Joanna would have to tell Lud.

Because he was working late, they met at the restaurant.

'Sweetheart, you look cool and beautiful. Makes me feel scruffy from rushing around like a madman all day, with so many damn frustrations.'

She listened sympathetically. He did seem hopped up and anxious. This was not the moment to tell him, but it would have to be some time that evening, since she had made an appointment for him at her doctor's office the following morning.

When their drinks arrived she lifted her glass and smiled at him. 'Thank God It's Friday.'

'Thank God It's Joanna,' he responded, giving her a look that turned her bones molten.

The drinks, and being together, eased both their tensions.

She ordered broiled salmon and a small salad.

'You must have had a big lunch today to be eating such a tiny dinner at this late hour.'

'Not really. I had a bite with Abby. I used to have lunch on Fridays with Nadine, until you appropriated her. How's she doing, by the way?'

'Just fine,' he said, paying careful attention to his drink. He didn't like to look at Joanna when he told a fib, and this was a whopper. Nadine wasn't doing fine at all. She was driving him up the wall.

'I'm so envious of all of you going off to New Hampshire. It's spring, everything will be in bloom.'

'Not like you,' he murmured, smiling at her. 'In fact, the weather report from New Hampshire isn't too terrific. There's unseasonably cold air coming down from Canada.'

'Better take your woollies.'

'Yeah. I wish I could take you, baby, but you know the setup. What's the matter?'

'Nothing.' She had jumped when he said 'baby'. Now she pushed away her plate.

'You've hardly eaten a thing.'

'I have to leave room,' she said softly, 'before I start getting a big belly.'

'You? Impossible. You eat like a bird.'

'But I make love like a rabbit.' Her heart was pounding, and she couldn't stop beaming at him.

He looked up as her words sank in. 'Christ! Joanna, is it – are you saying –'

She nodded. 'Are you pleased?'

He looked stunned. 'I guess so. It's such a surprise.'

'To me, too. I'd been on the pill, but when we went to Hawaii I forgot everything, never gave it a second thought. But if you – you don't want us to –' Joanna stopped and looked unsure for a moment.

'Of course I want us to.' Lud took her hands across the table, grinning sheepishly. 'Are you feeling okay? You've seen a doctor?'

She nodded and assured him she was fine, mentioning the blood test he was to take. About her miscarriages she would say nothing. There was no reason for him to worry unnecessarily.

'I don't want anyone else to know for a while, not even Nadine.'

Joanna didn't have to be concerned that he would impart that particular information to her sister, who was giving him a hard enough time. Lud had a moment of wishing the filming could be over before Nadine knew anything about a baby.

He was feeling very strange. The idea of having a child with Joanna was sort of exciting, and yet a little scary. He didn't know much about babies – except that parents could be awfully boring about them. Also, babies cried a lot, he remembered. Ed Storman, when his son was tiny, had been chasing starlets all over Hollywood, confiding to Lud that his wife was always too tired for sex.

Catching Joanna's eye on him, Lud smiled and mouthed a kiss at her. Then he took out his gold pen and an envelope and drew a line down the middle on the back of it. Marking one column B and one G, he wrote a name under each and passed the envelope to Joanna.

'Andrew. Andrea. Mm. Possible.'

'How about Belinda, Burt? Oh, Jesus, we're not talking about twins, are we, sweetheart?'

She shook her head, laughing. 'Not likely. Fraternal twins run in families but identical ones are a fluke. There's only one chance in two hundred and fifty of my having identical twins.'

Although Lud was smiling he was feeling quietly thankful that the odds were so much against twins. He no longer had any romantic illusions on the subject.

'I don't care what we call the baby,' he said, 'as long as it's not Ludwig junior.'

'Oh, I don't know. Ludwig the Second sounds kind of jazzy.'

'Not to me. Makes me think of Mad King Lud of Bavaria.'

'Isn't Ludwig German for Louis? We could call him Lou for short.'

'You're thinking of a boy?'

'Or a girl. How about Ludwiga?'

'How about getting out of here and going home to bed to make sure.'

That night, at Lud's, they made love very gently. Joanna didn't want to spoil it by telling Lud she wasn't as fragile as he seemed to think.

Afterwards he brought them ice cream in bed.

'I can't eat all that.'

'Course you can. If only we had a pickle to go with it.'

'You funny thing. That comes much later, and anyway, not all women crave such crazy combinations.'

'How's this for a crazy combination?' He put a dab of ice cream on her nipple and took it in his mouth.

'Beautiful, but don't get carried away. It's freezing. Hey! Ouch! Okay, two can play.'

Taking her spoon, Joanna drizzled ice cream on him from chest to knees and gently licked it off, teasing him, until he forgot her condition and pinned her down on the bed.

They made love again, fired by the knowledge that they had created a life between them.

Lying in Lud's arms, Joanna felt drowsy with contentment. This child was the outcome of the love she and Lud had for each other.

Lud looked over at his sleeping beauty and gently pushed a tendril of hair off her forehead. The sight of her lying there so vulnerable touched him.

He had never before, to his knowledge, made a woman pregnant and the fact that it was possible pleased him. Also, he felt deeply proud that Joanna wanted to bear his child. It would all work out fine, once he got used to the idea. He drifted off to sleep with his hand protectively over Joanna's stomach.

At the skiing lodge in New Hampshire, Lud was filming the episode in which Suzanne has gone away for a weekend with her colleague who is now her lover. But his estranged wife, jealous and vengeful, hires a helicopter to take her to their mountain retreat.

On the second day everything went wrong. It was unseasonably cold, and in the morning a water pipe burst in the middle of a tender love scene. By afternoon, Rick was complaining of a sore throat, and Nadine refused to kiss him and expose herself to a possible virus or infection. She was showing precisely the star temperament Lud disliked. Over dinner she was so provocatively flirtatious towards him that he cut the evening short, telling the cast they were on very early call the next day.

136

He escaped to his room, totally exasperated with Nadine. He didn't quite know what to do at this point, but it was clear he had to discourage her from public displays of affection towards him. Now, more than ever, when he had a responsibility to Joanna.

In her room, Nadine gulped from the bottle of wine she had filched from the kitchen. As wonderful as the day before had been, today had been hideous.

Although she had given up smoking years ago, she took out a pack of cigarettes and chain-smoked half of it. Her throat felt raw. Probably she was coming down with Rick's ailment, and she felt furious with him and with everyone and everything. Lud hadn't insisted that she go through with the love scene, but she had observed his impatience. It was obvious that he thought her unprofessional, and at dinner he had all but ignored her.

Nadine got into bed. Although she strained her ears, she could hear nobody stirring.

Every few moments she looked at her watch. Twelve thirty, twelve fifty, one ten. Everyone was asleep. Only she lay awake, agitated, her chest on fire, her extremities numb.

She stroked her body through her satin nightgown, pretending that Lud was touching her, but her imagination failed her, and she grew panicky. Barefoot, and without her robe, she pattered softly into the corridor.

A few minutes later she was back. In a daze, she reached for her tranquillisers and shook the contents of the bottle on to her night table. She began to pop them into her mouth and wash them down with wine.

At last she found oblivion.

Joanna had a very restless night, worrying about Lud and Nadine. Stop this nonsense, she kept telling herself. She was loved by a wonderful man and was going to have his child. What more did she want?

A commitment. The words formed in her head before she had time to deny them. She was being silly. Hadn't he said, at the very beginning of their affair, that he would ask her to go to L.A. with him? And now, especially, when she was going to have his baby ... Joanna took a deep breath and had a sip of the hot milk by her side. If she didn't rest properly it might affect the pregnancy. But she couldn't shake the feeling that all was not well with Lud, or with her sister. Joanna was so sure that she nearly picked up the phone.

Finished with her milk, Joanna lay back and began to do her breathing exercises. For the sake of her child she had to get over her own fears. The exercises helped her to relax, and she fell asleep.

She was at a huge party at Malibu, carrying a baby in her arms. Lud appeared, in front of a microphone. 'I want to introduce you to my wife.' He held out his hand to her, and she tried to take it, but couldn't. Suddenly the baby was no longer in her arms and although she strained until her arm ached, his hand always remained just a little bit out of reach.

Nadine heard her name being called from very far away. Her eyes felt as if lead weights were holding them shut. With an effort, she opened them.

'Naddie, for goodness sake, answer me.' The voice was outside her door.

Nadine raised herself on one elbow, feeling the room going around and around. 'Fern? I – I was asleep.'

'Well, hurry up. You've only got ten minutes.'

'Bring me some coffee, okay?'

Nadine forced her legs over the side of the bed, suddenly noticing the pills spilled out on her night table. She had been insane enough to think of killing herself but passed out before she could take more than two or three tranquillisers. Even so, looking at the half-empty bottle of wine she knew it was a miracle she was still alive.

All of last night's memories came flooding back, drawing tears of rage. Angrily she rubbed at her eyes.

Fern was at the door with her coffee. Quickly Nadine

scooped up her pills and got them and the wine out of sight before unlocking the door.

'Whew. Stale smoke. Nadine, what's the matter?'

Lud Haley, that's what.

Nadine forced a smile to her face. 'Nothing. Too much wine last night. Just leave the cup, thanks. I'll be there in a moment.'

Fern scrutinised her. 'You're puffy around the eyes. Didn't sleep worth a damn last night, did you? Believe me, it shows up on film. Lud will be furious.'

Lud can go to hell.

'I'll be fine, stop worrying.' Nadine heard the weariness in her voice and she forced another smile. 'Come on, I'm under enough pressure as it is. Just be supportive, if you're my friend.'

'Of course I'm your friend.'

However, Fern was Lud's assistant director first. She found him and tugged at his arm.

'Later.'

'It's important. Nadine's in bad shape this morning. You'd better do something.'

'What? What should I do, twist her arm? I can't be with her every waking hour.'

No, but if you had been with her during her sleeping hours she wouldn't have taken whatever she took last night. Fern didn't dare to say that to Lud. 'Just make her feel important, you know, like you care about her.'

'Of course I care about her. But there's a limit, Fern. There's no point giving her false hope, is there.' Lud was irritated with Fern for perceiving exactly what it was that Nadine wanted from him. Before Fern could say another word he walked away.

Nadine gulped her coffee while she threw on her clothes. Although she felt weak and dizzy she wasn't going to surrender to it. She was going to give the performance of her life and show Lud just how much of a pro she could be.

But when she was dressed her hands were shaking badly. Looking at herself in the mirror, she suddenly saw the

139

child Nadine, with Joanna always by her side, the two of them united by mysterious bonds against the terrors of the outside world.

'Oh, Jan, I wish you were here.' The words escaped Nadine's lips. Damn it, she needed something for her nerves. She shook out a Quaalude from her bottle and washed it down with a glass of wine.

On the set she concentrated by making an enormous effort and avoided looking at her director except when necessary. She did what he told her and didn't even complain of the cold, although she could feel goose pimples on her arms.

There was a fire going in the fireplace but it didn't do much good unless Nadine could stand directly in front of it. Unfortunately she was having to walk back and forth while Rick tried to convince her that his wife would eventually grant him a divorce.

'Attagirl, Nadine. Fine. Let's take fifteen. I want some changes in Rick's dialogue during the next scene.' While Lud went over the script with the writer, he wondered about Nadine's surprisingly credible performance, especially after what Fern had told him. He suspected his star was on something but as long as she worked well he would mind his own business.

Over lunch Nadine answered Jim Sweeney only in monosyllables. He was greatly infatuated with her and since she couldn't return the feeling he made her impatient.

Sitting next to Tommy, the helicopter pilot, who plainly admired her, Nadine began to flirt outrageously with him, every now and then glancing at Lud to see his reaction. Yes, he was an s.o.b. but she wanted him to care enough to notice that another man found her irresistible. She watched Lorrie, the lodge-owner's daughter, who was serving them, look tenderly at Lud every now and then. Lorrie was young and pretty but dim-witted. The stupid little bitch had about as much chance with Lud as a groupie with a rock star. Nadine saw the way Lud smiled at

Lorrie – just enough to keep her interested, not enough to give her any false hopes.

Nadine drank her wine quickly, glass after glass, while she ate almost nothing. She leaned against Tommy, her shoulder brushing his, her thigh connecting with his thigh.

He was only twenty-five, a country boy who had never met the likes of Nadine Barrett and was completely bewitched by her.

Fern was near enough to Nadine to see what was going on, and she was appalled. 'Naddie,' she called out in warning, but the actress ignored her.

In desperation, Fern scribbled a few words on a piece of paper, folded it, and had it passed to Lud at the other end of the long table, deep in talk with the writer over script changes. Unfolding the note, Lud read it, frowned, and crumpled it in his hand. He'd take care of it later.

But his train of thought had been disturbed. Although he tried to concentrate on what the writer was suggesting, he kept hearing Nadine's throaty laugh, which sounded to him like a hideous drunken parody of Joanna's. He looked over at Nadine, irritated. 'Don't you think you should go easy on that stuff, sweetheart?' he called to her, trying to put some affection in his tone. 'You have your big scene with Megan this afternoon.'

'Plenty of time,' Nadine said breezily. 'By then I'll be as sober as a lady lawyer.' She laughed extravagantly at her own joke. A moment later she put her hand on Tommy's knee and smiled impudently at him, hoping he wouldn't spoil it by looking flustered. He didn't. The wine had emboldened him, and he gave her an openly sexual look.

Lud sighed, shook his head, and looked away. If Nadine goofed this afternoon he would forbid wine at lunch from now on.

Lunch over, he assembled the crew and cast while Nadine, her arm around Tommy, enticed him to her room. 'Just want to change into something warmer. You sit there,' she said imperiously, indicating the bed.

Awed by her, he sat down, his breathing not quite under control.

She unconcernedly stripped to her bra and panties, then turned on her radio and began to dance in her uninhibited way. 'Going to take me for a ride in your 'copter?'

'Uh, gee, I can't do that. I'm on a job. Can't spare the gas. If anyone found out – '

'Who's going to find out? They're all working. I'll pay for the gas. Dance with me.'

He stood up, aroused by the suggestive motions she was making as she swivelled her hips in a way calculated to drive him crazy.

She danced closer, teasing him, until he grabbed her awkwardly and tried to kiss her. When she backed away he came after her again. This time she wound her arms around him and opened her mouth, pulling his tongue deeply into it, while she rubbed against him.

Tommy was breathing like a bull, his young face flushed with desire. He reached for her breasts and squeezed them tightly.

Nadine unhooked her bra in front and let him fondle her. Then she reached her arms around him and caressed his shoulders and back, moving her hands slowly down to his buttocks.

With a groan, he pushed her on to the bed, his fingers groping beneath her panties.

Slowly she swivelled her hips, letting her hand rest for a few moments on his crotch.

'Oh, baby,' he moaned.

Abruptly she squirmed out of his grasp. 'We'll have the main event after we come back from our ride,' she promised, moving off the bed and gathering her clothes.

Tommy lay motionless for a few moments, trying to catch his breath. 'But – but if we go for a ride it will be too late. By the time we get back and all – I mean, I have to be on the set by three-thirty.'

'That's hours away.'

While he watched, she ran her hands sensuously over her belly and thighs and slipped into her jeans. Then she

142

cupped her breasts for a moment before snapping her bra around them and putting on a heavy cable knit sweater.

Tommy was insane with desire for her, and ready to agree to anything, until the music was interrupted for a weather bulletin.

'Oh, boy, did you hear that? There are blizzard warnings. I'd better tell Mr Haley. We'll probably have to wait until tomorrow to film the helicopter scene.'

'You're not scared, are you? I don't believe there can be much of a blizzard in April.'

'There sure can. I've seen storms around here like you wouldn't believe – ' The rest of his words were lost in the kiss Nadine gave him.

Like naughty children they sneaked out of the lodge and, holding hands, ran for the helicopter.

Tommy started up the rotors with a great whoosh. Nadine held her breath as the tail of the 'copter rose into space and the machine angled off across the treetops.

She was exhilarated, loving the motion of the helicopter, and the crazy way it hovered in midair before continuing on.

Taking a cigarette from her purse, she lit it, puffing deeply. 'Hey, Tommy, how about some grass. This is dynamite stuff, Hawaiian, the best.'

'I can't,' he shouted, above the high-pitched squealing of the rotors. 'Not when I'm trying to concentrate.'

'Oh, come on, take a poke, it'll make you feel terrific.' Nadine held out the joint to him, putting her other hand on his thigh and letting her fingers creep slowly towards his crotch.

As he gasped, she inserted the cigarette between his lips and encouraged him to drag on it deeply.

They smoked the joint between them, while she continued to fondle him, laughing at his confusion as he tried to pilot the machine and at the same time deal with his erection.

The power Nadine could exert over Tommy added to her euphoria. She was on top of the world. It felt wonderful to sweep majestically over the hills. At moments she had the illusion that the rotors were attached to the top of her head.

Observing Tommy in profile, Nadine revelled in his youth, his sweet innocence. She smiled to herself. What if she were to lean down, put her head in his lap, unzip his fly –

Tommy's face suddenly froze, and Nadine saw him squinting into the white haze ahead.

'Don't worry, love,' she told him, nibbling his ear. 'We're floating in a beautiful cloud, and nobody can see us.' Slowly she rotated the palm of her hand on his crotch.

He struck her arm sharply with his elbow. 'Cut that out, will you? We're in big trouble.'

Looking up in surprise, Nadine became aware of snow swirling all around them.

Within moments the 'copter was battling a vicious wind.

Tommy was saying something, but Nadine couldn't make out the words as she was jolted in her seat.

'Hey, stop playing games,' she cried out to him. 'That's not fair.'

'We're heading back,' Tommy yelled. 'Oh, boy, I don't think we're gonna make it.'

Nadine had a moment of pure longing for Lud. It wasn't the same, being with Tommy. He was too young, too damn green. Now he was getting into a panic. Lud would have grinned at her and made sharp, sophisticated jokes while showing off his expertise as a pilot.

The air grew more turbulent, and the helicopter suddenly twisted sideways and spun downward simultaneously. Nadine felt the bottom drop out of her stomach as she held on to her seat with both hands.

'We can't make it,' Tommy screamed above the noise. 'I'll have to try to land.'

'Land then, you big baby,' Nadine said contemptuously. Or did she only think it? Who could hear anything over that racket, anyway? She wanted Lud, not Tommy.

144

What the hell was she doing here, being churned up like a milkshake?

Nadine suddenly didn't care what happened to her. If she couldn't have Lud she didn't want anyone or anything.

Shutting her eyes, she leaned her head back, feeling she had left her body over a distant hill. She never even noticed the precise moment the engine stopped.

Joanna was sitting in Winnie's office in the afternoon feeling pretty good. She had managed to get some sleep after all and although she hadn't been able to eat in the morning at least she hadn't been sick.

'I let Abby work on these two jacket designs for the Swiss book. She's really good, Winnie. All she needs is experience.'

He peered at Joanna from over his glasses, wondering if she was thinking of quitting her job. Lud would be returning to the Coast eventually and it looked as if those two were still going strong.

Winnie sighed. If she left he would be devastated but he couldn't expect her to give up her happiness for him or for Omega.

'This one,' Joanna pointed to an illustration of snow-capped peaks, 'gives a cleaner look, kind of austere, the way the Swiss are themselves. It's more like the Swiss edition, but I like the lake scene in a way, softer, more impressionistic.'

Winnie looked at her in surprise. 'Hey, I never thought you'd say that. You certainly are dreamy-eyed lately.'

Joanna gave him a radiant smile. 'That's because I'm pregnant.'

His eyebrows shot into the air. 'No kidding? You really are?'

She nodded. It was a little too soon to be sharing her good news even with her old pal but she just couldn't help it.

'I see,' Winnie said, looking reflectively at her.

Was that all? Not wonderful, the best thing he'd heard

all day? Joanna wanted him to be overjoyed that she was pregnant. Winnie, of all people, who knew about her miscarriages.

'This one is holding, Winnie. This time I'm going to make it. Lud is so happy, even more than I am, I think.'

Winnie nodded, abstracted.

'I wish we could stay in New York so I could work part time or something but of course his home base is L.A. Anyway, Abby will do a good job for you. You can see her potential from these designs. I probably won't be leaving for a couple of months, and in any case I'd be back here for the last two or three weeks before I give birth...'

Joanna trailed off and looked at Winnie, looking at her. 'Aren't you glad? About the baby? I thought you'd be happy for me.'

He paused a moment too long before saying, 'Sure.'

'Winnie, what's wrong?'

'I'm just taking it all in. We've worked together for a long time, kiddo. Much of the success of our books is due to your talent. I'll miss you as art director, I'll miss you as friend, that's all.'

'Oh, Winnie, I'll miss you too.'

No, that wasn't all as far as Winnie was concerned. He was hoping to hear the sentence, 'Lud and I are getting married,' but it wasn't said.

She talked about Lud's house in Malibu, his apartment, his friends, while Winnie remained silent.

As Joanna was reaching for her cup of tea she suddenly felt a dreadful pain across her back. 'Oh, God!'

'What is it, babe?' Winnie looked at her white face in alarm.

'Nadine,' she cried. 'I know something has happened to Nadine!'

17

When Joanna got through on the phone to the ski lodge Megan told her that Nadine had been in a helicopter accident. 'No, not a crash, a forced landing. She was thrown from the helicopter but there was snow on the ground, thank God.' All Megan knew was that Nadine had been taken to the hospital. Lud was with her and would call Joanna as soon as he could.

Winnie tried to get Joanna to sit down but she was too agitated. 'Winnie, she's really hurt, I know she is.'

This wasn't the first time Joanna had felt her sister's pain. Many years ago Joanna had been kept home from school because of a cold. Suddenly she had experienced a piercing agony in her elbow and she had cried out to her aunt. Sally, who believed in the mystical ties between the twins, had jumped into her station wagon and driven to Tyler, where she had discovered that Nadine had fallen in gym and broken her arm.

Lud called, finally, sounding grave. 'She's still in intensive care, but I don't want you to worry – '

'It's her back, isn't it? I felt the pain myself. Tell me the truth.'

He expelled a sharp sigh. 'Well, it's her kidneys and a couple of cracked ribs, but she'll be all right.'

'Lud, I want her flown to New York as soon as possible. Charter a plane, whatever it costs.'

Dominic Graham was making the rounds of the maternity section of St Anne's with two interns and some medical students when he heard his beeper.

He picked up a phone.

'Dominic, it's Abby. Listen, an emergency. Nadine

147

Barrett has been in a helicopter accident in New Hampshire.'

He listened, frowning at the news. 'I'll see that Nadine is promptly admitted. How is Joanna taking it? Keep an eye on her, Abby. And maybe check with Nadine's housekeeper about the children. Call me if there's anything more I can do.'

Dominic depressed his finger on the phone button and dialled Ted Halloran to give him a quick rundown. 'Lennox may have some problems. Identical twins, and with her history, stand by, just in case.'

Then Dominic phoned the director of St Anne's. 'How's Dr Mack's caseload? I'm going to have a patient for him.'

John Mack, born Mackiewicz, had begun life fifty-five years before in Pittsburgh, the youngest of six children of a Polish immigrant steelworker. An aggressive, husky street kid, John punched and pummelled his way through his early years until high school football gave him an acceptable outlet for his brute strength. He attended the University of Pittsburgh on a football scholarship, doing only the barest amount of work to squeak by. He planned a professional football career.

At a sorority bash, to which he was invited after helping his team beat Fordham, he noticed a very pretty, delicate-looking girl who smiled shyly at him. Dotty was different from the usual football-hero worshippers in that she was the first girl to show an interest in John for himself.

Middle-class Dotty admired the way he had lifted himself out of his beginnings by sheer grit. Also, she was awed by his strength, his vitality.

He appreciated her refinement, her sweetness, her soft sympathy towards him. They fell in love, but unaccountably she hesitated about becoming engaged. Believing it was because of his background, he broke off with her, hurt and angry. Although he missed her desperately, he refused to talk to her on the phone or to see her.

One day he was visited in his dorm by a man who looked like Dotty. It was her brother, and he told John that Dotty had been ill with kidney disease since childhood. After a period of relative good health, she was back in bed. John went to see her, observing with distress how sick she was. Still, he loved her and wanted to marry her. She felt she had no hope for a normal life and that it wouldn't be fair to marry him.

Refusing to accept her decision, he bought her a small diamond which she finally agreed to wear to please him. John determined to understand how a young and beautiful girl could be so sick, and he began to pore through medical texts at the library. With a quickness of mind he had never realised he possessed, he found his way through the medical jargon to grasp the nature of kidneys and their disorders. He was troubled that so little was known of what caused kidney diseases, and that almost nothing could be done to reverse kidney failure.

Glomerulonephritis was Dotty's problem, an inflammation of the kidneys. It followed a strep throat that hadn't been properly treated.

World War II interrupted John's education. Sent to Europe with the Army, he corresponded with Dotty until he received a letter from her brother telling him she had died of uremia.

When John Mack was demobilised he was an angry man who never touched a football again. He returned to school under the GI Bill, determined to become a doctor and specialise in kidney disease. With unfaltering application, he overcame his educational deficiencies, studied medicine at Cornell and Harvard, and turned into a brilliant surgeon.

Although he had entered the ranks of the upper middle class, Mack retained a distrust of it, especially disliking what he considered elitism and inbreeding. He wasn't at all pleased that a female friend of Graham's was going to be foisted on him as a patient.

Joanna stood forlornly at Nadine's bedside looking at her

sleeping sister. It hardly seemed like Nadine, so pale, and bandaged, with a drip attached to her arm.

The intern told Joanna that the bandages, for the cracked ribs, sprains, and bruises, would come off shortly.

Joanna was in the room for only a few minutes when the nurse led her out, saying that Dr Mack was going to be examining her sister.

Joanna couldn't sit still in the waiting room. She felt waves of fear with an undercurrent of guilt, certain that if she had been in New Hampshire with Nadine the accident wouldn't have happened.

After what seemed like an hour but was only fifteen minutes, Dominic appeared, looking at her with concern. 'How are you feeling?'

'I'm all right, but Nadine's so sick.' Joanna's voice was hushed.

He sat down next to her. 'All I know at this point is that as a result of the injuries to her kidneys, Nadine has gone into acute renal failure. Serious, but not as bad as it sounds. She's on hemodialysis. That acts as an artificial kidney. Certainly there's no immediate danger. And Dr Mack is an excellent kidney man.'

Joanna had turned pale.

'I want you to lie down, Joanna. You can't do anything for Nadine at the moment.' He put a pillow under Joanna's head, promising that the nurse would let her know as soon as the doctor had concluded his examination.

Joanna lay there, stunned, while the words 'acute renal failure' echoed in her head.

She dozed off for a few moments and awoke in a panic. Jumping off the couch, she tore down the corridor.

A tall, heavy-set grey-haired doctor was waving a set of X-rays at the admissions nurse outside of the Intensive Care Unit and shouting, 'What the hell kind of inefficiency is this, not to have a medical history of the patient – '

'We do have it, Dr Mack. I told Jean to give the workup to you but – '

Cursing under his breath, the doctor backed away from

the desk just as Joanna was approaching. 'Good God. Am I seeing things, or are you Nadine Barrett's – '

'Twin. Yes. Dr Mack? Please tell me how she is.'

'The lady has a twin. That's the best news I've heard all day.' He had a deep, booming voice which resounded along the corridor. 'Come with me, please. We have to talk.'

Dr Mack, at six feet three and two hundred and fifty pounds, seemed larger than life to Joanna. Even when he was sitting down, he exuded an air of authority bordering on menace, and his voice, with its harsh cadence, could be frightening. He was seldom seen to smile. For Mack, life was a serious business. He saw too many people die of kidney disease each year, and frustration sometimes made him tactless.

Sitting at the edge of her chair, Joanna whispered, 'Why is it good news that I'm Nadine's twin?'

'Because if your sister needs a kidney transplant an identical twin is the ideal donor.' As soon as he had spoken he saw it was a mistake.

Joanna wavered in her chair and turned very pale.

'Excuse my bluntness. I didn't mean to frighten you. Let me explain. Both of your sister's kidneys were seriously injured in the accident. That rarely happens but in this case – anyway, it means that a vital bodily function has stopped.'

He sketched a diagram of the kidneys and drew lines to illustrate his words. 'Blood enters the kidneys through this artery and is cleansed by passing through millions of nephrons, or blood filters. The wastes are filtered out through the ureter and then into the bladder. The newly cleansed blood returns through the veins to the blood-stream.'

Joanna listened in a daze.

'What happened is that because your sister's kidneys have stopped this filtering process, her body cannot get rid of water, salt, and other substances without help. So we now have her on a machine that does the work of the damaged kidneys.'

'Then why a transplant?'

'Well, I was getting ahead of myself. It's possible that one or both kidneys will return to a reasonable degree of functioning. Kidney cells can have wonderful recuperative powers.' He stopped and looked solemnly at Joanna.

She took a deep breath. 'But you don't think hers will, do you?'

'Well, to be honest, no, judging from the X-rays. I don't want to scare you, but if you want the facts, it's that if one kidney doesn't recover its function she faces a lifetime of dialysis, which is damned unpleasant. In fact, the veins tend to break down under repeated dialysis. You're both so young. Damn it, I don't even have your sister's case history yet. The inefficiency of hospital personnel,' he muttered, getting a pad from his desk. 'It will save time if you can give me some information.'

She asked when she would be able to see Nadine.

'Not for a few hours. You may as well go home. And I'd like your doctor's name, please.'

Joanna gave him the name of her internist, and then hesitated. 'I'm also a patient of Dr Halloran's.'

Mack looked at her with a frown. 'You aren't pregnant, are you?'

She nodded.

He stared at her with lugubrious eyes, which moved to her middle and back to her face. Apparently she wasn't very far gone.

What a lousy business. If neither of Barrett's kidneys returned to normal functioning she should have a transplant without delay. And she easily could, with a twin.

'Well, let's just wait and see, Mrs – '

'Lennox,' she whispered.

'Let's just wait and see.'

At the ski lodge Lud, drinking his fourth cup of black coffee, was talking to the telephone operator. 'Please, this is an emergency. I have to get through to New York. I realise the lines are busy because of the storm, but somebody is critically ill as a result of an accident . . . Yes, I'll wait for you to call when you have a line.'

Lud put down the phone and covered his face with his hands.

Fern, sitting white-faced next to him, patted his shoulder and said without conviction, 'She'll be all right, she just has to.' Hadn't Fern seen what was coming? Hadn't she warned him that Nadine was going to do something dumb?

Lud gulped his coffee. 'Just when she was really getting into the role, damn it.'

When the phone rang Lud made a lunge for it. 'Haley. Oh, Tommy. How are you? Sure you're sorry. We're all sorry. What in hell were you thinking of to take the chopper up in that storm? Yeah. I can imagine. She's a very sick lady. Kidneys. I don't know how bad because I can't get through, so hang up, please, Tommy. I'll get back to you.'

Lud suddenly jumped up. 'This is insane. Get packed and let's get out of here.'

18

Joanna called CBS and learned that Carl Barrett was travelling for them in Africa. She left a message for him to call her.

Then she reluctantly phoned her aunt in Texas, trying to relate the facts about Nadine's accident so as not to worry her and their father more than necessary.

Joanna sat beside Nadine for hours until she awakened. When she first opened her eyes they registered panic, until she could see her sister bending over her.

'I'm here, Dini.' Joanna kissed her cheek gently.

'Jan, how did you come here?'

'You're in New York, at St Anne's, where we can take wonderful care of you. Dominic has found the best doctor possible. No, dearest, don't try to move. You're all bandaged. How do you feel?'

'I don't know. Weak, a little nauseous.'

'I'll get the nurse to give you something.'

Nadine, with an effort, moved her hand to Joanna's arm.

'The children – '

'They're fine. I spent last night with them, told them as little as possible, reassured them.' As she spoke, Joanna was feeling reassured herself. Nadine didn't seem as bad as her doctor had intimated.

Nadine looked at her sister suspiciously. 'What's wrong with me? I'm not paralysed, am I? Oh, I couldn't stand that. If I've broken my back – it feels strange.' She tried to sit up.

'No! You mustn't move. You've only cracked three ribs. You'll be able to walk. You also hurt your kidneys.'

Nadine felt a surge of relief. As long as she could walk

it couldn't be too terrible. Then a throbbing pain through her back made her wince.

Joanna went for the nurse. 'Can you give my sister something for her back?'

The nurse assured her that everything possible was being done and painkillers were being administered under the direction of Dr Mack.

Joanna came back to her sister's bedside. 'Don't try to talk any more, Dini, just rest.'

Nadine closed her eyes. 'Stay with me.'

Joanna left her sister only for a few moments to have a sandwich in the hospital cafeteria.

Later that afternoon Dr Halloran drew Joanna away from her sleeping sister's bedside in order to check her out and caution her against overtiring herself.

She questioned him about the possibility of a kidney transplant.

He frowned. 'It's a little premature to be talking transplant. Let's hope that your sister's kidneys recover, as they probably will.'

While he soothed Joanna's anxieties he felt annoyed with Mack, who was known throughout St Anne's as brilliant but impossibly abrasive.

When Lud appeared at the hospital, Joanna flew into his arms, needing his warmth, his love, his reassurance. He held her close and kissed her tenderly, but she could see he was worried.

'They won't let me see Nadine. How is she?'

'Frightened and in pain, but not as bad as I feared.'

They had a drink at a nearby bar. Lud gulped a double scotch as if it were medicine. Joanna had never seen him so tense.

'Lud, how did Nadine happen to be up in the helicopter? I thought it was supposed to be Megan.'

'That's right.' He sighed. To some extent he felt responsible for the accident. Fern had told him to do something about his star and he had stupidly hesitated.

'Nadine went for a ride while the rest of us were filming.'

155

'Oh. I understand the pilot wasn't badly hurt.'

'Broken leg, arm and collarbone. Landing in soft snow helped. Unfortunately Nadine was thrown out of the 'copter altogether.'

'Isn't snow this time of year unusual? I mean, nobody had any warning?'

'Yes, they had. Tommy heard the weather reports, but Nadine insisted on the ride. I guess he was kind of taken with her and agreed.' Lud tapered off lamely.

'Are you saying that she knew about the blizzard and still –'

'I don't know the details, love. Weather predictions don't always come true. And the cast was under so much pressure. She had some free time and just wanted to have fun, I guess. We have such a tough schedule. Ironically, it was all in vain, since everything's shot to hell now. If Nadine can't work again pretty soon there won't be a series.'

During the next two weeks Joanna divided her days between the hospital and her job. Winnie, totally understanding as always, urged her to take all the time she needed, while giving Abby more responsibility.

Joanna would get to Nadine's room by lunchtime and eat with her, not leaving until her sister took a nap. Sometimes Joanna sat with Nadine while she underwent dialysis. Seeing her hooked up to the machine like a creature in a science fiction nightmare upset Joanna terribly.

Nadine, weak and shaken, spoke very little. Joanna was quiet as well. Often she sat beside her sister holding her hand and trying to will her own health into her. Joanna kept wanting to tell Nadine about her pregnancy but there never seemed to be an appropriate moment.

Joanna spent every evening with the children and she slept there too.

With Fern's pushing, Lud had decided to keep filming the best he could, so he was as busy as ever. Joanna snatched moments alone with him, promising herself that there would be all the time in the world, later.

Nadine recovered from the sprains and bruises quickly, and her ribs, taped to minimise the pain of movement, were healing nicely. However, she needed dialysis three times a week. Whenever she asked her doctor when she would be able to leave the hospital, he would reply, 'We'll see, in a few days.'

She didn't ask any specific questions, and he didn't volunteer any information.

When Lud finally was allowed to visit Nadine he was careful not to reproach her. Poor kid, she looked terrible. He kissed her forehead gently, aware of the frigid way she was holding herself.

'How's it going, love? Any better?'

'Anything would be better than being bandaged in seventeen places.'

'I know. I'm sorry. It hurts, huh?'

She grimaced. 'Like being kicked by a mule.' Looking at him, as dynamic and attractive as ever, she felt angry tears stinging her eyes. Only a short while ago she had been in one piece, too. If only he hadn't been so perverse.

He suspected that she blamed him for her recklessness. Well, he didn't deserve it. It wasn't his fault that she had wanted the impossible from him.

He took her hand and kissed it. 'Be a good girl and listen to the doctor. We need you back, as good as new.'

'What will happen with my scenes with Megan at the lodge?'

'No problem. The indoor stuff can be shot at the studio, and we've already filmed the helicopter sequence with another pilot. Your outdoor scenes, too, with an extra who has your build and can pass, in a long shot . . .' Lud talked on with an enthusiasm he didn't actually feel.

Nadine was well aware of how unattractive she must appear to him now, and she kept her face averted. All she wanted was to recover, get back to work again, and regain the ground she had lost. But she felt so weak. Could she possibly do it?

Joanna was growing more concerned every day because Nadine was better, and yet not better. Dominic was at a conference in Chicago and Mack had gone to Maryland to do a transplant. The intern monitoring Nadine's condition refused to tell Joanna anything except that her sister was holding her own.

Even when Mack returned, Joanna began to fear that he was avoiding her because he had no good news to report. Every time she thought she might have to lose one of her kidneys she broke into a cold sweat.

One morning, unable to stand the suspense any longer, Joanna accosted Mack as soon as he arrived at the hospital. 'I must know the truth about my sister. Please.'

'I can't talk now. I have patients to see, damn it.'

Barrett's twin had caught him at the worst possible time. Only minutes before he had learned that the kidney transplant in Maryland had failed. Not only had the organ been rejected but the patient, a man of forty-two, had suffered an unexpected heart attack.

'In any case, Mrs Lennox, I should speak to your obstetrician, who will then speak to you –'

'Please just tell me in one sentence how my sister is doing.'

'I can tell you in one word. Lousy. Her condition has gone from acute to chronic renal failure. Until she has a transplant she'll have to stay on the dialysis.'

'I see,' Joanna whispered, utterly crushed. 'I was so hoping for complete recovery.'

'Believe me, so was I,' he responded grimly.

'She – she really does need a transplant?'

'Yes. Excuse me. I've got to go.' He continued down the hall, Joanna following.

'Oh, God! She won't get better, maybe in a little while?'

He shook his head. 'She won't get better. I've told you

158

what you wanted to know. I'll talk to Dr Halloran as soon as I can.'

Joanna, upset, continued to walk beside him. 'But the dialysis will help her, won't it?'

'Not to recover. It will just keep her alive.' He realised how brutal that sounded, and he stopped impatiently and tried to explain. 'Look, a person with kidney failure never feels really good. Your sister won't be able to attend to normal daily living. As the toxins and fluids build up in her body, she'll feel fatigue, loss of appetite, depression. I understand she's an actress. Keeps asking me when she can go back to work. I've been stalling her but I might as well tell you she won't be able to stand the strain of acting. A simple office job, maybe. But I can't let her return to her profession without a functioning kidney.'

'Oh, no!'

If Nadine couldn't act she would be so miserable. And *Sister In Law* would be doomed.

'If – if she had the transplant, how long would it take her to recuperate enough to go back to work?'

'Barring complications, she probably would be all right in three, four, five weeks.'

Joanna felt a flush of guilt rise to her cheeks. She loved Nadine, she wanted desperately to help. But deep within her, to her horror, was a fear of losing a part of her own body.

'Can a person be all right with only one kidney?'

'Yes. One kidney is so constituted as to do the whole job. You might say that the second kidney is a spare.'

Mack's beeper went off, and he picked up the nearest phone. 'Goddamn-son-of-a-bitch!'

Joanna shrank away, frightened at the violence of his response to what obviously was bad news.

When he hung up he passed his hand over his eyes, so distressed he nearly cried. After all his painstaking work, the Maryland transplant patient had died.

When Mack noticed Joanna hovering nearby he let out his frustration on her. 'Will you go away, please?

All this is just talk. You can't do anything for your sister now unless you terminate your pregnancy because we couldn't possibly take a kidney from a pregnant woman.'

19

Nadine awoke one morning frightened and shaky from a bad dream she couldn't remember.

'Nurse, I want to see Dr Mack.'

'I'm sorry, Mrs Barrett, he's not due here until this afternoon. Can I get you anything?'

'Yes.' Nadine sank back in bed. 'A new body.'

Nurse Robinson, having spent several years in the kidney unit, looked with sympathy at her patient. 'We could all use a new body, hon, but in the meantime yours would feel better if you ate some breakfast. You haven't touched your tray.'

'I can't look at food. I feel sick just thinking about it.'

She had no desire even to get out of bed. This had been going on for almost three weeks. Every couple of days she would be attached to that boring machine for four or five hours. Afterwards she felt much better and was convinced the worst was over. For about a day she could walk around, felt much stronger, almost back to normal. But instead of continuing to improve, she would unaccountably grow weaker. The headache would return. She would lose her appetite and the nausea would begin again.

She was worried about Jeff and Kate. When she talked to them, twice a day, she found them sulky. They missed her, she knew, and she missed them. But she felt so rotten. How would she be able to cope with their incessant demands? If Joanna hadn't been staying with them Mrs Wilson probably would have quit.

Nadine had tried to get in touch with Carl (who had never returned Joanna's call) without success, and she was furious with him. The children were his, too, and he ought to be able to take time off to be with them.

Aunt Sally phoned every few days to see how she was. Nadine tried to minimise her illness to her aunt, as well as to her father. When she hung up she would feel sick just from the effort to sound cheerful when she felt so awful.

Fern phoned Nadine later that morning. 'Hi, Naddie just checking in. How're you feeling today?'

'Bored. I'm sick of being sick. I want to get well and get the hell out of here.'

'Oh, you will, I'm sure you will. We're fixing it so when you come back to work you won't have to wait for your scenes. Lud wants to say hi, and Megan, and Rick.'

Nadine forced herself to sound better. She appreciated the cast's interest. Lud was being as sweet as he could possibly be. Still, when she hung up gloom descended.

When Mack finally arrived, Nadine pounced. 'I want to know exactly what's wrong with me. Why I seem to get better and then move back to square one.'

He told her.

'A kidney transplant!' She was genuinely shocked, never dreaming it could be as bad as that. Like many people who had scarcely ever been ill, she knew next to nothing about illness.

Nadine's heart began to pound, and she felt weak with fear. Just imagining such an operation made her feel sick. And yet, without it, to go on like this from day to day . . .

'You mean a person gets killed or something,' Nadine whispered, 'and carries a card saying to give a kidney to someone like me?'

'Well, that's more difficult than it sounds.' Her doctor explained about compatibility of blood and tissue, about the way the body rejected foreign organisms.

'Are you saying it's hopeless?'

'No, not hopeless at all. In fact, you're luckier than most because you have an identical twin.'

'You mean if Joanna – you mean she could give me a kidney?'

'Yes.'

'But, but why haven't you told her? Just letting me lie here, week after week.'

'I've been waiting to see if one kidney at least would recover its function. A transplant is a last resort.'

'But I have to go back to work! The whole television series depends on me. I'm the star, and all those people are waiting, and it's costing so much money – '

'Calm down. Excitement is bad for you.'

'Jesus Christ. You've just told me I can't act, can't leave that goddamn machine for more than a couple of days at a time, and a little excitement is bad for me! God, I'm practically dead, aren't I? Without dialysis I'd be dead, wouldn't I?'

Without answering, the doctor frowned at the chart the nurse handed him showing Nadine's latest blood-pressure reading.

'At least talk to my sister about the transplant. Or I will, but I don't know all the details.'

'No more talk now, please – '

'You *have* told her, and she refuses!'

'No, that's not true.' His eyes softened. 'Nadine, we'll talk about it tomorrow.'

Before she could object he was gone, and the nurse was giving her an injection.

Joanna sat in Dr Halloran's private office long after office hours, numbly trying to make sense of everything.

Halloran, doodling on his prescription pad without being aware of it, was trying to contain his irritation towards Mack and talk calmly to his patient. Although he firmly believed in the demystification of medicine and that a patient ought to understand as far as possible the ramifications of a particular illness or required surgery, he deplored the way Mack had been unable to keep his big mouth shut, even if Lennox had demanded to know the truth. After all, she was his patient, not Mack's.

'Mrs Lennox – '

'Could you call me Joanna, please?' The Mrs made her feel like a phony.

'Joanna, without speaking to Dr Mack first I can't give you any information about your sister's condition.'

'But it must be serious if he told me she definitely needs a transplant.'

'That may be. But if the donor is pregnant it's usual to wait until she gives birth. Unless it's an emergency, the patient can be on dialysis for several months.'

Joanna almost cried with relief. 'Why can't a pregnant woman donate a kidney? Is the operation that bad?'

'Well, any operation to a pregnant woman is inadvisable. Aside from possible complications, the foetus can be damaged by the anaesthetic. Kidney surgery is particularly tricky because during pregnancy the kidneys are under a special strain.' He explained that the wastes from the foetus returned to the mother's bloodstream via the placenta and had to be removed from her blood by her kidneys. 'I want you to go home now, get some rest, and try not to worry. I'll talk to Dr Mack first thing tomorrow and call you at your office.'

At Nadine's Joanna found Jeff and Kate more anxious than ever. They felt abandoned, and although they knew their mother was recovering from an accident they were resentful and difficult.

'I want to see Mommy in the hospital right now,' Kate demanded.

'Children under ten aren't allowed,' Joanna said gently. 'I've told you that.'

'If she doesn't come home soon I *will* be old enough,' Jeff commented petulantly.

Joanna contained an impulse to hug the breath out of them both.

'Don't you kids have homework to do? Come on, I'll bet neither of you can spell "Mississippi".'

She joked them into forgetting their mother for a while, and in the process of cheering them up she felt better herself.

It wasn't until Lud and she were having a light dinner, after the children were asleep, that thoughts of Nadine returned to depress her.

'Dr Mack told me she needs a kidney transplant and I'm the ideal donor. The catch is that – that I'd have to have an abortion.'

Lud stared at her, seeing her lovely eyes fill with tears. He pulled her into his arms and held her close, feeling her heart beating against his.

Lud was silent for a time, stroking her hair. Then he tilted her sad face and kissed her lightly. 'Why can't another donor be found? I've read about remarkable tissue matches through kidney computer banks, something like that. I mean, thousands of transplants take place every year, but how many people have a twin to help out? There must be another way, and we'll find it.'

Her heart filled with gratitude. He wanted the baby as much as she did. But she hadn't yet told him everything.

She swallowed hard. 'The thing is, Nadine won't be able to return to work unless she has a transplant. Dr Mack thinks she couldn't stand the strain. So if we can't find another donor almost immediately – '

'Oh, Christ!' Lud ran his fingers through his hair.

Joanna looked tensely at him. 'Lud, I don't know what to do. Dr Halloran said he'd speak to Dr Mack but I can tell it's really serious. I know she's not at all well. I can't stand to see her like that. I haven't been able to tell her about the baby, but I suppose I must. Oh, God, how can I let her down? And let you down? But not to have the baby!'

'Sweetheart,' Lud murmured, pulling her close again.

After a while he held her away from him. 'There is one way, one thing we could do, temporarily.'

Halloran rang Mack as soon as he got to the hospital in the morning but his colleague was making rounds. By the time Mack got back to Halloran he had been called to an emergency delivery.

Joanna, frustrated that the two doctors were unable to confer, phoned Nadine from her office. 'How are you today?'

Nadine could hear the tension in her sister's voice.

'Better,' she mumbled. 'I always am, after the dialysis. Did you speak to Dr Mack by any chance?'

Joanna felt a pain in the pit of her stomach. 'Yes, very briefly. I have to hang around here until about three today, but I'll come as soon as I can.'

'Whenever,' Nadine responded glumly. 'I'm not going anywhere.'

Joanna sat at her desk with her face in her hands, feeling awful. She didn't know how she was going to tell Nadine what she had to tell her.

'Something wrong?' Winnie asked from the doorway.

'It's Nadine.'

'I thought she was doing pretty well.'

Joanna shook her head. 'I was hoping for the best, but it hasn't happened. Her kidneys haven't improved.'

Winnie frowned in sympathy. An uncle of his had been on dialysis for several years, and he knew how serious and uncomfortable kidney trouble was.

He confined himself to patting Joanna's arm.

Joanna hadn't intended telling anyone but Nadine what Lud had discussed with her, but she somehow found herself unburdening herself to her old friend.

'Nadine is too sick to finish the series. Her doctor won't permit it, and that means the end of the production unless – unless I take Nadine's place. It would make her so miserable. But because most of the episodes have already been filmed, it would be impossible to start over with another actress. The cost would be prohibitive. But I don't know how I can possibly do it, even if Nadine goes for the idea. Yet, to see Nadine and Lud lose everything, when it's in my power to help – ' Joanna stopped to gulp air.

Winnie put his arm around her shoulder. 'I have complete faith in you, babe. I really believe you can do anything you really want to do.'

'Thanks, Winnie. I guess I must. There's no alternative. But I'll have to take some time off. The two weeks of my holiday, anyway. Unless you'd rather I quit now and let Abby take over altogether.'

'No, no, of course not. Take what time you need. We'll

work it out. But I think we'd better tell Abby what's going on.'

'Yes. But not that I'm going to try to take over Nadine's role, if she agrees. That has to be a secret.'

Abby, summoned to Winnie's office to learn that she was going to be acting art director, felt a mixture of emotions. Joanna had told her about the pregnancy and Abby had hoped eventually to move into Joanna's job, but not so soon.

Leaving Winnie's office, Joanna felt strange when she looked back and saw Abby and Winnie with their heads together. Already Joanna felt like an outsider, and after thirteen years it was terribly unsettling.

At the hospital she was intercepted by Mack.

'I've been trying to get hold of your doctor without any luck. As long as you're here, can you spare a moment?'

Joanna went with him to his office.

'I'm sorry I was so rough on you yesterday. It was a bad day for me. Anyway, it's my duty to your sister to tell you that the sooner she has the transplant the better it will be for her. Now, your kidney would be the best match by far. However, it's your decision. If you don't feel you can do it, I have to start looking for another donor, and it may take months. So what I'd like to know is if you'd consider giving her a kidney after your baby is born.'

Joanna opened her lips to say yes, but the word seemed to stick in her throat. A cold panic gripped her. 'I – I don't really know. It frightens me, the idea of losing a piece of myself, even though I want to help my sister. Maybe if I can get used to the idea.' She swallowed painfully.

He looked at her with sympathy. 'I understand how hard it is, Joanna. But I must repeat that the best chance your sister has for a normal life is your kidney. Next best might be another sibling, if there were one. Your aunt is probably too old, and your father definitely is.'

Joanna was shaken by a chill. She hated her cowardice, and yet she was so genuinely frightened. 'I've heard that there are donor centres, where tissues can be matched up.'

'Yes. In fact, we have a transplant coordinator right here at the hospital. But matching kidneys to patients is difficult. It's a question of compatible immune systems, of the blood and tissue antigens of donor and receiver being the same or similar. You see, there are hundreds of thousands of possible combinations. Unfortunately, your twin is extremely difficult to match – and that goes for you, too, of course. Your B positive blood is rare; only a little more than eight people out of a hundred have that type.'

'I know,' Joanna whispered.

'Believe me, Joanna, I wish I could be more optimistic, but normally the chances of finding a reasonable tissue match between unrelated people is only about one in a thousand. In your sister's case, the chances are much worse.'

Looking at how white Joanna had turned, he saw that he had frightened her even more. And yet she had to know the truth, damn it. The pregnancy was such a difficult complication.

'We won't say anything more now. I've given you something to think about, to speak to your husband about.'

Mack was dismissing her, but Joanna found herself unable to move. She sat miserably in her seat, twisting the leather strap of her handbag and feeling lower than a worm.

'If I gave her a kidney, could I ever have another child? I mean, with one kidney?'

'Certainly. One healthy kidney can do the work of two. There's no reason not to have a normal pregnancy.'

'I see. Is a transplant a – a serious operation?'

'Of course it's serious. Any operation is serious. But the risk to you would be small. I've done hundreds of kidney transplants and never lost a donor yet.'

'Oh. But what about Nadine? My sister would be all right, wouldn't she?'

'Probably, but nothing is certain. The main trouble with any transplant is that the body tends to reject all foreign substances. But because identical twins have the same

168

genetic makeup, the chances of rejection are minimised. Your kidney has a better chance of not being rejected by your sister than any other we could find. With a kidney from an unrelated dead person, the chances for long-term function are only about fifty percent. With your kidney, the chances would increase to more than ninety percent. I've done four transplants involving identical twins. Men in three cases, women in the fourth. So far – and it's more than four years – all the recipients are leading normal lives. Nobody can predict far into the future at this point, Joanna, but right now four people are alive who otherwise might have died. Of course, new medical discoveries are constantly being made.'

'I see.' Joanna felt torn in two.

'I think we've said enough for now. Go home, take it easy, think about it.'

'I – I don't need to think about it any more,' she said in a firmer voice. 'I'll do it. After I have my baby, I'll give Nadine a kidney.'

Joanna went to the bathroom and was sick to her stomach.

Mack stopped in briefly to see Nadine and read her chart. 'Feeling better today?'

'Yes, thanks to the iron maiden.'

He allowed himself a rare smile. 'I'm glad to see you've got a sense of humour.'

'Yeah.'

'I've just seen Joanna.'

Nadine's heart began to pound. 'Did you ask her?'

'Yes. She'll give you the kidney.'

Nadine untensed her muscles as relief flooded through her.

'Of course, you understand that can't be until she gives birth. It means another six or seven months on dialysis because we can't do such an operation on a pregnant woman.'

Nadine felt as if she had been socked. She sank back against the pillows and shut her eyes.

'I see that you're disappointed to have to wait,' Mack said, watching her. That his patient hadn't known of her twin's pregnancy never even occurred to him.

'Tell my sister,' Nadine whispered, turning her face to the wall, 'that I don't want her kidney.'

He stared at her, startled. 'You don't know what you're saying.'

'I do know.' She sounded weary, defeated. 'I'll stay on dialysis until you find a donor. Anyone but my sister.'

When Joanna got to Nadine's room she found her in bed facing the wall. Thinking she was asleep, Joanna sat down to wait.

'Who is it?' Nadine asked irritably.

'Me. I didn't realise you were awake.' Joanna bent over to kiss her sister's cheek and got no response. 'Are you feeling bad?'

Nadine slowly rolled over and looked at her.

Joanna suddenly knew that Mack had told her sister everything.

'I – I was waiting for you to feel better before I told you about the – '

'Bullshit! You must have known you were pregnant before I went to New Hampshire.'

Joanna forced herself to meet her sister's accusing gaze. 'Yes, I did know. But I didn't want to tell anyone so soon – '

'Anyone!'

'Dini, I made a mistake. I'm sorry. I – I was being superstitious, afraid to say in case it didn't stick – '

Nadine glared at her. 'But this one is sticking, isn't it? Well, congratulations!'

A nerve in Joanna's temple started to throb.

'Does the father know? Or is he "anyone" also?'

'He – he knows.'

'Since when?'

'Before New Hampshire,' Joanna admitted. 'He had to take a blood test. I had to tell him, because if he hadn't

170

wanted the baby – but he does. Oh, if only this weren't happening! I never wanted it to be like this!'

Lud had known before New Hampshire. Nadine couldn't stand to see Joanna's happiness, behind the so-called 'concern'. She turned her eyes to the ceiling.

'Dr Mack told you about the transplant?' Joanna asked.

'Yeah.'

Looking at Nadine, Joanna felt a rising panic. Her sister had already taken on the pallor of a chronic invalid, and her face was so puffy. She was supposed to be better after dialysis, yet only a few hours had passed. If she looked this bad now, how about tomorrow, and the day after?

'Then you know that I'll give you a kidney as soon after the baby is born as I possibly can.'

'That won't be necessary.'

Joanna's hopes shot up. 'What do you mean?'

'I mean I don't want your kidney. I'll manage without it.'

'You can't! The dialysis –'

'You're not the only one in the world with kidneys. Dr Mack will find me one, so you can stop worrying about it.'

'Of course I'm worrying about it! I'd do it right now if I weren't pregnant.'

'Will you stop going on about it?' Nadine demanded querulously. 'I said it's all right, didn't I?'

'Oh, Nadine, you make me feel like a monster! But it's my third month. I already feel the changes in my body. The baby –'

Joanna stopped and looked miserably at her sister. 'I want to help, but you – you don't want me to – to –'

'No! Just shut up about it, okay?'

Nurse Robinson bustled in with a huge bouquet of flowers from Jim Sweeney. Nadine had talked to him on the phone, but she refused to let him see her. She didn't want to face anyone from the cast looking as she did.

Joanna's anguish increased by the moment. Nadine's fury was masking her despair and her fear. How could

171

Joanna tell her that Lud wanted her role taken over too? Loyalty to Lud vied with loyalty to her sister. Nadine looked terrible and she was so weak. All the will in the world couldn't help her to get out of bed and go to the studio. Joanna had turned away while the nurse was arranging the flowers.

Nadine, glancing at her sister's back was irritated to know that she was weeping. As if *she* had anything to cry about! Joanna was going to have Lud's baby. And Nadine was practically dead. The seriousness of her illness was only just beginning to get to her. Her life was hanging by a thread, a wire attached to the dialysis machine. Without a transplant she wouldn't be able to travel anywhere for more than a couple of days at a time. And with a transplant, she would have to worry about her body's rejection of the new kidney.

Every time she thought of her sister, healthy and pregnant, she wanted to scream.

'I'm tired and I'm expecting a call from Lud. I wish you'd go now,' Nadine said flintily.

Joanna brushed at her eyes and turned around slowly. 'He won't call you until tomorrow. He asked me to discuss something with you first.'

Nadine felt a weakness over and above her illness. She sat up and Joanna hurried to arrange the pillows behind her.

'He's not thinking of replacing me? He absolutely can't!'

'No. I mean, not exactly. You're the star, Dini, nobody but you, and your name would appear as the star, but—'

'No!' Nadine shot Joanna a look of undisguised hatred. 'I know what you're going to say and I don't believe it!'

Joanna had to control her voice. 'It would only be for the remaining episodes,' she whispered miserably. 'Just so Lud can hand in a finished series. Ed will have to get a network, and by the time the pilot is screened months will have passed. In the meantime you'll have had the transplant. I mean, before the last episodes are aired. You could even reshoot my scenes.'

She was stopped by the expression in her sister's eyes: a combination of despair, anger, and contempt.

'*You're* going to take *my* place?'

Joanna heard the quaver in Nadine's voice. 'Only if you agree, Dini. You don't think I want to do it, do you? I'd give anything not to.'

Anything! How did Joanna dare say that when she could have an abortion and give Nadine her kidney right now!

'You know how scared I am of acting. I don't know how I'll ever do it, but there's no other way.'

Nadine stared straight ahead at the small blank television set, seeing her big scene with Megan, played by Joanna; the final courtroom scene, played by Joanna; and the final clinch with Rick, played by Joanna.

Nadine looked down at her hands, noting irrelevantly that she needed a manicure.

Joanna, her hands clenched, wanted to go to her, embrace her, tell her everything would be all right, the way she had done when they were children. But she couldn't, not unless . . .

When Nadine had finally mastered her voice, she looked at her sister with dull eyes. 'Okay.'

For Joanna there was no relief. She felt the pain her sister was suffering, and tears sprang to her eyes.

Dry up, Nadine willed.

Joanna dabbed at her eyes. 'The children keep asking when you'll be coming home.'

'Next week – until I have to return to the hospital three times a week for my fix.'

Joanna didn't blame her for being bitter.

Wincing, Nadine got out of bed and walked slowly to the window overlooking Madison Avenue. The days were growing longer. She saw strolling people looking in shop windows. It was spring, a time for renewal, romance.

Joanna said goodbye without daring to touch her sister.

173

Outside the door, she cried silently, her fist over her mouth.

Nadine leaned her head against the window. Finally the tears came.

Joanna was going to get it all: Lud, his baby and *her* role.

20

'Naddie, darling, I won't stay more than a moment, I promise. I was in the neighbourhood. The dentist. And I just had to see you.' Fern embraced her friend.

'Careful of my ribs,' Nadine cautioned. 'They're still all taped up.'

Fern took a seat, trying to hide her shock at Nadine's altered appearance. Her hair was a mess, and she was unhealthily pale and puffy. Fern's heart sank. No amount of makeup could enable Nadine to step in front of the camera looking like that.

'When's the doc letting you out of here?' Fern asked, in as breezy a tone as she could muster.

'A few days. But I'm not well by any means. My kidneys are shot. I need a transplant.'

'Jesus.' Fern felt a cold shiver. A transplant, to her mind, belonged in the realm of medical fiction. Just the thought of such an operation was horrifying. She had to take a few deep breaths before she was able to speak. 'God, that's terrible, Naddie. But don't worry, honey pie. Nowadays doctors can perform miracles. I'm sure everything's going to be just fine.'

'Yeah. Dandy.'

Nervously Fern lit a cigarette, ignoring the no smoking sign. 'If only there were something I could do.'

'If you were my twin you could give me one of your kidneys.'

Fern looked at her, amazed. 'You mean that Joanna could – and she won't? Lordy. How does she have the heart to see you this way and not do something about it? I mean, if you were my twin I'd be in the operating room right now.'

175

'Even if you were pregnant?' Nadine broke in miserably. 'And it meant having an abortion?'

Fern stared at her. 'Joanna's pregnant? Oh, shit!' All the implications were immediately clear. 'If she thinks Lud's going to marry her just because she's knocked up –'

'He wants the baby,' Nadine said tightly. 'He's known about it since before New Hampshire.'

Fern, licking her suddenly dry lips, reached nervously for another cigarette.

'Don't smoke, please. It makes me nauseous.'

Fern crushed out her cigarette, as Nadine slowly reclined against her pillows. 'Do you know that Lud wants my sister to finish the series?'

'What! Oh, Naddie, no!' Even as she made the denial, Fern's practical intelligence was grasping Lud's reasoning.

'My doctor won't let me work,' Nadine said in a flat voice. 'I'd go against his advice, if I could, but I feel lousy most of the time. Three times a week I'm on a dialysis machine four or five hours. It makes me feel a little better but I'm still hardly in shape to play the role of a feisty lawyer –' Her voice broke.

Fern, dying for a cigarette, cracked her knuckles. Maybe she had been stupidly speaking off the top of her head. The more she thought about it the more sense it made for Joanna to take on the role.

Nadine, watching Fern, could almost see her computerised brain feverishly clicking away. Even her friend, much as she disliked Joanna, was coming up with the same answer as Lud. Nadine felt the fight going out of her.

Fern took a deep breath. 'Don't give up, Naddie. Look at the bright side. Even if Joanna finishes the series, you'll be the star. By the time it's shown and becomes a hit, you'll be ready to go on to bigger and better acting jobs.'

Nadine tried to take heart but she couldn't do it. She couldn't even hope that her sister did poorly in the role. Too much was at stake.

When Fern saw that Nadine had closed her eyes, she tiptoed out of the room.

Fern found Lud in the cutting room at the studio. 'I wish you'd told me you asked Joanna to take over Nadine's role. I was just at the hospital and I'm afraid I put both my feet in my mouth, like an idiot.'

'Sorry. I was waiting until Joanna had cleared it with Nadine. Joanna just phoned a while ago to say Nadine agreed. How did she seem to you?'

'Oh, disappointed but willing, of course. She's a pro. The question is how Joanna's going to do it. She's no actress, and – '

'Don't you worry, Fern. Joanna will come through beautifully.'

Fern swallowed back her retort, believing that the only reason Lud didn't tell Joanna to have an abortion now was that he couldn't have both sisters out of commission at the same time.

Later that night Joanna was lying in Lud's arms, tense and fearful about the acting ordeal ahead of her. 'I've been studying the lines, but I'm afraid that as soon as the cameras start to roll it will all be a blank.'

'No, it won't. I'll be there, helping you. You're a natural for the part. I told you that right from the beginning.'

She hugged him tightly, aching to believe him. 'I want to be good enough, but not so good that Nadine will feel even more hurt.'

It was Lud's opinion that Joanna's performance would outstrip Nadine's, but he didn't say so. He patted Joanna's stomach affectionately. 'How's Esmeralda liking it in there?'

'Just fine,' Joanna said, momentarily cheered. 'But I think it's going to be Ludwig Two. I'd kind of like a little you. The most frustrating thing about meeting a man fully grown is that you missed his infancy and childhood.'

'That's how I feel about you, so don't blame me for wanting a miniature Joanna, cute as a newly hatched chick.' He caressed her gently.

'Don't, please, Lud. I'm sorry but I'm really worried about Nadine. She's being so brave, even though she's frightened. And so angry at me. Imagine telling me she doesn't want me to give her a kidney later, when I can. Of course, if someone else could be found in the meantime, so she wouldn't have to wait...'

'The doctor's probably exaggerating. Naturally it would be easier to use your kidney. But if he has to find another donor he'll do it. It may cost money.'

'I'll pay anything, Lud. I simply can't stand to see her suffer.'

Dominic looked up from his desk to see John Mack standing in the doorway of his office.

'Sorry if I'm interrupting. I know you've just returned from a conference to a backlog of work, but I was wondering if I could talk to you for a minute about Lennox and Barrett because I understand you know them personally.'

'Yes. Let's talk by all means.' Dominic indicated a seat.

John Mack eased his bulk into the chair. 'Upsetting case, this one. Complicated by the pregnancy. What I wanted to ask you is if there's any chance that Lennox could terminate. I know there are no other children but she's still a young woman.'

Dominic's ears grew warm. 'The problem with terminating in this case is three previous miscarriages.'

'Oh, hell. That's it, then, I guess. Although I'm almost tempted to hope she miscarries this time, brutal as that sounds.'

It sounded brutal, indeed. 'Is there any reason Nadine can't stay on dialysis until Joanna gives birth?'

'A couple of reasons. Nadine's growing hypertension and her abnormally weak vascular system. Joanna's terrified, understandably, but she did agree to donate. However, I'm worried sick about Nadine's blood pressure.'

Dominic felt terrible. He hadn't realised how bad Nadine was. And when he thought of Joanna having to lose a kidney . . . Her bravery only endeared her to more.

'Dr Graham, do the twins like each other?'

Dominic looked at him, shocked. 'What a question.'

'Well, it's not an idle one. Maybe you can tell me why Nadine's acting so peculiar. One minute she was begging me to line up her sister's kidney, the next minute she was saying she wouldn't take it, period. It doesn't make sense. Unless she wants her sister to abort and is sore she can't have the operation right now.'

'I can't believe that,' Dominic murmured. 'As far as I can tell, they're extremely close and loving with one another.'

'I wonder.'

'Maybe Nadine feels she can't wait several months because she's in the middle of an acting role. Or she may not want her sister to have to go through an operation—'

'No, I don't think that's it. Not altruism. Sorry to disagree but I have a hunch it's jealousy. You know, lots of love/hate stuff.'

'Is it productive to speculate along those lines?' Dominic's tone held just a tinge of reproach.

Mack remembered that the three were friends, and no doubt Graham felt he was overstepping. 'Well, anyway, I'm going to try to find a kidney through our computerised donor system. Not that it will be easy. Nadine has the lowest histocompatibility I've come across in years.'

'Oh, God, no!'

Mack pounded the arm of his chair tensely. 'Well, let's hope we get lucky. Of course, it may take months, probably as long as it takes Joanna to give birth. By then I think Nadine will be grateful for her sister's kidney. In fact, by that time she'll be ready to accept a kidney from the devil himself.'

For Joanna the first rehearsal was hideous. The trauma of being in front of the camera came back to haunt her and no matter how hard she tried, she remained stiff and found it difficult to get her words out. Her voice sounded like a monotone in her own ears, and she was aware of every limb in her body, and where it was at any given moment.

Lud directed her patiently, trying to ease rather than force a performance out of her.

Fern, smoking nonstop, derived satisfaction from seeing Joanna squirm, even though her failure might jeopardise the series.

Over lunch Fern and Lud discussed with Joanna the possibility of starting with a less demanding scene than the confrontation with Megan.

Joanna said thoughtfully, 'I think I'd rather stick to the sequence because it develops the characterisation. I'm sorry to be such a drag. I just feel so awkward and on view.'

'Never mind, sweetheart, you're doing beautifully.' Lud smiled at her encouragingly.

Joanna was determined to justify his faith in her, which was more than Fern had. Fern's presence, in fact, reminded Joanna poignantly of her childhood self and made it even more difficult for her to relax.

When they returned to the sound stage, Joanna felt a little looser, possibly because of a growing familiarity with the role. Earlier it had been terribly unnerving to face Megan's hostility as the jealous wife who came flying at her.

Joanna's motions were more fluid and her voice better controlled.

She would practise, practise, practise until she got it right.

For the next week she thought Suzanne every minute of the day when she wasn't thinking about Nadine, now at home, or talking to her on the phone.

'Nadine, I don't know how you manage it. Acting is the hardest thing I've ever done in my life.'

Her sister was silent.

'Well, I'll get through it somehow. I must. How are you feeling?'

'As usual.'

Joanna detected the profound despondency in her voice.

'I'll be up to see you as soon as I get a moment. I don't have to tell you what it's like at the studio.'

'No.'

It occurred to Joanna, when she hung up, that Nadine was ignoring her pregnancy completely.

Joanna and Lud spent their evenings at home rehearsing.

'You're fine when it's the two of us alone, sweetheart. If you can just forget the camera – '

'I can't. That's the trouble.'

He was very supportive and understanding and so were the crew and cast. They appreciated Joanna's valiant effort to save the production.

Rehearsals were over far too soon. 'We have to complete the big love scene before Esmeralda gets between Rick and you,' Lud teased.

'I'm not ready to film tomorrow, Lud. It's too soon.'

'Now stop, sweetie. Don't you trust me to know?'

'Yes, but – '

'But nothing. Look at it this way, love. You won't be on stage in front of a live audience. It will just be us, family.'

She wanted to be reassured, but she had a restless night all the same.

In the morning she ignored her nausea and chewed on some dry crackers. While Lud was shaving she crept back into bed and rested. She was not going to let them all down.

In the taxi out to Long Island City she held Lud's hand tightly and mouthed her lines. 'I'm so scared,' she murmured.

He squeezed her hand. 'You're going to do just fine. I had to tear my hair out to get the right stuff from Nadine, actress or not.'

Just before Joanna went to her dressing room, Lud held her close. 'Think of me loving you every moment.'

'If I mess it up – '

'I'll still love you. And Esmeralda.' He patted Joanna's tummy. 'Okay. Go.'

181

As soon as Joanna stepped under the hot lights, with the cameras on her, old fears immobilised her features and drove the words right out of her head. Yet she heard someone speaking her lines, and after a split-second, realised that it was she.

'Look at Megan, not at me,' Lud called out. 'Forget me. Forget everything but defending yourself to a woman who's lost her husband and is blaming you.'

Joanna tried her best. When she was dressed for the role and moving around the rustic lodge set, with its fire burning in the hearth, she found it a little easier to go with the illusion.

'Cut. Not bad, Joanna, not bad at all.' Lud and Fern did some rearranging of props.

'Take two.'

Joanna tried again and again, each time getting it a little better, and losing some of her fright and awkwardness.

During the fifth take, she knocked over a vase. The crash startled her, and when she saw the broken crockery at her feet, in the puddle of water, she burst into tears.

'I can't, I just can't – '

'Of course you can,' Megan said, putting her arm around Joanna sympathetically.

'You're doing great, honest,' Rick told her. 'Do you think this is the first prop destroyed during this production? Shit, I did worse than that. I backed into a bookcase that had glass doors, and for days I was picking slivers of glass out of my behind.'

Joanna laughed through her tears.

Lud called a break, insisting that Joanna eat something and lie down in her room and rest for half an hour.

She awoke with a start to see that an hour had gone by. On the set Lud was filming another scene. Fern told Joanna to get her face and hair done and stand by.

Joanna, combed and made up, stood watching the scene between Rick and Megan and she became involved in their drama. On cue, she stepped in front of the camera and glided into the role of Suzanne, the words coming of their own accord. She was an inspired lawyer, an intriguing, charming woman who had earned her colleague's love because of her unusual qualities. He had long since ceased to care for his possessive wife who had given nothing new to her marriage in years.

Suzanne defended herself with spirit, tempered with compassion. She was using her fine mind to get the wife to see that she was doing herself an injustice, not only by trying to hold on to a man who was tired of her but by not growing herself, becoming her own woman.

'Cut.'

Joanna turned, startled, at the sound of spontaneous applause coming from the cast and the crew.

Megan kissed her, and Lud called out, 'That's the way to go, Joanna. Terrific.'

Her eyes welled. For the first time in her life she understood the appeal of acting.

21

Although Nadine had come home expecting to feel much better, she actually felt worse. The contrast between the normal energy and uninterrupted good health she used to take for granted and her present condition plunged her into a deeper depression.

Kate and Jeff, relieved to have their mother back, behaved themselves initially, but when the novelty wore off they regressed, fighting, strewing their toys all around, ignoring her pleas for order and quiet.

Nadine could see the difference between her former occasional psychological fatigue and the real thing. No matter how hard she tried, she could do almost nothing without having to rest for a long while afterwards.

Joanna, worried about her sister's emotional state as well as her health, talked to Mack about installing a dialysis machine at home.

'Sure, why not,' he said sardonically. 'A machine only costs about five thousand dollars. You know, most of your sister's care is paid for by the government.'

After he explained, Joanna volunteered to contribute double that amount to the Kidney Foundation.

As long as Joanna could take her wealth for granted, Mack had no qualms in influencing her in the direction of kidney research.

Nadine was perfunctory in thanking Joanna for the machine, a gift she felt was motivated by guilt. The machine at home would make her life a little easier but it wouldn't keep her from having to be on a special diet or taking complicated medication.

A dozen times a day Nadine stood at the window of her tenth floor apartment wondering if there was any point in going on. She had failed in her marriage, wasn't much good at mothering and just when a career as an actress had seemed possible she had done the most stupid thing of her entire life.

To be an actress required stamina as well as talent. It was gruelling work that took a toll on a normal body. And hers, in that condition . . .

Joanna's daily calls were brief and, Nadine felt, only dutiful. Her sister didn't offer many details about the filming and Nadine didn't press her. Nobody from the cast had called – not Megan or Rick or even the perfidious Fern. That meant Joanna was doing well.

Nadine's suspicion was confirmed when Jim Sweeney spoke to her on the phone and innocently praised Joanna's performance. Unbearable waves of jealousy made Nadine tremble.

Just after she hung up, after speaking to Jim, the phone rang again. Nadine, hoping it was Lud so that she would have an opportunity to talk away some of her anger at him, instead heard Dominic's voice.

'I'm doing great,' she reported, unwilling to be entirely deprived of the chance to make somebody share her misery. 'I've become a dialysis addict, haven't you heard?'

'I have and I'm terribly sorry, dear. But the chances for success with a new kidney are very good, as Dr Mack has undoubtedly told you.'

'Sure. I feel like a prisoner sentenced to death who's been told he's only going to get life imprisonment.'

Dominic, in spite of his sympathy, grimaced at her self-pity. 'Is there anything I can do? Maybe spend time with Jeff and Kate?'

'Oh, if only you would!'

He arranged to come by that evening. Nadine invited him for dinner, since Mrs Wilson was cooking anyway.

Dominic was pleasant company, as always. Jeff and Kate were captivated at the way he sat on the floor with them, relaxed and enjoying himself.

185

'You ought to have your own kids,' Nadine said, as she saw him to the door.

He smiled ruefully. 'I hope I shall, some day.'

'Why didn't you and Alexis?'

Dominic was embarrassed at having been asked such a personal question, one he couldn't bring himself to answer.

He kissed Nadine's cheek. 'Follow doctor's orders and try to hang on. Don't hesitate to call me if there's anything I can do.'

Throwing a last concerned glance at her, he walked away quickly. No matter how many unfortunate patients he ministered to – women who had cancer, or who had given birth to defective or still-born infants – every tragic case distressed him. Now he had seen for himself that Mack hadn't exaggerated about Nadine's condition. A transplant would make all the difference.

Nadine shut her door, feeling depressed and abandoned. A sudden nausea took hold of her. She told Mrs Wilson to put the children to bed and went to lie down herself.

After two weeks at home with the cheerful nurse and the machine, Nadine was climbing the walls. On Sunday, when Joanna appeared to take the children, she observed that Nadine's patience was stretched to the limits. The realisation gripped her in anxious conflict. It was in her power to put an end to Nadine's suffering now, but at what a price.

Nadine resentfully contrasted herself with her sister. In the past, Joanna's pregnancies had made her a wreck. But this pregnancy, at the worst possible time and with the worst possible man, was indestructible. She saw on Joanna's face an aura of bovine anticipation, and she suddenly and ferociously loathed her. If only Mack could come up with a donor quickly.

And yet, Nadine had an aching need for Joanna. She felt so isolated, at home alone with her illness. 'How's the series going?' she forced herself to ask.

'It's tough but I'm squeaking by. Endless takes, and

coaching and infinite patience on the part of the pros. Sometimes I forget my lines. Sometimes I look at Lud or at the cameras. Or my timing is off.'

'How many episodes to go?'

'I'm not sure. Three, I think.'

Nadine felt a weight descend on her chest and lodge there like a boulder. They were proceeding almost as quickly with her stand-in as with her. That meant Joanna had to be as good an actress, maybe even better. But then Nadine reminded herself that her sister was a special friend of the director's.

Rising wearily, Nadine went to get the children.

Joanna stood miserably toying with her fingers, praying that Mack would come up with a donor. She didn't think she could stand to see Nadine like this for several more months.

Mack was seeing one of his transplant patients at his private office for a checkup. 'Everything's fine, Harold, but you look worried.'

The plump forty-year-old man sighed and leaned forward over the doctor's desk. 'You won't believe this. The mother of the boy whose kidney I got? She's been following me all over the place. The lady's off the wall, flipped out, loony. She thinks I'm the reincarnation of her kid or something. Keeps calling me, wanting to know how I'm doing, wanting to see me.'

Mack shook his head sadly.

'At first I felt sorry for her, you know. My wife even invited her over to the house and we looked at pictures of her kid. She's got no husband. She was driving the car when her son got killed. I guess she feels guilty. And she has a little money, enough to keep buying me things. A gold watch for my birthday, for chrissake. I told her I couldn't take it but she made such a fuss. I don't know what to do. My wife's fed up altogether.'

Mack was interrupted by a call from Stan Marsden, the kidney transplant coordinator at St Anne's. An accident victim in Frankfurt had an immune system that was compatible with Nadine Barrett's. The potential donor's blood and tissue antigens had been keyed into a teleprinter terminal and transmitted to the New York computer.

Mack hung up, highly excited. 'I'll see you next month, Harold.'

'Sure. Good news?'

'Possibly. I've got a potential donor in Germany.'

Harold got up and moved towards the door. 'Good luck. I sure wish my kidney came from over there.'

Mack phoned Nadine at home. 'Now, don't get your hopes up because a lot still can go wrong. I just wanted to alert you to be on hand, ready to go to the hospital at a moment's notice.'

He went through the rest of the day on tenterhooks.

At six-thirty Marsden phoned him back. 'They jumped the gun in Frankfurt. The patient has critical injuries – that's right, has – and is on life-support equipment. There's some disagreement among the doctors as to whether there's any remaining neurological activity. I know you're keen on giving Barrett a kidney, and this match seems too good to be true, but what can I do? The parents of the patient haven't given up hope.'

After checking with Nadine, Mack caught a night flight to Frankfurt.

Joanna had offered to remain at Omega on a consultant basis for a few hours each week, to which Winnie readily agreed. She was at her desk working when Nadine phoned, sounding happier than she had in weeks. 'I've had some good news for a change.'

Joanna listened with growing excitement. 'Oh, that's wonderful.'

On her way home, Joanna stopped in front of a children's shop on Madison Avenue, her eye arrested by a dress displayed in the window. Because Lud seemed to want a girl so much, Joanna had begun to think of their baby as female also. On an impulse she went into the shop and asked to see the dress. It was white, made of fine Egyptian cotton, with hand-tatted lace trimming, and a pink rosebud adorning the collar. Of course the dress was highly impractical and outrageously expensive, but Joanna fell in love with it, visualising it on 'Esmeralda'.

While the saleswoman was wrapping up the dress, Joanna also picked out a matching hand-knitted sweater, hat, and booties. It was supposed to be bad luck to buy baby clothes in advance, but she didn't care and in fact didn't believe it. She hadn't done this sort of thing before and it had made no difference.

Now Joanna felt things were going to improve on all counts. Mack had intimated to Nadine that the compatibility between her and the donor was nothing short of miraculous.

This baby was going to be born, Joanna was certain of it.

Mack was conferring with doctors at the hospital in Frankfurt.

'We can't rush this thing,' the chief neurologist told him, through an interpreter.

'But you say there's no neurological activity at all.'

'We must be certain. The boy is twenty-two, victim of a motorcycle crash. His parents are devastated, and he's an only son.'

'But the parents have agreed to a transplant.'

The neurologist shook his head. 'The victim carried a donor card. In fact, he was a medical student.'

After an entire day of indecision on the part of the doctors, Mack was finally persuaded to return to his hotel. He had hoped the matter could be settled quickly, but now he saw that at least another day would pass. It was an unfortunate situation. Usually the transplant unit wasn't notified until after the potential donor had been pronounced dead.

Mack phoned New York to report his progress to Stan Marsden and Nadine, and to tell them he was still very hopeful.

Mack was awakened by a phone call. The doctors had

concluded that the boy was dead and had disconnected the machines.

After a cup of coffee, Mack rushed to the hospital, only to find himself accosted by the hysterical parents of the dead boy. It wasn't necessary for the doctor to understand a word of German in order to glean that the parents disagreed with the decision.

The father, especially, was enraged, claiming that the life-support system had been disconnected too soon merely because their son had foolishly signed a donor card. The father accused Mack of bribing the German doctors to declare his son dead prematurely.

While the father railed, the mother wept. This was their only child, she kept saying. They were shopkeepers, and they had scrimped every cent to pay for medical school. Just because their son's motorcycle had skidded on a wet night, all their work and hope and love had been in vain.

Mack was becoming frantic. The victim's kidneys had already been removed and packed in a pulsatile-perfusion machine which circulated a special preservative solution through them. However, they could last only about fifty-four hours.

He tried to reason with the father, saying he had bribed nobody. He was a doctor and believed every human life to be sacred. But the young man's injuries had been to the head. Even if a miracle had kept him alive, he would not have become a doctor but a vegetable. And Mack had a patient who could benefit from a transplant.

The father kept shaking his head. 'Tell him,' a frustrated Mack shouted to the interpreter, 'that I'll reimburse him for the cost of his son's schooling. Damn it, my patient is a millionaire.'

The interpreter, a young, sensitive-looking girl, was appalled. 'I can't say that, it will only make matters worse.'

Unfortunately, the father understood enough English to have got the gist of Mack's offer. The word 'millionaire' stuck in his throat.

'Never,' the father yelled. 'Never! Donor card or no

donor card, I won't allow it. I'm getting a lawyer. I'm going to sue the hospital for killing my son.'

Mack, trying to control his anger, saw that his offer of money had caused all the hospital personnel to draw away in contempt.

Damn it, he'd gone too far. He appealed to the interpreter. 'Can I talk to the mother?'

'Not now. She's lying down. The doctor gave her a sedative.'

The chief neurologist beckoned to Mack and said haltingly in English, 'Aside from kidneys, people have hearts.'

Mack muttered that he knew that, and he was sorry. He requested an audience with the boy's mother when she awoke and the neurologist said he would try. Mack's impatience was understandable, but the hospital didn't want to be sued.

Mack wondered privately if the parents of the victim possibly had a lingering hatred of Americans because Frankfurt had been practically destroyed by bombing during World War II.

The situation was maddening. This kidney match was about one in a million.

Mack didn't dare leave his hotel. He ate in the dining room, leaving instructions that he be paged if any call came for him. The rest of his time he spent at the window of his room looking out at the Main River.

When the hospital did contact him it was to say that the parents' lawyer had got a court order to prevent him from taking possession of the kidney.

Since the organ had been removed from the victim, nine hours had elapsed.

Lud sat in Nadine's living room drinking a scotch and discussing the series.

'After the transplant,' Nadine said, 'I'll need a couple of weeks to recuperate. What are the chances of refilming Joanna's scenes?'

191

He hesitated. In his opinion, Joanna was as good, if not better, than Nadine. There was no need to reshoot at all.

'Well, the chances are poor without more money. It's costing almost half a million to produce each one-hour of viewing time – '

'And if I pay?'

He set down his glass. 'There are still difficulties. Megan has another commitment starting in a month, and our writer has contracted for another series. We just can't go on indefinitely. We're so late as it is – '

'You owe it to me, Lud.' Nadine looked steadily at him, satisfied that he was the first to lower his gaze.

For the hundredth time he wished he had never set eyes on Nadine and had given the role to a reliable, experienced television actress. The other problems he would have faced were nothing compared with the fix he had got himself in with this impossible woman.

'Have you seen the takes?' Nadine asked.

'Yes. Of course I can tell the difference between the two of you. Among the cast members, opinion is divided. But I also had some innocent viewers look at the takes and it never crossed anyone's mind that two actresses were playing one role.' After a moment's hesitation, Lud continued. 'If you're willing to pay for the reshooting, we can probably do it when you're ready.' Although he was sure it would never come to that, there was no harm in telling Nadine what she wanted to hear.

What she hadn't wanted to hear was the implication that Joanna was as good an actress as she was.

Nadine's euphoria at the thought of the new kidney receded and a rage against Lud rose within her, for so many reasons. But now was not the time to show it. First she had to get well.

As her third month ended, Joanna began to suffer from terrible fatigue. She had to have many rest periods to enable her to stand up on the set, and by nine in the evening her eyes were closing. She had to cut down at Omega, and saw little of Lud in the evening, feeling it was unfair to keep him hanging around if she was going to fall asleep so early.

'Lud, when this is over I'm going to go to sleep for a month. Maybe even hibernate all summer,' Joanna told him, the evening she had nearly dozed off in the restaurant.

'When the series is finished we'll take a holiday. Rent a cabin in Maine for a week. I'll wait on you hand and foot – and maybe a few other places – and you'll just lie back and keep Esmeralda happy.'

Mack prowled his hotel room like a caged beast. Although he had run into other delays involving kidney transplants, he was used to dealing with American donor centres, where people spoke the same language, where things were done in predictable, acceptable ways.

Now, waiting for an autopsy to be performed on the kidney donor, he ached with helplessness and frustration. Never in his life had he seen such quantities of red tape. The fear of authority was so strong in these Germans that they would let two healthy kidneys die rather than expedite a simple thing like a goddamn autopsy.

In the meantime, valuable time was passing, not only for Barrett but for another renal-failure patient in Birmingham, England, awaiting the other organ. Twenty-four hours gone. The boy's mother had refused to see Mack, and that was that.

The autopsy yielded the predictable conclusion that the life-support machines had not been prematurely disconnected because the patient's brain had died of injuries received in the accident.

Otto Becker, head of the kidney unit in Frankfurt, intervened on behalf of Mack and got him an audience with the subdued but still-grieving parents. Becker also acted as interpreter.

'I apologise for the distress I caused you,' Mack began. 'I am sorry for your loss and for the loss of a potential doctor. Let me tell you about my patient. She is only thirty-four years old and a mother of two.' He could be

193

as persuasive in calling forth positive feelings as negative ones. And any roughness was smoothed into conventional speech by Becker.

Mack described graphically what kidney failure meant, what sort of life a sufferer could look forward to.

He closed with the reminder that their son had understood and that his card constituted a desire to give someone a chance for a new life. Were the parents going to deny their son's last wish?

As he made his impassioned plea, Mack saw and felt the parents' grief. Both seemed to have shrunk in two days. They sat side by side, not touching, not moving, staring at the floor.

Becker nudged Mack and drew him out of the room. 'They must think it over.'

'Think it over, hell! Man, it's thirty-nine hours!'

Becker commiserated, but there was nothing to do but wait. This Mack did at his hotel, his bag packed. Every so often he pounded his fist into the mattress.

At one in the afternoon the parents agreed to release the kidneys.

Mack was left with less than thirteen hours to return to New York and perform the transplant.

22

Nadine packed her bag and went off to St Anne's for what she hoped would be the last time. While she joked with the nurses and orderlies in the kidney unit, a pre-operative workup was done and everything made ready for the transplant.

Dominic stopped by her room in the late morning to say hello. He had been keeping in close touch with her condition since his conversation with Mack.

She put aside the book she was reading. 'Take a last look at the "before". I'm going to be transformed, transplanted, whatever. I can't wait.'

Dominic smiled, hoping she wouldn't be disappointed. Mack might not have adequately explained to her that although a healthy new kidney was a great deal better than her nonfunctioning ones, it was not the same as the two organs one was born with. Nadine, Dominic suspected, tended to indulge in wishful thinking.

'Children okay?'

'Yes, but grumpy because I've come back here.'

'I could drop in for half an hour on my way home tonight. I'd stay longer, only I have theatre tickets.'

'Even a short visit would be great, Dominic. They think you're terrific.'

After phoning Nadine at the hospital during a break from filming, Joanna returned to the set feeling hopeful. The operation would be over by this evening and she had promised to be at her sister's bedside.

They were shooting Suzanne's last big courtroom scene. Joanna was more relaxed in front of the camera than she had ever been and after only four takes they achieved a satisfactory result.

She was through for the day and not feeling tired, for a change, so she decided to spend some time at Omega. She had not yet told Winnie of the new developments in her sister's case.

He was very happy, of course.

'It's not over yet, Winnie. The kidney has to get here, and then not be rejected.'

'I know, but that doctor seems to know his business. It's about time things broke your way. You deserve it.'

Afterwards Joanna stopped at a toy store to buy her niece and nephew a new Monopoly set. As she passed the stuffed-toy counter, she was attracted by a white baby elephant with a pink ribbon behind its ear. Joanna immediately had a picture of her daughter cuddling the toy, and she had to have it to add to her collection.

Mack sat on the aisle seat of his first-class flight out of Frankfurt, every few minutes looking next to him to be sure that the battery-operated machine containing the kidney was securely strapped in.

A little after two pm Frankfurt time the plane took off. The flight was going to be eight and a half hours long, which would get him to Kennedy at five-thirty pm. Stan Marsden would have a helicopter to meet him. If the kidney was at the hospital by five forty-five the operation could be done by the fiftieth hour. It was too close, damn it.

Mack simply couldn't relax. He wanted a drink badly but stuck to tonic and juice because he always allowed at least eight hours without liquor before performing surgery.

Listening to music over his earphones, he picked at his meal and drank two cups of coffee. Then he thumbed through the pages of the in-flight magazine, tried to do a crossword puzzle, and finally put everything aside and shut his eyes.

He dozed off, only to awaken with a start as he felt a jolt

beneath him. The pilot was asking all passengers to fasten their seat belts because of turbulence.

Later, Mack was awakened by the pilot's announcement that they were encountering strong headwinds and the flight would be delayed by at least twenty minutes.

Swearing under his breath, Mack checked the machine beside him. He was perturbed to note that although it was already five-fifteen, New York time, no announcement about landing had been made. The flight attendant, who knew the situation, agreed to check with the captain, and her news was not reassuring. 'There's a rain storm over New York and outgoing flights are being delayed. But that doesn't mean we will be, give or take a few minutes.'

'That few minutes may make a difference to somebody's life.'

She relayed his message to the captain, who promised to do the best he could.

However, the plane didn't touch down until six pm, and by then Mack was truly alarmed. A wheelchair was waiting at the disembarkation point. The kidney was strapped into it and wheeled, at a trot, by an airport employee, Mack running alongside it. Special papers prepared in advance enabled the two to get through Customs on the run.

Stan Marsden met Mack at the gate. 'Couldn't get a helicopter. There's been an electrical storm, but I have an ambulance outside and a police escort.'

'Oh, no!' It was already six ten. Fifty hours and twenty-five minutes, which meant less than four hours of safety.

Mack sat in the back of the ambulance with Marsden, the two of them gazing at the machine strapped to the stretcher. The sirens of the police escort screamed as the vehicle shot along the expressway.

'Storm's kept the traffic down, and anyway, we're going against most of it,' Marsden commented.

'I'm worried. Fifty-four hours is only an approximation. Shit, why are we stopping? Where the hell are we?'

Marsden moved to the rear of the ambulance and stuck his head outside. 'Queens Midtown Tunnel. Oh, hell, there's a solid line of traffic waiting. We can't move in any direction. And now the storm's over. We could have had a helicopter after all – '

'Will you stop second-guessing?' Mack shouted.

A policeman got out of his car and approached the ambulance. 'Sorry, sir, there's been a watermain break. Just what we needed after this downpour. Anyway, there are about eight square blocks flooded.'

'Radio for a helicopter right now,' Mack demanded. 'I don't care where it lands. On top of this buggy, if necessary.'

The traffic was slowly clearing by the time the helicopter arrived, twenty minutes later. It made a landing on a nearby rooftop, while Mack, Marsden, and a couple of policemen manoeuvred the wheelchair out of the ambulance, hurried it across the lanes of traffic, held up by other policemen, into the building, the lift and up the flight of stairs to the roof. Mack and Marsden joined the pilot in the 'copter.

'Get some speed up,' Mack shouted at the pilot, aware of the irony that the kidney was being rushed to someone who had damaged hers in a helicopter crash. 'Come on, man, this is vital.'

'Doing my best,' the pilot shouted back, 'but there's no shorter distance between two points than a straight line.'

The helicopter landed on the roof of St Anne's, where several orderlies were waiting. The kidney was rushed to the laboratory for checking and last-minute tissue retyping.

It was seven-thirty – fifty-two hours and ten minutes since the kidney had been removed from the donor.

Joanna was getting ready for a game of Monopoly with Jeff and Kate when she heard the bell ring. Moments later, Mrs Wilson was showing Dominic into the living room.

Joanna and Dominic smiled at each other a little shyly.

'Come and play with us, Doc,' Jeff called to him.

'I can only stay half an hour.'

'That's okay. You can sell me your property.'

'He's going to sell it to me, aren't you, Doc?'

'In any case,' Joanna told them, 'we won't get to finish the game today. I'll be going to the hospital any minute.'

'First, Aunt Joanna, you have to go straight to jail,' Kate announced happily. 'You don't pass Go, you don't collect two hundred dollars.'

'Poor me.' Joanna smiled at her niece. 'How do you expect me to win this game, anyway?'

'I don't expect you to win, I expect you to lose,' Kate assured her, drawing laughs from both adults.

'I'm going to win,' Jeff declared, 'I usually do.'

When the phone rang Joanna jumped up and ran to it, but the call wasn't from the hospital. While she was near the phone, she dialled St Anne's. 'It's after seven,' she said tensely to Dominic, who had quietly approached the foyer. 'The operation should have started by this time. Hello, yes.'

She frowned and put down the receiver. 'Dr Mack hasn't even got there yet. I don't understand it, unless the rain delayed everything.'

'It's your turn, Aunt Joanna,' Jeff called to her.

She was feeling faint with worry, and Dominic silently shared it.

'I want to trade Marvin Gardens for Boardwalk, but Jeff won't,' Kate complained.

'Because that'll give her a monopoly, and I'll still need to buy Atlantic Avenue,' Jeff countered.

'I'll sell you Atlantic Avenue,' Dominic declared, looking at his watch. 'I have to go in a few minutes.'

Although he had planned to leave by seven-thirty at the latest, Dominic couldn't bring himself to abandon Joanna, looking so upset because there had been no word from the hospital.

Instead, he phoned his date to tell her there was an emergency and she was to leave his ticket at the box office.

'It's after eight,' Joanna said at Dominic's elbow. 'Something's wrong.'

'Let me try the hospital. I believe it's your turn to play.'

Dominic waited until she had left the hallway before making his call. Mack couldn't be reached but Dominic was put through to Stan Marsden.

'We were too late, damn it. The kidney was no longer viable.'

Dominic felt terrible. He stood near the phone for a few minutes, phrasing to himself the words he would use to tell Joanna.

It turned out to be unnecessary, because the front door opened and Nadine walked in.

Dominic went to her. 'I just heard. I'm so terribly sorry.'

She nodded and continued to the living room.

'Mommy's back,' Kate yelled happily. Both children rushed to their mother.

Nadine, staring at Joanna over the children, looked ghastly. Slowly she shook her head.

Joanna forced herself to remain calm. 'Go on with the game, kids. Mommy has to lie down.'

She went to her sister and put her arm around her. Without speaking, the two walked to Nadine's bedroom, past Dominic, who was still standing in the hallway. He went back to the children.

Nadine sat on the bed, allowing Joanna to help her get undressed.

When she had her nightgown on, Nadine crept under the covers. 'The trip took too long,' she said simply. 'The kidney didn't last.' Closing her eyes, she turned on her side, her back to her sister.

Joanna, feeling deeply distressed, left the room.

Dominic was waiting for her in the hall. 'Anything I can do?'

She shook her head. 'No point in missing your play,' she said dully. 'I'll stay here tonight, in case Nadine needs me, or the children.'

He put his hand on Joanna's shoulder for a moment.

'I'm a friend of the family, remember. Please call for help if ever you need it.'

She forced herself to finish the game with Jeff and Kate, telling them their mother was asleep.

It took hours for Joanna to fall asleep herself.

She was going to be filming for two or three more days, if all went well. Then the series would be finished.

Joanna helped Mrs Wilson get the children ready for school in the morning and left Nadine still sleeping.

Lud had been in frantic conference with the writer in order to make last-minute changes in the script, which meant that Joanna had to learn new lines.

'Sorry to do this to you, love, but there were some problems. And we're in a rush because Storman is going to be here to look at a rough cut. He has to see your performance for himself.'

The cast made an enormous final effort, Joanna taking time out only to check with her sister.

Nadine, on the phone, was subdued and, Joanna knew, profoundly depressed. After the series was finished, she promised herself, she would devote her time to cheering Nadine up. As it was, their conversations were short and somewhat unreal.

'Mack will find another kidney, maybe closer to home,' Joanna told her sister, trying desperately to believe it herself.

'Sure,' Nadine answered without enthusiasm. She had begun to feel that the odds were stacked against her. In everything.

Two days stretched into three, then four, but finally Lud said, 'Cut. This is it, gang, we've done it.'

The cast cheered, immediately beginning to plan a celebration for that evening.

Megan offered her apartment, a huge place on West End Avenue and Lud said if she could get a caterer for the food, he would pay for it.

Joanna, sitting and resting, was quietly sharing in the euphoria.

'Are you tired, sweetheart? Need a snooze before the party?'

'I wonder if I could beg off. I really should go to see Nadine and the children. She's been feeling so awfully let down over that transplant business.'

'You can spend all day tomorrow with her, but this party's for you as much as anyone. Without you there wouldn't be a series. Showbiz people are superstitious, so you'd better show up or else.'

She smiled. 'I'd better, if you put it that way. I don't think I'd like or else.'

Lud gave her a long, passionate look that hit her like a laser beam. 'Yes to everything,' she murmured.

Taking her by the arm, he hurried her into a cab.

Instead of returning to Manhattan, they went in the other direction, out to the airport.

'Where in the world are we going? Not Hawaii again. We'd never make it back for Megan's party.'

'Hawaii doesn't have a monopoly on bliss,' he whispered, kissing her.

They pulled up at a motel.

'We haven't any bags, Lud.'

'Just puff out your stomach a little. They'll understand.'

Laughing, she went along with the game.

The clerk rented them a room for one night which Lud paid for on the spot.

They ordered drinks, sitting across the room from each other and exchanging hot looks.

'Joanna, it's been such a long time. I've been missing you.'

'Me too.'

Gradually they drew nearer, but still postponing the moment. When finally they came together their passion reached exquisite heights after their abstinence.

Joanna fell into a relaxed sleep. Lud, who only dozed for a short while, got up, showered, and went out to make some neglected phone calls, one of them to Ed Storman.

When Joanna woke she found a piece of the motel's

202

stationery pinned to Lud's pillow. 'Stick around. I'll be back for more.'

Lazily she got out of bed, stretched and had a shower. By the time he returned she was dressed and made up.

'Heavens, there's a girl in my room. The question is what to do about it.'

He pulled her into his arms, kissing her gently and holding her close. 'I love you, baby. And I love *you*, baby,' he added, patting her tummy.

On the way back to Manhattan, Joanna leaned her head against Lud's shoulder and daydreamed about being a mother. She visualised 'Esmeralda' in the adorable clothes she had bought.

Lud's face, which Joanna couldn't see, was tense. Ed Storman had been subpoenaed in connection with another show and couldn't leave L.A. The timing couldn't have been worse because Ed expected Lud to bring the rough cut with him to be edited there. The producer was also toying with the idea of using the truth about the twins as promotion material. Lud was vehemently opposed to what he felt would be a cheap shot at publicity. The series was good enough without that. But Ed could be damn stubborn.

Lud waited until they were nearly at Megan's before telling Joanna that he was leaving for California after the party.

She was unaccountably frightened.

'It can't be helped, sweetie.' He explained, assuring her he would be back within a week or so, leaving out the part about his producer's publicity scheme, since he was determined to talk Ed out of it.

'Please don't sulk. Haven't we stored up lots of love for those lonely nights?'

'Lud, did you know – '

He stopped her question with a kiss. 'No, love, I called him while you were sleeping.'

Trying to cheer her up, Lud began to sing, 'Joanna and me and baby make three, we're happy in Malibu heaven.'

Joanna laughed and hugged him, and he kissed the tip of her nose.

Nadine lay in a single bed in one of the spare bedrooms, a tube in her left arm hooked up to the dialysis machine. With her right hand she turned the pages of *Cosmopolitan*, trying to interest herself in the new line of makeup for the summer, in clothes, in an article dealing with female sexuality. However, she couldn't seem to concentrate on anything.

She had been attached to the machine for only an hour. That meant almost four more to go. The thought of being subjected to this stultifying imprisonment three times a week for many months was unbearable.

When Mack had come to tell her the kidney from Germany was no longer usable, she had wanted to scream her frustration and impotent rage at him, but he had done it for her, stomping around the room, casting imprecations on German bureaucracy, the donor's parents, the weather, Stan Marsden, for not having arranged for a helicopter regardless of the storm. Mack had finished by telling her that although he would keep trying, the chances for another good match were really remote. She would have to reconcile herself to five more months on the machine and then the acceptance of her sister's kidney.

She didn't see how she would be able to stand it. Feeling like hell, looking like hell, with no work to do. And Joanna would grow bigger and more bovine by the day. She would move away from her to California with Lud. Nadine would be left alone here, to cope with the children and her non-life.

'Miss Sims,' Nadine called.

The smiling black nurse hurried into the room. 'What can I get you, hon?'

'The telephone, please.'

After it was jacked into the wall by her bed, Nadine phoned the Astoria studio. Everyone had already left. In fact, the communicative person who answered the phone told her they had finished shooting and were somewhere at a party to celebrate.

Nadine had never felt so wretched, so isolated, so hopeless in all her life. Whenever anything bad had happened to her, Joanna had always been there. Now her dear sister was out enjoying herself and not giving her a thought.

Nadine flicked on the television, tuning in to a film made for television about how a former athlete, paralysed from the waist down as a result of an accident, goes on to make a wonderful adjustment. She watched part of it, impatient and incredulous. Without bodily mobility, she felt there was no point in being alive.

Switching off the set, she picked up the phone again, dialling Joanna, Fern, and even, in desperation, Jim Sweeney. Nobody was at home.

Just as she was about to give up, she decided to call her folks in Texas. Aunt Sally answered, and before Nadine could stop herself, she was spilling out all her troubles.

Aunt Sally promised that she and A.W. would come to New York as soon as they possibly could.

Joanna, holding a glass of tonic and ice, was trying to join in the celebration at Megan's but finding it difficult. Having made an appearance at the party, she wondered if she could slip away unnoticed. Then she decided she had better stay for Lud's sake. He was enjoying his relaxed contact with the cast and crew, now that the discipline of the filming could be set aside.

Three times Joanna went to the phone and tried to reach Nadine, each time hearing a busy signal.

Lud came up to her. 'I'm leaving now, sweetheart.'

'Can I go out to the airport with you?' she asked wistfully.

'No need, love. Better go home and rest. I'll be in touch as soon as I can, but don't worry if you don't hear from me for a few days. I'm likely to be rushing around like mad, keeping crazy hours and sleeping with my phone off

205

the hook. Anyway, you can always leave a message for me with Ed's office.'

She walked him to the door, feeling panicky for no reason she could clearly define. He held her close for a moment, kissed her and was gone.

Joanna decided to leave as well, but before she could say goodbye to Megan she was caught up in a discussion with Rick about acting, her opinion sought after. She couldn't just be rude and walk away. Maybe if she took her mind off Lud and Nadine she would lose the terrible feeling that something awful was about to happen.

By the time Nadine was unhooked from the machine she felt ready to jump through the roof. She now regretted having spilled her guts to her aunt. Sally was a nice lady but there was nothing she could do in New York. In fact, she would only get in the way and Nadine's father was even worse. Not in such good health, and so old-fashioned. He hadn't been to New York since the double wedding of the twins and then he had grumbled and moaned during his stay about the godless ways of the corrupt big city.

Nadine was also feeling disloyal to Joanna for having told their aunt about her pregnancy. Aunt Sally would never say anything against Joanna, but Nadine knew she had been genuinely shocked.

Mrs Wilson stuck her head out of the kitchen. 'The children want hamburgers and french fries for supper, but we have no hamburger. We're also out of bread. I'd order up from Gristedes but they're already closed.'

Nadine sighed. 'Could you possibly pick up what we need at the corner market?'

Taking off her apron, Mrs Wilson left to do her errand.

Nadine felt physically stronger, after the dialysis, but still down in the dumps. Against doctor's orders she mixed a gin and tonic and drank it quickly. It made her feel so much better that she mixed herself another. Since her accident she had stopped taking pills, but she wished she had something now. Getting smashed would help her forget her troubles.

'Mommy,' Kate appeared at the kitchen door, 'I'm hungry.'

'We'll eat soon,' Nadine promised.

The frozen potatoes were waiting to be dropped into the oil. She put a light under the pan. Then, pulling some paper towels off the roll, she positioned them on the counter next to the stove.

The children usually ate in the kitchen. Nadine set the table, deciding to eat at the same time. Mrs Wilson could go home as soon as she had brought the groceries.

Nadine sipped from her drink. When she saw that the oil wasn't bubbling, she impatiently raised the flame.

The phone rang in the kitchen. 'It's Carl. What's going on?'

Nadine told him.

'God, how awful. I'm sorry. Look, I'm going to be in New York tomorrow on my way to Palm Beach. Everything's on very short notice. I'd like to take Kate and Jeff to spend a few days with my folks – '

'But they'd miss school.'

'Only a couple of days. I'll bring them back next week. Mom and Dad would like to see them very much. It's been almost a year.'

The rage towards her ex that Nadine usually kept under control now erupted, helped by the alcohol.

'You haven't seen your children in months but you can't stand to be alone with them! You have to dilute the experience by dragging in other people – '

'I didn't call you to argue. If I don't take Kate and Jeff to Florida I'll only have about two hours to be with them. So just say yes or no.'

Nadine felt frightened. Without the children she'd be all alone with the goddamn machine. Carl didn't give a damn about her. Nobody did.

'Nadine, I can't stay on the phone. I'm in Dar-es-Salaam.'

She suddenly had a picture of Kate and Jeff asking

wistfully about their father. It wasn't fair to keep them from him, and from their grandparents.

'Okay, take them,' she told Carl angrily, slamming down the phone, just as Mrs Wilson returned with her shopping.

'I can't find the ketchup, Mrs Wilson.'

'Oh, it's not in the fridge. I keep it in the cupboard. Don't you bother, Mrs B., I'll get it as soon as I hang up my coat.'

The cupboard was no place for the ketchup, Nadine thought, irritated. Opening the doors overhead, she saw it on the highest shelf, just in front, near the edge. Damn that incompetent woman for putting everything in an inconvenient spot.

Impatiently Nadine stood on tiptoe and reached for the ketchup.

Suddenly she slipped and grabbed the counter to keep from falling.

The paper towels, pushed closer to the stove, went up in flames.

Joanna, saying goodbye to Megan at the door, was assailed by a horrible searing sensation.

23

Joanna spent the night in Nadine's room, where Kate and Jeff slept at opposite ends of their mother's king-sized bed.

Sitting in a chair, Joanna never closed her eyes once. She simply sat there, numb physically and emotionally, while the night passed as in a dream.

If Mrs Wilson hadn't been here to beat out the flames, her sister might be dead. As it was, Nadine had suffered first- and second-degree burns to her arms, chest, abdomen, and legs.

Joanna had thought it more important to remain with the bewildered children than go to the hospital, but she had been on the phone to St Anne's several times.

Nadine was in Intensive Care. On top of her kidney problems, the shock from the burns and the possibility of infection had made her condition critical.

Fortunately, the children had been at the other end of the apartment watching television. By the time Joanna had arrived, Nadine was on her way to the hospital. Mrs Wilson had fed the children in the dining room but hadn't had a chance to clean up the kitchen. Joanna, finding her sister's gin and tonic, knew that she had been disobeying her doctor.

Nadine had been understandably devastated at losing the new kidney at the last moment. And Joanna knew how much her sister had hated not being able to finish the series. But to have another near-fatal accident! Joanna was beginning to think forces were at work in Nadine that she couldn't fathom, and it scared her.

Joanna didn't even realise it was morning until Mrs

Wilson arrived at seven-thirty. 'You've been sitting up here all night, poor thing. How's Mrs B.?'

'I don't know. I'll phone the hospital.'

The children stirred, and Joanna leaned over the bed and kissed each one awake.

'Mommy?' Kate asked, looking sleepily at her.

She didn't answer but hugged her niece tightly.

'Mommy's in the hospital,' Jeff explained stoically.

Joanna held him close for a moment also, knowing how frightened he must be feeling not to have referred to his mother as Mom.

'Resting comfortably,' Joanna reported to Mrs Wilson after her call to the hospital. She and the housekeeper exchanged a sober glance. The words didn't mean much.

Joanna was going to St Anne's to see for herself.

The downstairs buzzer sounded just as she was getting ready to leave.

'It's Mr Barrett,' Mrs Wilson reported. 'Doorman says he's on his way up.'

Joanna stood in the foyer, feeling uncomfortable. When the bell rang she opened the door.

'Hello,' Carl said coldly, striding past her. 'Are they ready?'

'Carl, wait. There's been an accident.'

He turned in astonishment. 'Joanna? What happened?'

She told him, watching his features grow more tense and anger cloud his eyes. 'What's she trying to do to herself, anyway?' he muttered.

'Did she know you were coming today?'

'Of course. I just got off a plane. I wanted to take the children to Florida to visit my folks.'

'Oh, do. They're so upset, and they miss you. This would be the ideal time.'

She said a few more halting words. Although so many years had passed, she had never been comfortable with Carl from the day she had learned he loved her sister.

'Joanna, you look exhausted and upset yourself. Take care, and let me know the news about Nadine.' He wrote a phone number on the back of his card and handed it to her. Suddenly he kissed her cheek, something he very seldom did.

As Joanna let herself out, she could hear the children crying, 'Daddy, Daddy, Daddy!'

At the hospital, she was permitted to see Nadine for only a few minutes. Although Joanna had braced herself, she still was shocked and pained at the sight.

Nadine was conscious, her face pale, her arms, chest, and abdomen completely bandaged.

The sisters looked at each other for a moment.

Nadine tried to smile. 'Pretty stupid, huh?' she said weakly.

'Yeah, pretty stupid,' Joanna echoed, stroking Nadine's hair. 'Are you in much pain?'

'No. I'm shot full of dope. If I pull through all this I'll probably be an addict. Only good thing is I didn't burn my face. The children must have been terrified.'

'They're all right. They didn't actually see anything. I stayed the night in your room with them. And this morning Carl came.'

'Oh, that's right. I'd forgotten. It's just as well.'

The nurse interrupted and led Joanna from the room.

Joanna tried to phone Lud, but there was no answer at his house or apartment, so she called Ed Storman's office and left a message.

Then she made her way to Mack's office. He had told her to come and see him. She found him looking grave.

'Dr Graham and Dr Halloran are on their way down so that we can have a conference.'

The two doctors arrived together and seated themselves on the couch, while Mack sat in the easy chair, half-facing them, half-facing Joanna.

'Nadine has suffered first- and second-degree burns on her arms, legs, and abdomen, preventing vascular access. Dialysis is now impossible.' He paused to let his words sink in.

Joanna felt a flutter of apprehension, but only hazily, as if everything were happening under water. Mack's voice sounded very far away.

He continued to speak, pointing out, for Joanna's benefit, what happens to the body when wastes and fluids cannot be removed normally by functioning kidneys, or artificially by machine.

'Do you have any questions, Joanna?'

'No,' she whispered, aware that the three men were looking at her with strange expressions.

'Nadine needs an immediate kidney transplant in order to survive.' Mack sighed profoundly and waited.

There was a long, eerie silence.

Joanna looked from one doctor to another, her befogged brain unable to comprehend. 'Have you found another donor?'

Mack shook his head. 'There is no donor but you. That we almost had someone was a miracle. It's not likely to be repeated. Kidneys are in short supply. More than thirteen million people in the US alone suffer from kidney disease and almost eighty thousand die every year.'

He shut his mouth and looked for help to the two obstetricians sitting tensely on the couch. One of them was going to have to tell this poor woman what was what. He had practically hit her on the head with the facts and still nothing had registered.

Halloran said gently to Joanna, 'You have to make a very difficult decision.'

She stared glassily at him.

'Your sister will die unless she has another kidney. Yours is the best she could have. And it's the only one available.'

Joanna blinked rapidly at him. 'That's what Dr Mack said last time, only he did find one.'

Mack squirmed but kept his mouth shut.

'There isn't time, Joanna,' Halloran continued softly.

'NO!' The cry of anguish came from Joanna automatically. The numbness was gone, and a nightmarish terror was gripping her backbone.

Dominic sat clenching his hands to keep from going to Joanna.

212

'How can you ask me to kill my baby?' she cried, looking in turn at each of them.

'We're not asking it,' Mack said. 'The decision is yours and your husband's. But I must repeat that without a transplant your sister cannot survive.'

Joanna heard him but she couldn't believe it. 'The burns will heal, won't they? The nurse said they weren't so bad –'

'By the time they heal it will be too late,' Mack interrupted through tight lips. 'The longer we wait, the worse it will be for your sister.'

'I – I simply can't believe it. It's such a shock. To have to decide right here, right now...' Joanna's voice broke.

Halloran closed his eyes for a moment, wishing he were anywhere but here, and that Joanna were anyone's patient but his. He knew how she must be feeling, after her miscarriages. His wife was in the sixth month of her first pregnancy. They had a name picked out, the layette purchased...

Dominic, looking at Joanna's bent head, didn't trust his voice at that moment and had to remain silent.

Mack's compassion for Joanna vied with concern for his patient. 'Discuss it with your husband, Joanna. In fact, bring him to see me.'

'I can't. He – he's in California. I've left word, but so far...' Joanna lifted her head and took a deep breath, forcing herself to look Mack in the eye. 'He's not actually my husband.'

'God give me strength!' Mack rose to his feet. 'What is this, feminist chic or something? Joanna, we're talking about your sister's *life*!'

Agitated, Dominic also stood up. 'I'd like to speak to Joanna alone, please.'

Mack threw up his hands. 'She's all yours!'

After the two doctors had left the room, there was a long silence as Dominic tried to choose the right words.

Joanna felt a terrible weakness throughout her body and her throat ached. Nobody except Lud cared about her baby.

'It's so unfair,' she whispered, 'it's so unfair. After all these years, all the hell I've been through, when finally . . .' Her voice faded, unable to rise above the pain in her throat.

'I know, dear, I know,' Dominic said softly, resisting the impulse to put his arms around her. He took Mack's seat facing her.

'How can anyone ask me to volunteer to do away with my own baby?'

'At this stage, Joanna,' he murmured, 'it's an embryo, less than six inches long and weighing only about six ounces.'

'To you it's an embryo, but to me it's a human being, a life growing inside me. I feel protective of it.'

Emotion spilling over into her eyes, she looked at him tearfully. 'You know the scientific stuff but you don't know how it *feels* to be pregnant.'

Dominic was filled with compassion. 'That's true. I can only imagine, and sympathise. Very much so. It's a terribly painful choice, Joanna, but you must deal with the reality of your sister's predicament.'

'I'm not the only one in the world with two kidneys,' Joanna burst out. 'Dr Mack said the same thing last time, but he came up with something. Couldn't Nadine be given a kidney that would last a year? Even six months? By then she could have mine.'

'It's not that simple. There needs to be a minimum of histocompatibility, and Nadine is difficult to match. Dr Mack can't put her through major surgery and sew in a kidney that he knows in advance will probably be rejected, can he?'

'Of course not,' Joanna cried, 'but he doesn't even see me as a person. Or my sister either. She's sick kidneys, I'm well kidneys. He's simply inhuman.'

'I think he's all too human. He wants to keep people alive the only way possible. Twenty years ago almost all people who had irreversible renal failure died. So now, when it's in his power to save a life – '

'He's willing to sacrifice another life? If I end this

pregnancy I'll never have another child, I just know it. Especially with only one kidney.'

'That's not necessarily true. With one kidney you would be able to conceive as well as with two, and carry to term.'

'Then why can't they take one kidney now and leave me my baby?'

'Because any major surgery is too dangerous, especially to the embryo.' He repeated what Mack had told her weeks ago.

'Joanna, your miscarriages could have been caused by any number of factors. One possibility is an unknown genetic incompatibility with your husband. The fact that this pregnancy is normal would bear that out.'

'I can't think of possibilities now. All I can think of is this child growing within me. Not an it, a she. I feel it's a girl, and –'

'Please, Joanna.'

'No! No, I can't. It's not your child we're talking of killing.'

A tremor of pain flitted across Dominic's features and Joanna saw that she had trespassed on a private sorrow. 'Oh, Dominic, I'm so sorry,' she cried. 'I had no right. I hardly know what I'm saying.'

'I understand.' He expelled his breath sharply. 'Can't you reach Lud? If you discuss it, the two of you –' He broke off, the words sticking in his throat.

'Lud wants this baby as much as I do.'

'Even so, don't you think he has a right to know the facts and to share in your decision?'

Joanna nodded. She was remembering Lud, patting her stomach, joking about Esmeralda.

'No matter what he says, I can't do it, Dominic, I just can't. I'd feel like a murderer.'

'And if your sister dies?'

'She won't. I don't believe it. Dr Mack's a magician. He can pull kidneys out of a hat. I think it's now a moral question with him, accusing me of feminist chic. He doesn't know anything about me or Lud, or how very much he wants this baby.'

Dominic looked piercingly at Joanna. 'Are you afraid that if you don't have the baby, Lud won't want you?'

When Joanna Magid became pregnant for the third time she was full of optimism. Although Ben remained sceptical, he perked up and was kinder to her than he had been since her second miscarriage.

The morning of Ben's thirty-first birthday, he reacted to her kiss of congratulations by grunting that he didn't want any fuss. Joanna's idea of a birthday celebration was for her and Nadine and their husbands to go to the theatre and then a really good restaurant, but she knew better than to force her wishes on Ben.

He didn't much like Nadine, and he was very resentful of Joanna's closeness with her. Yet, when Joanna tried to get close to him he held her at emotional arm's length.

The most Ben would permit in the way of a birthday celebration was a quiet dinner at home for just the two of them.

On her lunch hour, Joanna picked up her gift, a wallet embossed with his initials in gold. The wallet contained slots for his credit cards and a writing pad because he was always jotting down bits of formulae in connection with his hobby of inventing.

The housekeeper had done the shopping and set the table. Joanna had only to arrange the fresh flowers and put out the pâté, toast, and champagne.

Ben announced his arrival from the hall and went to the bathroom to wash. Joanna was hoping he would come into the living room immediately after but she heard him going towards the bedroom.

She followed slowly, trying to contain her disappointment.

'Hello, dear,' he said, giving her a perfunctory kiss. 'Everything okay?' He meant the baby.

'Yes, fine. Are you going to change your clothes before dinner?'

'Of course. I always do.'

'But today is special.'

'To you, maybe, not to me.'

'Ray called to wish you a happy birthday. I think he and Judy would like to come by, maybe for coffee – '

'I'd rather not. My brother will only bore us with his political shenanigans, and Judy talks nonstop about her boys as if nobody else ever had children.'

Joanna sighed. 'It's your birthday, your choice.' Still, she felt a little bad. She liked Ray and Judy and their kids. Maybe if Ben had his own son to boast about . . . Joanna was ashamed to admit to herself that she was hoping for a boy because she sensed that a daughter, after all this time, wouldn't please her husband quite as much as a son.

Ben put on old clothes and finally went with Joanna to the living room. He sat down on the couch, regarding the pâté, the champagne cooling in the bucket, and the gift on the cocktail table. 'Such a fuss over a birthday,' he grumbled, smiling tightly.

Unlike most people Ben looked best with his face in repose because his smile was so pained it seemed to Joanna more of a grimace.

'It's not as if I didn't have a birthday every year,' Ben continued. 'I told you not to make a big production out of it.'

Joanna put her arms around him. 'I know you never had birthday parties as a boy and I think that's pretty terrible. If I want to fuss over you a little, why can't I?' She kissed him, getting no response.

'We're soon going to have plenty of expenses without throwing money around on – my God, Mumm's. Really, dear, I guarantee that if you did a blindfold taste test you wouldn't be able to tell this stuff from Taylor's. Well, this isn't bad,' he granted, chewing on the toast smeared with pâté that she had put into his mouth.

'Come on, admit you like it,' she said, smiling at his obvious pleasure.

'Sure I like it, but I also like plain liverwurst.'

Joanna, eating her own portion and holding out her glass

217

for champagne, didn't reply. She had never been able to understand Ben's stinginess. He objected to living off her money so would accept from her only as much as he put into their joint account. In fact, they would have been able to manage beautifully on his assets, both from his job and from various inventions. The most recent was an anti-shoplifting device consisting of an invisible substance stamped on an ordinary tag affixed to the product. If a customer tried to leave with the goods, bypassing the sales clerk, an electronic buzzer was set off at the door. For this invention, Ben had been paid half a million dollars. Yet, he insisted that Joanna buy no-name brands of everything from soap to soup, and he always decanted cheap scotch, wine, and brandy into crystal containers, claiming that nobody could tell the difference. Joanna could and so could people like Winnie and her brother-in-law Carl. However, she had learned early in her marriage that it was fruitless to argue with her husband.

'Aren't you going to open your present?'

Gingerly he removed the paper and took out the wallet, turning it over and over, examining the compartments, noting the perforated paper on the writing pad for easy removal.

'This must have cost a fortune.'

'Oh, Ben! Can't you just say "Thank you." Try it,' she teased.

He made a face at her. 'Okay, thank you. It's nice, but I could have done with something half as fancy.'

The champagne made her more expansive and him more withdrawn. Instead of coming into the kitchen to talk while she cooked, he began to read a technical journal.

Joanna sighed. Ben just wasn't the kind of man who rose to occasions, she thought, spooning saffron rice into the serving dish and topping it with shrimp in butter sauce.

'Dinner,' she told him, on the way to the dining room.

As usual, when she cooked, tasting and worrying to get things just right, by the time she sat down she had little appetite left.

218

'You're hardly eating,' he observed. 'That's not what the doctor ordered. Have you been sick today?'

'No, I'm fine.' She put a shrimp in her mouth, containing her disappointment that he hadn't commented on the dish. She knew if she asked him how he liked it he would say, 'Not too bad. Reasonably edible.' That was his little joke.

She had always tried so hard to please him. In the beginning of their marriage he had been quite agreeable and although his was not a demonstrative nature, she felt that he loved her. Why else would he have married her? Certainly he hadn't been after her money.

She had noticed a falling off of his interest after each miscarriage. The sex would be almost non-existent for a while, until he gradually worked up to their customary twice a week.

Joanna was trying her best to eat her dinner but her tastes had become quirky. Anything rich didn't appeal and the shrimp had been for him. Now, it seemed, neither of them was particularly happy about her choice.

'You aren't going to leave all those shrimps, Joanna. At these prices? You should hear my brother talk about the cost of raising three boys, how much they eat, how expensive their clothes are, and doctors and now nursery school for Bucky . . .'

The more Ben said, the worse Joanna felt. She was going through agony to have just one baby, and he was talking about having three, as though that were their plan too. It made her terribly anxious.

After dinner Ben turned on the television to watch *MASH* and he laughed at almost everything. Although Joanna tried to enjoy it with him, she felt she might just as well not have been in the room.

Joanna's hope that Ben would want to make love that evening rapidly evaporated. When they had first been married, a couple of glasses of champagne would have had him dragging her into the bedroom. But that had been eight years ago.

219

If only everything went well with this pregnancy. If only it was a boy, big and healthy and the image of Ben.

The bell rang, making them both jump. 'Who can that be? You didn't tell Ray to come by, did you?'

'Of course not. I wouldn't do that without checking with you.'

But it *was* Ray, with his wife and their oldest son.

'We're not staying,' Ray said. 'Bucky just wanted to give his Uncle Ben a present himself.'

Five-year-old Bucky, grinning with importance, held out a package that obviously contained a book.

'Thanks,' Ben mumbled, not sounding very gracious. He could barely look at the child and Joanna was struck for the first time by the disturbing thought that Ben might not really like any of his nephews.

Although she wanted to offer their guests coffee, a drink, something, she feared that Ben would be furious. The three guests, standing around in their coats watching Ben unwrap his present, caused Joanna acute embarrassment.

'Sit down for a minute,' she said finally. 'Bucky, do you want a cookie?'

'Birthday cake,' the boy replied, grinning at her.

She hugged him. He was so adorable. 'I'm sorry but there isn't any. Your Uncle Ben doesn't like birthday cake.'

'Uncle Ben doesn't like birthdays,' Ray added without rancour. He was a state senator. Two years younger than his brother, Ray actually looked older because he was balding and growing paunchy. There was no resemblance, physical or otherwise, between the brothers.

Ben glumly thanked his relatives for the book, a big expensive one about sports, the sort of thing he would never have bought for himself.

After a few moments, Judy, exchanging a glance with Ray, stood up and took Bucky's hand.

Joanna felt mortified.

'Don't you think it would have been nice, Ben, as long

as they took the trouble to drop in with a present, to offer them coffee?'

'No, I don't,' he snapped coldly. 'You're all over the place, the hostess with the mostest. That's not your job right now. Your job is to produce a child.' Ben stopped, practically choking with anger, walked into the spare bedroom and shut the door.

Joanna remained in the living room, crying quietly. Did Ben want the child for its own sake, as she had always assumed? Or did he need a child to show his brother he was as good, and as manly?

She cried herself to sleep. Towards morning she awoke violently ill. It was the start of the old symptoms. Unable to sleep every night, sick every morning, wretched most of the rest of the time.

Three weeks later she lost the baby.

One month afterwards she lost her husband.

Ben stood at the door, all his bags packed, saying coldly, 'There's something wrong with you. I can't keep going through this year after year. As far as I am concerned, a childless marriage is a pointless marriage.'

Dominic could have kicked himself for adding to Joanna's upset by his impertinent question. He was surprised when she made an attempt to answer it.

'I suppose I'm particularly sensitive because my miscarriages drove my husband away. Immediate cause, anyway. But my relationship with Lud is very different.'

There was a pause.

'You think I should have an abortion, don't you?' Joanna's voice was calm, but she trembled inside. Dominic was a rational man, unlike her sister's mercurial, prejudiced doctor.

Dominic thought about her question, looking down at his hands in his lap. His watch was ticking away, second by second. Seconds in which Nadine's body was accumulating fluids and wastes, with no means of cleansing her blood. A transplant was the only way, and soon.

That was the professional judgement of Dr Dominic

221

Graham. But Dominic the man was more than a little fond of Joanna and at bottom didn't want her to have Lud's baby. This was the first time he had been able to admit it. Was Dr Graham being prevented from thinking of other possibilities besides abortion because Dominic had a personal feeling for Joanna?

He diagnosed himself as unfit to make an ethical judgment.

Joanna, watching his face, suddenly gleaned that in this particular case the level-headed English doctor might very well be prejudiced – especially if he had a long-standing infatuation for her sister.

'You – you can't advise me, can you?'

He lifted his head and regarded her sadly. 'No.' His voice was barely a whisper. 'No, I can't. I'm sorry.'

Joanna nodded. 'Thanks for talking to me.'

Nadine had been moved out of Intensive Care back to the kidney unit. She was out of immediate danger from her burns. Otherwise, her condition was unchanged.

The nurse allowed Joanna to visit for a few minutes. She sat mutely by the bed as her sister slept, her eyes filling every few moments.

What was she to do? What in the world was she to do?

24

Joanna's father and aunt were sitting in the waiting room outside the kidney unit. Joanna embraced them, shocked and pained at how much her relatives had aged. Her father looked like a fugitive from an old Hollywood Western. Strands of long white hair escaping from his Stetson made his wizened face seem even more shrunken. He sported cowboy boots under an ancient black suit shiny with wear.

Sally looked her sixty-four years. Her parchment skin was finely lined and she, too, seemed to have shrunk. Although her Nieman-Marcus suit and blouse were expensive, they didn't fit well. She looked like a farm woman wearing hand-me-downs.

'Did Dr Mack send for you?'

'No, Naddie did. Only yesterday she called us on the phone,' Sally explained. 'She sounded so unhappy we got the first plane we could.'

Yesterday. Before the accident, obviously. Joanna realised how panicky Nadine must have felt to get the family here. The sisters had always tried to keep their folks from unnecessary worry.

'We've been praying for Nadine's recovery,' A.W. said. 'We're still praying, which is more than you do, I reckon. What's this I hear about y'all being in the family way and with no husband?'

Joanna flushed.

'Lordy, A.W., can't you let our gal catch her breath before you start lecturing her?'

'No, I can't.' At seventy-five, A.W., in spite of his thin, frail appearance, had lost none of his irritable energy. 'This is serious business. The way you and your sister live, it's

223

no wonder the Lord brings misfortune on the whole family. She, getting divorced and taking the kiddies away from their daddy. And you, also divorced. The only two in the history of the Lennox family. And now y'all got yourself in trouble. Is this what you learned in church and Sunday school? To shame yourself and your family?'

'A.W., there's no use going on like that.'

'I'll tell you what did it,' A.W. continued, raising his voice. 'That durn-blasted college education, that's what. They were decent girls before they started thinking they were smarter than everyone else.'

'Will you hush now, A.W.? The point is that Naddie needs a new kidney and she needs it immediately. And the only way she's going to get it is if Jo –'

'But I can't,' Joanna interrupted quickly. 'Another donor can be found, I just know it. Dr Mack said the same thing last time.' She described the fiasco of the German kidney.

Aunt Sally listened with pursed lips. 'I know all that but you aren't thinking straight, Jo. He used up his chances, can't you see that? Anyway, your kidney is still best because you're twins.'

'Please, please, Aunt Sally, Daddy, please don't tell me to kill my baby!'

'I don't hold with abortions,' A.W. said grimly. 'I also don't think doctors have a right to mess around with folks' insides. Not when they go this far. Taking a kidney from one, giving it to another. That's playing God and I'm against it.'

'Y'all are talking foolish, A.W., like some born-again Christian.'

'Sal, you're rilin' me,' he shouted. 'I was born a Christian the first time around, hear? I know what's right and what's wrong!'

'Don't you understand that Naddie's fixing to die unless she gets a new kidney?'

'Aunt Sally, if it were anything but this baby! I'm going into my fourth month. She – she feels alive to me. It's the first time I've ever held this long. With Ben I miscarried three times before the fourth month.'

'Three times? Mercy. You only told me once.'

'I didn't want to upset you. There was nothing you could do. But now, when I've been waiting so long –'

'Waiting, have you?' her father interrupted harshly, 'but not waiting until you were wed again!'

Joanna looked at her father guiltily. 'We probably will get married, eventually. Please try to understand, Daddy. The father of my child is a wonderful man, and he wants the baby –'

'Wonderful! How dare you say that, when he's willing to bring a bastard into this world! Anyway, from what Nadine tells us about him, he's too fancy to get wed. A big television director playboy.'

Joanna felt the resentment rising. '*She* tells the truth and *I* lie, right?'

'She doesn't sass me like you've always done.'

'She doesn't have to because you've always taken her part. You've always loved Nadine better, both of you,' Joanna whispered, looking from her father to her aunt.

'That isn't true,' Sally said, genuinely surprised.

'It is. Even though you could hardly tell us apart you got her believing she was weak and I was strong. What if the situation were reversed? What if I were the one who needed a kidney? Poor Naddie would be too weak, wouldn't she? You wouldn't expect it of her, would you?'

'Jo, I'm real shocked to hear you say that. With the Lord as my witness, I love you both the same. Your daddy does too.'

'I can't listen to any more.' A.W. stood up. 'I've got an aching head like a rattler was putting the squeeze on it. I'm going to find a church to pray in.'

Aunt Sally looked after him, shaking her head. Then she turned to Joanna. 'I guess I made some mistakes, but I never meant to do anything but my very best by both of my gals.'

Tears came to Joanna's eyes when she saw how hurt her

225

aunt was. 'I'm sorry, Aunt Sally. I know you did your best. I'm just so upset over everything.'

Sobbing, she rushed into her aunt's arms. Sally held her, patting her head. 'I bet you didn't sleep hardly at all last night and what you have to decide is real hard, but Jo, I don't think you have a choice. And believe me, gal, I'd be saying the same to Naddie if it were you lying in that bed.

'Look, Jo, I'm not smart like y'all. I've got no education but I know some things. When my Charlie was going overseas I knew he might never come back. Don't you think I wanted us to be as close as we could? Well, I didn't do it because it wasn't right. All these years, whenever I wondered if I'd have been comforted having his child, I always said to myself that I did right not to go against the Lord. And that's the way I still feel. I don't see any joy in having a child without a daddy. And how much joy are you going to get if you lose your twin?'

Joanna had no answer. She bent her head and wept.

Aunt Sally patted her shoulder. 'Don't fret so. Maybe there's another way. I didn't want to tell you before I knew for sure, but in fact I'm going to be tested to see if I'd be a good match for Naddie. If I am, I'll give her my own kidney.'

Joanna caught her breath. 'Oh, Aunt Sally, it could be so dangerous at your age.'

Sally held her off. 'Then what are you suggesting we do, gal? Wait until it's too late?'

Joanna went home to lie down. She was feeling wretched. All afternoon she kept hoping that Lud would call, but he didn't. She phoned the hospital. There was no change in Nadine's condition.

Too restless to stay at home, Joanna took a taxi to Omega. It was almost five. She hoped she would be able to catch Winnie before he left.

'Hey, babe, just tried to reach you,' Winnie greeted her. 'Lud phoned about fifteen minutes ago with the message that everything's fine, and the rough cut is brilliant. He and

Storman are editing it.' Winnie was consulting a hastily scribbled note. 'He said not to worry if you didn't hear from him for a day or two. He's going up to San Francisco, but he should be back here next week.'

'Oh, God.' Joanna sank into a chair and put her head in her hands.

'Any trouble between you two?'

She shook her head and told him about Nadine.

Winnie was appalled. 'I don't know what to say, babe.'

'And I don't know what to do. Even if Aunt Sally is a good match, I'm afraid her age would make the operation too dangerous. Oh, Winnie, if only I knew what to do!'

He peered sadly at her over his glasses. He would need the wisdom of a Solomon to advise her. Dr Mack had already cried wolf and yet had found a kidney. Doctors weren't infallible. He had two sick parents to prove it. But still, doctors knew more than laymen.

'Thanks for listening, Winnie. I have to think it out for myself. If only I hadn't missed Lud.'

Winnie thought she should call Storman's office and leave an additional urgent message, which she did. Unfortunately, his secretary didn't think her boss could be reached until the next day in San Francisco.

Winnie patted her arm. 'Stop in and say hello to Abby. She's working like a dog, designing the jacket for the Belgium book.'

Joanna had a spurt of nostalgia for her old job, her old life. Imagine having nothing more pressing to think about than designing a book jacket.

Winnie walked with Joanna to the door, his arm around her shoulders. He was very subdued. 'I'll talk to you tomorrow, babe. Try to take it easy.'

Winnie shut his door and picked up the phone.

Abby, bent over her drawing board, was chewing a lock of her hair while she concentrated. She looked up to see Joanna standing in the doorway. 'Hey, how nice to – what's happened?'

227

'Everything.'

Abby listened, horrified. 'Oh, that's so awful. Did you speak to Dominic?'

Joanna nodded. 'He can't help. Nobody can, except someone with the right kidney.'

Abby looked at her with compassion. 'I'm just on my way home. Why don't you come too and have dinner with me and my date? Nobody special. Last year's hunk, who moved to Chicago. He's been here for a week and we've mostly eaten out so I thought I'd cook for him tonight.'

Joanna smiled wanly. 'Thanks, Abby, but I'm not in a social mood. And I couldn't eat anything.'

'Sure you could. I haven't quite worked out the menu yet.' Abby put on her jacket and linked arms with Joanna. 'I've cooked for so many men I lose track of who likes what. Remember my Greek friend, Costa? He wouldn't eat anything with butter, cream, or mayo. Stan liked butter but hated olive oil and marge. Frank was allergic to shellfish. Chris turned as green as an avocado if he ate one, and what's-his-face, last month, hated garlic and loved onions. Or was it the other way around?'

Joanna began to laugh, and then to sob.

Abby, concerned, offered to cancel her date and keep Joanna company at home.

She kept shaking her head, feeling it was cowardly to have blurted out her problems to her friends. It was her decision, hers and Lud's. She was just making Abby feel bad.

Telling her she would be fine, Joanna joined the throng of people leaving their offices on this beautiful, soft May evening.

Her chest was heavy with anguish. From a pay phone she called the hospital. No change. Then she called Nadine's house. Her aunt answered sounding let down. She had been tested and found not to be a good match.

Joanna hung up feeling as if she were going to crack into little pieces. She couldn't think straight. If only she could talk to Lud. Just hearing his voice would be so comforting. She simply didn't feel real.

228

Her head was in a muddle. She kept hearing Lud singing, 'Joanna and me, and baby make three.' How could she do away with their child?

The next moment she had a picture of Nadine in bed, pale, puffy, bandaged, deathly ill. How could she refuse to save her sister?

Winnie sat in the hospital waiting room chewing hard on a piece of gum, trying to stop himself from shaking.

When he was ushered into Mack's office he was still not in control.

'Irwin Kranick,' he said nervously, holding out his hand.

Mack, looking curiously at him, shook his hand and found the palm moist.

'What is your relationship to Mrs Barrett?'

'Uh, no blood relationship. Her sister, Joanna Lennox, has been my art director at Omega Publishing for ten years.'

Mack put down his pen. 'The chances of an unrelated person being compatible with the patient are miniscule.'

'I realise that, but I want to be tested.'

'When was the last time you had a physical, Mr Kranick?'

'I have a checkup every six months. So it would have been in January. I'm healthier than I look,' Winnie assured him. 'My blood pressure is 130 over 70. Pulse rate, generally 70.'

Mack took the man's history, knowing it was practically pointless. When he was through, he looked at the quaking, sweating man in front of him and didn't know whether to yell at him to go home or pin a medal on him.

'Are you sure?'

'I'm sure. I'm scared to death but that doesn't mean I won't do it. This is a terrible business, I know. I had an uncle on dialysis for several years and I was tested as a donor for him. So let's proceed, please.' Winnie sat up straight in his chair, his voice strengthened by dignity.

Mack was touched. Joanna was pregnant by another

man she was apparently crazy about, and this unromantic-looking fellow was offering to make a terrific sacrifice to keep her from losing her baby. That was the kind of unselfish love Mack could respect. He buzzed his nurse.

Nadine slept on and off, each time waking and feeling an immediate, excruciating panic to find herself trussed up, her skin burning, her back aching, and remembering what had happened to her.

She tried to talk to the nurse, who kept checking her condition, but she was so weak she found it difficult to get any words out.

At intervals, the nurse injected Nadine with painkillers. It was all happening to someone else. Nadine was acting the part of a critically ill woman, but before the end of the story, there would be a miracle. The doctor would save her, or a new medicine, just invented... She fell asleep again, awaking to see Dr Mack's face peering at her.

Suddenly she knew that this was real. She was dying. In her delirium she felt that it would be better to die. Actually, she should never have been born.

When Aunt Sally came to stay with them, after the twins' mother had died, Nadine was glad, but also a little afraid of the aunt she hardly knew.

One day, going in search of her doll, she saw it half-crushed against the back of a chair a neighbour lady was sitting in. Nadine hesitated. Her mother had taught her that it was rude to ask grownups to move, even if they were in the way of your toys.

Nadine decided to wait for her sister. Maybe if they both asked...

Aunt Sally and the neighbour were talking about how the twins' mother had died in childbirth. Nadine, like Joanna, was still getting over the shock of learning that babies, like farm animals, came out of their mothers' stomachs.

'Poor Kathy wasn't meant to have any more babies,' Aunt Sally was saying. 'Doc Brady told her it might kill her. But my brother wanted a son. See, when the twins were coming Doc Brady didn't know there were two of them. Jo came first and she was real tiny, six pounds. But Kathy was still hollering so Doc took another look. Lordy, there was Naddie trying to get out. She weighed only five pounds seven ounces. Anyway, twins were too much for poor Kathy. They wore her out, and she was never the same again. Doc should've gone into Kathy's belly with a knife.'

Nadine, hidden from the grownups, leaned against the door jamb sucking her thumb. The words 'should've gone into Kathy's belly with a knife' scared her. Did Aunt Sally mean that the doctor should have killed Nadine? Was it her fault that her mother had died? Joanna came first, so she wasn't to blame.

Nadine didn't tell her sister what she had overheard. She was too scared. Instead, she began to mind her aunt and her daddy a lot more. She smiled a lot and was a good girl so that they would love her and wouldn't send her away for her wickedness.

When her phone rang Joanna jumped. A man's voice said, 'Joanna?'

'Oh, Lud, I've been trying to reach you – '

'It's Carl. I'm calling from Palm Beach.'

Tears of disappointment filled her eyes. 'Yes, Carl. Yes, I've been to the hospital. Nadine is very sick.'

'That's terrible. What are you going to do?'

'I don't know. I'm waiting to hear from – from the baby's father. And I'm praying the doctor will find another donor.'

Before Carl could comment, Joanna heard shouting, and the next minute Kate was on the phone.

Joanna took a deep breath. 'Hello, Katie, are you having fun?'

'Oh, yes. We go swimming and everything.'

'How's Jeff?'

'He's okay. He's eating supper. I'm waiting for my soup to get warm.'

231

'You mean cool, darling.'

'No, I don't. My soup is hot now, and I'm waiting for it to get warm.'

'Oh, I see.' Joanna, overcome by emotion, had to put her hand over the mouthpiece so that Kate wouldn't hear her sobs.

Jeff came to the phone, and finally Joanna spoke to Carl again. He was planning to bring the children home the next day.

'That will be fine because my father and aunt are at Nadine's and would love to see them.'

When Joanna hung up she was on the edge of hysteria. How would she ever face Kate and Jeff if she let anything happen to their mother?

Joanna phoned Mack's private number.

'No, no change as yet. But she'll grow weaker, and by tomorrow – '

'Isn't there a kidney that could be transplanted temporarily, one that would last just until – '

'No! For God's sake, if there were I'd be in surgery now.'

'Then take my kidney, but without sacrificing my baby. At least it would have a chance.'

'No, I don't think it would. I can't accept such a responsibility. What if it were born damaged?'

Joanna's teeth were chattering. 'I can't reach the baby's father. I don't know what to do.'

Mack wished he could slap some sanity into her. 'What can I say that I haven't already said? Believe me, I'm doing everything I can. I have an international call out for a kidney, but our chances are almost zero. Unfortunately we struck out on your aunt and on Mr Kranick.'

'Who?'

'Kranick. Your boss. Came in offering to be a donor. I knew there wasn't a hope, but we tested him anyway.'

Joanna was struck dumb. Winnie had offered a kidney to her sister!

Joanna hung up the phone and crept under the covers of her bed. She was trembling with cold, even though she had her clothes on. Curling herself up tightly, she shut her eyes. If only she could sleep for a little while.

Hours later she awoke with a start, bathed in perspiration. It was pitch dark, and her heart was hammering against her ribs. For a moment she didn't know where she was, or who she was.

And then it struck her.

Winnie had offered to give his kidney to Nadine. To her sister, someone he hardly knew.

Winnie was a stranger. Joanna was Nadine's TWIN, closer to her than anyone else on earth.

Joanna got out of bed and picked up the phone. Immediately she put it down.

'Oh, God,' she cried. 'Oh, God!' Nadine was dying, she knew it.

She pulled on her coat and ran out of the apartment. When she was halfway down the stairs she thought she heard her phone ringing but there was no time to go back.

25

The streets were deserted, as in a nightmare. Joanna ran into an apartment building on Seventy-second Street and accosted the doorman. 'Get me a taxi, please. My twin sister is dying!'

The doorman loped into the street, blowing his whistle. A taxi with its off-duty sign on slowed when the doorman stepped into the gutter waving his arms.

Joanna shoved a five-dollar bill into the doorman's hand and got into the taxi. Within minutes she was at St Anne's.

She flew past the guard and the nurse at the front desk and into the elevator.

Nadine's night nurse jumped up as Joanna rushed in. The nurse was flustered. She had dozed off, just for a moment.

'Dini!' Joanna threw herself on her sister's bed.

The nurse, looking at her patient, saw that she had grown worse.

'Do something!' Joanna shouted. 'Call Mack.'

While Joanna knelt at Nadine's side the nurse gave her an injection and ran for help.

'Dini!' Joanna held her sister's hand tightly and willed life and strength into her.

Nadine opened her eyes. 'Jan?'

'I'm here. I won't leave you.'

'I'm leaving you,' Nadine whispered, her eyes glittering.

'You mustn't! I'll do it! As soon as Mack comes –'

Nadine shook her aching head. 'It wasn't meant to be. I wasn't meant to be.'

'Dini, don't talk nonsense. Don't talk at all.'

Nadine's hot hand moved in Joanna's icy one. 'Do you remember Miss Nason?'

Joanna nodded, jolted by the same memory.

Joanna and Nadine sat next to each other in high school biology listening to Miss Nason talk about conception and birth, and in that connection, twins.

She explained the difference between fraternal and identical twins, and that the first type was more common. On the blackboard she demonstrated the way more than one ripened egg cell could be fertilised by different sperm, forming fraternal twins who would be no more alike than ordinary siblings. However, if a single egg split in two after fertilisation, identical twins resulted.

'At the beginning there are usually two placentas. But as the foetuses grow there's a constant struggle for nourishment and jockeying for space. The placentas are so pushed together that they fuse, and towards the end of the pregnancy most twins are sharing one placenta.'

Everyone in the class kept turning to look at the Lennox twins.

Fern Brunner raised her hand. 'You know, I always thought that I had a twin sister. When I was real little I used to imagine she had been kidnapped and was growing up far away, and some day we'd meet.'

Miss Nason nodded at her. 'That's quite a common feeling, and it may even be based on a truth. It may be that although two embryos start to develop, one is reabsorbed by the mother's body and only one baby is actually born.'

Nadine, trying to take notes, found her hand faltering. She didn't dare look directly at Joanna at that moment, but could see, from the corner of her eye, that her sister wasn't writing in her notebook either.

A warm flush suffused Nadine. She was the smaller one, the one that shouldn't have been born.

'Oh, Dini!' Joanna cried. 'I remember feeling terrible about being bigger! I wondered if it was because I had

235

taken some of your share of the placenta, and of the nourishment. If that was why I was stronger than you.'

'I wasn't meant to be,' Nadine repeated in a whisper. 'Twins are bad luck. The Haida Indians kill one.'

Joanna ran into the hall and learned that Mack was on his way.

She returned to her sister.

'Jan,' Nadine whispered feverishly. 'I killed Mommy.'

Joanna gasped and took her sister's hand. Nadine was simply delirious. In a faraway whisper, Nadine described overhearing their aunt telling about the twins' birth.

'Aunt Sally meant a Caesarian, of course. Anyway, it hardly mattered which of us was born first. For that matter, I was bigger and could have caused more damage than you did.'

Nadine was silent, and Joanna didn't know if she had heard or been able to understand.

If only Mack would get here! Joanna crouched over her sister, kissing her forehead, stroking her cheek. Now Joanna could understand why Nadine had never been able to talk about their mother's death. Her terrible secret had caused her to become goody-goody in order to compensate, making Joanna resentful of the greater attention Nadine received from everyone.

Nadine's breathing became heavier. She slipped into unconsciousness.

'Oh, God, no!'

Two nurses and an intern hurried into the room wheeling equipment.

Gently the intern pulled Joanna away from the bed. 'You must leave now.'

'I can't. I can't let her die.'

'We're doing everything we can.'

Joanna saw Mack get out of the elevator. 'You must save her! I'll have the abortion! I'll have it right now and give her my kidney.'

He nodded and hurried past her.

Joanna was led to the waiting room by a nurse and

236

persuaded to lie down. She shut her eyes, gradually feeling calmer.

When Joanna woke Mack was standing beside her.

'Nadine's better. As a desperate measure I gave her peritoneal dialysis. That means actually running a catheter through the wall of the abdomen into the peritoneal cavity and flushing out the wastes that way. But we can't do it again, especially with her burns. There's a real danger of peritonitis.'

'Can I see her?'

He hesitated. 'Well, actually Dr Halloran is waiting for you in OB, if you meant what you said about the abortion.' Taking Joanna's hand, Mack looked at her with compassion. 'We're fighting against time, Joanna.'

She looked sadly back at him. 'I'm ready.'

After the abortion Joanna felt sorrowful but calm. The tension she had been under because of the indecision was now relieved. Nothing mattered as much as saving Nadine's life.

Afterwards, Joanna fell into a deep sleep. When she awakened at noon she asked about her sister.

'She's as well as can be expected,' Halloran reported.

'When can we have the operation?'

'That depends on how you're feeling. Tomorrow, maybe, or the day after.'

'As soon as possible,' Joanna said quietly. She never wanted to see Nadine so ill again. 'What sex was the – the embryo?'

'Male.'

She nodded sadly. Her phone rang, and the doctor left the room.

'Sweetheart, what's wrong?' Lud's voice sounded frantic. 'I've been so worried, trying to reach you at home. I called the office and Winnie told me what had happened to Nadine. How is she? How are you?'

Joanna felt drained of all emotion. 'Nadine almost died last night. She must have a new kidney, and mine is the only possibility. Lud, I – I had an abortion this morning.'

'Oh, sweetheart!'

'I had to do it. The embryo was only thirteen weeks old, but Nadine and I have shared our lives for thirty-five years, starting in the womb. I couldn't let her die.'

'I understand, angel. I'm so sorry. But do you feel okay?'

'I'm very sad. Otherwise all right. I tried hard to reach you so you could share in the decision, but we kept missing each other.'

'I know. Never mind. I know you did what you had to do.'

He stopped speaking.

Joanna, listening to the expensive silence, began to tremble. 'Lud, I know this must be a shock.'

'Yes, but I'll get over it. I'm only concerned about you. And Nadine, of course. Try not to worry, sweetheart. I'm sure things will turn out just fine.'

'When will you be back?' Joanna asked in a small voice.

He hesitated. 'Not as soon as I expected. We've been editing like crazy, and finally have something to show. Had to chase up to San Francisco to see someone Ed felt could get us in the door at NBC, and in fact they're interested.'

'Lud, that's wonderful.'

'Tell Nadine the good news. That should cheer her up.'

'I will. We're going to have the operation tomorrow.'

'Good luck, sweetheart. I wish I could be there but it's not possible.'

'Oh.' Lud sounded so remote, so far away. Didn't he realise that if something went wrong he might never see her again?

Another silence took up precious moments. The telephone was a cruel instrument. If only she could see him, feel his arms around her.

Lud, I need you. Somehow she couldn't bring herself to say the words, to beg him.

'I'll be back as soon as I can make it, angel. You're being very brave. Everything will be fine, I know it will. I'll call every day to see how you're doing. Remember that I love you.'

'Whatever that means,' Joanna murmured.

'Of course I love you, baby,' he said, making her wince. 'I'm sorry we lost Esmeralda, but we'll make another one. And just think of the fun we'll have trying.'

Joanna shut her eyes. How could he be so insensitive?

After their conversation she went slowly into the bathroom to wash her face.

The mirror revealed to her that the mother-to-be was no more. Gone was the glow, the anticipation.

Lud had never even asked if their child would have been a girl or boy.

When Lud hung up he wiped his sweating forehead with his palm, as several emotions collided within him. He wasn't going to be a father after all. At least not yet. He felt ashamed of the surge of relief. At the same time he was fearful for Joanna, having to lose a kidney. Although he had planned to come back to New York in a couple of days, he simply couldn't face being there. He had no stomach for illness, for hospitals.

He remembered how terrible it had been when his father, swollen beyond recognition, was dying of sclerosis of the liver. His mother had been in Hawaii with her third husband. Lud, as the only living relative, had had to deal with doctors, nurses, and his impossible parent who had brought the whole business on himself.

As Nadine had done on herself, involving Joanna so unfairly.

Well, he was going to put the whole thing from his mind and concentrate on selling that series. That was the best thing – the only thing – he could do for the twins at present.

*

Nadine woke up, amazed to be alive.

Nurse Robinson smiled at her. 'Feeling better?'

'Yes,' Nadine said, uncertainly. 'What happened, Robbie?'

She explained the peritoneal dialysis.

When Joanna appeared, Nurse Robinson left the twins alone.

'Joanna, I had such a strange dream that you came here in the middle of the night and we talked about Mother.'

'That was real.'

For a moment Nadine studied Joanna's pale, sad face. 'You've lost the baby?'

Her sister nodded.

'Oh, Jan. Because of me, because of the worry –'

'No.' Joanna took a deep breath. 'I've never been able to carry even this long.' She had to conceal the truth from her sister, who was feeling guilty enough.

'Anyway,' Joanna forced herself to smile, 'we're going to be able to bore a lot of people about our operation. It's tomorrow.'

Nadine's face registered panic. Joanna took both her hands and kissed her forehead. 'There's nothing to worry about, dearest. We're going to go through this together, and we have the best chance in the world.'

Nadine grimaced and suddenly turned her head away.

Nurse Robinson bustled in. 'She needs to rest now.'

Joanna went in search of Mack, learning that he was in surgery and expected to be there most of the afternoon. 'Please have him check with me before he speaks to my sister. It's very important.'

Joanna was given a room in the kidney unit and told to remain there for her pre-op workup.

While she was waiting, she phoned Winnie.

'I've rejoined the human race, thanks to you, you sweet, wonderful man. I'll always love you for what you tried to do for me.'

Winnie grew warm with embarrassment. 'I told Dr Mack not to say anything. Seemed pointless, since I wasn't any use –'

'Oh, but you were. Mack had to tell me because I needed to see how childish and unrealistic I was being. You made me feel so ashamed. Especially as Nadine almost died last night.'

Winnie's sensitive ears heard the pain in Joanna's voice. 'You had the abortion?'

'This morning. There really wasn't any choice. I guess I knew it all along. I couldn't have sacrificed Nadine. It would have been like committing suicide.'

Winnie was relieved that Joanna had come to her senses. Then he bristled quietly when she told him Lud wasn't going to be with her for the operation. Increasingly he had felt that Lud wasn't doing right by Joanna.

'How about I drop by later, kiddo? I might even bring over the Belgium material so you can take a peek. No rush, of course. Only when you're feeling up to it. And Joanna? I'm very, very sorry. I know what that sacrifice meant to you.'

'Thanks, Winnie,' she whispered.

When she hung up, she felt restless, unable to concentrate on anything.

How she wished Lud could have flown in even for one day.

Aunt Sally tiptoed into the room and kissed Joanna. 'I saw Naddie and she told me you lost the baby. Poor Jo, it will all be for the best, I'm sure of that.'

Joanna sighed. 'Did you tell Daddy?'

'Not a word. He's in church. Found himself a Baptist preacher and is really going at it. I'm not going to say a thing until the transplant's over. I don't think his heart can take the strain. Better to wait until I can tell him both his gals are okay.'

Joanna remembered that Carl would be bringing Nadine's children home. Sally was very pleased. 'Don't worry, Jo. We're set up just fine, and Mrs Wilson makes us feel right at home. We'll hang around until it's all over and both our gals are strong and well again.'

When Sally had gone, Joanna picked up a deck of cards and laid out a game of solitaire. She was feeling terrible, and part of it was anger. Anger at Lud and even at her aunt. Neither gave a thought to how much she had wanted her baby.

Dominic stuck his head in the door. 'Just thought I'd see how you were.'

'Thanks. Fine.' She kept her eyes on her cards.

'How about some gin?' he asked at her elbow.

'Terrific. Make it with tonic, two cubes, and a twist of lime.'

He smiled. 'I meant a game of gin rummy.'

'No, thanks. I'll play these.' She put the queen of clubs on the king of hearts, only vaguely aware of transferring her resentment towards Lud on to Dominic.

'I see. What's a nasty girl like you doing in a nice place like this, anyway?'

She looked up at him, and suddenly her face crumbled. 'I'm sorry, Dominic.'

The tears began to come, dripping off her cheeks on to the cards.

He took the chair next to hers. 'It's a terrible loss, a terrible disappointment. I know, my dear, I know how much it hurts.'

'One minute I was pregnant,' she whispered, 'and the next I was – empty.'

He sat with her, and she found solace in his presence. At least he didn't drop platitudes to the effect that she would get over it and that there would be other babies.

Dominic had comforted many women in this situation, but it always affected him deeply. He had a personal reason, too. And this was Joanna.

When she glanced at him, she saw the tears in his eyes.

He swiped at them, embarrassed. 'When I was married,' he explained huskily, 'we lost a baby.'

Joanna began to cry again, and this time she surrendered herself to her sorrow and clung to Dominic.

He forced himself to gain control of his feelings, to hold her as a doctor or friend might, and not as a man with his arms around a woman whom he cared for deeply.

What Dominic didn't tell Joanna was that Alexis,

worried about her dancer's figure, had aborted their baby without even consulting him. He had never been able to forgive her.

Of course, Joanna's situation was vastly different. She had had no choice. He had come from seeing Nadine moments before. That Joanna hadn't told her sister the truth only increased his admiration.

Just keep it that way, he told himself sternly.

Halloran gave Joanna a final examination in the morning, and then Dominic appeared. 'You must be bored with doctors, so I'll stay only long enough to wish you good luck.'

Mack grimly pushed his way into the room. 'We're all going to need luck, lots of it,' he bellowed, turning angrily to Joanna. 'Why the hell didn't you tell me you wanted your sister to think you miscarried?'

'Oh, Dr Mack, you didn't tell her the truth! I left word for you to check with me first.'

'Yes, well, I got the message too late. You two are the first twins I ever met who don't tell each other everything.'

'But what's the problem?' Dominic asked.

'The problem, damn it, is that Nadine is refusing her sister's kidney again. She's having hysterics. I'm at my wit's end in this case.'

'Go away,' Nadine greeted Joanna. 'Oh, go away, I can't stand to look at you.'

'Dini, I didn't want to upset you even more by telling you everything. Please understand that I want to give you my kidney because I love you.'

'No!' Nadine cried. 'No! Don't! You can't love me! You won't, after you hear what I've done to you.' Nadine began to sob convulsively, her hands over her face.

26

The day after the sisters' argument, when Joanna and Lud had returned from Hawaii, Nadine went to work, to Fern's surprise.

'Are you well enough?' Fern asked her.

'My laryngitis is better, so I can get some words out today. Otherwise, I feel awful and look it too. Any more questions?'

Fern, who thought Nadine looked all right, realised she must be very depressed to speak to her like that.

Lud was already on the set with the writer and stage designer.

Both women looked towards him. 'Bastard,' Fern muttered. 'He's had himself some fun in the sun, leaving me to do all the worrying. I'd like to wipe that lovesick grin off his face.'

'Me too,' Nadine murmured.

Fern looked guardedly at her. 'It would be for the good of the series and all of us. Because let's face it, Naddie, your sister's got Lud eating out of her hand like he was a pigeon, and we're the ones getting dumped on.'

Careful not to say too much, Fern walked away, leaving Nadine looking thoughtfully after her.

Nadine played her first scene well and Lud was pleased. But during her second scene, she began to falter, and finally she broke down in tears.

'Lud, I can't go on,' Nadine whispered, looking at him balefully. 'I – I know what it will mean if I quit now, but I just can't help it. I'm so miserable.'

Lud called time and took Nadine out for coffee.

She peered at him from a tear-streaked face. 'It's just –

seeing you every day. It's too hard, Lud. I've tried my best, but I just can't.' She broke into fresh tears.

'Nadine, please.'

'You know how much this role means to me, but to be tortured for several more weeks would be unbearable.'

'If you pull out now, it means the end of the series.'

'Don't you think I know that?' Nadine cried. 'It also means the end of me. I've sold almost everything I had to put up the money and if I quit I'll be out a fortune. But I don't know what else to do, Lud. I never thought, when we agreed on the deal, that you and Joanna – ' Nadine, choking on her tears, couldn't go on.

Lud rubbed his hand across his face. 'Nadine,' he said softly, turning his compelling eyes on her, 'try to bear up this afternoon, please, for me. Tonight we'll have dinner, talk.'

Nadine heard the seductive promise in his tone, and she inwardly rejoiced, forcing a tearful little smile. 'I'm not sure I can get through today, but I'll try.'

'That's my girl.' Lud put his hand on her arm and pressed it slightly.

They resumed filming. Wan as Nadine appeared, when the cameras were rolling she acted very well. In fact, she prided herself on being much more of an actress than Lud dreamed.

In the evening Lud, looking dashing in a charcoal suit with a pale grey shirt and a grey-and-red ascot, picked Nadine up in a chauffeur-driven limousine.

Nadine had dressed for the occasion in a Laura Biagiotti dress, unlike anything Joanna would wear, which was precisely why Nadine had chosen it. The two-piece dress was beautifully feminine, leaning towards the demure. Made of white silk jacquard, it had long sleeves, a mandarin neck, and a gold belt that tied in front.

'You look lovely,' Lud said, examining her with an appreciative eye.

She murmured her thanks shyly.

Lud lit a marijuana cigarette, took a poke and handed it to her.

245

She smoked her share and then leaned back, half facing him, so he could see the outline of her breasts against the white silk.

The limousine let them out at the World Trade Center. After a quick ride in the lift to the one hundred and seventh floor, Nadine and Lud were led to a window table of the Hors D'Oeuvrerie.

'How high the moon,' Nadine said dreamily, looking out at it.

'How high Nadine,' Lud joked, making her laugh. He sipped his martini, looking at her with eyes that made her feel she was the only woman in the world.

'Nadine, you have a great future as an actress. Natural talent, to go with the grace and beauty. I've never seen anyone progress from novice to pro in so short a time. I mean that, love.'

She felt an exquisite warmth envelop her, but she remembered to lower her eyes and say shyly, 'That's a wonderful compliment. I'll treasure it. I've always wanted to be an actress, ever since I can remember.'

He nodded. 'Tell me, Nadine,' he murmured, 'tell me about you as a little girl, living on a farm and dreaming about another kind of life.'

'Well, unlike my sister I wasn't very strong. I was more like my mother, fragile and kind of dreamy.' She told him about their poverty, about their first days in front of a camera in the Dallas television studio and how she had loved everything about the experience. Nadine was careful to mention Joanna as little as possible.

Lud ordered a second round of martinis. Nadine talked on, loving the way he sat looking at her and listening attentively.

She crossed her legs and felt her knee touch his. She didn't move her leg away, and neither did he.

Nadine came to the part about switching from drama to art at college, only she made it seem as if it were Joanna's dominant personality that drew her unwillingly from her chosen career, instead of her own dependence.

'It wasn't until I met you, Lud, and you saw my

246

potential, that I began to have any confidence in myself as an actress.'

He smiled at her, a smile that turned her inside out. She had never met a more fascinating man, had never wanted anyone as much as she wanted him.

When Nadine finished her narrative she grew momentarily unsure, and covered it by lowering her head so that she could force tears into her eyes. When she lifted her face, her eyes were glistening, her lips trembling. 'It's been wonderful, working with you, learning from you, but – but – ' She broke off, as a sob rose to her throat.

He reached across the table for her hands. 'There mustn't be any buts, sweetheart. You have what it takes, and I'm here to help it happen. As I helped – ' He named a famous star.

Nadine looked wide-eyed at him. 'I didn't know that,' she lied.

He explained that he had been only an assistant director at that time. Nadine looked raptly at Lud, appearing to drink in every word but actually plotting her next move. After weeks of pumping Fern, Nadine knew everything she needed to know about Lud Haley and his meteoric rise from bit actor to promising director.

Lud had had a three-month affair with the famous star he was telling her about. And now it was Nadine's turn.

'Hungry?' Lud asked, finally.

'I guess so.' Nadine looked lovingly at him, as if she could listen to him talk forever.

When he helped her on with her coat, she leaned against him for a moment, feeling his hands tighten on her arms. She was getting to him.

'Look at the glittering lights of the city imitating the brilliance of the stars,' he murmured in her ear. 'You're going to be up among them, I promise you.'

The limousine drove them to a heliport on East Thirty-Fourth Street.

'I thought it might be fun to ride by helicopter up to Connecticut for dinner.'

'Fantastic.' Nadine felt exhilarated when the rotors

started with a roar, but she feigned fright, grabbing on to Lud as the machine took off straight up like a rocket and banked sharply into a hairpin turn.

The lurching ride gave Nadine the opportunity to press against Lud, to whisper hotly in his ear, to lean her face close to his to hear what he was saying. She looked at him with adoration, keeping her lips moist and slightly parted.

Finally Lud drew her close, pressing his mouth insistently on hers.

She moved out of his embrace, knowing she had aroused him, and pretended to be interested in the landing of the machine.

Lud was quiet in the taxi and even more so in the restaurant.

Outside, Nadine turned to look at him, face upturned, lips waiting. He pulled her into his arms.

They took a taxi to a motel. Nadine, drunk on triumph more than on wine, played her role skilfully, hanging back at first, then gradually throwing herself into lovemaking with passionate abandon.

Over breakfast, Nadine couldn't help throwing him an impudent smile. 'You think I'm wicked, don't you?'

'Wonderfully wicked.' He looked at his watch. 'We'd better hustle, love. We'll be late as it is.'

They returned to New York by helicopter.

Nadine didn't mention quitting again.

On the set Lud treated her very carefully, tempering his criticism with compliments. He didn't want the cast to know about their affair, and Nadine agreed not to rock the boat – not yet, anyway.

Nadine and Lud continued to be together a couple of times a week at his house. Because of the children she returned home to sleep. She and Lud never talked about Joanna. Nadine knew, of course, that he was still seeing her sister but she was sure it was only a matter of time.

Although Nadine had made up with Joanna, she saw little of her sister during this period, out of low-level guilt and because of hard work. This series was going to take off. It had to, or she would be bankrupt.

Nadine anticipated the next stage in her affair with Lud when they went on location in New Hampshire. Here, with almost a week in which to charm him, she would succeed in replacing Joanna.

The first night Lud came to Nadine's room, but the delights she had longed for didn't materialise. He seemed withdrawn and perfunctory. She redoubled her efforts to please him, and it went all right, but only mechanically.

When everything was a disaster the next day, Lud turned totally impersonal and professional again. Nadine began to be anxious.

That night, after waiting in vain for him, Nadine tiptoed to the door of his room. She heard his low, seductive voice, and then a distinctive feminine giggle. Lud was in bed with Lorrie, the ski-lodge owner's daughter.

Nadine told Joanna how she had flirted with Tommy to try one last time to have an impact on Lud. She described her reckless drinking and pot-smoking, her foolish attempt to recapture with Tommy the joy of the helicopter ride she had taken with Lud.

Joanna, white-faced, was sitting tensely at the edge of her chair.

'After the crash, I wanted to tell you about Lud and me, but I just couldn't. And then when I found out you were pregnant –' The tears began again. 'Jan, I'm rotten. I don't want to live. I don't deserve to live.'

Joanna stood up, feeling dizzy. Looking at her sister as if she had never seen her before, she walked out of the room.

'Oh, Mrs Lennox,' the nurse at the desk called, 'Dr Mack wants to speak with you –'

'Later.' Joanna moved like a sleepwalker to the lift.

On the way to her room she saw Halloran conferring with a nurse.

'Not now,' she headed him off. 'Please, not now.'

249

'Are you all right?' he asked, concerned by her expression.

'No, goddamn it, I'm not all right!' She went into her room and slammed the door. Flinging herself on the bed, she lay on her back staring at the ceiling.

The question that rotated in her head was why, why, why? Why had Nadine done it? Lud's motivations were clear enough. He had started out to keep Nadine from quitting. Joanna saw that he would have done anything to prevent that. Nadine had been seductive, as only she could be and apparently Lud was a pushover.

Now Joanna understood his strange behaviour after their return from Hawaii, his neglect of her, his claim to be 'working' too hard to see her very often. The two nights after he had started with Nadine, he and Joanna hadn't made love at all. And then he had cancelled their Friday date. To be with Nadine.

In New Hampshire, he had spent the first night with Nadine, having come from Joanna's arms, after learning he was to be a father.

Joanna's door opened and Mack came through it.

'Not now,' she said morosely.

'When then? Time is running out. Your sister says no transplant, but she's beginning to grow weaker. Damn it, I'm worried, Joanna. If we don't act by tomorrow morning she's going to be very ill again, making the operation very risky.'

'All right. I'll talk to her.' Joanna got up shakily. She had lost her trust in her lover and in her sister, as well as her baby. To lose a kidney now seemed to her almost anti-climactic.

As soon as Joanna approached Nadine's bed, her sister began to sob. 'You hate me, and I don't blame you. I hate myself.'

'No, I don't hate you,' Joanna replied in a flat, sad voice. 'Only what you did. And I don't know why you did it.'

'I don't know either,' Nadine sobbed softly. 'Jealousy, I guess. You've always been better in everything – tennis

250

and swimming and bike riding. Stronger. Good in every subject at school – '

'But you were a better actress. I was jealous of you for that. And for being more popular with boys.'

'That popularity, it was only because I was a phony.' Nadine spoke so low that Joanna had to bend closer to hear her. 'A phony,' she repeated. 'It was important to me to be popular. And when I had to quit acting classes to be with you I learned I had no art talent.'

'Why did you quit?'

'Because I couldn't do without you,' Nadine confessed. 'My dependence made me furious, not only with myself but with you, too. I thought you wanted it that way. Wanted to control me, to take advantage of my weakness.'

'That was never true. I wasn't really any stronger. Plenty of times, when we were little, I was as scared as you but I didn't dare show it because – '

'Aunt Sally wouldn't let you,' Nadine finished. 'I wish I'd known that. I thought you were jealous of my acting talent and kept me dependent so I'd follow you in art, where you could shine.'

'I was jealous of you. I've already said so, but I guess by the time we got to college that ended when I became excited about art. I suppose when sisters, especially twins, are compared, not allowed to be individuals, it leads to misunderstandings. I know Aunt Sally didn't mean us to be this way – '

Nadine burst into tears.

'You must stop upsetting yourself now, Nadine. No matter what you've done, it's over, and this isn't the time to worry about it. We have to prepare for the operation.'

'No, I can't let you,' Nadine cried. 'Because of me you lost your baby. I can't let you lose a kidney. I couldn't go on, if anything happened to you.'

'And I couldn't, if anything happened to you.'

'You could. You're still better at everything, a better actress, even.'

'Don't be silly. It was terribly hard for me.'

'You'd be a better mother to Jeff and Kate.'

'Dini, stop it! Of course I wouldn't. An aunt isn't the same. They need you. Think of that, and forget everything else now, please.'

'I can't. I can't get over what I did.'

'If I can, you can. Lud bears his share of the blame, too. He's been irresponsible to both of us. Hush, dearest, hush.'

'Jan, I don't see how you can forgive me, when I can't forgive me.'

'Because I love you,' Joanna said quietly, her eyes welling. 'The bonds are so strong. I feel your joy and I feel your pain.'

'I deserve to be punished.'

'Don't you think you're *being* punished? God, just look what you've done to yourself.'

'Yes, but I've also done it to you. Oh, Jan, I'm so sorry. And so afraid.'

Joanna lay down on the bed next to her sister and kissed her cheek. 'Whatever happens, it will happen to us together.'

Gradually Nadine's sobs ceased and she became drowsy, feeling like a little girl again. Joanna had forgiven her and would take care of her. She always had.

Abby knocked at Dominic's office door at the hospital. She had her arm through Winnie's.

'Hi, Dom, here we are, ready to give our life's blood.'

He smiled. 'It's very good of you to offer. Probably they won't need it, but someone will. Winnie, do you feel quite up to donating?'

'No,' he admitted, 'but I'll do it anyway. Don't mind me. I always get a little nauseous in hospitals. They're going to be all right, aren't they?' he asked nervously.

'Joanna, undoubtedly. With Nadine there's always a chance of rejection but I believe that's rare when an identical twin's kidney is involved.'

Mack's nurse recognised Winnie and stopped to say

hello. 'I've mailed you the kidney donor card, Mr Kranick.'

Winnie thanked her, looking uncomfortable.

'Winnie!' Abby exclaimed. 'Did you offer to give Nadine a kidney?'

Winnie and Dominic caught each other's eye, and the doctor realised that he and the editor suffered from the same malady in regard to Joanna.

'I had the right blood group,' Winnie mumbled, looking away from both of his companions. 'Anyway, the other factors didn't match.'

Abby hugged him. 'I think you're wonderful.'

Dominic thought so too.

'Cut that out,' Winnie said gruffly. 'If you make a martyr out of me your cousin over there is going to expect me to give a British Imperial pint of blood.'

Joanna and Nadine lay on stretchers side by side, waiting to go into surgery. Both were pleasantly relaxed after their pre-op injections.

Mack appeared. 'We're all set, ladies.'

Nadine eyed him playfully. 'Don't you have to warm up or something?'

'Sure,' he replied, his face deadpan. 'I've just been juggling a couple of kidneys to limber up my fingers. So there's nothing to worry about. I've performed hundreds of transplants. You're going to feel like a new woman shortly, Nadine.' He turned to Joanna. 'And you'll be about a quarter of a pound lighter but otherwise the same.'

'Great. I can stop dieting.'

Mack's face twitched in the approximation of a smile. 'Now, my beauties, we're on our way.'

He walked between them as they were wheeled into surgery. Then he took a hand of each and squeezed.

'Is that my hand shaking or yours?' Nadine joked.

'Yours, of course. I wouldn't let you loose in here with a butter spreader.'

'That's the unkindest cut of all,' Joanna said.

'I save my kindest cuts for the surgery.'

'Dr Mack's not kidding,' Mrs Shaw, the anaesthesiologist, confided as she readied the anaesthetic.

'Only kidneying,' Joanna murmured.

The last thing she remembered was Mrs Shaw's tinkling laughter.

27

'Dr Mack, I'm feeling so much better,' Nadine greeted him from her bed. 'It's wonderful to have a working kidney again. Have I thanked you lately?'

He took her pulse. 'Every day for two weeks, but don't stop. Surgeons need as many curtain calls as actresses.'

As he began to examine her, Nadine winced.

'Hurt?'

'Yeah. Like someone was sticking pins into a pin-cushion.'

'You'll feel that for a while because some small nerves had to be cut when I made the incision.'

'I can stand it. At least my burns are healed. Now all I have to do is hope the kidney won't find its way back to my sister like a homing pigeon.'

Mack actually smiled, and Nadine was pleased. 'Joanna's kidney is doing wonders for my wit. Just think what I could do with her funny bone.'

Joanna, entering the room she was sharing with Nadine, laughed appreciatively. 'Hey, why not take all of me?'

'Cut it out, you two,' Mack demanded, his mouth twitching. 'You're destroying my reputation as a serious surgeon. I'm going to have to let you out of here. Joanna, you're going home tomorrow.'

The twins looked at him anxiously.

'And you,' he said to Nadine, 'are doing fine, but we'll keep you one more week just to make sure.'

Although disappointed, she tried not to show it.

Joanna followed Mack out of the room. 'She's going to be all right, isn't she?'

'I think so. That's all anyone really can say at this point. She has the best possible chance for a normal life.'

'I see. I want to thank you again for everything, Dr Mack. And I apologise for giving you such a hard time.'

'Yes, well, decisions like yours are always tough.'

Joanna, looking uncomfortable for a moment, suddenly thrust a cheque at him, made out to the National Kidney Foundation. She smiled shyly at his look of astonishment. 'We wouldn't like to lose you to hearts, or something.'

'Never fear,' he said gruffly, staggered by the amount she was donating. He put his arm around her shoulder briefly before moving down the corridor.

Dominic entered the twins' room holding a large envelope. 'Nadine, you look better every day.'

'Colour me rapidly recovering. What have my little monsters been up to?'

'This, speaking of colouring.' He showed her the pictures the children had made. 'These are for you, those two for Joanna.' He glanced towards her empty bed.

'She's already recovered. Going home tomorrow, and she'll be staying at my place with the kids. Dominic, thanks a million for stopping by to see them. They always have so much fun with you.'

'No more than I do with them. It's still a flower garden in here, I see. Looks and smells wonderful.'

'Yes, doesn't it. Since we're missing the best part of spring our friends are making sure at least we get some of the flowers that bloom in the season. Let's see, the mums are from Winnie and Abby, the big mixed bunch from the television gang and the roses, from Lud.'

Dominic gloomily regarded the enormous scarlet arrangement next to Joanna's bed, as she returned to the room.

She halted near the door. 'If I'm interrupting I'll come back later.'

'Don't be absurd,' he said crisply. 'You do live here. I came to see both of you and to deliver Kate's and Jeff's latest artistic efforts. Good, aren't they?'

'Oh, yes.' Joanna, studying them, smiled fondly, giving Dominic a pang of longing. Flowers weren't the only thing that bloomed in the spring.

Joanna began to look over some Omega material, but she felt a little uncomfortable. However Dominic might deny it, she was sure he came mainly to see her sister. And he kept visiting the children. He would be a wonderful stepfather, the best possible. In fact, Dominic was a lovely person altogether. He had dropped in to see the twins every day, bringing prettily wrapped delicacies of fruit and nuts and cheering them up with amusing talk.

Joanna's eye fell on Lud's roses. He sent flowers and phoned, but she suspected he wouldn't return to New York until she was out of the hospital.

'What did you make of Daddy and Aunt Sally?' Nadine asked Dominic.

'They were quite friendly and to me, highly interesting. My first real Texans, actually. You two have left most of it behind.'

Dominic remained for a while longer. At the same time he enjoyed being there, he was under a strain to hide his feelings for Joanna.

He didn't know what had been wrong between the sisters. Whatever it was seemed to have been put right and he was glad. At times, though, when Joanna didn't see him looking at her, she went into a brief reverie. He wondered why Lud had not yet come back to New York. If it had been Dominic . . .

When the phone rang, Nadine answered it. 'Hello. Yes, fine, Lud, better every day. She's right here.' Nadine handed the phone to Joanna. Dominic intercepted a strange look between the sisters.

He said goodbye quickly and left, not wanting to hear Joanna talking to her lover.

Idiot. Stop thinking of her in that way.

Nadine slowly got out of bed, put on her robe, and went for a walk. Every time Lud phoned she felt guilty.

Joanna hung up after the briefest of conversations. Lud believed her sister to be present and although she seldom was, Joanna didn't tell him. She couldn't have an intimate talk with Lud long-distance. All the things she had learned about him had caused her emotions to feel encased in cement.

Joanna went in search of her sister. 'May I have this waltz, ma'am?'

'Sure, but make it a minuet. Not that I'm complaining. I'm just glad it's not dance macabre.'

Joanna put her arm around Nadine's waist. 'You'll be doing the hustle in no time. But now, hadn't you better go back to bed?'

'I guess so.'

Joanna helped her sister off with her robe.

Nadine's face was strained. 'Jan, every time I try to thank you –'

'I say you're welcome. That about covers it. You'd have done the same for me.'

'But the point is what you did.'

Joanna sat on Nadine's bed. 'Not so very much, all things considered. Knowing what I now know, the baby wouldn't have been such a terrific idea. As for the kidney, I don't miss it at all. Gives the other lazy thing a chance to show its stuff.'

Nadine, beginning to laugh, wound up in tears.

Joanna held her, patting her shoulder. 'Don't cry, Dini, it's all over now.'

'I'll never be able to forget it,' Nadine sniffled. 'The whole episode with Lud makes me feel so ashamed. I don't know how I could have done such a thing. You know, when Fern first called me and took me to see Lud, she'd talked up the part until I wanted it so badly I was willing to do anything to get it. Like – like sleep with the director. Only he didn't seem to want that. He was very professional, businesslike. He told me that even if I had the right look and the talent, there wasn't any point in testing me because he'd never get backers for an unknown who did some television commercials as a kid.'

'I can understand your excitement, but to go ahead and sell everything and invest so much, without even telling me. Dini, I would have helped you.'

'I know.' Nadine moved away to blow her nose. 'But

I couldn't admit to anyone that it was an ego trip for me, buying my way into the role the way I did. I never even told Fern. Only Lud and Storman knew. And my accountant.'

Nadine began to cry again. 'I've messed up my whole life, and yours, too.'

'Let's forget the past.'

'Not until I tell you everything, Jan. Since the operation I've been thinking about it all and not lying to myself for a change. About Carl, for instance. I used to convince myself that it was already over between you when – when I got involved. But it wasn't, I see that now. You were devastated, and you married Ben on the rebound. That horrible man, who made your life hell with his coldness and stinginess. Every time I think of what you went through with all those miscarriages – '

'Please, Dini, please stop crying.'

'I broke up your romance with Carl and – and as soon as I had him I didn't really want him any more! I hated being the stay-at-home wife, while he travelled everywhere.'

'Then why didn't you go with him?'

'I couldn't,' Nadine cried. 'If I'd gone with him it would have meant leaving you behind. I know it's dumb but I couldn't do it. So I did the only thing I could think of to keep him home. I got pregnant, accidentally on purpose.'

'Oh, Nadine.'

'I know. It was so unfair. Anyway, it not only didn't work, it backfired. Carl began to travel more than ever. There was so much bitterness. And then I got pregnant with Kate. That really was an accident, but Carl stopped sleeping with me. And after Kate was born, he wouldn't. Or couldn't.'

Nadine's face crumbled, and she sobbed uncontrollably. 'My poor children! I've ruined their lives, too. They hardly have a father because he didn't really want them. I think he tries to feel deeply about them but he just can't. That's why he doesn't see them too often.'

Joanna felt a chill up her spine.

'It was such a terrible marriage! Oh, Jan, I've never really been able to love a man. Not even Daddy, after I felt so guilty because of Mom's death. I've always wanted to have every man crazy about me. I suppose I hoped that some day, somehow, I'd be able to feel something real.' She stopped to gulp down her tears. 'Do you know what happens? At first I feel smug, when I get a man interested, and gleeful and triumphant. And then – and then it turns to contempt. Because at bottom I know I'm rotten and I can't respect any man who doesn't think so too.'

Joanna, sitting on the other end of Nadine's bed, felt hot tears sliding down her cheeks, as her sister spilled out her painful confession.

'Jan, I didn't leave Carl. He left me. I lied about it to save face. And not only that. The last thing he said to me before he walked out was that he'd made the worst mistake of his life when he gave you up for me. If that's any satisfaction to you.'

Looking at her sister, so miserable and repentant, Joanna could feel only deep sorrow.

'Oh, my God!' Nadine cried. '*I'm* the one who's been holding Carl against *you* all these years! Because I never really won him and you never really lost him. I've been hating you because of Carl and that must be the real reason I went after Lud!'

28

'Taxi, madam?' Dominic was sitting in his dark green Austin Healey convertible parked in front of the hospital.

Joanna smiled. 'Well, that would be nice, if I won't take you out of your way.'

'No, your way is my way.'

She slipped in beside him. 'It's a beautiful day to be getting out of the hospital.'

'Yes, it is, but don't breathe too deeply, at least not here. The country is the place for that.'

Dominic started the car. 'In fact, I have an old farm near Woodstock. A bit rustic but reasonably comfortable. I'd be so pleased if you and Nadine and the children would spend a weekend there with me.'

He glanced at her, still pale but looking wonderful to him, as her hair blew softly back from her face.

'That's awfully nice of you. I'd like that, and so would they.'

Dominic's spirits lifted. 'The weekend after next would be good. Nadine may still be feeling a bit fragile, so it won't hurt to have a doctor on the premises.'

At Nadine's building, Dominic helped Joanna out and gave her bag to the doorman.

'Thanks for everything,' she said warmly. 'I appreciate how kind you've been to both of us during this crisis, and how wonderful to Jeff and Kate, too.' Impulsively Joanna kissed his cheek.

Dominic returned to his car, smiling ruefully. A kiss to be treasured. One of a kind, no doubt. And yet she had agreed to go away for a weekend. Where was Lud? Still in California?

As Dominic drove away he lectured himself silently. Lud had business on the Coast and Joanna's acceptance of Dominic's invitation didn't mean a thing. She liked him, sure, but only as a friend. God, he was thirty-nine years old, and still he behaved like a fool over a woman he knew loved someone else.

Dominic continued to visit Nadine daily, glad she was doing well and would be released from the hospital on schedule. Also, he was relieved that she had agreed to the weekend in the country because Joanna might have been unwilling to come alone.

Towards the end of the second week Dominic allowed himself the luxury of phoning Joanna to see how she was feeling and to make final arrangements.

She sounded warm, sweet and cheerful. Most important, she actually told him she was looking forward to the weekend.

Dominic hung up, feeling young and foolish and something close to reckless. Although he generally was not given to daydreaming, he couldn't help picturing Joanna on the farm, projecting how he would show her around and somehow contrive to be alone with her part of the time. Imaginary dialogue kept popping into his head. Maybe if she saw him in that setting, when he was at his most relaxed, being truly himself instead of merely Dr Graham, friend of the family . . .

Early Friday afternoon, Dominic parked his rented station wagon in front of Joanna's building. Impatiently he bounded up the steps two at a time.

She was standing in the doorway wearing shorts and a striped T-shirt.

'You look cool and comfortable, as well you should.' He greeted her with a smile, daring to peck her on the forehead.

'Dominic, I tried to reach you before you left the hospital.'

'Oh. I left my beeper behind for the weekend. What's wrong?'

'I'm afraid I won't be able to go after all,' she apologised.

He stiffened with disappointment, barely able to take in her explanation. Following her to the living room, he saw piles of clothes on the sofa and chairs.

Joanna was going to California. That had to be it.

'. . . learned only this morning that Lud is back. I'm sorry, Dominic. I tried to head you off so you wouldn't have to climb all those stairs on such a hot afternoon.'

He took a deep breath. 'That's quite all right.'

Joanna quickly shifted some clothes. 'Excuse the mess.' Someone from the cleaners was supposed to pick up her stuff hours ago. 'Let me get you something cold to drink.'

Dejected, Dominic glanced around the room, noticing that her taste in decor was as excellent as he had imagined it would be.

Joanna returned with two tall glasses of lemonade.

'Thanks.' He managed a faint smile as he took the drink and sipped from it. 'Aha. Not frozen from a tin but the real stuff, just like Mother used to make.' He tried to keep his tone casual, to disguise his agitation.

He might not see Joanna again for years. Maybe never.

Observing her, sitting at the edge of a chair piled with garments, Dominic had a terrible, aching feeling of loss. In spite of all his warning lectures to himself, she had really got to him. Especially in the hospital, when he had seen her at her most vulnerable. He loved her all the more for the honest expression of her grief, for the way she had clung to him, trusting him to soothe her.

Dominic stood up. 'Thanks for the lemonade. I'm disappointed, of course, that you won't be joining me – I – I mean us – after all, but I quite understand.'

What he didn't understand was why she looked so thoughtful, almost abstracted, and not particularly happy. Shouldn't she have been, with her lover back in town?

When she apologised again he decided her discomfort was the result of having taken him out of his way.

263

At the door Dominic kissed her on both cheeks. If this was to be the last time he saw her, what the hell.

He couldn't keep from giving her a rueful parting glance.

Joanna shut the door, frowning. Dominic had seemed really upset that she had changed her plans. And he had kissed her hello and goodbye, something he had never done before.

Was it possible that she, not Nadine, was now the main attraction?

'Joanna, you look wonderful,' Lud exclaimed, holding her off and scrutinising her. 'I want to give you a real hug but I'm afraid of hurting you.'

She smiled wryly.

They were sitting in her living room, with all the windows open and the sounds of the street wafting into the apartment.

To Joanna Lud seemed unfamiliar, after more than a month apart. This tanned, relaxed man in slacks and sport shirt, unbuttoned halfway down his chest, was like a stranger to her.

As Lud looked at Joanna, his apprehension was eased. She was still beautiful, still his woman.

He reached for her hands. 'Sweetheart, I've missed you terribly. Trying to communicate over the phone was so impossible.'

'I know. Have you sold the series?'

'Yes, to NBC. For a decent price, though not as much as we wanted. But let's not talk about that now. You don't seem pleased to see me. Met someone else while I was gone? Fell in love with your doctor or something?'

Lud didn't like the way she was staring at him. 'Joanna?'

'I know about you and Nadine.'

He sucked his breath through his teeth and tightened his hands over hers. Not that he was really surprised Nadine couldn't have kept her mouth shut. 'I was planning to tell you.'

264

'When? After the baby?'

'After the series. Nadine threatened to quit. She was driving me crazy, but maybe she's told you a different story.'

'No. She told me her part in it. After sharing our kidneys it's become easier to share our feelings.'

Joanna related what had led up to Nadine's confession.

'All right, then you've heard it straight. I didn't know what else to do. If she'd walked out in the middle of everything – believe me, it didn't mean a thing. You were the one I loved, the one I still love.'

Lud took Joanna gently in his arms and kissed her face all over, gradually applying pressure to her arms, burying his warm face in her neck. He cupped her breasts and moved his hands down to caress her hips, her thighs. 'It's been so long,' he murmured. 'I've been going crazy thinking about you and wanting you.'

Joanna didn't stir. She felt a mechanical pleasure in his touch, but that was all.

Perturbed by her lack of response, Lud drew back, frowning. 'You've been through a terrible ordeal, but that's over now, love. This plot is meant to have a happy ending, namely Joanna and me.'

And baby make three. A deep anguish washed over her. 'My plot goes something like this. While I was pregnant with your child you had an affair with my sister.'

'An affair, no. For God's sake, it was blackmail.'

'You had other options. For one thing, you could have called her bluff. She never would have quit. Her part meant more to her than anything. Not to speak of the investment. She sold almost everything she had for money to back the production.'

'I didn't realise that. She assured me she had many millions. Even if she hadn't quit, she was making my life a misery.'

'If only you'd told me the truth, we could have worked it out by ourselves. Knowing I was pregnant would have made a difference.'

265

'Would it? She might have been worse. She was so jealous of you.'

'Yes. But she knew how much I wanted a baby. There's been jealousy but also love. The bonds between twins are special, and nobody else can really judge. Oh, Lud, anything would have been better than what you did, calculating your chances, and using both of us.'

'I never used you, sweetheart. You must believe that. I've been crazy about you ever since we met. You know that.'

'Sure. And you were indifferent to Nadine, but you were able to make love to her.'

Lud put his hands through his hair. 'That's the sort of thing women can never understand.'

'I'm trying. Explain it to me.'

'I didn't start out to do anything but flatter her into not quitting and into giving the best performance she was capable of. But when a beautiful woman – and she's your twin, after all – sets out to be seductive, and both people have been drinking and so forth, biology has a way of taking over.'

'I see. Biology. That's all it was. No curiosity? You didn't wonder what Nadine might be like in bed?'

Lud sighed sharply and rubbed his palms on his trousers. 'Of course I wondered. A man and woman can't have any sort of dealings without at least a tinge of sexual curiosity. Maybe women don't think this way but men do.'

'Some women do,' Joanna responded, remembering Abby, 'but they don't necessarily have to give in to their curiosity.'

'I don't see what I did as giving in. I told you that I didn't plan it, but when it happened I just couldn't take the risk of drawing back and making your sister even angrier.'

Joanna looked steadily at him.

He swallowed. She was being so calm, so reasonable, so grown-up. 'It wasn't like being with you, if that's what you're thinking. I didn't love Nadine.'

266

'That she's my twin had something to do with your fascination, didn't it?'

'Of course. All through history men have been fascinated with sisters. You know, in some cultures when a man's wife dies it's the custom for him to marry her sister. In fact, a common form of polygamy is for a man to marry several sisters at once. So be grateful you have only one.' Lud gave her his most appealing smile.

Joanna was seeing him with unblinkered eyes for the first time. 'Lorrie isn't the least bit my sister.'

'Who?'

'New Hampshire Lorrie, the lodge-owner's daughter.' Joanna was unable to keep a tremor from her voice.

Lud looked uncomfortable. 'Okay, I'll tell you the honest truth. I was happy about the pregnancy, but I guess a part of me was also scared. I got up to New Hampshire and Nadine was on the verge of a breakdown. The first night I thought I'd get her soothed down.' Lud took Joanna's unresisting hand. 'I wanted you, and missed you, and there I was making love to your clone. In fact, I had to pretend Nadine *was* you in order for it to work at all.'

'That contradicts what you just said about being attracted to sisters.'

'Okay. I didn't want to admit it, but I really did pretend she was you, honest. And the next day was one disaster after the other. By evening I was around the bend. I couldn't be with you and I just couldn't stand to be with Nadine. Believe me, I knew I'd made a mistake. I was feeling guilty about you, sorry about Nadine – '

'So you handled the problem by involving a third woman?'

The irony he heard in her tone chilled him. Maybe it would have been better if she had flown at him hysterically, all out of control and wanting to be reassured. 'Please, love, hear me out. The vibes I was getting from Nadine were that she was playing for keeps, and it scared the shit out of me. I deliberately asked Lorrie to my room so that Nadine would decide I wasn't worth mooning over and she'd get off my case.'

Joanna looked incredulously at him. 'I see. Lorrie didn't attract you either, but men being what they are, somehow you were able to have sex with her anyway.'

'Joanna, please. Believe me, there's a difference in intensity. Sure, I can do a mechanical thing, but it's not the way I make love with you.'

Putting his arm around her, Lud whispered in her ear, 'I didn't kiss anyone the way I kiss you, or where I kiss you.'

Joanna broke away. 'It's no good, Lud. I can't ever feel about you as I did. That you could have made love to two women, even after you knew about the baby – but I'm forgetting that you didn't really want it.' Her eyes were stinging.

'I did want it, but I was a little afraid of the responsibility. Most men feel that way. It works itself out eventually. I would have got used to being a father. And I will in the future. Joanna, I don't want any other woman. Only you.'

He took her in his arms, and she felt herself weakening. He could be so damned persuasive. Until she began to wonder about his activities during the past month, the parties, the starlets, and would-be actresses surrounding him, enticing him. Once, in a moment of honesty, he had admitted he had never in his adult life gone longer than two weeks without sex.

'Joanna!' Lud held her away from him, a look of disbelief in his eyes. 'You aren't saying that you're through with me?'

'I just can't feel the same,' she whispered unhappily. 'Not after Nadine.'

'To hell with Nadine! That was meaningless. I'm talking about us.'

'Nadine is part of me, now more than ever. I can't say to hell with her.'

'I'm sorry. I didn't mean that. I'm upset. I thought you loved me.' He stopped, looking wounded.

Joanna wondered if it was real or if he was playing the

role of aggrieved lover, directing himself as he would an actor.

Okay, take it from the top, Lud. Try to convince her not to shoot you down just because you made a couple of goofs.

'Joanna, I love you.'

'Whatever that means. I said that on the phone to you, when I really needed you to mourn our baby, to just be here for that, and for the operation.'

'I'm so sorry, angel. I didn't realise. Anyway, I'm here now. I'll make up for everything.'

He put his hands on her shoulders. 'If you've forgiven Nadine enough to let her have your kidney, surely you can forgive me and come and live with me in California. We belong together, you know that.' Drawing Joanna closer, he began to caress her very lightly across her neck and her ears, knowing it aroused her.

'Have you forgotten,' he whispered, pressing against her, 'how much you like what you call my bits and pieces?'

'No, I haven't forgotten,' Joanna answered, in a sad low voice, moving away, 'but they've been too many places.'

'Oh, God! The one thing I can't believe is that you've stopped loving me!' Lud put his face in his hands.

For a moment Joanna was touched. Then she pictured him embracing her sister, and Lorrie, knowing that Joanna was carrying his child.

'I thought I loved you, but infatuated may have been the right word. I was simply swept away.'

He looked up unhappily. 'You didn't enjoy being with me? We didn't have wonderful times together?'

'Of course we did, only real life has a way of intruding on fun and games.'

'I'm not playing games, Joanna. I love you. I want you. I've asked you to live with me.'

'Does that include marriage?'

He looked truly amazed. 'Isn't that a bit old-fashioned? It never occurred to me that you wanted to get married. You never said a word.'

'No. I was waiting for you. I guess I am old-fashioned at that.'

'But it's only a piece of paper.'

'I see marriage as a commitment, a trust. I know it's no guarantee, but at least it shows good faith. Living together seems too mistrustful. It implies that nothing can last, but it's okay for a couple to make the arrangement of the moment more convenient by hanging their clothes in the same closet.'

'Look, my mother's married for the fourth time, so the document didn't help, did it? In fact, I think it hurt. It locks people into something legally that has nothing to do with their feelings.'

'You don't want to marry me, do you?'

Lud threw open his hands in a gesture of helplessness. 'I want you every which way, believe me, love, but I have an aversion to weddings and everything they represent. I think statistics are going to show that live-in couples last longer. Do you want a conformist dull married man who resents his captivity? Or a lover who will wake you every morning by sprinkling rose petals on your head. Who will drizzle champagne all over your belly and adore you madly because he's free to do so, knowing that you stay because you're free to.'

Lud's questions were meant rhetorically. He took Joanna in his arms and pressed his mouth to hers, murmuring, between kisses, how much he loved her.

She saw that if he kept that up she might succumb to the fantasy. But fantasy was not what she wanted.

Gently she moved out of his embrace. 'It's not only marriage. It's you, me, us. I'm simple and straightforward and loyal. I was to Carl and to Ben, and I would be to you, even if things weren't perfect. But trust is important to me.'

'Nobody, not even you, can promise fidelity.'

'Maybe not. But there have to be reasonable expectations. You've never been with any woman longer than a few months, you told me. We've only been together five months, counting your absence, and during that time you've slept with Nadine and Lorrie, at the very least.'

'Joanna, you're making me angry.'

'That's not my intention. I'm only trying to clarify, so I can understand.'

'Okay. Understand this. When Fern brought Nadine to me I saw another you – not as intriguing, but with the right look, whom I could teach to act. The fact is I was in a hell of a fix when we lost Gina because we also lost most of our backers. Either I had to come up with an experienced actress in a hurry, to get new backers, or lose the series. Along comes your twin, not only with acting ambitions but with money to invest. I knew it might not work, but I was going by what I'd seen of you, and by what Fern told me. She praised Nadine to the skies. And at the beginning, your sister was as sweet as syrup. I didn't know she'd turn out to be such a calculating bitch. Okay, okay, I know you two are close and maybe she has a lifetime of credit with you but she had very little with me. And I wouldn't have slept with her if she hadn't held me over a goddamn barrel. Same thing goes for Lorrie.'

Lud's gaze wavered, and he grew embarrassed. 'I met Lorrie last winter, before Christmas, when I was skiing up there. We had a little thing, and I arranged with her father to use the lodge for the series. Lorrie saw to it that we were paying almost nothing in exchange for keeping their name and giving them publicity.'

Joanna stared at him. God, he was slippery. First he had told her that he had slept with Lorrie to discourage Nadine. Now he was saying that he had done so to keep Lorrie happy, so she would honour their deal.

Joanna smiled at Lud sardonically. 'Are you telling me that your experiences with both women had to do with work rather than pleasure?'

'Absolutely.'

'So, in the future,' Joanna said slowly, 'if a similar situation should arise, you'd go ahead and –'

'No! Christ! It won't arise. This was my big chance to

break into serious drama. After *Sister In Law* I'll be able to write my own ticket. Joanna, please!'

'Lud, tell me about the girl you loved in your youth. The one who died.'

He frowned. 'What girl?'

'The small redhead you knew at college.'

He was still puzzled. 'I don't remember. I'm not interested in the past.'

'But surely if she meant as much to you as you said on the first night we were together, you couldn't have totally forgotten.'

'Look, I don't want to rehash past history. It's the future that interests me. Our future.'

The look of naked need on his face made Joanna sad but strengthened her resolve. Was there ever really a redhead, or had he said that simply to gain her sympathy?

Joanna had no doubt that he needed her at that moment. But what if he needed another woman at a future moment?

He saw the doubt in her eyes. 'Joanna, all I can go by is how I feel for you right now.'

'I'm afraid that's not good enough for me, Lud. A couple should make a conscious effort to build a life together. I didn't know it until a short time ago, but what I want is to get married and have a child. Two children if possible. I want to stay home and care for them for a few years. And also, paint, read, and just *be*. I'm not cut out for intrigues, for Malibu parties.'

'Joanna, this doesn't sound like you. Everyone loved you in Malibu.'

'I don't want everyone to love me, just my husband and my children.'

Lud stood up and thrust his hands into his pockets. 'What happens to your domestic dream if there aren't any children?'

Her glance didn't waver. 'I'd want to adopt.'

He frowned and sat down again. 'Are you so insecure that you need to surround yourself with institutions and kids and stuff instead of relying on your feelings?'

'But I am relying on them. I learned something during the last few weeks about true caring.' She told him about Winnie.

Lud became exasperated. 'I see. So now you're in love with Winnie, right?'

'No. My point is only that character counts, all other things being equal. I would trust Winnie come what may. But I don't love him romantically, so we're only friends. I could have loved you romantically but I no longer trust you.'

Lud stared at her. 'I can't believe you really mean all this. You're still not recovered from your operation, and I think maybe you're scared.'

'Of course I'm scared! I'm scared of not really living! I don't want to drift from one sensual amusement to another. I want to build something solid with someone solid. Last week I was thirty-five.'

'God, I forgot. Sweetheart, I'm so sorry. My only excuse is that I had so much on my mind. That's what all this is about, isn't it? Angel, I'm going to buy you something so spectacular it will take your breath away. Damn me for forgetting. I know how important birthdays are to women.'

Joanna shot him an ironic look. 'To *people*. When people care about each other, they listen, and they remember.'

'When's my birthday?' he challenged, grinning.

'October fourth.'

'Okay, score one for you. I'm better at remembering feelings, and situations. I can describe every nook and cranny of your body. I can tell you what you did with me, and how it felt, and how much you liked it when I – '

'Lud, this isn't a disagreement about sex,' Joanna broke in softly. 'But wonderful sex by itself doesn't make a relationship work. Other things matter. It's not the birthday present I missed, it's your forgetting the significance of the day, especially this year. Do you know what Nadine and I did on our birthday? We ate a quiet dinner at home with the kids and just celebrated being alive.'

Lud nervously began to walk back and forth. What had happened to his beautiful, sensual, adorable funny girl? Nadine, that's what. Nadine and her fucking scheming had dragged Joanna down into sickness and morbidity.

'Do you realise,' Joanna asked, 'that this is the first serious talk we've ever had?'

'Yeah, and it can be the last, as far as I'm concerned.'

'It's not a barrel of laughs, is it?' Her question was sardonic, but he missed the nuance.

'No, goddamn it, it's not.' Lud suddenly turned his hypnotic gaze on her, and for a moment she held her breath, feeling the old magnetism.

'When we're in California, love, I'll have to keep you in my inside pocket because the moment I let you loose you get brainwashed.'

He smiled his wonderful, charismatic smile. 'Beautiful Joanna, you can punish me as much as you like. I've made a mess of things, okay. But I don't think I deserve to be thrown away, and if you do that we'll both be very sorry.'

She sighed. 'I'm sorry already, in a way, but I simply can't help it. At this point I place a greater value on sensitivity and reliability than on charm. You were three thousand miles away when I needed you.'

His smile faded. 'I've explained to you. Christ, I was up to my ears in the series and trying to keep Ed from doing crazy things. I wasn't going to tell you but he actually wanted to advertise that Suzanne was played by Nadine *and* you. He thought it would be a terrific publicity gimmick.'

The more Lud said, the more defensive he seemed. Joanna didn't interrupt. When he had finished, he looked at her searchingly.

She remained silent.

'Okay, I guess I could have spared a couple of days to be here, but honestly, love, I'm useless around a hospital. I worry, I feel sick myself, my humour deserts me. I saw my father die.'

'I'm sorry, Lud. I know illness is unpleasant. But it does

274

happen. That's the reason for the "sickness and health" clause in a marriage contract. Think of this. I have only one kidney now. If something should ever go wrong, I'd be in the same predicament as Nadine, only with no hope of getting a new kidney from my twin. I'd be an invalid. And where would *you* be?'

29

'Thanks, cousin Dominic, for taking time out from your busy day to have lunch with me.' Abby lifted her glass of wine raffishly.

'My pleasure,' he said, returning the gesture.

'How do you manage to keep so cool in the middle of this heat, anyway?'

Abby's wilted look made him smile. 'An Englishman, m'dear, never gets hot, but he might just admit to being somewhat discomforted by the unseasonably warm weather.'

She laughed at his self-mockery. 'Except that in New York ninety-nine is perfectly seasonable in August.'

'It sounds as if your holiday is past due.'

'It is. I can't take it until after Labor Day. Winnie's away at the moment and his assistant is impossible, the kind of gay guy I just can't stand. Thinks I'm his mommy or something.'

Dominic listened in vain for a word about Joanna. Since taking her home from the hospital at the end of May he hadn't set eyes on her. It had seemed pointless to call. Perhaps she had already gone to California.

He had spoken to Nadine a couple of times, asking about her health and Joanna's. Aside from telling him they were both fine, Nadine hadn't elaborated.

'I was hoping you'd invite me up to Buckingham Palace one of these weekends but you never did,' Abby accused Dominic.

'I'm so sorry, Abby. I'd no idea that would appeal to you. I'm very quiet on my farm, actually. Thirty acres and nothing to amuse except for a bubbling brook. I thought you might be bored, but if you really want to dangle your feet in the pond, go for a run with my unruly dog, collect eggs in the hen house, Lady Chatterley style – '

'I'd love to, if you'd agree to be my Mellors.' Abby threw Dominic a baleful look.

He laughed uncomfortably. 'We're back to that, are we? Abby, we wouldn't suit each other. Surely you must know that by now. What's wrong? Are you between men and feeling midsummer sadness?'

'Yes to both questions. I met this terrific guy, in advertising. Boy, was he neat.'

'Mm hm.' Dominic smiled encouragingly and buttered a roll.

Abby was struck by the beauty of his hands. 'What? Oh, it turned out to be a bummer. After a couple of dates I called him and invited him to go sailing with some friends, and he hemmed and hawed and said he couldn't. Two days later I got a note in the mail saying I was getting too serious. Can you imagine? And he wasn't ready to see one woman exclusively, and more of the same kind of bullshit.'

'Abby, if he didn't appreciate you as you deserve you're probably just as well off.' He was addressing his remark to himself as much as to her.

She immediately picked up on it. 'Who hasn't been appreciating you lately? That lady doctor? Or is that over?'

'I suppose you could say so but it never really got started.'

'How come you can't seem to settle down any more than I can?' Abby wondered. 'It's time, isn't it? Unless Alexis soured you on women.'

'No. Only on Alexis-type women.'

'You don't think I'm like her, do you? I suppose you find me horribly promiscuous.'

'I don't think you're selfish like Alexis. That you're not exactly a vicar's daughter is strictly your business. I'm not inclined to be judgmental.'

'Dominic, I really do have a thing about you. Seriously. And you've never given me a chance.'

He put down his fork and looked with uneasy compassion at this woman he thought of as good-hearted and sweet but undeniably scatty. 'Abby, my dear, I wish I could say something encouraging. I don't even think I can analyse it. I'm terribly fond of you, but not in that way.'

'How do you know?' she challenged. 'You've never kissed me except like a cousin, damn it.'

He tried not to smile. 'The kind of kissing you suggest is a result of everything else's being right, not the starting point.'

'You want to bet? Some of the best affairs get started with a kiss, not to mention a romp in bed. Joanna and Lud, for instance, and wow, was that dynamite.'

Dominic lowered his eyes and concentrated very hard on the wine in his glass.

'I dare you to kiss me, Dominic. I mean really.'

He looked up at her, his penetrating grey eyes assessing the lengths to which she was prepared to go, and he to follow.

'Just do it right now,' she repeated, her pert little face serious for once, 'if you're not afraid.'

He swallowed. He hadn't 'really' kissed a woman in a couple of months. He just hadn't felt like it. Perhaps he was in the mood to be tempted, but did he want it to be by Abby?

'Nobody will care, in this spaghetti palace. They're used to young lovers. Come on. I dare you, doctor.'

He leaned across the table and put his mouth on Abby's. Immediately she opened her lips, and her tongue searched for his. She moved her hands to the back of his head and held it.

'Okay,' she said breathlessly, leaning back in her chair. 'Was that so terrible?'

He exhaled slowly. 'No,' he answered carefully, 'it was very nice, but I don't know that it proves anything except that you're very attractive and desirable, which I've known all along.'

'Then for God's sake why can't we take it to its logical conclusion? I mean, I've got nobody and you've got nobody. There's a lonely weekend coming up, and we each might have somebody, if – Oh, shit, listen to me begging the man!'

Abby lowered her head and put her hand in front of her face.

Dominic felt like a swine. He touched her arm. 'I'll be in town this weekend. My sister and her husband are arriving from England. You remember Pam and Cyril. Would you like to join us tomorrow for drinks and dinner?'

Abby's fingers separated to show her mischievous dark eyes, and then her mouth, curved into a happy smile. 'Terrific. I'd love to. Whew. What a struggle this has been. Seriously, are you sure it's okay? I mean, I really don't want to twist your arm.'

'It will be just fine,' he muttered, put off by her quick recovery. In fact it would be somewhat awkward. Pamela and Cyril would think he was daft, dating Alexis' cousin, after all these years. He could tell them it wasn't actually a date. Of course, Abby might make it clear that she was hoping to share his bed. And he had practically agreed.

'Cheer up, Dom. It'll be fun, and you might even learn a trick or two.'

'Without a doubt,' he replied dryly, making her laugh.

'I know I'm not your type, being neither blonde nor beautiful.'

He looked at her curiously. 'Is that what you think I'm after? Alexis was brown-haired, remember. Although she was beautiful what attracted me to her initially was her vitality.'

'Sure, but you don't exactly like ugly, do you?'

He smiled. 'Does it have to be the extreme? Let's just say I admire attractive qualities in general.'

'Yeah, so they all say, but I don't believe it. Certain types are in, and others are out. Like mine. Short brunettes have been out since the fifties. Now it's skinny blondes with mosquito bites for boobs and gorgeous legs.'

Dominic grew pensive, and he poured more wine. Unused to drinking at lunch, he felt quite light-headed. He

279

hoped he wouldn't get any emergency calls that afternoon.

'I saw you before, looking at a slim blonde like you
could have devoured her and don't deny it.'

'Okay, I won't.' He had, in fact, thought for a moment
that the woman was Joanna.

'See? That type is the rage –'

'Doesn't mean a thing to me.' He sighed and mumbled,
'If it did I'd console myself with her sister.'

He had thought his last words were inaudible, but he
caught Abby staring at him with a strange expression.

Good lord, he really had drunk too much wine. 'Some
dessert?' he asked quickly, hoping to distract her from his
stupid remark.

'Whose sister?' Abby frowned in concentration. 'No
dessert, thanks, just coffee.' Her mouth suddenly flew
open in belated comprehension. 'Joanna! Oh, my God, it's
Joanna! In Amsterdam you – oh, how stupid of me. But
don't you know that –'

'Please! Please just shut up about it,' Dominic commanded tensely in a low voice. 'Not one word more. I
insist.' He summoned the waiter.

Abby sat toying with her spoon, glancing at him from
under her long eyelashes. His high colour had deepened.
She had never seen Dominic so ill at ease or so angry.

She busied herself with putting milk in her coffee, and
then she said mildly, 'I understand Nadine's doing very
well with the kidney and is going to acting school.'

'Oh, yes?' He gulped his coffee black, making a face as
the hot liquid burned his tongue.

'I take it you haven't talked to Nadine lately?' she
persisted.

Damn the woman. 'We've exchanged a few words on the
phone once or twice.'

Abby drank her coffee slowly. In spite of the air-condi-
tioning, she was feeling warm all over again.

Apparently he didn't know that Joanna had broken up
with Lud. Was it Abby's place to give him that piece of

280

information? Especially after he had cut her off about Joanna?

Abby cast her mind back to the hotel room in Amsterdam. What had Joanna said about Dominic? Abby couldn't exactly recall, but her friend hadn't been in the least interested. Would she be now?

Abby had waited years for Dominic. And tomorrow night she was going to get her big chance.

'The more I look at your hair, the better I like it that way.' Joanna was admiring Nadine's centre parting and the way she had pulled her shoulder-length hair slightly back with two barrettes. 'It's forties-looking and yet contemporary, and with the print dress it works beautifully.'

Nadine was gratified. She poured Joanna more coffee. The sisters had just eaten dinner at Nadine's.

'I got tired of being such a copy-cat. It's enough I've got your kidney. The least I can do for myself is pick a hairstyle and clothes.'

'Maybe I'll do my hair your way,' Joanna teased.

'Go ahead, if you think this is the real you.'

Joanna shrugged. 'I don't know what the real me is anymore.'

Nadine looked at her guiltily. 'You miss Lud, don't you?'

'No, not really. I sort of miss having somebody, but not Lud in particular. It was fun while it lasted, but Lud Haley isn't the kind of man to grow old gracefully with. And—'

' — California's not the place to grow old gracefully in. You haven't heard from him yet?'

Joanna shook her head. 'I don't expect to. He called me from the airport just before he left, saying he wouldn't accept my decision, etcetera, but I felt he was only reacting to being rejected for once in his life.'

'Yeah. No doubt he hit Los Angeles in a blaze of energy, all his sexual antennae out, ready to play charming scoundrel to any star-struck idiot eager to let him.'

Joanna glanced at her sister. 'That sounds awfully bitter. I hope you don't really feel that way.'

281

Nadine sighed. 'You may not be bitter, but I am, just a little, wrong though I was. Actually, in your position I'd be furious.'

'Well, I went along with Lud's madness without a whimper. It's not really his fault that I wanted more than he could give. He was doing his thing all along. I simply failed to recognise just what it was.'

'That goes double for me.'

'One thing came out of it, anyway. *Sister In Law* will be screened in January.'

'Yes, and everyone will see what a lousy job I did. In class I'm learning just how little I know about acting. I won't be able to stand watching myself as Suzanne.'

'Then watch me.'

'In fact, if you wanted to do a really sisterly thing you'd make Storman credit you with the part, so that my brilliance as a serious actress can emerge in a year or so after I've done all my homework.'

Joanna laughed. 'If I did that I might be asked to play another lady lawyer. The hardest thing I ever did in my life was to finish up those episodes.'

'Oh, sure. The easy part was giving me the kidney, right?'

'Yup. Oh, what did – '

'Mack said I was fine. Greets me these days with a kidney punch, just to dare it to budge. Apparently it's taken up a long-term lease, if he's to be believed.'

'I believe him. That man tells the truth until he draws blood.'

'I know,' Nadine agreed, 'but he's a – '

' – wonderful surgeon. And really a nice man, as long as his transplants stay put, as this one will.'

Nadine looked off into space. 'I hope so. I haven't ever appreciated being alive the way I do now. There's something to be said for knowing you may have only five more years.'

'Don't be goofy. There hasn't been a sign of rejection.'

'Not yet, but it can always come. Anyway, I'm on

constant medication. Strong stuff, steroids. The side effects can weaken my health in general.'

'You'll just have to do what Mack tells you until they know more about transplants,' Joanna said quickly. She had given enough money for them to manufacture kidneys out of solid gold.

'Yes. But I have to face the fact that I may not live out my normal life,' Nadine insisted quietly. 'If it hadn't been for you I'd have no life at all. Anyway, I don't intend to waste a moment. I'm trying to get a part in a stage production.'

Joanna, eyes lowered, blinked back tears. 'That's pretty demanding, isn't it? I mean, having to give one performance a day, sometimes two.'

'I know, but I wouldn't be onstage all the time. I'm not aiming for romantic leads. I'm too old, and anyway I think character roles are more interesting, now that I finally got myself some character. You know a lead I'd be a natural for? *Whose Life Is It Anyway?* At least I could lie in bed during the whole performance.'

Joanna smiled and swallowed the lump that kept forming in her throat.

Jeff and Kate appeared at the door of the dining room.

'Ah, just the ones I wanted to see, speaking of bed.'

'Not for me, Mom,' Jeff said. 'I still have an hour.'

'Yes, but drink your milk now anyway, with Kate, and not too many cookies. And please watch the crumbs.'

The children continued on to the kitchen.

'The little monsters have become angels,' Joanna said.

'Nobody told them how close they came to losing me, but they must have known. They're into obedience, long may it last. Oh, they've been invited to a birthday party on Sunday. Me too, since I'm friendly with the girl's mother. I hope you don't mind.'

'No, of course not.'

Nadine sensed Joanna's disappointment. The only undisrupted pattern in recent weeks was Joanna's Sunday with the children. 'Of course you're invited to the party

283

too. The children would be disappointed if you didn't join us.'

'We'll see,' Joanna said lightly. They wouldn't be disappointed at all. Since Nadine had taken full charge, they needed their aunt less. Although Joanna was glad, she couldn't help feeling a little hurt.

'Kate,' Nadine called, as her daughter tried to sneak past, 'bed, please.'

'Oh, Mommy, I go to bed early every single night. Why can't I have a holiday for just tonight?'

Joanna and Nadine smiled.

'Stop laughing at me,' Kate sulked.

'We're not laughing at you,' her mother said. 'What you said was amusing.'

'It was? Then can I stay up? Please, Mommy.'

'Ten minutes only.' Nadine looked at her watch. 'After that no more arguing, okay?'

'Okay.'

Joanna walked home, feeling restless. Her structured life, encompassing job and Lud, had collapsed all at once, and she wasn't meeting many people. Abby, the perennial bachelor girl around town, invited her to make the rounds of bars and discos, but Joanna had less taste for that kind of life than ever before.

What she needed, Joanna decided, was to start painting, take up tennis again, and find some new interests.

Joanna was awakened by the phone.

'Hi, it's Abby. Sorry to get you up so early but I'm leaving town in a terrific hurry. You aren't busy tonight, I hope.'

'Well, no.'

'Smashing. Do me a favour. I forgot I was going away for the weekend – and I can't get out of it. I was supposed to meet Dominic tonight, but I can't reach him to tell him I won't be able to make it. Be a pal and fill in for me, please.'

'Abby, I couldn't do that. If he's expecting you it will be so embarrassing. Can't you phone him?'

'I did, but he's out. Probably went to pick up the Pendletons at the airport. They're super, you'll love them. Please, Joanna. I think Dom mentioned tickets for a play,' Abby fibbed.

Joanna, only half-awake, finally agreed. A little later she regretted it. This was absurd. The last thing she felt like doing was substituting for Abby at a family reunion.

30

Dominic, having tea with his sister and brother-in-law in the Gold Room of the Helmsley Palace Hotel, was filling them in on its history.

Suddenly he stopped and stared. Was that actually Joanna Lennox walking towards their table? So often he mistook females of a similar type for her that he had begun to distrust what he called his Joanna mirages. But this was not one of them.

He stood up slowly, not knowing or caring how Joanna happened to be here. Only extremely happy that she was.

When she saw Dominic's receptive smile she felt less awkward.

'Abby couldn't make it and had no way of getting in touch with you,' Joanna murmured.

'Well, she couldn't possibly have picked a more welcome substitute.' Dominic introduced Joanna to his sister and brother-in-law.

'Pleased to meet you, Lady Pamela, Sir Cyril.' Joanna shook hands shyly.

'Please call us Pam and Cyril. So much easier,' Dominic's sister requested, smiling at her. Pamela didn't much resemble her brother, being rather plain, small and fair, with light-blue eyes. She was several years older than Dominic, and her husband was older still, a pleasant-looking pudgy man with a round face and a genial smile under his greying moustache.

'I'll only stay for a moment.' Joanna noted Dominic's look of disappointment.

'But you must have a cup of tea,' Cyril maintained, while his wife poured for Joanna. 'Best thing about tea time,' Cyril confided, 'is that what you call the happy hour follows closely on the heels.'

'Cyril and Pam are coffee lovers, actually,' Dominic explained, 'but I thought they'd enjoy the experience here. I was hoping the harpist might be playing this afternoon. This used to be a music room in the old Villard Houses.'

They all looked at the balcony under the magnificent vaulted ceiling.

'I can do without a harpist,' Cyril said. 'I came to New York to hear jazz, and that's what I mean to do. Not that I don't appreciate this lovely place with its gold-leaf opulence.' Cyril pushed aside his cup and the remains of his cake. 'To paraphrase the great Dorothy Parker, cake may be jake but liquor's a helluva lot quicker,' he said in his best Americanese.

Joanna and Dominic laughed, touching eyes. Abby had been right in assuring Joanna that the baronet and his wife weren't in the least bit stuffy.

'As you can see,' Dominic said, 'I'm not the only Brit who responds so enthusiastically to America, though I like to think I was one of the first.'

'On the heels of the Pilgrims,' Joanna teased. She was enjoying herself enough to be talked into having a drink.

Dominic explained that Joanna had been the one to bring Abby into Omega, giving Joanna the opportunity to regale her listeners with amusing anecdotes about her job, laced with generous praise for Abby.

'Have you left Omega?' Pamela asked.

'Well, I'm remaining as a consultant.'

'Joanna and her twin, Nadine, have been through quite an ordeal recently,' Dominic said, hoping Joanna didn't mind.

'I'm particularly interested in twins.' Pamela went on to explain that she was a paediatrician and had been doing research into the medical problems of twins. She was very skilful in drawing Joanna out and getting her to talk about the transplant. Joanna found herself speaking freely as if to an old friend.

During the discussion, Dominic wondered why Abby

287

had sent Joanna in her place, after she had been so eager to come herself. And why Joanna happened to be free on a Saturday evening. Could Lud still be in California? Was something amiss between them? Just being with Joanna caused a rush of adrenalin and Dominic cautioned himself to slow down. It might be that Joanna was planning to go to California, and that only Nadine's health had held her back.

Joanna was having a wonderful time and didn't need much persuasion to agree to join them for dinner at The Coach House, in the Village.

'My brother-in-law, fond as he is of cocktails, maintains there's no American food worth eating,' Dominic told her. 'I'm hoping to change his mind.'

'So far, so good,' Cyril murmured. 'This Maryland crabmeat is quite palatable, don't you think, Pam?'

'I do. And the cornsticks are so compelling I simply can't stop nibbling.'

'Just as long as you leave room for the best pecan pie you'll ever taste,' Dominic said.

'Oh, you beast, you're creating havoc with my slimming. If only I looked like Joanna,' Pamela lamented.

'If you did, my dear,' Cyril said in her ear, 'you'd have to fend off an unnaturally attentive brother. He's potty over her, don't you agree?'

Pamela laughed and nodded, poking her husband with her elbow.

Dominic, glancing at Joanna as often as he dared, thought her beauty had been enhanced, as if her suffering had lent a new, thoughtful quality to her loveliness.

After dinner Cyril lit a cigar, pretending not to notice his wife's disapproving frown.

Suddenly Dominic began to cough.

Cyril apologised and immediately put out the cigar.

'It's all right,' Dominic said, between coughs.

'It is *not* all right,' Pamela insisted.

'Sorry. I thought as long as it was a Havana – '

Dominic excused himself from the table.

'Really, Cyril, you know how sensitive he is to smoke.

My brother had tuberculosis some years ago,' she explained to Joanna. 'He insisted on attaching himself to a hospital in the north of England where doctors are in such short supply that he worked himself nearly to death. Rotten diet and hardly any sleep.'

Noting Joanna's look of sympathy and concern, Pamela continued with her story of Dominic's dedication to medicine, which he would have been much too modest to tell Joanna himself.

'I truly don't think Dominic would have survived if he'd stayed up north. If he hadn't happened to be at the theatre one night in Liverpool, where Alexis was dancing in a show . . .'

Talking of Alexis reminded Pamela of how much she had disapproved of her sister-in-law. Dominic's taste in women had definitely improved. When Dominic returned to the table, Joanna was asking Pam how she managed to combine her career with running their country estate.

'Labour-saving devices, mostly, and a few dailies. Of course things are easier now that our daughters are up at university.'

'Pamela was my inspiration,' Dominic declared. 'I chose obstetrics so that I could assure her of a steady supply of patients.'

Joanna smiled appreciatively, looking at Dominic with increased respect.

They took a taxi to Fat Tuesdays, where the blind British pianist George Shearing was featured.

Pamela hugged her brother. 'You sly thing, to arrange this for us. We almost never get to hear him live.'

'But we have all his records,' Cyril added. 'I hope he'll play *Up a Lazy River*.'

'I do, too,' Joanna said. 'Shearing is one of my favourites. I didn't realise jazz was so popular in Britain.'

'Among a select group,' Pam replied. 'Even if we've lost Shearing to the US we have Humphrey Lyttelton and Johnny Dankworth. You know, when I was a child I had a mad crush on Hoagy Carmichael and that's what started me on jazz. Sometimes, in fact, I sing along while Dominic plays the piano. Of course, he's much too good just to accompany me.'

'Not really.' Dominic sounded embarrassed. 'I just play for my own amusement.'

'I had no idea you played,' Joanna said, surprised.

'Then we must pursue that some time.' Dominic gave her a long look.

Joanna was relieved when the music began.

The four listened to George Shearing and his bass player, Brian Torff, conducting a sprightly musical dialogue. Part of the fun was recognising the tunes. Dominic whispered to Joanna, *Love Walked In* after the first few notes. She nodded, murmuring, *Speak Low* as soon as she recognised it. They smiled at each other.

Shearing did play *Lazy River*, to the Pendletons' delight.

'That was marvellous,' Joanna said afterwards. 'He played it up and down and all around. Even threw in a little stride.'

They continued their discussion in the taxi. Dominic dropped the Pendletons at their hotel and then gave the driver Joanna's address.

She grew very quiet, cautioning herself not to go overboard again. Yes, Dominic was an attractive man and she felt increasingly drawn to him. But initially he had wanted Nadine. She couldn't go through that ever again.

Dominic paid the driver and insisted on walking Joanna to her door.

'Thanks for a wonderful evening, Dominic.'

'It was for me, too. I'm having a little drinks party at five tomorrow for Pam and Cyril. I hope you can make it. They so enjoyed meeting you and would love to see you again before they leave for Washington.'

'I enjoyed meeting them too. But tomorrow I take Jeff and Kate out.' As soon as she spoke, she remembered that they were going to a birthday party, but she didn't bother to mention it.

'Come afterwards, with Nadine.'

Joanna's face grew warm. 'I'll tell her but I doubt I can make it. Thanks anyway.' She reached into her handbag for her keys.

'You're annoyed with me, aren't you? Because I didn't invite Lud? If he's in town do bring him of course,' Dominic said, keeping his tone even.

Joanna aimed her key at the lock and missed. 'That's over,' she said quickly.

Dominic held his breath and then exhaled slowly. 'May I ask since when?'

'Since the – the operation.' Joanna turned towards him. 'It had nothing to do with the abortion. We simply had gone as far as we could go, given the different things we want.' Joanna felt flustered. Why was she telling all this to Dominic anyway?

So it had been over for two months, and Dominic hadn't known. That was why Abby, bless her, had sent Joanna to him. He moved a step closer and put his hands on her shoulders.

Joanna drew back fearfully. 'I'm not Nadine, remember.'

He gave her a puzzled smile. 'Of course not. I do believe I can tell you apart, most of the time.'

Joanna wasn't amused. She had had enough to drink to blurt out, 'She's your first choice, and just because I'm her twin – '

'WHAT? Hold it one moment. What the devil gave you that idea?'

'Well, Nadine was your friend first.'

'Of course, since I got to know her well, as her doctor. But you're my friend now. And you could be more, much more,' he added in a low voice.

Joanna slowly shook her head. 'Just because Nadine turned you down – '

'Jesus. I don't know what you're on about, Joanna. Nadine never had an opportunity to turn me down because I never dreamed of approaching her romantically. Yes, I know you're twins but I don't think of you as being at all alike. You have an entirely different personality from hers,

291

and a special quality that has always appealed to me. However, as long as you were involved with Lud I couldn't very well –'

Dominic was stopped by Joanna's doubtful expression, and her deep sigh. 'I'm so tired of making mistakes,' she murmured, as much to herself as to him.

He felt a sudden rush of resentment. 'Mistakes, plural. I see. Charming. In other words you've been putting yourself about all over the place but you're going to make an exception of me. Damn you, Joanna, how did I get to be so unlucky?'

His crisp, almost angry tone made her respond flippantly, 'Bad timing, I suppose.'

There was a pause.

'When and where did I miss my cue?' he asked.

She suddenly realised that he was really hurt. 'I'm sorry, Dominic. I don't know. It's not because I'm not fond of you, but I'm so afraid of being disappointed again.'

Could she be referring to Lud? Dominic grew hopeful, and also reckless. He threw her one of his special looks. 'For what it may be worth, Joanna,' he said in a low voice, 'I've been in love with you for so long – since Amsterdam – that it makes me ache just to think of it.'

Joanna stared at him. Her breathing was so uneven she couldn't utter a sound.

She didn't resist when he took her by the shoulders and gently kissed her lips. Then he held her against him for a moment.

Joanna felt protected and cherished, but she didn't trust her feeling. Lud had taught her that talking about love didn't mean very much.

Dominic, eyes shut, holding Joanna, sensed how vulnerable she was, and at the same time stiff and scared. He worked his fingers over her shoulders and back, feeling the tension in her muscles. Sighing, he kissed the top of her head and released her.

'Forgive me, Joanna. I have no right to importune you. I thought you'd guessed how I felt, but apparently it comes as a shock. I'm sorry if I've made you uncomfortable.

292

Whatever happens, count me as a friend, always. I do hope you'll come tomorrow. Good night.'

He turned and went briskly down the steps and up the street without looking back.

'Don't they look adorable,' Joanna said to Nadine, admiring Jeff and Kate, who were dressed up to go to their party.

'I don't look adorable!' Jeff objected loudly.

'Oops. Sorry, big Jeff. I meant tough and handsome,' Joanna amended.

He grinned at her. 'That's better.'

'Where's the present?' Nadine asked them.

The children went to get it.

'Sure you won't change your mind and come with us, Jan?'

'No, thanks. I'm a little headachy today. I don't think I could take twenty children screaming at a party.'

What Joanna didn't say was that she would find it too painful to be the only adult there without her own child in tow. Anyway, she was feeling terribly unsure of herself in general.

It was strange, the way the sisters had changed places. Nadine was pursuing her acting, positive it was what she wanted, whereas Joanna was in a state of confusion. She had talked herself out of a job, and in truth, didn't really want to go back to Omega full-time. During the night she had tossed restlessly, dreaming of Dominic and the other men in her life, all jumbled up.

'Do you want to walk over with us?' Nadine asked. 'It's on Fifth and Sixty-fourth.'

Joanna went along.

'If you want to stop up later for a quick dinner, please do, Jan. I'll have to rush because I'm learning a part.'

'I won't, if you don't mind. In fact, Dominic Graham is having a cocktail party at five for his sister and her husband. You're invited.'

'Uh uh. No time for parties. I mean, whose life is it,

anyway?' Nadine linked arms with her sister, while the children ran up ahead.

'Did Dominic ever ask you out?' Joanna was surprised at the way her heart was pounding while she waited for the answer.

Her sister was plainly embarrassed.

'We tell the truth nowadays, don't we, Dini?'

'That's right, we do. I'm not making up any lies. I'm just a little ashamed to admit I flirted like hell with him on more than one occasion. I don't remember when. Not recently, you can believe me. He never even noticed. Oh, Kate, don't you dare cross that street!'

Nadine tore down the block after her daughter. 'Jeff, you're supposed to take care of her.'

Joanna followed slowly, feeling better than she had all day.

After seeing her sister to her destination, Joanna went for a long walk in the park. She wound up sitting at the boat pond, people-watching.

When she thought about Dominic she could remember nothing unfavourable.

In Amsterdam Dominic had been very attentive, hinting that they might see one another in New York. She had ignored the suggestion. He had been such a good loser. Concerned about her pregnancy at that museum opening, when Lud was otherwise occupied. And it was Dominic who had comforted her in the hospital when she cried for Lud's child.

Should she go to Dominic's party? If she did, could she keep their relationship on a friendship level? And was that all she wanted?

When Dominic opened the door for Abby and she saw his face, she knew she had done the right thing.

He kissed her cheek. 'Thank you for Joanna, even if nothing comes of it.'

'Don't thank me. I really did go away.'

He put his hand on her arm. 'Come off it. You had no weekend plans.'

294

She shook herself loose. 'Okay, so I took myself to a friend's house overnight. Do I have to leave now, or will you lead me to the booze and let me say hi to Pam and Cyril?'

Dominic hugged her. 'Incorrigible thing.'

'Not for long. I intend to become corrigible very soon.' Abby, her arm around his waist, walked with him to the kitchen where the bar was set up.

'You know, Dom, our little lunch helped me more than you can guess. Because when you finally called my bluff, after all these years, I began to get cold feet. I suddenly realised that whenever I meet a really available man I back off with some excuse. The ones I take up with usually have something wrong with them. My exes turn up every once in a while, reminding me of where I've been and who with. I have this recurring nightmare that one day they'll all appear on my doorstep at the same time.'

Dominic smiled, looking at Abby with understanding.

'Anyway, I got started thinking about my whole life and why it's not working. Shit, I'm almost thirty. Not only can't I get with a man, I can't get with the job. Joanna talks about "exchanging ideas", but the good ones are really hers. Winnie knows, of course, but he's giving me every chance. I've got two terrific people cheering for me, but I don't come through.' Abby's voice caught a little. She covered it by taking a long swallow of the drink Dominic handed her.

'Frankly, Dominic, I'm a mess, and I've decided to take myself to a shrink. That's our little secret. Oh, and don't you ever dare tell Joanna that I set up last night for her or I'll stick pins in your effigy, I swear.' Abby swiped at his cheek with her lips and moved off to talk to the Pendletons.

Touched by Abby's confession, Dominic poured himself a drink and looked at his watch. It was after six. Joanna wouldn't be coming, and he felt a stab of disappointment.

Sighing, he backed into his brother-in-law. 'Sorry, Cyril.'

'Cyrry, Sorrel,' the baronet responded, laughing heartily. 'Don't quite know where I'm at, as you yanks say. Some colleague of yours plied me with dope. Doctors. How about tickling the ivories for a bit to soothe the savage beast in me?'

Dominic put his arm across Cyril's shoulders and led him to the living room, dominated by a baby grand. 'Okay, but behave yourself. No dancing on the piano.'

Cyril sank gratefully on to the couch, as Dominic began to play, encouraging his guests not to stop talking, insisting he was only providing a little background.

Pamela opened the door for Joanna. 'I'm so glad to see you, dear.' She hugged her. 'We were afraid you weren't coming.'

Joanna was pleased to be greeted so warmly. However, she was feeling nervous and she made for the kitchen and a glass of wine. There she ran into Ted Halloran, who was delighted to see her looking so well. He sheepishly introduced her to his very pregnant wife.

Joanna allowed herself to feel a pang of envy, which quickly passed. She thought Ted was a really nice person, as well as a good doctor, and his wife seemed very sweet.

Abby joined them on the way to get another drink. 'The joint is crawling with medics. This definitely is the place to get sick on a Sunday.'

The sounds of a piano drew Joanna into the living room. Dominic looked at the keyboard when he played, so Joanna could watch him unobserved. She could see that he enjoyed playing, and he did it extremely well.

Joanna moved to the front of the piano. He still hadn't seen her. His heavy dark hair was half in his eyes, and she watched, fascinated, as his beautiful fingers moved gracefully over the keys.

Dominic finished the number, looked up, and saw a vision of loveliness leaning on the piano.

Joanna smiled and said, 'Play it again, Dom.'

He just stared at her.

296

She felt her face colouring. '*I Got It Bad, And That Ain't Good,*' she murmured, giving him the title of the song.

With his face beginning to reflect the joy he was feeling, he played the opening chords. 'That's supposed to be my line.'

Joanna laughed. 'Okay. How about I've got it good, and that ain't bad?'

It was his turn to laugh. 'Do you really want an encore, or may I play something else?'

'Of course play something else. You're in charge, here.'

He started with *Sweet and Lovely*, immediately going into *Taking A Chance on Love*. He didn't care that he was being obvious. He didn't care about anything except that Joanna was leaning on his piano, where she belonged.

'That was super,' Joanna said. 'I love the way you play.'

'I love the way you listen.'

Pamela sat down next to Cyril. 'Look at those two, isn't it splendid?'

'Yes, m'love, it is.' Cyril was stoned but retained his dignity. 'I say, Dominic, how about *Up a Lazy River*.'

Dominic, beginning to play, called to his sister. 'I could use some words. Come on, enough stalling. Time for your New York debut.'

Pamela held back shyly until her husband pushed her forward. 'Go on, Pammie my love, let's show these yanks.'

She sang *Lazy River* and then *These Foolish Things*, her voice and phrasing very pleasant, Joanna thought. She told Pam so when the number was finished.

When Dominic's guests began to leave he saw them to the door.

Abby had been hanging out in the foyer, observing Joanna and Dominic. She kissed her friend's cheek. 'You're in excellent hands, Joanna. I must rush. See you in the office on Wednesday.'

'We'll be going as well,' Pamela told her brother.

'Oh? I thought we'd all have a bite of dinner – '

'I couldn't, truly, Dominic. I'm still digesting what I ate last night. And my lord is fading fast, aren't you, sweets?'

'I'm afraid so,' Cyril confirmed blearily. When he hugged Joanna goodbye, Cyril whispered, 'You'll be good to our lad, won't you? He's a very decent sort, really, and frankly, that wife of his messed him about something awful – '

Pamela firmly led her husband away.

Dominic shut the door and leaned against it, looking steadily at Joanna.

Slowly she came towards him. 'It seems customary to kiss the piano player.' She touched her lips to his for just an instant.

He put his arms around her gently, feeling her trembling. 'You smell wonderful. You feel wonderful. You are wonderful. And probably hungry for some dinner.'

Joanna laughed at the nonsequitur and relaxed. 'I could eat something, I suppose. What do you have?'

They looked in the refrigerator. 'Not much, I see. I'm no cook, and mostly I eat out.'

'Just leave it to me.' Joanna assembled ingredients, and by the time Dominic had emptied ashtrays and gathered glasses she had set the table in the dining alcove, lit two candles, and made them ham-and-cheese omelettes and sliced tomatoes.

Dominic poured wine into their glasses. 'Here's looking at you, kid.'

She smiled, remembering Amsterdam. '*Proost.*'

'The omelette is lovely, Joanna.' He felt a burgeoning of happiness so strong that he didn't dare say anything more at the moment, and instead concentrated on eating.

'Did you ever consider being a professional jazz pianist?' she asked after a while.

'Only in my wildest fancies. Fact is I only like to play when I'm in the mood. And when I'm going well I can forget where I am. Once played the watch right off my wrist,' he finished, making Joanna laugh.

298

They talked about other aspects of jazz, and Pam and Cyril, and Dominic's medical studies at Oxford.

Joanna felt very comfortable with him, liking his gentle humour, his eclectic interests.

Finally the bottle of wine was empty, and the candles had burned down to their wicks.

There was a long silence. Dominic, holding his wine glass, regarded the few drops remaining, while Joanna watched the faltering candlelight cast a glow on his dark hair and finely chiselled features.

She suddenly found his penetrating eyes upon her. 'I'll take you home, Joanna.'

She nodded, slight disappointment mingled with great relief.

He was a very attractive man, but she wasn't inclined to rush into anything. It was just as well that he shared her caution.

31

Joanna and Dominic began to see each other a couple of times a week. They had dinner in quiet restaurants and went to the theatre and to jazz clubs. Although Dominic often put his arm around Joanna, or held her hand, his kisses were gentle and chaste, and he made no passionate advances.

She wasn't quite sure what to make of his reticence, after three weeks. He had said he was in love with her. Did he expect her to be the one to indicate she was willing to advance to the next stage? Or was he simply profiting from his mistakes with Alexis and proceeding very slowly this time?

Joanna's emotional barometer was unsteady during this period. It was a relief to feel no pressure. Yet, at times she knew that if Dominic were to give her the slightest encouragement she would willingly surrender herself.

Her interest in him grew with each encounter until it became almost an obsession. He had showed her many sides of himself: the compassionate doctor, reliable friend, humorous, affectionate, sensitive companion. But she saw from the way he looked at her and the careful manner in which he touched her that he was holding back his sexuality. Perversely, his restraint excited and intrigued her. If she had known how to conquer her shyness she might have behaved in a seductive manner, but that really wasn't her style.

Abby, questioning Joanna on a weekly basis, was astonished. 'You mean he hasn't even kissed you?'

Joanna shook her head.

'That's extraordinary. What's he doing anyway, trying

reverse psychology? How do you stand it? I mean, if it were me I'd be climbing the walls.'

Joanna smiled and deftly changed the subject. She was reluctant to trivialise her feelings about Dominic by discussing them with anyone. There was much more to their friendship than a quiver of the flesh.

Just how much more she learned one evening during the fourth week. She had invited Dominic to dinner and decided to cook something special. However, he not only phoned to say he was going to be detained because of an emergency but when he did arrive and sat down to eat he could hardly touch a thing. He apologised and explained that he was terribly worried about his patient's post-operative complications.

Joanna, looking at Dominic's anxious expression, forgot how hard she had fussed over the food. She felt ripples of tenderness for him and had a sudden impulse to stroke his face and kiss away his anxiety.

It was then that she realized she was in love with him.

Before she could do or say anything, Dominic's beeper went, and he was called back to the hospital.

'I'm so sorry, Joanna,' he murmured at the door. 'I'll make it up to you this weekend.'

Joanna, shutting the door, wondered about her changed feelings and how to deal with them.

Dominic had invited her to the country for the weekend and she was looking forward to it with a heightened sense of anticipation.

The renovated eighteenth century stone farmhouse was situated on a slight rise and shaded by an old oak and two large maples. There were four bedrooms, a dining room, living room, large kitchen, and bathroom.

Dominic showed her to her room and then gave her a tour of the house, which was simply furnished with rustic tables and chairs and whatever he had been able to turn up at country auctions and antique shops. Joanna liked his taste enormously and quickly felt at home here.

301

'And now for the vintage room in the basement. The wine shares with medical instruments.'

'How wonderful,' Joanna exclaimed. The exhibits scattered over several display tables practically constituted a small museum.

Joanna slowly examined a set of cupping instruments with valved glasses; a steel-and-ivory forceps; a large brass syringe; and a set of silver scales. She picked up a telescopic ear trumpet, opened it and put it to her ear.

'What's that? What's that?' Dominic said into it, making her laugh.

He was amused to observe her moving quickly past a pewter bleeding bowl, a lancet with a tortoise-shell folding guard, and an amputation saw fitted with a carved bone handle.

'They're fascinating, Dominic, but a little scary. Everything looks early nineteenth century.'

'That's right. After Lister introduced antisepsis, in the 1860s, ivory and tortoise shell couldn't be used any more because they couldn't be sterilised. Actually, my great-uncles started the collection. I brought some things over with me and I've continued to acquire pieces. Whenever I get discouraged about medical advances I look at these old things and see just how far we've managed to come after all.'

Joanna picked up a steel stethoscope, noting the ivory earpieces and ebony chestpiece. She looked at Dominic uncertainly.

Smiling, he beckoned to her and undid a few buttons of his shirt. 'Go ahead, try it. Stethoscope means, literally, "I look into the chest".'

Joanna quickly put the chestpiece against his bare chest and listened. 'Sounds strong and steady,' she murmured, suddenly noticing an increase in the speed of his heartbeat. Or was that her own pulse pounding in her temples?

She could feel his breath ruffling her hair, and it gave her a tremor of physical desire.

'If you keep this up, it will start missing beats, I promise you,' he murmured.

She backed away abruptly and replaced the stethoscope.

The airedale, Duncan, had followed them and was now going from display to display, sniffing and barking.

Joanna and Dominic laughed, breaking the tension.

'Poor beast. He thinks he's wandered into a canine torture chamber, don't you, Dunc.' Dominic petted the dog, inviting Joanna to do so as well.

Later, on the wide expanse of lawn they threw a Frisbee back and forth, Duncan running between them and leaping for the disc. He was proud of himself when he was able to catch it in his teeth.

In the early evening it turned cold, and a heavy rain began to fall. They ate dinner indoors and then Dominic built up the fire. 'Intimations of autumn,' he said softly, smiling at the sight of Joanna bundled into one of his Shetland sweaters. She looked like a little girl dressed in grown-up's clothing, and she touched him deeply.

The last period of time spent with her had confirmed his feelings. Joanna was everything he had imagined. He was glad that his disturbingly increasing passion for her was tempered by tenderness.

Joanna joined Dominic in front of the fire. 'Listen to the wind howling.' She shivered delicately. 'It's nice to be warm and cosy in here.'

'There's nowhere I'd rather be, nobody I'd rather be with,' he said softly.

Her heart jumped, and she quickly glanced at him, in profile, marvelling at how handsome he was, more than she had thought.

Finally averting her eyes, she sipped her brandy, watching the fire and listening the logs snapping in counterpoint to the rain pattering on the roof.

Joanna was acutely aware of Dominic's physical presence, of the lean length of him, of his elegance and grace.

The wine and brandy had made her languorous.

Duncan curled up between Joanna and Dominic, and as

they both reached out to pet him, they accidentally touched fingertips.

An electrical charge shot through her and her skin began to tingle warmly.

Dominic felt an excruciating surge of desire which he tried to will away. But as he stroked Duncan's back he imagined what it would be like to run his hands over Joanna's body. Although he sensed a certain amount of receptiveness to him on her part, he hesitated to initiate lovemaking because he feared his vulnerability. If they became lovers only in the physical sense, his longing for all of her would become even more unendurable.

Joanna watched, mesmerised, as Dominic's hand moved sensually across Duncan's fur. She wanted that hand to stroke her. Becoming aware of a moist pulsating between her legs, Joanna sat up slowly and turned to look at Dominic.

He gazed back at her.

For a long moment waves of desire shimmered back and forth between them.

Joanna forgot how to breathe.

Abruptly Dominic stood up, walked to the window, and remained looking out at the rain.

Trembling with longing, she studied him from the rear, noting the way his square shoulders tapered to narrow hips and long, strong legs.

She had a compelling wish to come up behind him, pull his shirt out of his jeans and cover his bare back with kisses. Becoming caught up in her fantasy, she visualised tearing off the rest of his clothes, touching him all over, and dragging him on to the pillows in front of the fire.

Suddenly he turned and caught her expression of naked desire.

With the blood pouring into her cheeks, Joanna jumped to her feet, in her haste stepping on Duncan's paw. The dog let out a short yelp.

'Oh, Dunc, I'm so sorry!' She knelt and put her arms around him, burying her burning face in his fur.

Dominic, after several deep breaths to return his

pounding pulse to normal, said in his coolest voice, 'He'll be all right. Tougher than he looks.'

Slowly Dominic walked back towards her.

A loud crack of thunder made them both jump. Dominic smiled and dared to draw Joanna into his arms, holding her close and motionless for some minutes, letting his humours flow into her body, and hers flow into his.

She experienced a heady moment of feeling the protection of his arms. Then she tightened her muscles against her surge of physical desire, which started in her fingertips and toes, quickly spreading through her limbs to her very core.

As he tilted her face and kissed her forehead, Joanna trembled imperceptibly. Sliding her arms around his neck, she offered her lips.

'Dominic,' she murmured huskily.

He was absolutely unable to resist kissing her deeply for the first time, a kiss that turned her flesh to liquid desire.

When they paused for breath, he shivered slightly and looked at her with burning eyes.

She returned the look. 'I love you, Dominic.'

He shut his eyes for a moment.

'I love you,' she repeated.

His face worked with emotion and, holding her tightly, he kissed her forehead, her eyelids, her cheeks, and then her mouth, long and deep until they both were breathless.

'Oh, God, Joanna!' Fiercely he pulled her down to the rug and kissed her neck, his hands gripping her shoulders and moving to her breasts. Her nipples were so hard she thought they would push through her clothes.

She fumbled with the buttons of his shirt, while he took her sweater off and unhooked her bra.

The moment she felt his lips on her breasts she had a shuddering orgasm that made her cry out. He covered her bare skin with hot kisses, while pulling off her jeans.

Then she tore at his clothes, kissing his chest and belly, completely in the grip of her passion.

When he pushed her back on the rug she lay there, softly

305

moaning, feeling his hands and lips and tongue on the inside of her thighs, moving higher and higher.

Forcing herself to hold back, she drew him on to her. Their bodies fused, slowly rocking in a gradually increasing rhythm.

He threw his head back, breathing hoarsely, and slowed his motion.

Joanna was very close. 'Dominic,' she gasped, clutching his arms. 'Dominic!'

As she started to come, he thrust urgently into her until he climaxed in spasms so strong they left him trembling.

For a while Joanna lay in his arms, smoothing the small patch of fine, dark hair on his chest. Her stomach constricted when she realised that she very much wanted to have Dominic's child.

She began to kiss his shoulder and his chest, moving her head slowly down to his belly, loving his lean, taut body and the salty taste of him.

He was fully aroused even before he felt her mouth caressing him, and he tightened his hands in her hair, while he groaned and sucked in his breath. 'Oh, darling.'

He pulled her on top of him so he could watch her ecstasy, as well as hear it and feel it. Her pleasure triggered his so intensely that he was unaware of digging his fingers into her back until his tremors had subsided.

Joanna leaned forward and covered his face with soft kisses.

The fire had burned to embers and it had grown chilly.

Dominic took her by the hand and they started upstairs, stopping every couple of steps to kiss gently.

He turned down the covers of his bed and looked at her. 'You really are unbelievably beautiful, Joanna, as beautiful in body as you are in spirit.'

'Even with my scar?' she asked, her eyes brimming with emotion.

'Of course.' Dominic traced it gently with his finger. 'It's minor, and you came by it most bravely. I love it

306

because it's part of you.' As he kissed the length of it softly she grew weak with love for him.

Drawing her down on the bed he began to kiss her everywhere, touching her lightly and drawing from her a deep sensuality. His kisses and touches made her writhe in exquisite agony. When she could no longer bear it she took the initiative, exploring his body with loving hands and lips.

Tenderly undulating together in slow motion, they extended their pleasure as long as they could before release came in a long, delicious orgasm.

Locked in each other's arms, they dozed off, awakening only when their limbs became stiff.

Dominic pulled up the covers and drew Joanna close. He kissed her hair and cheeks and forehead. 'I love you very much, Joanna.'

'I love you just as much.'

She fell asleep curled up beside him like a snail in its shell.

Hours later they awoke and smiled at each other.

'The sun's out,' she murmured, kissing him.

'It's in, too – inside of me.' He put his arm around her. 'How are you this morning?'

'Wonderful.'

He laughed and kissed the top of her head. 'You are, rather.'

Joanna smacked him playfully. 'Okay, okay, I *feel* wonderful. Would you like breakfast in bed?'

'I wouldn't dare, not with you beside me. I'd surely wind up with egg on my face.'

They ate in the kitchen. Joanna, watching Dominic polish off his bacon and eggs, felt consumed with love for him. Everything he said, everything he did seemed exactly right to her.

He caught her eye and gave her a long look in return, biting his lip, his fork suspended.

Joanna was suddenly shy, and a little fearful of the

intensity of her feeling for him. Quickly she stood up and poured them more coffee. 'Do you want anything else?'

'Yes.' He took the pot from her hands and put it on the trivet. Then, moving her close to him, he leaned his head against her stomach. 'I want you. For the rest of my life.'

Her heart contracted, and she put her hands on his head, twining his heavy hair between her fingers.

'I want you, too,' she whispered.

He stood up and took her by the hands, looking down at her with eyes that glittered with love. 'I'm asking you to marry me.'

Her heart stopped in mid-beat.

Smiling almost apologetically, he continued, 'I hope you won't think it too British and boring of me to believe that the wedding should come before the pregnancy.'

Joanna began to tremble. 'Oh, Dominic,' she cried, flinging herself into his arms.

He held her close, stroking her hair, cherishing the moment.

After a while she gently withdrew from his embrace and looked sombrely at him. 'There might never be a pregnancy, you know.'

'Improbable, but irrelevant. You're the only woman in the world I want. If you can have my child it will be serendipity.'

'And if I can't?'

'I won't love you one whit less, my darling. And if we must have a child, we'll adopt one.'

After a moment, he tilted up Joanna's chin and kissed her damp eyes. 'Was that a "yes" I heard?'

'Yes,' she murmured huskily.

He took her left hand and slipped a ring on her third finger.

'My grandmother's.' He kissed Joanna's forehead.

She stared at the ring, an emerald in an elegant Victorian setting. Simple, but breathtakingly beautiful.

'I've been carrying it around, just in case.' He was enjoying her happy astonishment.

'Since Amsterdam?'

'Of course.'

He drew her into his arms once more and held her pressed to him, the mutuality of their love confirmed.

Later they walked in the woods, with Duncan romping alongside. Dominic pulled Joanna beside him on a rock and threw a stick for the dog to fetch. 'No doubt you'll find the subject of money quite unromantic but we must discuss it. I have a decent income but in no way does it approach your millions.'

Joanna stopped his words with a kiss. 'I don't care about my millions or even if you're marrying me for my money.'

'Well, that's all right, then. I'm relieved, since there could be no other possible reason.'

'Just remember that I haven't earned most of the money, Dominic, it earns itself. I'll marry you only if you agree to halve everything.' She leaned forward to pet Duncan. 'I'll take his head, you can have the part that wags.'

'Be serious, darling.'

'I am. Absolutely. We can use the money for medical research. For anything we both decide. What I don't want to give up is my name. Would you object to Lennox-Graham?'

'Of course not. As long as you don't mind having to write all that on cheques.'

'Joanna Lennox-Graham,' she mused. 'I like it.'

'I like her.' Dominic paused and sighed. 'Now we come to the other serious stuff – the frustrations of being a doctor's wife. There will be times like the other night when I must stop whatever I'm doing to go where I'm needed. Dinners will congeal on the plate and films and plays will have no ending for me unless you fill me in. And your sleep will often be disturbed by that beeper going off.'

'I know,' she said softly.

'You'll be irritated, impatient, sometimes downright furious, wishing I had a nine-to-five job like other men.'

'No,' she murmured. 'I won't. Not for more than a few moments, anyway. Because part of what I most admire

309

about you is your dedication to your work, the way you really care about people. It's only because I love you so very much as a human being that I can love you so much as a man. Love you and trust you, and want to be with you always.'

Dominic wrapped his arms around Joanna and held her close for a long time. Duncan, as if he knew his future, dropped his stick and reclined next to the couple, wagging his tail and resting his chin on Joanna's knee.

EPILOGUE

Their daughter, Victoria, was born a little more than a year after their marriage.

For hours Joanna gazed at her baby, still in awe of the miracle weeks after her birth.

'Dominic, she's getting to look exactly like you.'

'Not at all, darling.'

'She does so, especially when she smiles.'

'You know she doesn't smile yet, if you've been reading your Dr Spock. In any case, she'll change and go on changing the first few months.'

'You're just being argumentative,' Joanna scolded.

'I most definitely am not. To prove it I'll say categorically that Vicky doesn't in the slightest resemble Duncan. Now, can we agree on that or are you going to be difficult?'

Joanna began to laugh, just as Dominic's beeper went.

'Nuisance,' he said, after phoning the hospital. 'I wanted to spend a peaceful Sunday with my lady and my little girl.'

'I know, darling. Anyway, Nadine's coming over soon, with the children. She's studying for a role in a television film and wondered if she could leave Kate and Jeff here for a few days. They're so excited over their new cousin. Would you mind?'

Dominic smiled. 'Of course not. You know how fond I am of the little monsters. Besides, we might as well train them to babysit properly. I'm glad for Nadine. Good role?'

'Pretty good, but not the lead. Acting is so competitive. She wins some, she loses some. At least she's feeling all right. That's the most important thing.'

Dominic slipped into his coat and went back into the kitchen, where Joanna was sitting and breast-feeding Vicky.

He leaned over to kiss the baby's cheek, and then Joanna's lips.

'Bye, darling. Do good work, as always,' she said.

He turned for a last look at his madonna and child, emotion making him say gruffly, 'Don't move until I get back.'

'At the rate she eats, we'll be right here when you return.' Joanna looked at him with adoring eyes. 'We love you.'

'I love you too, you two.' He blew them a kiss.

'And then,' Joanna murmured to her daughter, 'they all lived happily ever after.'

HEYWOOD BOOKS

TODAY'S PAPERBACKS
– AT YESTERDAY'S PRICES!

Heywood Books is a new list of paperback books which
will be published every month at remarkably low prices. It
will range from glitzy, up-to-the-minute women's novels
to compelling romantic thrillers and absorbing historical
romance, from classic crime to nerve-chilling horror and
big adventure thrillers, presenting an outstanding list of
highly readable and top value popular fiction.

Look for this month's new titles:

THE BIG X	*Hank Searls*	£1.50
THE SUMMER DAY IS DONE	*Robert Tyler Stevens*	£1.75
TWIN CONNECTIONS	*Justine Valenti*	£1.75
THE SHAPIRO DIAMOND	*Michael Legat*	£1.75
A RATTLING OF OLD BONES	*Jonathan Ross*	£1.50
MIRROR IMAGE	*Lucille Fletcher*	£1.50

MIRROR IMAGE
Two sisters –
One rich but unhappy,
the other missing since she was a small child

Lucille Fletcher

For all the great wealth and luxury with which Robin
was surrounded by her fabulously beautiful film star
mother and her famous conductor father, none of
the family could forget the shatteringly sudden disap-
pearance of her small sister many years before. For, on a
beautiful Sunday morning in 1969, eight-year-old Robin
Chodoff and her four-year-old sister Marya went for a
walk in Central Park, but only Robin came back. Marya
had disappeared, never to be seen again . . .
So when her mother receives a letter from France
suggesting that Marya has been found, Robin is dis-
patched to look for her. And so she becomes caught up
in a trail of terror and deception more sinister and more
frightening than the worst nightmare.

HEYWOOD BOOKS

FICTION

One Little Room	*Jan Webster*	£1.50
The Winnowing Winds	*Ann Marlowe*	£1.50
The Root of His Evil	*James M Cain*	£1.50
Criss-Cross	*Alan Scholefield*	£1.50
Lovenotes	*Justine Valenti*	£1.75
Perahera	*Julia Leslie*	£1.50
Alone Together	*Sherrye Henry*	£1.75
The Summer Day is Done	*Robert Tyler Stevens*	£1.75
Twin Connections	*Justine Valenti*	£1.75
Mirror Image	*Lucille Fletcher*	£1.50

SAGA

Daneclere	*Pamela Hill*	£1.75
Making Friends	*Cornelia Hale*	£1.75
Muckle Annie	*Jan Webster*	£1.75
The Windmill Years	*Vicky Martin*	£1.75
Seeds of the Sun	*Vicky Martin*	£1.75
The Shapiro Diamond	*Michael Legat*	£1.75

HISTORICAL ROMANCE

The Caretaker Wife	*Barbara Whitehead*	£1.50
Quicksilver Lady	*Barbara Whitehead*	£1.50
Ramillies	*Barbara Whitehead*	£1.50
Lady in Waiting	*Rosemary Sutcliff*	£1.75

THRILLER

KG 200	*J. D. Gilman & John Clive*	£1.75
Hammerstrike	*Walter Winward*	£1.75
The Canaris Fragments	*Walter Winward*	£1.75
Down to a Sunless Sea	*David Graham*	£1.75
The Big X	*Hank Searls*	£1.50

HORROR

The Unholy	*Michael Falconer Anderson*	£1.50
God of a Thousand Faces	*Michael Falconer Anderson*	£1.50
The Woodsmen	*Michael Falconer Anderson*	£1.50

CRIME

Here Lies Nancy Frail	*Jonathan Ross*	£1.50
A Rattling of Old Bones	*Jonathan Ross*	£1.50

NAME ....

ADDRESS ....

....

Write to Heywood Books Cash Sales, PO Box 11, Falmouth, Cornwall TR10 9EN. Please indicate order and enclose remittance to the value of the cover price plus: UK: Please allow 60p for the first book, 25p for the second book and 15p for each additional book ordered, to a maximum charge of £1.90.

B.F.P.O. & EIRE: Please allow 60p for the first book, 25p for the second book, 15p per copy for the next 7 books and thereafter 9p per book.

OVERSEAS: Please allow £1.25 for the first book, 75p for the second book and 28p per copy for each additional book.

Whilst every effort is made to keep prices low it is sometimes necessary to increase cover prices and also postage and packing rates at short notice. Heywood Books reserve the right to show new retail prices on covers which may differ from those previously advertised in the text or elsewhere.